WHAT REMAINS OF YOU

WHAT REMAINS OF YOU

A Novel

KIMBERLY HENSLE LOWRANCE

This is a work of fiction. Names, characters, organizations, places, events, and incidents are either products of the author's imagination or are used fictitiously.

Text copyright © 2026 by Kimberly Hensle Lowrance
All rights reserved.

No part of this book may be reproduced, or stored in a retrieval system, or transmitted in any form or by any means, electronic, mechanical, photocopying, recording, or otherwise, without express written permission of the publisher.

Published by Lake Union Publishing, Seattle

www.apub.com

Amazon, the Amazon logo, and Lake Union Publishing are trademarks of Amazon.com, Inc., or its affiliates.

EU product safety contact:
Amazon Media EU S. à r.l.
38, avenue John F. Kennedy, L-1855 Luxembourg
amazonpublishing-gpsr@amazon.com

ISBN-13: 9781662539817 (paperback)
ISBN-13: 9781662539824 (digital)

Cover design by Joanne O'Neill
Cover image: © AndTheyTravel / Shutterstock; © Yulia Naumenko / Getty

Printed in the United States of America

For Rob

Things are always different from what they might be.

—Henry James, The Portrait of a Lady

Chapter One

Widowhood isn't the worst part of my life, Diana Morgan thinks as she jogs up her driveway. With each step, her lungs burn and bright spots of pain shoot up her calves. *This run might be even more terrible.*

Intrigued by the ridiculous idea she can find an upside to losing her husband, Diana limps onto her porch and begins to make a list to answer the question *Why Isn't Widowhood the Worst?* She imagines writing the list on the Notes app on her phone, the place where she tracks what she needs at the grocery store. Instead of "grapes," "cheddar cheese slices," and "juice boxes," she could write:

Tom was the one who liked to run, not me. I don't have to jog anymore.

I can sleep in the middle of the bed if I want; no more sticking only to the right side.

Shivering from the frigid New England weather, Diana opens her front door. She peels off her gloves, along with her hat and insulated vest, and drops them on the bench in the cluttered hallway next to her son's basketball gear.

There's no one to disagree with me.

Well, her kids, twelve-year-old Duncan and nine-year-old Phoebe, regularly disagree with her, so that's not a true silver lining to her current situation. As she closes the door and kicks off her sneakers, she tries again.

I can keep the heat as high as I want. No more putting on an extra layer to accommodate Tom's obsessive need to keep the thermostat at sixty-three degrees.

I can keep the heat as high as I want, but I have to pay the heating bill myself.

I'm the only parent Duncan and Phoebe have.

I'm alone.

Diana bends over, heaving. The breath in her chest is violent and sharp.

"Mom?" Duncan calls out.

Diana presses her hand against the wall and slowly pulls herself up. A moment passes before she can speak. "Coming."

She finds her children in the kitchen, clustered at the island. Duncan is clad in workout pants and Tom's old Van Halen concert tee. It's too big for him, but he wears it all the time. Diana dutifully washes it whenever she finds it in the laundry, envisioning a college-age Tom wearing the shirt while singing along in a crowded concert hall.

She blinks to erase the image and turns to her son. "How was practice?" Duncan likes nothing more than to talk about basketball and his cocaptain position on his middle school's team.

"Coach made us run extra laps because—"

"Mama," Phoebe interrupts, hopping from foot to foot and brandishing a manila envelope, her ponytail swaying with each jump. Her coat and boots are piled on the floor next to her backpack and favorite stuffed animal, Bear Bear. "I found it! I found the time capsule!"

For the past week, Diana's kids have been pestering her to locate a family time capsule they assembled four years ago. It was Duncan's homework assignment, but Diana barely remembers it. Duncan is clear they're supposed to open it today, Leap Day, February 29, 2016, and he's persuaded Phoebe to help him convince Diana to find it. She's looked everywhere—dressers, cabinets, the attic, even the bathroom linen closet—but without success. Tom would have known where it was, which makes this simple request all the more difficult.

"Where was it?" Diana asks, waving her arms in circles to interrupt her thoughts and to release the remaining tension from her run.

"For homework," Phoebe begins, "I have to write a paragraph about winter, and I don't know how many *z*'s are in 'blizzard.' I think it's three, but when I asked Duncan, he wouldn't tell me." Phoebe stares pointedly at her brother, aggravation etched across her face.

"Mom makes me look up words I can't spell, so you have to do the same, Pheebs. It's only fair," Duncan says.

Phoebe shakes her head, and Diana stifles a laugh. Phoebe has figured out that her brother sometimes claims the need for sibling equality to disguise his reluctance to help her, and she is not on board with this approach.

"So I went into the office to get the dictionary," Phoebe continues. "One shelf down from it was the time capsule, tucked behind the photo albums. Can we open it, Mama?"

Diana takes the envelope from her daughter. On the front, in red marker, is Time Capsule: Do not open until February 29, 2016. Her breath grows shallow, and the hair along her forearms rises. "Strange. I thought I checked there."

In the eighteen months since Tom died, Diana has tried not to think too much about the past. That's probably why she didn't find the time capsule when she searched the office; she must not have wanted to go near those photo albums documenting their years together. Now that Phoebe has found it, however, looking back is unavoidable.

"Mom?" Duncan asks. "You okay?"

Diana forces a smile. "Of course," she lies. She needs more time to prepare, to reinforce the walls she's built around her grief. She drops the time capsule onto the island. "Let me get dinner started first? I'm starving after my run."

"But it's Leap Day today, Mama. We have to open it *today*." Phoebe's face crumples, tears threatening.

"Don't worry. We will." Diana kisses Phoebe's forehead. "You and Bear Bear start your homework while I figure out what we're eating. You get to work, too, Duncan."

Mollified by the prospect of food, Phoebe heads to the table, dragging Bear Bear by the ear, his furry bottom bouncing on the floor. Bear Bear has been Phoebe's great joy since her third birthday, when she opened a pink polka dot box from Diana's parents to find him inside. Diana still remembers Phoebe kissing his turquoise nose with delight, whispering, "Bear Bear." If Diana doesn't watch closely, Phoebe will smuggle him to school in her backpack, sticky with the remains of her breakfast.

Duncan grabs the laptop from the counter, where it sits on a pile of unopened mail, newspapers bound for the recycling bin, and notices from the kids' schools that are probably important. "Can I use the computer? I have to research the Supreme Court for history class." Before, the computer was Tom's, but now Diana and the kids share the device. She keeps it in the kitchen, instead of across the house in what was Tom's office. Diana needs everyone to be close by, in the same room.

"Yes, but no video games."

"Mom," he groans. That one word has endless meanings, and in this instance, she knows Duncan hopes to convey his frustration with her rules. He tells her all the time that none of his friends have parents as strict as her, but she won't relent. She's extra cautious about everything related to her kids. She'd be a different mother if Tom were still alive. More lenient, probably. And not so insecure.

As Duncan passes by on his way to join Phoebe at the table, his hand lightly grazes Diana's shoulder, and she smiles. When he was little, Duncan would never leave a room without kissing or hugging her. That stopped for a few months when he turned ten, much to Diana's regret. Then Tom died, and everything changed. Now, Duncan is always aware of where she is in the house, always touching her as he walks by, as if to ensure she's still there.

"Mama, I forgot. Lakshmi sent home food for us," Phoebe says. "She said it was Daddy's favorite. I brought it home from my playdate with Mira. It's by the back door."

Lakshmi, Diana's close friend and Mira's mother, has cooked for Diana and her kids once a week for months now; it's one of the ways she looks out for them. Often the meals are the Indian dishes Lakshmi makes for her own family—dal, biryani, sambar—but sometimes, she cooks food that reminds her of Tom.

After putting away Phoebe's coat and boots in the foyer closet, Diana brings Lakshmi's dish into the kitchen, peeking under the foil to find homemade macaroni and cheese. *Definitely Tom's favorite,* she thinks, placing the dish on the counter.

"I still don't know how to spell 'blizzard,'" Phoebe says, her voice vibrating up toward a full-fledged whine. "Can't one of you tell me?"

"As we already discussed, you have to get the dictionary," Diana says, opening the refrigerator to assess what else they have for dinner. She pushes aside the milk—still good, amazingly—and finds her mother's fruit salad. A bag of baby carrots in the back of the crisper will work, too.

Phoebe sighs dramatically but gets up, stealing a carrot as she skips by.

Diana closes the refrigerator and eyes the time capsule. She should have let the kids open the envelope and get this over with. Whatever is inside—probably some old photographs—won't be that upsetting, right?

Eager for a distraction, she checks her phone and finds texts from her family. How far did you get on your run? her sister, Andrea, asks, her message peppered with sneaker emojis. Don't forget to replenish your electrolytes! Diana's mother's text is no different in its sentiment: I hope you made time for that jog, sweetheart. You'll be grateful you prioritized your health and well-being.

To Diana's sister and mother, exercise is a sign Diana hasn't fallen back into the debilitating grief that eclipsed her after Tom's death, a time when she couldn't take care of Duncan and Phoebe, pay her bills, or remember to eat. The darkest of those days are behind her, Diana believes, but she isn't sure her family is ready to let go of being the ones who hold her together.

Phoebe returns to the kitchen, lugging the dictionary. "It's one *z*, right, Mama?"

"Look it up, Phoebe," Diana says, sticking her phone into her pocket. "Mac and cheese good with you for dinner, Duncan?"

Duncan doesn't answer, keeping his eyes on his homework and acting as if she isn't there. The mood swings of adolescence: One moment Duncan is affectionate and responsible, the next, grumpy and sullen, communicating only in grunts or eye rolls. *The teenage years are going to be long,* she thinks.

As soon as Diana places the mac and cheese in the oven to reheat, Phoebe looks up from her homework. "*Now* is it time to open the time capsule?"

Diana picks up the envelope and lets its crisp edges slide across her palm. Her focus compresses, as if she's looking at the time capsule through a telescope. Everything around her blurs. She's not interested in seeing what's inside. In fact, she's scared by the pain this innocent assignment of Duncan's might dredge up. She'd rather shred the time capsule into small pieces and throw it into the trash than remember. She can feel her hands twitch in anticipation, imagining the sensation of ripping the envelope apart.

But Duncan and Phoebe want this, and her children's needs come before her own, so Diana closes her eyes and counts to ten, using the circular breathing both the parenting and grief books suggest for tough situations.

"Mom?" Duncan asks, his fingers paused over the computer keyboard.

Diana opens her eyes and reluctantly walks over to the table, where she hands the envelope to Phoebe. "All yours, honey."

Once Diana is seated, Phoebe glances from her brother to her mother and arches an eyebrow, a trait she's inherited from Vivian, Diana's mother. In a flash, an adult Phoebe is before them, time jumping ahead too quickly.

"Come on, open it," Duncan says, shoving their homework off to the side.

Phoebe flips over the time capsule. It's unsealed, with only a silver metal clasp holding the flap in place. She hunches over, her tongue sticking out and her feet swinging, as she urges up one arm of the clasp. Her movements are methodical, and Diana's anxiety grows.

The second arm opens, and Phoebe looks up, triumphant. She unfolds the flap and removes a piece of cream-colored construction paper. Shaking her head, Phoebe examines the drawing. "You can tell I was really little when I made this. I'm a much better artist now." She hands the paper to Diana and helps Duncan remove the other items from the envelope.

Looking at Phoebe's drawing kick-starts the muscle that pulls memories from where they live in Diana's brain, hidden under all the loss and sadness. Out of shape and abandoned, the muscle struggles to locate the night they assembled the time capsule, four years earlier. The memory is there but fragmented, like a puzzle missing several pieces.

Diana remembers Duncan coming home from school with the time-capsule assignment, adamant they put it together that night. No waiting for the weekend, when they would've had more time; he wanted the Leap Day time capsule completed on Leap Day.

Tom joined them for dinner, the first time in weeks. Still dressed in his good gray suit from court, his tie askew, and the sleeves of his blue oxford shirt rolled up to the elbows, he looked tired, with hollows under his eyes like half-moons. Diana remembers rubbing his back and feeling the knots in his muscles, the stress from the day not yet released.

After the dishes were cleared, Tom and Duncan conferred about which items to include in the time capsule, while Phoebe, a newly minted five-year-old, worked on her contribution, a crayon-colored picture of a family of kittens. At Phoebe's direction, Diana labeled each one, the names written in thick lines of purple: MAMA, DADDY, DUNCAN, ME.

When Phoebe started yawning, Duncan and Tom agreed to finish assembling the time capsule while Diana handled bedtime. As she and Phoebe said good night, Tom ruffled Phoebe's hair, kissing both her and Bear Bear, his other arm curled around Diana's waist. He held her there for a long moment, before leaning away and opening a beer, the crack and fizz of the can finishing off her memory like an exclamation point.

Diana puts the drawing to the side. "What else do we have?"

"Here's some of my math homework." Duncan shows her a worksheet with a smiley face on top. "I made some dumb mistakes when I was younger."

"Everybody makes mistakes," Diana says absently. She scans the front page of *The Boston Globe* from 2012; stories about the presidential race and winter snow dominate the headlines, not too different from today.

She and the children pass items back and forth: a photo of the four of them apple-picking, along with Duncan's school portrait, a snap of Phoebe in her preschool classroom, and the ticket stubs from Duncan's first Celtics game.

"Here's the interview I did with Dad." Duncan holds up a paper stained with burnt-orange spots. *Tacos,* Diana remembers. *We had tacos for dinner that night.*

"Read it," urges Phoebe.

"Go ahead, Duncan," Diana says, the ominous feeling rising inside her again.

"Name: Tom Morgan. Age: 47," Duncan begins. "Address: 90 Newton Road, Alcott, Massachusetts. Occupation: attorney. Hobbies: playing basketball with Duncan. Hope for the future: My son will pick up his Legos."

Duncan pauses and bites his lip. Diana tries not to cry.

"Daddy was funny," Phoebe says.

"He definitely was," Diana agrees, swallowing hard. "He was also right about your brother's inability to pick up his Legos."

"Seriously, this is not an issue anymore," Duncan says.

"Your room is the messiest," Phoebe says, giggling.

"Mine is messy? Have you ever cleaned your closet? I'm pretty sure something's *living* in there."

Diana interjects before a fight ensues. "Is that it for the interview, Duncan?"

"Two more questions. Favorite vacation: Cape Cod with my family. Favorite season: winter." Duncan smiles. "Dad liked winter because we'd all go sledding down the hill by Grandma and Grandpa's house."

"I don't remember that," Phoebe says.

"You don't remember sledding with your dad?" Diana says. A memory sneaks through the fragile barricade she's constructed against the past. She sees Phoebe nestled between Tom's legs as the two of them fly down the hill, their plastic sled picking up speed as it bounces against the packed snow, Tom laughing, Phoebe shrieking with delight.

"I miss Daddy," Phoebe whispers.

"Do you want us to stop?" Diana says, hoping Phoebe will say yes.

"Nah, you're okay, right, Pheebs?" Duncan says. "You want more of the time capsule, don't you?"

Phoebe nods as she tightly squeezes Bear Bear.

Duncan thrusts a white, letter-size envelope across the table. "This is for you, Mom."

Diana's name is written on the front in Tom's handwriting. "It's from your dad."

"Maybe it's a love letter, Mama."

"Please open it," Duncan whispers.

Duncan's "please" jolts through Diana. She inserts her finger into the corner of the envelope and rips. From the jagged opening, she withdraws a sheet of paper filled with Tom's handwriting, all right angles and clean lines. Smoothing the page out on the table, she begins to silently read.

Dear Diana, If you've found this letter, I'm gone. I shouldn't say "if," as it's clear there's no miraculous recovery for me waiting around the corner. I am so sorry for leaving you and the kids.

"Mama?" Phoebe asks. "What does it say?"

"He's talking about being sick. But—"

"But what?" Duncan asks.

"Your father wasn't sick when we put together the time capsule. He wasn't diagnosed until later." Diana's teeth chatter, as if an icy wind has found its way into the warmth of her home. She turns back to the text.

I'm also sorry for something else, something I've never told you. I should have accepted responsibility a long time ago, before I met you. Maybe if I tell you now, it will be enough. It's also possible I'm making things worse for you by writing this letter, but I owe it to you to tell you the kind of man I really was.

When I was 18 years old, I did something criminal. Something so terrible I can't even write the details here.

People died. It's all my fault.

The rest of the words tumble across the page, and Diana feels a headache take hold behind her eyes. *Oh my God, oh my God,* she thinks, the words a frantic chant in her head.

Duncan and Phoebe look at her, waiting.

"Mama?" Phoebe asks hesitantly.

Diana stands up and stuffs the letter into her pocket. "Why don't we celebrate finding the time capsule? How about ice cream?" Her voice is too loud and too high, and she's afraid her children can tell she's hiding something. "Duncan, check which flavors we have, and Phoebe, get the scooper. I'll look for sprinkles." She rushes across the kitchen to the pantry closet by the back door.

"But we haven't had dinner," Phoebe says.

"*Shhhh,*" Duncan hisses, opening the freezer. "Mom? We have strawberry and mint chip."

Hidden behind the pantry door, Diana holds on to the shelf stocked with oatmeal and cans of black beans and pushes down a wave of panic. Sweat breaks out along her hairline, and her legs shake.

She has no idea who died, what Tom did, or why he left this letter for her. But in front of her children, she has to pretend nothing has changed and that she didn't read the words "sorry," "criminal," and "my fault." She grabs a container of rainbow sprinkles. "I'll be right there."

Chapter Two

As soon as the kids are asleep, their bellies filled with unexpected dishes of ice cream and Lakshmi's macaroni and cheese, Diana carries a bottle of wine and a glass into the living room. In the dark, she sits on the floor against the sofa.

She considers calling her sister to tell her about the letter, maybe even have Andrea come over while she reads it, but if she does that, the focus will shift from what Diana needs to what her sister wants her to do. Her parents will react similarly. This letter is for Diana; she has to read it on her own.

A list starts up: *What Did Tom Do That's So Bad He Left Me This Letter?* Inside her sweatshirt pocket, she runs her fingers along the envelope, stopping when she comes to the hastily torn opening.

Diana started making lists as a kid. She pitched *Why Should My Bedtime Be Later?* to her father at age seven. He laughed and gave her fifteen more minutes. She presented *What Makes Me the Better Daughter?* to her parents in high school after they caught her sister sneaking out to meet a boy. Her parents had been amused by that one; her sister, not so much.

Her list-making continued during college, waning after graduation, as her adult life began to take shape, and it's only now, at forty-three, that the lists have reappeared. They are meant to offer the answer to a question, but occasionally, Diana's grief co-opts her lists into something else, something revealing, something she tries hard not to see.

Did he drive drunk and cause an accident?
Was it a hit-and-run?
Did he intentionally hurt someone?

The branches on the tree in her front yard slap against the house as the wind picks up. Diana and Tom met on a blustery night like this one, a storm in the forecast. She was at a bar on Boylston Street with coworkers from the Boston Public Library, drinking margaritas and shooting pool. After her second drink, the tequila tiring her out, Diana said her goodbyes. As she came out of the restroom, coat in hand, calculating how often the subway ran at that time of night, she found him waiting.

"You're going? Right when I got the courage to talk to you?" Leaning against the wall, wearing a red tie and a blue shirt that matched his eyes, he had his arms crossed at his chest, and his mouth was turned up at the corners in a hesitant smile. Tom had a beard then, and when she looked at him, his smile grew and he stepped forward. She remembered inhaling, and his scent—the crisp, grassy smell of the moment before snow fell—filled her head, all the blood rushing to her toes, leaving her skin tingling.

He said later he noticed her when she walked through the door. He hoped she would step away from her group so he could say hello. This confession came after they'd been dating for three months. She made a crack that maybe he was a stalker, but he didn't laugh. "I knew you were special," he said, and she kissed him.

That night in the bar, she almost turned away from Tom, from their future together, but a quiet and insistent hunch made her push through her sleepiness to stay. He bought them a round of margaritas and told her about his job at a prestigious law firm and his dream to go out on his own. She sipped her cocktail and noticed the way his hair curled around his ears. She wanted to run her fingers through those curls and rub her cheek against his beard, the hairs tickling her skin, slowly at first and then harder. She wanted to inhale the scent of him again

When Tom asked about her life, Diana entertained him with stories about the library's patrons and shared her dream of earning her PhD in library sciences and working at, or perhaps even leading, a grand library like the ones she'd visited during a vacation to England. He listened carefully, asking such smart and thoughtful questions she forgot they'd just met. And then there was Tom's laugh: the way his eyes lit up when he found something funny, the way he clutched his stomach when the joke was exceptional, the musicality of his unexpected giggle. She fell for him that night, though it would be a while before she realized it.

They talked until the overworked bartenders kicked them out. Not ready for the night to end, he walked her home, the wind whipping around them on the empty Boston streets. It was a magical, chance meeting, and every anniversary, Tom made them margaritas to summon up that first night when they found each other.

It's time to read this letter, Diana thinks. Shifting up onto the sofa, she leans over to the side table and turns on the lamp. The red liquid in her glass glints in the pale light. She takes a large swig of her wine—a pinotage, Tom's favorite—and places the empty glass on the table. As the wine seeps through her body, Diana rubs her hands over her face. *I can do this.*

She removes the envelope from her pocket. He wrote her name as if in a rush, the letters crooked, the envelope dented with the marks of his pen. She pulls out the letter and begins to read, starting with the first line in case she misunderstood the words earlier.

Dear Diana,

If you've found this letter, I'm gone. I shouldn't say "if," as it's clear there's no miraculous recovery for me waiting around the corner. I am so sorry for leaving you and the kids.

I'm also sorry for something else, something I've never told you. I should have accepted responsibility a long time ago, before I met you. Maybe if I tell you now, it will be enough. It's also possible I'm making things worse for you by writing this letter, but I owe it to you to tell you the kind of man I really was.

When I was 18 years old, I did something criminal. Something so terrible I can't even write the details here.

People died. It's all my fault.

I never owned up to what I did, a decision that was another mistake.

Others know about my past. After my death, around the time you find this letter, when I hope you've moved on from me, they may come into your life. Don't let them in. Keep them away from Duncan and Phoebe.

If we had been different people, or maybe if our relationship had been different, I might have told you all this sooner. I tried, but I wasn't sure how you'd react. Would you have been disappointed in me? Or angry? How could you trust me for lying to you for our entire relationship? For so long, I blamed you for my inability to come clean. I saw you as the obstacle to being truthful when it clearly was me. I'm sorry for so much.

Perhaps this cancer is the universe fixing my wrongs. If it is, I understand, though I wish leaving you was not the debt I had to pay.

When you speak of me to Duncan and Phoebe, tell them their father was imperfect, but he loved them, and you, more than anything.

Tom

By the third paragraph, Diana stops breathing. At the end, she finds herself lightheaded, choking for air.

I hope you've moved on from me.

I blamed you.

I'm sorry.

She turns over the page and examines the envelope again. This is definitely Tom's handwriting. He wrote this letter, though the tone of it is odd, as if he anticipated the words would be dissected and analyzed.

An idea comes to her, and Diana is up, running into the kitchen, the letter clutched in her hand. She grabs the time capsule from the top of the toaster oven and dumps the contents onto the black granite countertop. She haphazardly pushes the items apart, almost ripping Phoebe's drawing in half with her frenzied movements. Everything is there: Tom's interview, the newspaper, the apple-picking photograph. All the other items are from 2012, when they assembled the time capsule.

Except this letter. It's from a different time, likely right before Tom's death in 2014.

A surge of nausea, all that wine acidic and angry, roiling in her gut, makes Diana briefly think she will vomit all over the kitchen floor. She squeezes her eyes shut and presses her fingers into her temple.

"Go back to the beginning," she says, as if it's that easy.

With her belly pressed against the counter, Diana recreates finding the time capsule. She sees Phoebe run in from the office with it in her hands. She remembers sitting at the table with the kids as Phoebe opened the envelope.

That's when Diana remembers an important detail: Phoebe labored over the time capsule's clasp, not its seal. The adhesive was untouched. It could have been possible, therefore, to add a letter . . . later.

"Some *love letter* this is. What happened?" she pants. "Why doesn't he explain what he did?"

Diana shuffles again through the time capsule's contents, her brisk movements turning the papers and photographs into a disorienting, dizzying blur. She imagines the panic she's feeling is similar to what it's like to drown, or to get caught in a tornado: everything swirling around, nothing to hold on to.

Whatever Tom's cryptic message is, she is sure of one thing: It is indeed a disaster, a man-made storm violently barreling into her life, seconds away from splintering her to pieces.

Chapter Three

Tom reaches across the warm and rumpled sheets and pulls Diana close. She draws circles on his forearm, his hair rough under her fingers. He kisses her temple, trailing his lips down to her neck and then her shoulder, where he rests his chin. She loosens her body against his and relaxes into a sort of melting contentment that happens only when he embraces her.

He murmurs; his message is indistinct. She fights her way through the layers of sleep to hear him. The words grow more insistent, and then they are clear.

"Mom, Mom!"

Diana groans and rolls over.

"Mom?"

She opens her raw and sticky eyes to Duncan standing next to her bed, wearing his parka and carrying his sneakers, a worried look on his face.

"Hey, honey."

Too much wine last night, she thinks, her tongue darting around her dry mouth. *And not enough sleep.*

"Mom, it's 7:36. Aren't you supposed to be up for work by now?" Duncan turns the bedside clock around so the red numbers blink in Diana's line of sight. She's overslept by more than an hour. She pushes off the covers and sits up so fast she feels a sloshing in her head, as if her brain is swimming the breaststroke in her skull.

"Dammit, I have an 8:30 meeting. Where's your sister?"

"Sleeping."

"Okay, I got this." Diana forces a smile. "Thanks for waking me up." She heads toward the bathroom, calves still aching from yesterday's run. "You better get going. You don't need to be late, too."

"Mom?" Duncan doesn't move from his spot next to the bed. "What did Dad's letter say?"

The letter, she thinks, looking at her bedside table. She stashed it in the top drawer only hours earlier. *Phoebe might forget about it, but Duncan never would.*

"He wanted me to tell you he loved you." Diana grasps the doorknob for support. "And that the three of us were the best part of his life."

She can't tell Duncan all of it. She didn't fall asleep until after 4:00 a.m., imagining what Tom did that was so bad he couldn't tell her about it when he was alive.

Duncan purses his lips into a stiff line. She wants to wrap her arms around him, but she's learned to wait for him to let her in.

"Can I read it?"

"The letter was for me. I've told you what he wanted me to share."

Duncan twists his sneakers in his hands, the laces swaying.

"You should get going. We can talk about this later."

"Uncle Evan's taking me to that basketball clinic tonight. I'll be home late."

Since Tom's death, Diana's brother-in-law, Evan, has stepped in to help with Duncan, driving him to out-of-town games and taking him to buy new basketball shoes when, thanks to a substantial growth spurt, his old pair became too small. The irony, Andrea pointed out, was that Evan hadn't known a bank shot from a fast break when Tom died. He learned, though, studying basketball websites to find ways to engage Duncan in shop talk during their drives from games in one eastern Massachusetts town to the next. It was one of many ways Diana's family built a safety net underneath her and her kids.

"We'll talk tomorrow then," Diana says. "I love you. Have a good day at school."

Duncan slips out of her room without responding. She listens to the stairs creak under his feet and the front door open and close before moving into the bathroom.

Tom still hovers on the edge of her thoughts. Diana's dream was so vivid she can still feel his body against hers, and the sensation makes her off kilter and jumpy.

Oversleeping doesn't help either. She planned to get up early to prepare for her meeting with the library's communications team, but that's not going to happen. She'll have to wing it.

After relieving her bladder and washing her face, Diana brushes her teeth, the bristles scraping against her gums, blood staining her toothbrush. She steps into the shower and trembles under the cold water, scrubbing away last night's run and forcing herself awake.

Toweling off, Diana avoids glancing at herself in the mirror, certain if she does, she'll see the deepening grooves in her forehead and the web of fine lines under her eyes. She's seen a worn version of herself for months. Sometimes, when she remembers how she was before—more vibrant, more hopeful—she cries.

Back in her room, Diana checks the clock: 7:41 a.m. There isn't time to do much with her shoulder-length, wavy hair, other than sticking it in a ponytail. She opens her closet, avoiding looking to the left, where Tom's clothes still hang. Her mother used to urge her to clear out his belongings, but Diana said no every time Vivian brought it up. Eventually she stopped asking.

As if she's aware Diana is thinking about her, Diana's phone rings, and her mother's face appears on the screen. Diana debates silencing the call, but Vivian will only call again and again until she answers.

"Mom, I'm running late for work. I can't talk," Diana says. She puts the phone on speaker and rips the dry-cleaning bag off a pair of black wool pants and a beige cashmere sweater. She has no idea when her mother took her clothes to the dry cleaner and placed them in her closet, though she appreciates the help.

"Sweetheart, I wanted to touch base about Family Dinner."

Diana is scheduled to host her parents, Evan, Andrea, and their son, Noah, later in the week for what Vivian calls Family Dinner. Even in texts and emails, she capitalizes both words, as if they've been trademarked or declared a national holiday. Diana has completely forgotten about the dinner. *Finding a letter from my deceased husband will do that,* she thinks as she takes her underwear, bra, and socks from the bureau under the window and begins to dress.

"I haven't done any planning yet, Mom. I've been kind of slammed at work."

Family Dinner began when Tom and Diana moved to Alcott. Fed up with noisy neighbors and rising rents, they decided it was time to buy, and there was no better place to live than Alcott, near her parents and sister. The two-story yellow house with the magnolia tree in the front yard was the last one they saw on a whirlwind tour of available homes, and Tom and Diana knew it was theirs as soon as they walked through the door. Diana wrote a letter to go along with their offer, and their story—hometown kid looking to raise her own family in the place where she grew up—made them the winners of an intense bidding war. The first Family Dinner was held the week they closed on their house.

Since Tom's death, Vivian and Andrea have alternated hosting Family Dinner, while waging a low-level campaign for Diana to volunteer to do so as well, certain such a commitment would demonstrate she and the kids have overcome their grief. Aware one dinner couldn't possibly make Tom's death any easier, Diana resisted their appeals. That worked until two weeks ago, when her father called to ask if she might change her mind. Vivian and Andrea had checkmated her; Diana could never say no to Francis.

"Let me make it easier for you, Diana."

As she pulls her sweater over her head, Diana considers asking her mother to host. However, such a last-minute request would concern her family, and the questions would inevitably start: *"Are you okay? Do I need to come over? What's really going on?"* She can't handle that level of invasiveness.

"Maybe you could bring dessert?"

"I'll make lasagna."

"That's too much. The host is supposed to do all the cooking."

"Everyone loves my lasagna."

Everyone does *love her lasagna,* Diana thinks as she zips up her pants. She doesn't have time to continue this negotiation, and her mother will get what she wants anyway. "That would be great, Mom," she says. "I really have to get going."

Diana hangs up the call and selects earrings from the bedside table, next to the small blue dish where Tom dropped his loose change. It's still filled with coins, now covered in dust.

A glance at the clock indicates it's 7:48 a.m. As she clips in her earrings, Diana hustles to Phoebe's room. "Honey, wake up. We overslept." Diana turns on the overhead light as she steps over a pair of panda-shaped slippers. She finds Phoebe perfectly still under the covers, Bear Bear clutched in her arms, long hair covering her face.

"Pheebs? I can't do this today. I have a meeting, and we're late. I need your help." Diana's voice rises higher and higher. "Phoebe? *Please.*"

Phoebe squirms out from under her blanket. "Hi, Mama." She opens her eyes and blinks. "You're already dressed."

"Did you hear me? We're running late. I have to get you to Mira's so I can make my meeting. I need you to get up and get dressed. *Now.*"

Diana adds the "now" for emphasis, but it's lost on Phoebe, who, instead of getting out of bed, stretches her arms above her head. "I'm comfy, Mama."

"Let's go." Diana opens Phoebe's dresser to select her clothes: rainbow-striped leggings, a purple sweatshirt, underwear, and pink socks. She turns back to the bed to find that Phoebe hasn't budged. "Phoebe!" Diana's tone takes on a biting edge. *"Get out of bed."*

Phoebe frowns but sits up, swinging her feet over the side of the mattress. "I want breakfast first."

"Get dressed. I'll make you a sandwich." Diana gestures to the pile of clothes on the dresser. "I'm not kidding around, Phoebe."

She runs down the stairs, stopping briefly to unearth both her boots and Phoebe's from the pile in the front closet. 7:51 a.m. Nine minutes to get out the door. *Nine minutes.* She grabs the ingredients for Phoebe's breakfast, slathering peanut butter and jam on two slices of bread and smooshing them together.

Hearing the water run upstairs, Diana wraps a paper towel around the sandwich, leaving the jam and peanut butter jars on the counter. No food or coffee for her; she'll eat later, whenever she can find the time. She removes Phoebe's lunch box from the refrigerator, stuffs it into her backpack, and glances at the microwave clock: 7:53 a.m.

"Phoebe?" Diana paces at the foot of the stairs, clutching the sandwich and Phoebe's backpack. She shouldn't yell at Phoebe; it isn't her daughter's fault they're late, but can't the kid move faster?

"Phoebe!" This time Diana shrieks, a sound that, as it comes out, rattles her. Her agitation is really about Tom's letter, but she can't calm herself. She can't let go of the feeling that a grenade has been thrown into her life, sabotaging the order and control she's carefully built.

Phoebe appears at the top of the stairs, still in her nightgown. "I'm coming."

"Why aren't you dressed?" Diana places the backpack and sandwich on the bottom step and runs up the stairs. She pushes Phoebe down the hall and into her bedroom, undressing her as they go. "I can't believe you, Phoebe Francesca Morgan! We're in a rush. Come on!"

Not even the deployment of her full name motivates Phoebe. She stands naked in front of Diana, listless and looking down.

Diana pulls Phoebe's purple sweatshirt over her head, handling her daughter as if she's a toddler again, stymied by armholes and buttons. She yanks Phoebe's left arm through the shirt, then her right. She turns back from picking up the rest of Phoebe's clothes to find that her daughter is crying, tears silently falling.

"Oh, baby." Diana drops to her knees.

"Why are you yelling at me? Why are you mad at me?' Phoebe sniffles out the words, wiping her face.

"We overslept, and I can't be late today. I have a meeting I'm leading, and it starts in"—Diana looks at her watch—"thirty-two minutes. I still need to deliver you next door and get to work. It's not a lot of time. I *really* can't be late. So I'm stressed out, and that makes me yell." Her face is hot with the shame of losing control.

Phoebe lets Diana slide on her underwear, socks, and leggings. When she's dressed, Diana hugs her. "I love you, Phoebe. I'm really sorry I'm a grump today."

"I love you, too, Mama."

Diana kisses Phoebe's cheek and stands up. "Can we go?"

"I didn't brush my hair." Phoebe tugs at the knots tying up her hair, a crown of chaos atop her head.

Diana again checks her watch. No time. "We'll ask Lakshmi to brush it for you, okay?" She picks up Phoebe, something she rarely does now that her daughter is nine, and carries her downstairs, where they pull on their coats and zip up their boots. Handing Phoebe her sandwich, Diana picks up their bags and opens the front door: 8:01 a.m.

Sunlight reflects off the snow covering the front yard, and a trail of Duncan's footsteps leads to the curb. Diana and Phoebe hurry across the small strip of land separating their house from Lakshmi and Mira's. Phoebe is silent until Mira opens her door, squealing her name. Phoebe greets her friend with a squeal of her own and skips inside.

"Would you mind trying to get out the knots in Phoebe's hair?" Diana drops Phoebe's backpack inside the door as Lakshmi steps up to the threshold in bare feet with a roomy WBUR fleece on her slender frame. "I'm afraid it's a mess. Sorry."

"Of course."

Diana waves a relieved thank-you and turns to go.

"Diana, have you had any coffee? Breakfast?"

Diana stops on the bottom step. "Not yet."

"One second." Lakshmi disappears inside, the door left ajar. Diana watches the second hand on her watch click forward: 8:04 a.m. If she drives fast enough, she'll have time to print out the meeting agendas before the other attendees arrive.

"Here," Lakshmi says when she returns. She hands Diana a travel mug and banana, a perceptive look in her warm brown eyes. "Coffee, with extra milk, the way you like it. Eat the banana, Diana. Don't throw it in the bottom of your bag and forget about it."

"Thank you, thank you." Blowing Lakshmi a kiss, Diana rushes off to her minivan and into the busy morning traffic.

She arrives at Alcott Memorial Library with a few minutes to spare, sliding into her reserved space in the far end of the parking lot. Leaning her head against the steering wheel, Diana takes several steadying breaths. Her anxiety today reminds her of the early days after Tom's death. Back then, everything—a clogged toilet, an oil change for the car, the tax bill—sent her into a panic, wrapping around her like a heavy blanket in a heat wave.

She sits up and flips open the visor to check herself in the mirror. In the morning light, her face is blotchy and drawn. *I look like I overslept, and I forgot to put on deodorant. Dammit.* Diana picks up her purse from the passenger seat. *I'll set three alarms for tomorrow. And I won't think about the letter for the rest of the day,* she vows, opening her door into the biting cold.

Chapter Four

If Diana were to make a list of what she loves about her job as the assistant director of Alcott Memorial Library, at the top would be the library itself: the way the building smells, like stories yet to be told, or the unturned pages of a brand-new book. She loves how walking through the doors fills her with a sense of familiarity and safety, and how the library, after all these years, still seems like magic.

Completed in 1901, Alcott Memorial Library is a Tudor masterpiece, an odd architectural choice for a town that had been a Revolutionary War battleground, but Alcott lore is that the library's main benefactor was a serious Anglophile. He wanted the recognizable dark trim and timbered ceilings and withheld his funding until the town agreed. He tried for a moat as well; town leaders finally stood up to his bullying when he made that proposal.

To Diana, the library is the heart of Alcott. Senior citizens return their books in the mornings, gathering by the circulation desk, while in the late afternoon, teenagers camp out at the wooden tables on the lower level to finish their homework. Diana remembers visiting the library with her mother when she was a child, and that she works here now reminds her both how rapidly time speeds by and how the past has only just happened.

Diana takes the elevator to the fourth floor, eyes on her watch: 8:26 a.m. After dumping her bag and coat in her office, she snatches a pad and pen from her desk and sprints to the conference room. Of course, the one morning when she would have welcomed late arrivals, everyone is on time. In the rear of the room, the department's administrative assistant sets up the projector and laptop, and another colleague passes out agendas. They stepped in for her, again. She says a voiceless prayer of thanks and walks through the doors.

Ninety minutes later, Diana sits at her desk, sipping the coffee Lakshmi gave her, now room temperature, and listening to her stomach growl. She should have taken Lakshmi's advice and eaten that banana on the drive to work. She also should have remembered to bring in the banana from her car.

The meeting, thankfully, went well, though Diana makes a mental note to avoid scheduling early-morning appointments again. Her guilt about the way she interacted with both of her children this morning gnaws at her. Hopefully, all she needs is a good night's sleep to parent better tomorrow.

Yet sleep alone can't fix the real reason she snapped at Phoebe.

Despite her vow to not think about the letter, halfway through her meeting, it crept back into her thoughts. Ignoring it, Diana understands, will be impossible. Without the truth, she'll worry about Tom's secret and obsess about all he might have done.

The only option is to decipher this strange, unsettling news. She has to figure out what Tom was really trying to tell her. The letter is more than a vague warning about unknown people. Or, at least, it has to be . . . right?

What's the first step people take on those British crime shows when they're charged with solving a mystery? They call in a smart detective with a charming accent. She doesn't have one of those, so Google will have to suffice.

Diana wakes up her computer and navigates to her internet browser. She enters *"Thomas Morgan"* + *crime* into the search bar and hits Return.

Diana hopes nothing will appear, that this whole mess is a dream, a nightmare, a lie.

Quickly, too quickly, the screen loads with the results. *Hundreds of results.*

So many different Thomas Morgans have committed so many different crimes, from mail fraud to theft to tax evasion to child pornography. Diana grows queasy with each result. She studies an article about a Thomas Morgan seeking a prison pen pal and spends too much time looking at the mug shots of Thomas Morgans. None of these men are her husband. A revised search—*"Thomas Morgan" + crime + 1982*, the year Tom turned eighteen—also doesn't turn up what she needs.

Trying to decide where and what to search for next, she doesn't notice when her office door, which she left slightly ajar, is pushed open. The library's director, Camille Taylor, appears in the doorway. "Diana?"

Nearly six feet tall with her hair in long, thin braids gathered in a bun, Camille has dark eyes and freckles along her high cheekbones. Today, she wears a white tunic and slim-cut navy pants with sparkling teardrop earrings and silver bangles on her wrists. The two women first met a decade ago, when Diana, sick of the commute into Boston, interviewed to work at Alcott Memorial. As the first female head of the library, Camille diversified the collection to include more writers of color, hired staff experienced with technology and social media, and raised record-setting donations for the library. Along the way, Camille and Diana bonded over their children, their vision for Alcott Memorial, and their shared love of historical fiction.

"Are you free?" Camille asks, bracelets jingling against one another as she closes the door.

"Of course." Diana minimizes the internet browser and turns her computer screen slightly away.

"You seemed distracted in the meeting, and I wanted to check on you."

Diana fidgets with the pen lying on her desk. "I had a terrible night's sleep, and it must have thrown me off. Do you think the team could tell? Should I send an apology email?"

Camille's shoulders relax, and she lowers into the chair. "An apology isn't necessary. I doubt anyone noticed other than me. Is there anything you need to talk about?"

Diana considers telling Camille about Tom's letter, but every one of her instincts, no matter how dulled by the hangover of insomnia and all that wine, begs her to stay silent. After all, she has no idea what she's dealing with. Camille and the rest of the library staff were generous with their time and patience while Tom was sick and in the months after his death, but there's a limit, isn't there?

"No, nothing's bothering me," she lies. "Nothing at all."

After Camille leaves, several additional online searches bring Diana no closer to deciphering Tom's letter, so she calls down to the reference desk for help accessing the library's online research consortium. The librarian, in quintessentially gruff New England fashion, chastises her for never registering for the service. She rectifies Diana's oversight in seconds, grumbling all the way. "If you have other questions, we're here," the librarian, a neighbor of Diana's parents, adds before she abruptly hangs up.

"No thanks," Diana mutters, moving back to her computer screen. She stops at the framed photo of Tom on her desk. She snapped it on their honeymoon in Greece, the blue and white buildings of Santorini aglow in the waning rays of a sunset that reached on into forever. It's as if the photo has captured his essence, as if she could bring him back to the living with it if she only tries hard enough.

Another list comes to her: *Why Didn't Tom Tell Me What He Did?* Why go to the trouble of writing—and hiding—this letter and keep the whole truth to himself?

He meant to tell me but got too sick to do so.

He was scared.

He was afraid of what would happen if I knew the truth.

He—

Diana is pulled out of her list-making by animated voices in the hall. She sticks her head out of her office to find her mother in conversation with the department admin. Afraid Vivian is asking her colleague highly personal questions or offering unsolicited advice, both of which her mother is wont to do, Diana interrupts her mid-sentence. "Mom? What are you doing here?"

Vivian nods goodbye to the admin and lugs two shopping bags to Diana. "I'm here to see you, of course."

"I'm working."

"I'm sure you can take a break to talk with your mother, can't you?" Vivian kisses Diana's cheek and breezes into her office, rose perfume trailing along behind her. She drops the bags next to the desk. "These are for the children. A new sweatshirt and jeans for Duncan. Socks, too. Pajamas and new dresses for Phoebe."

Diana pokes through the bags. "You didn't need to do this, Mom."

"I wanted to." Vivian sits down across from Diana and removes a glass container from her large purse. "An egg salad sandwich, your favorite. You forgot your lunch, didn't you?"

"Mom—"

"I thought more about Family Dinner. I'll bring everything, not only the main dish. All you need to do is prepare the house. You can do that, yes?"

"Yes, of course I can." Diana and her sister call Vivian "The General" behind her back, so efficiently does their mother run her life, their father's, and the rest of the family's. As a teenager, Diana chafed under her mother's extensive efficiency and competence; as a widow with two kids, she knows The General is one of the reasons she manages to remain a functioning member of society.

Her mother has always had the uncanny ability to anticipate her family's needs. Diana knows that if she looked inside that large purse, she'd find the typical items, like aspirin, mints, tissues, and lipstick, but also a number of surprises. Over the years, her mother's purse has been home to items significantly more unexpected than an egg salad sandwich: a pocket copy of the US Constitution, used to settle a heated argument about the Bill of Rights during a family road trip; a pepper grinder to add flavor to the rubbery chicken served during Duncan's basketball banquet; and a stapler she happened to have on the day Diana needed to turn in the kids' summer camp registration forms. The General has never produced a lamp from her bag like Mary Poppins, but Diana wouldn't put it past her mother to try.

"Thanks for the clothes. I'm sure the kids will love it all." Diana drains the last of Lakshmi's coffee. "What's on your schedule for the rest of the day?"

As Vivian describes the luncheon she's due to attend with an old college friend, the errands that will follow, and a Zumba class she's eager to try at the senior center, Diana remembers a moment, a few months after Tom's funeral, when she overheard her mother and sister whispering in her kitchen. Diana stood in the shadows on her stairs, bare feet pressed against the cool wooden floor, as they discussed what to do about her unrelenting sadness.

"It's gone too far," Andrea said. "She needs inpatient treatment."

"A hospital?" Vivian said, her voice breaking.

"It won't be long, Mom. A few weeks at the most."

Vivian began to weep. "We have to help her, but a hospital stay would be disruptive to the children. I . . . I don't know how to make this better for them."

Her mother's pain was a weight Diana hadn't expected. It made her see, for the first time, what her descent into grief was doing to everyone around her. She decided then to hide her feelings, letting them emerge only when she was alone. She began right away, forcing herself to change out of the pajamas she'd worn for the past five days and shower. She cried as she blow-dried her hair and made her bed, but when she came downstairs to help make dinner, Diana was clear-eyed and somehow managed to stay upright. Her mother declared "she'd turned a corner," and her family eagerly embraced this pretend Diana, a fantasy she's kept going ever since.

So ingrained is she in this pretense that Diana doesn't tell her mother about Tom's letter, opting to keep this development to herself.

After her mother leaves, Diana spends the rest of the afternoon preparing next year's budget, approving licenses for more young adult e-books, and answering overdue emails. Another time, she would have described the day as productive; today it feels more like procrastination. When the clock turns to 5:00 p.m., she reluctantly heads out, already wishing it were tomorrow.

After a drive she can't remember making, Diana arrives home, parking in her driveway and listening as her car pings and hums as it shuts down. Like most nights, she hasn't planned ahead for dinner, so she'll most likely fall back on what she secretly refers to as "the widow's special": dumping a box of pasta into boiling water and waiting impatiently for it to cook, as a jar of tomato sauce burns across the stove.

Her phone beeps with a text from Evan: Hope Duncan's feeling better. Too bad he had to miss the basketball clinic. Give a call if you need anything.

Feeling better? What's wrong with Duncan?

Before she can act on Evan's message, an alarm on her phone sounds, reminding her that she's due to collect Phoebe from her after-school program. Diana walks across the street to the elementary school, where Phoebe is waiting at the side door with her bag packed and coat zipped. She is not the last child to be picked up, though she has been plenty of times before.

As Diana waves to the after-school coordinator, Phoebe barrels into her arms, nearly knocking the two of them over. "Mama, I'm happy to see you."

"I'm happy to see you, too," Diana says, rescuing Phoebe's hair from where it's stuck in her coat collar.

Phoebe's face shines up at Diana, and for an instant, bathed in her daughter's love, Diana forgets about Tom's letter, work, her ongoing grief, and stress. She stares at her daughter, as if meeting her for the first time. The elements that make up Phoebe's face come into clear focus: the swell of her cheeks, the beauty mark under her left eye, the curve of her upper lip. *This is what matters,* Diana thinks, kissing the top of Phoebe's head.

"Let's go home," Phoebe says, impatiently tugging at Diana's hand. "Bear Bear doesn't want to be alone anymore."

When they cross the street into their yard, Lakshmi comes out on her front porch. "Do you want to join us for dinner?" She gestures into her house. "I have enough."

Diana does want to go inside, more than anything. She needs to tell someone about the letter, and Lakshmi may be the only person in her life who will be able to hold conflicting ideas of Tom in her mind, remembering the man independent of his secret.

But that will have to wait. Diana needs to track down Duncan.

"Mama." Phoebe tugs at her arm.

"Not tonight, Lax. Let's catch up tomorrow? After Phoebe goes to bed? I'll bring the wine."

"Of course. Ramesh will be in DC." Lakshmi tightens her fleece against her body. "I could use the company."

The house is dark when they enter, and as Phoebe chats about her day, Diana flips on light switches and hangs up their coats. "Duncan?" she calls out.

She's met with silence, but she has a feeling he's nearby and something is wrong.

"Pheebs, I'm going upstairs for a minute."

"I have to get Bear Bear. I left him in my room."

"I'll bring him down for you, honey. You unpack your backpack in the kitchen."

When Diana steps onto the upstairs landing, she hears a sniffle. Duncan's room is empty, the bed still unmade from his morning rush to school, his laundry basket on its side in the corner, socks and boxers in a heap on the floor. It takes a moment—seconds, really—for Diana to realize where he is. She sprints down the hall, past Phoebe's bedroom, the window seat her father built for them, the bathroom the kids share, and into her bedroom. That's where she finds Duncan, crumpled on the floor, clutching Tom's letter.

Chapter Five

When all this is over, Diana will reflect upon her hasty and ill-considered decision to stick Tom's letter in her bedside table. What if she'd taken it with her to the library instead? Or locked it up, as she later did, in the fireproof box in the office, with their passports and birth certificates? Would Duncan have given up on his need to know what his father had written? Would he have accepted that Tom's message wasn't for him and moved on?

She doesn't think any of this when she finds him on her bedroom floor, curled up on the braided area rug, his long legs squashed into his chest. Instead, terror rockets through her nervous system, down her spine, and all the way to her toes.

"Duncan?" She falls to her knees. "What's happened?"

Diana leans over him, her hair falling out of her ponytail and across her face. She pushes the strands behind her ears and slowly turns Duncan over, not wanting to worsen his pain. Her brain hasn't fully calculated that Duncan + letter = a problem she can't easily parent her way through. In a fruitless attempt to believe something other than the letter is causing his distress, she searches his body; there's no blood, no broken bone poking through the skin. His eyelids are scrunched together, his face red and twisted. She settles next to him on the floor, cross-legged, one hand on his shoulder, the other on his knee. "Duncan?"

He opens his eyes. They are bloodshot, the lashes clumped together in unhappy spikes. He thrusts the letter at her and sits up, his legs sprawled in front of him. "What's this, Mom? What does it mean?"

She has no idea what to say. How does she explain this to Duncan when she can't explain it to herself?

"He says people *died* because of him." Duncan jabs at the letter. "Who died? Who?" He's yelling at her, his voice filled with fear.

Before Diana can respond, Phoebe is in the doorway, holding Bear Bear. "Mama? Why is Duncan upset?" Weeping, she runs to her mother's lap as Diana takes the letter from Duncan and pushes it under the bed. Phoebe's sobs are sympathetic, unconnected to Duncan's discovery, or maybe she's been holding them in for some time. They're relentless, too, soaking the front of Diana's sweater. She starts to hyperventilate, her chest heaving and her body twitching. Duncan's emotions abate the more upset Phoebe becomes, and soon he's wrapped himself around his sister, trying to soothe her.

They've been here before. After Tom died, they each fell into grief in unsettling, yet different, ways. Phoebe cried unceasingly, exhausting herself until she passed out every evening. Duncan withdrew, nearly failing out of school. Diana fell into a stupor, sleeping for days at a time. The thought of returning to that period fills her with dread.

"Phoebe, honey, you're all right," Diana whispers, holding her children tight to her body, one arm around each of them.

When Phoebe calms down, she's limp in Diana's arms, eyes puffy and hair matted against her face.

"Duncan, let me put your sister to bed, and then we can talk." Diana lurches up onto her left leg and then her right, Phoebe's weight making her off balance and awkward. "Okay?" She looks at Duncan as she leaves the room, and he nods with one curt tilt of his head.

She expects he'll listen to her, that he'll wait, but after she's escorted Phoebe to the bathroom, changed her into pajamas, and tucked her into bed, Diana hears the front door slam.

Through Phoebe's bedroom window, in the darkening twilight, Diana watches as Duncan runs onto the basketball court of Phoebe's elementary school. Up he goes, tossing the ball into the net; he sprints to save it from rolling into the snow. He runs to the other side, dribbling all the while, only changing which hand bumps the ball up and down. Back to the net and up, stretching to direct the basketball through. Over and over, Duncan barrels across the court. As if compelled to keep his body in motion.

Diana knew nothing about basketball before Duncan picked up the sport. Tom, a freshman starter on his high school's varsity basketball team, hoped Duncan would be similarly inclined, so he registered him for Alcott's recreational basketball league before the boy could tie his sneakers. From the second the orange ball was placed in Duncan's hands, he was captivated. Whenever Tom could get away from work, he and Duncan would be on this court, sometimes joined by other kids from the neighborhood. More often than not, it was the two of them alone, strategizing plays, improving Duncan's jump shot, and practicing rebounds. When the winter weather forced them inside, they watched Celtics games on television together, wearing matching Larry Bird jerseys, perched on the edge of the sofa. The sport bonded the two of them, with Tom passing on his love of the game to his son as a kind of legacy.

During those first few months without Tom, when Duncan clammed up and wouldn't talk to anyone, Diana, barely able to function herself, sat silently next to her son on the sofa while he watched countless basketball games, including old playoff series broadcasting on cable channels she didn't even know they had. After a while, she started to talk to him during the commercial breaks. At first, Duncan ignored her. Then, slowly and begrudgingly, he started to answer her inquiries about zone defense, the three-second rule, and traveling. Sometimes, he even mocked her ignorance ("Mom, how do you *not* know this?"), rolling his eyes when he thought her question was particularly ill informed. Those were her initial glimmers he would be okay.

Diana hurries out of her house, pausing at the edge of the yard to wait for a car traveling down the street to pass by. The driver, a slight figure hunched over the steering wheel, steps on the gas as the car approaches Diana, tires squealing. Before Diana can yell at the driver to *slow down*, the car is gone, and the lights around the basketball court click on, making her blink.

Intent on his game, Duncan doesn't waver as she runs across the road to him. She made a mistake asking him to wait. While she may have needed a few minutes to take care of Phoebe, the delay was too much to ask of him. So, of course, he came here. He always comes to the basketball court when he's upset.

Diana stops at the edge of the court, clearly visible to her son, and watches him. Lately, she's been distracted, not ignoring her children, but not giving them her full attention either. Her grief is to blame, as is her job. She's given both of those areas of her life more energy and space than she should have. *No parenting awards for me,* she thinks.

"Duncan? Why didn't you wait for me?"

He bounces the ball harder against the blacktop, scowling.

That's the wrong question. Why did I ask that? "Do you want to talk about what you found?"

Duncan stops, gripping the ball. He starts to speak but abruptly turns to the net instead. Up he jumps, and the ball goes through. *Swish. Swoosh.*

"Are you worried I'm mad at you for lying to Uncle Evan about being sick? Or finding the letter?" Diana asks, trying again. "Don't be. I wish you hadn't, of course, because it wasn't for you. I'm not mad at you, though."

Duncan captures the ball as it exits the hoop and bounces once near her feet. Diana asks herself whether it's possible to mess up this conversation more. "What I mean is that I don't understand the letter myself. Not yet. Since you've read it—" Diana is interrupted by her son's anguish.

"Why, Mom? Why did he have to die? Why did he leave us?" Duncan drops the ball, clenching his fists and looking down at his feet. "Why?" he asks, the tears coming fast, falling to the ground and disappearing into the blacktop.

Diana is at his side, wrapping her arms around him. "*Shhh,* honey. I'm here." They rock together, their weight shifting from one foot to the other, not unlike how Diana soothed him late at night when, as an infant, he emerged from a satisfying slumber to the shock of being awake. "*Shh, shh.*"

"Why, Mom?"

"He was sick, honey, and the doctors didn't have the medicine to help him."

"He had cancer." Duncan's voice is so low Diana strains to hear him.

"Yes, cancer." Only months between diagnosis and death; not enough time to get better. But enough time to write that letter.

"He gets fuzzier in my mind." Duncan gulps as he grabs for air to fill his constricted lungs. "Sometimes, I can't remember him on my own. Like he's only a story someone told me, not a real person. Why, Mommy? Why?"

Duncan hasn't called her Mommy in years. She pulls him closer, his shoulder blades taut under her hands. She inhales his twelve-year-old-boy scent, drenched with sweat and sadness.

This is the truth of their lives: An enormous loss has reshaped all of them, forcing the kids to grow up in ways they shouldn't have, at least not so soon. While she would give anything to be able to take away Duncan's grief, to lessen his pain would be, in some ways, dishonest. What Diana can do—what she *has* to do—is validate his emotions. He needs to believe the parent he has left is there for him.

"Why did your dad die? I don't know. He should be with us, helping you and your sister with your impossible math homework, teaching Phoebe to ride a bike, and, of course, playing basketball with you."

As Duncan's breathing calms, Diana slides her thumb along his cheek. "There's nothing we can do to change the fact he's not here.

What we can do is keep going and look out for one another. Remember your dad loved us, and loves us still, wherever he is."

Duncan sniffs. "Where do you think he is?"

This isn't the first time Duncan has asked this question. A few weeks before he died, Tom was having a good day, so Diana set him up in the backyard, on a chaise under the shade from their beech tree. Despite the eighty-degree temperature, she wrapped him in a blanket and put on his head the straw sun hat with a lavender ribbon she wore to the beach.

"I look like a farmer," Tom said, as she straightened the blanket around him.

"Not at all, love. In fact, you're wearing the latest in vacation sun hat fashion. No self-respecting farmer would wear this to toil in the fields." Diana bent down under the brim to kiss him, her lips gentle against his.

As Tom touched her cheek, Duncan burst out of the house, the *Boston Globe* sports section in hand. "Can I sit with you?"

"Sure, buddy," Tom replied, patting the edge of the chaise. "Like my hat?"

"That hat is dumb."

"Duncan!" Diana said. They were all tentative around Tom, around each other, too. They chose their words carefully, didn't criticize or make noise, and didn't think beyond the next few minutes.

"You should wear mine." Duncan settled his Celtics ball cap on Tom's head, tossing the straw hat to Diana. "Better, right?"

"Much better. Thanks." Tom looked at Diana with a faint smirk.

"I'll get you two a snack." Diana paused on the top of the deck stairs to watch Duncan and Tom huddle over the newspaper, already oblivious to her. Increasingly, she could see they were getting closer to the end, and that she and the kids weren't ready. She worried Tom sitting outside would confuse Duncan and Phoebe. They might believe he was improving; they might hope he'd make it.

In the kitchen, Diana poured two glasses of lemonade and placed four of her mother's chocolate chip cookies on a plate. They were Tom's favorite, though he ate so little. She returned outside, but the conversation between Duncan and Tom froze her on the other side of the tree.

"You feeling good today? Maybe better than yesterday?" Duncan's questions for his father were full of longing.

"Duncan, I'm not going to get better," Tom said, softly, so softly. "I love you, buddy. More than anything else."

"Even more than basketball?"

"Even more than basketball."

Duncan sobbed, the first time since Tom's diagnosis, and a stinging pain filled Diana's chest. She wavered, the tray shifting in her hands, and the lemonade spilled, drenching the cookies.

Tom held Duncan to his chest. The more Duncan shook, the tighter Tom's arms grew around him, until Duncan quieted, Tom's mouth at his ear murmuring words Diana couldn't hear.

Eventually, Duncan sat up, wiping his hand across his face. "What happens? After, I mean."

"I'm not sure. But I'll be with you. You can talk to me. I'll listen, though I won't be able to respond." Tom took Duncan's hand in his. "I will always, always love you. That doesn't change because you can't see me. I promise."

Standing on the basketball court with Duncan now, Diana remembers how people said the acute pain she and the kids experienced when Tom first died would dissipate. It would get easier, everyone said. She's still waiting.

"I'd like to believe your dad is somewhere good, where he can shoot hoops and watch *Star Wars*. Maybe he's still with us, listening and hoping we won't be this sad for too much longer. Maybe he's here on this basketball court with us. No matter where he is, he loves us."

"This sucks," Duncan says, pulling away from her to stand on his own. He gestures in the direction of his basketball, hidden in the shadowy snow piles along the court. "Dad gave that ball to me for my sixth birthday. I loved it so much I slept with it next to my bed. That Paul Pierce poster I have in my room? Dad gave it to me, too. I have all this stuff he gave me—*but I don't have him.* What the hell, Mom?"

Diana lets "hell" go by without comment. "The weeks after your dad died, I walked around our house taking an inventory of our possessions, like our books and his CD collection and the snowblower. These objects were here, all around us. And your dad wasn't. I was so mad about that.

"I was especially furious about a bottle of hot sauce. Your dad used it only once. Too spicy, he said, even for him. I found it in the back of the fridge. It made me so angry. I thought about driving the car over it but was afraid I'd puncture the tires. Instead, I put it in a Ziploc bag and smashed it to pieces with the hammer one night after you and Phoebe went to bed."

Duncan stares at her, his mouth hanging open.

"I was better after. Only a little bit, though." Diana never planned to tell anyone that story, especially not Duncan.

"Does this mean I can break something?" Duncan offers Diana a small grin, and she understands she was right to open up.

"If smashing a bottle of hot sauce will make you feel better, then yes. Ask me first, though, so we can keep you safe." Diana smooths his sandy-colored hair back from his face and holds his chin in her hands. "I appreciate you shared all of this with me, honey. Thank you."

"Mom, that letter . . . What does it mean? What did Dad do? Who's coming for you?"

Diana feels a rush of fear. This can't be one of those times she says or does the wrong thing.

"This letter," she begins. "It could all be a misunderstanding." Diana wants to believe this, and she wants Duncan to as well.

So many emotions—sorrow, anger, and confusion—ripple across his face. "How am I supposed to remember him, or try to remember him, if he was someone else?" Duncan asks, kicking at the ground, pebbles ricocheting across the court.

How am I supposed to remember him if he was someone else? The words burrow into Diana, staking their claim on her memories of Tom. She wants to be alone, to hide in her room and scream into her pillow.

Instead, because her son needs her, she offers Duncan the assurance they both crave. "I'll figure it out. Make some phone calls, do some research. But Duncan, this has to stay between us."

"I can help." He squares his shoulders in a movement that could have been cloned from Tom.

"No, this letter is my responsibility. Your job is to go to school, do your homework, and play basketball. It may take me a while to sort this, so you have to be patient. You're staying out of it. No discussion. And we'll keep this between you and me, for now. No talking about it with anyone else. No worrying Grandma or Grandpa, or Uncle Evan and Aunt Andie. Deal?" She holds out her hand, and he shakes it.

"Good," Diana says, swaying on her feet. She mentally adds a large glass of wine to her to-do list for the evening. "Let's go in. It's chilly, and your sister's by herself. I don't want her to be frightened if she wakes up alone."

"I have to get my ball." Duncan runs to the far side of the court. He picks up the basketball Tom gave him, and because he can't help himself, he pivots and tosses the ball up to the hoop.

Swish.

He catches it before it hits the ground and returns to Diana, taking her hand in his.

Chapter Six

Preteen boy clothes are disgusting, Diana thinks as she loads Duncan's basketball shirts into the washer. It's best to do the laundry each day, lest the odor kills them all.

There is much Diana hates about maintaining a house: mopping the children's breakfast crumbs from the kitchen floor, managing the unending saga of dusting, and scrubbing toilets. The list of her least favorite chores is tiresome and infinite. Laundry, however, is an altogether different task.

Diana loves the way clothes smell brand new when they first come out of the dryer, and she appreciates the satisfaction of folding towels into a perfectly straight pile, all the corners lining up. Most of all, she loves the brief look back at the days that have already disappeared as shown through her family's clothes: her daughter's muddy leggings from playing tag with the neighborhood kids, her son's basketball jersey damp with perspiration from one of his many games, her kitchen towels marked with traces of Lakshmi's latest meal. When Diana drops the items, one by one, into the washing machine, she says a soundless goodbye to those rapidly fading moments and watches as the clothes swirl together, preparing for what is yet to come.

With those images clear in her mind, Diana closes the washer door, fills the dispenser with detergent, and turns on the wash cycle. Then she heads upstairs with a white plastic basket piled high with clean clothes. Arriving on the landing outside their bedrooms, Diana checks on the kids. Phoebe is already asleep, with Bear Bear in her arms and lullabies playing on Tom's old iPod. Duncan sits at his bedroom desk, finishing up his homework. While they haven't discussed the letter since last night's conversation on the basketball court, he gave her a long hug this morning as he left for school, embracing her so fiercely her ribs ached afterward.

Diana puts the laundry basket on her bed and begins folding. Occasionally, when she comes across items of Tom's the kids have taken as their own—his law school sweatshirt, a pair of cozy argyle socks—she groups them separately, as if forgetting he no longer needs them.

After Duncan agrees to listen for Phoebe and go to bed as soon as his homework is done, Diana leaves for Lakshmi's. Once she's inside her friend's house, Diana's tension fades away. Unlike her own home, which is more of a way station, at Lakshmi's, she finds succor and stability. She can leave her life behind.

Lakshmi is in front of her stove, stirring a bubbling pot and dancing to pop music playing from her phone. Diana pauses to take in Lakshmi's artwork, framed in gold and arranged together on the wall. The paintings are only ten by ten inches, and the subject matter is prosaic—a peony in full bloom, a pile of books, a beach ball—but the canvases have a liveliness that draws people in.

Diana's favorite of Lakshmi's pieces hangs in her own kitchen. It's an earlier work, and while Lakshmi's technique has improved since then, to Diana, it's by far her best. Three peaches nestle in a blue bowl, sunlight falling across them with a shadow at the edge. Diana has added the painting to the list of things she'd save in an emergency, a categorization at which Lakshmi, ever humble, scoffs.

Lakshmi glances up. "How long have you been there?"

"A minute or two. Looking to see if you've added any new paintings." Diana holds out a bottle of wine. "Pinot grigio."

"My favorite, thank you." Lakshmi accepts the wine and gestures to the stove. "I'm making chai. Or would you prefer the wine?"

"I can't handle caffeine this late."

"I made it decaf," Lakshmi says, her smile indicating she anticipated that concern. She places the wine inside the refrigerator and hands Diana a bowl of pistachios. "Why don't you settle in, and I'll be over with our drinks."

Diana dumps her tote bag on a chair and takes a seat at the oval kitchen table. "Celine Dion?" she asks, gesturing to Lakshmi's phone.

"Of course, Celine. I keep telling Ramesh we have to go to her concert in Las Vegas, but he's not as big a fan as me." Lakshmi turns down the volume on the music and hands a cup of steaming chai to Diana. "Celine lost her husband, too. She took some time off from performing afterward, but thankfully she's returned to the stage."

Diana holds the mug up to her face, letting the chai's steam warm her skin as she inhales its luscious ginger-and-cardamom scent. "I'm afraid I'm not up to speed on the ins and outs of Celine Dion's life." Hoping to change the subject, she points to the corner of the room, where a canvas sits on an easel in front of a north-facing window. A profile of a person is sketched in the center, the lines tentative, as if the artist is still formulating her idea. "A new piece?"

Lakshmi crosses her arms as she examines the easel. "I'm trying to paint Ramesh. Capturing him is hard, though. He's too impatient to sit for me. I thought I could do this from memory, but I may have to refer to a photograph. Or maybe I have to give up and start another project."

That's the secret of painting, Diana has learned from Lakshmi: If you don't like the direction of a new piece, all it takes is a paintbrush to wipe it away so you can begin again.

Begin again. Diana lets that thought roll around in her mind until it's close to the surface. What if she could begin again? What if she could relive all the years with Tom? How would they be different now that she knows he had a secret so significant he kept it from her until he was gone? That he withheld part of himself? That he didn't trust her? She pushes away these thoughts from their hold on her and returns her focus to Lakshmi.

"Does Ramesh want you to paint him?" She considers what it would be like if Lakshmi asked to paint her. She'd be flattered. And nervous to have her friend look that closely at her.

"He doesn't have a choice," Lakshmi says, grinning. "I'm the artist, after all."

Lakshmi hasn't always been an artist. Before painting, she was associate general counsel for a tech company in Boston. One late night at the office, her boss hit on her, and when Lakshmi turned him down—"as kindly as I could," she explained to Diana—he retaliated. Her office was reallocated without explanation, rumors spread that Lakshmi slept around, and she was blamed for a colleague's mistake when all the evidence was to the contrary. With her reputation and career in jeopardy, Lakshmi sought Tom's help. When her company learned she was willing to forgo the public embarrassment of a lawsuit for a quiet, yet lucrative, settlement, Tom made sure the matter was speedily resolved.

Afterward, Lakshmi enrolled in a painting class to lift her spirits, and she turned out to have a natural inclination for matching color and light on canvas. She now teaches the class that ignited her interest and finds herself busy with commissions and pieces of her own.

Lakshmi takes a seat next to Diana. "How are you? I've done all the talking since you arrived."

"Work is hectic," Diana says. "I miss Tom all the time. It's like I'm not remembering him as much as I'm imagining." She runs her tongue along her teeth, trying to clear the sourness that fills her mouth when she speaks of her grief.

"Imagining?"

"What life would be like if he was still here. Or what could have happened. It's as if my future memory bank can't turn off. I see him at Duncan's high school graduation or walking Phoebe down the aisle at her wedding or holding our someday grandchildren. He's there, part of our lives, not only in our memories." Tears roll down Diana's cheeks and onto her scarf. She wipes them away with the chunky fringe. "You'd expect I'd be better at responding to a simple 'How are you.' It's been eighteen months, after all."

Lakshmi puts her hand on Diana's forearm. "It's all right, I'm the one who asked."

"You did. It's your fault."

"Yes," Lakshmi says, smiling. "It's all my fault."

Diana returns Lakshmi's smile, and the two women fall into a comfortable quiet. They've been close since Diana and Tom moved in next door, their friendship an unforeseen boon no real estate agent could have predicted. In the days after Tom's death, when Diana felt herself drifting, unable to function, she listed the people who were still in her life, saying their names over and over, like a mantra: Phoebe and Duncan; her parents; Andrea, Evan, and Noah; Camille; Lakshmi, Ramesh, and Mira.

Lakshmi clears her throat. "Can I make a suggestion? What about trying therapy again? Maybe it might help this time?"

Diana tried therapy once, joining a grief support group after Tom died. It met on Sunday nights at Saint Florian's, a church in a town where she knew no one, sharing space with AA meetings. An untouched box of sugar wafer cookies sat on the table in the center of the room, and paintings by the church's nursery school students lined the walls. The group was run by a social worker whose voice sounded like an oboe, wistful and expressive. It was clear from the way the members diligently attended, always on time, that many found the group beneficial. Slowly, though, what was supposed to be a tool to lift Diana up became an albatross, weighing her down.

Listening to those other people talk, Diana learned everyone carried some kind of grief, and her pain wasn't special. The commonness of the shared loss repelled her. She stopped attending the meetings and never returned the social worker's follow-up phone calls. Maybe quitting was a mistake; maybe she would have found solace in that group like the others had. She'd never know. Since then, she's worked to forget the stories she heard in that room, sitting on the metal folding chairs around the untouched box of cookies. Sometimes, usually late at night, they come back to her, adding to her own grief and expanding her pain.

"It's not for me, Lax."

"What about a therapist? One-on-one with someone?"

Diana shakes her head.

"Will you at least tell me what's going on? You've been doing so well. Has something changed?"

If she tells Lakshmi about the letter, she will never be able to hide from the fact Tom did something terrible and kept it from her.

"Diana?"

Diana meets her friend's kind, worried eyes. She came to Lakshmi for help. She can't get that help if she keeps this story to herself. She has to trust someone, and there's no one better than Lakshmi. With shaking hands, Diana removes the letter from her tote and places it on the table.

"This is a letter from Tom. He wrote it before he died. I just found it. Will you read it, please? I could use some advice."

Lakshmi nods. A moment into reading, she reaches for Diana. Diana laces her fingers between her friend's, Lakshmi's cool skin against her own. She examines the paint on Lakshmi's hand—mustard yellow, black, flecks of gray, a little spot of pink on her thumb.

When Lakshmi arrives at the last sentence, she squeezes Diana's hand. "This is . . . Are you okay?"

"No, I'm not."

"You didn't know about this? This crime?"

"I have no idea what this is about."

"What about these 'others' Tom mentions? He says"—Lakshmi releases Diana's hand and points to the letter—"*they may come into your life*? What does that mean?"

"Another thing I don't understand."

"No one's come by the house or work? Or sent a letter or package? Or called you?"

"No to all of that," Diana says, "but now that you ask, I didn't check the landline. I never give that number out, though, so I doubt anyone's called there."

"You have a landline?" Lakshmi looks at her quizzically, head tilted to the side.

"We got it when we moved in; it came with the internet. The tele-marketer calls and hang-ups got so bad last year that I turned off the ringer." Diana sips her chai. "He hid the letter for me to find; did you catch that? I don't understand any of this."

"Where did you find the letter?"

"In a time capsule from 2012 that the kids and I opened two days ago. The letter was written in 2014, sometime after he was diagnosed in May and before he died that September."

Lakshmi sits back, staring at Diana. "I have no idea what to say."

"I did some research at work yesterday and again today. I didn't find anything useful." Diana pulls out her laptop. "I thought maybe you could help me. Two heads are better than one and all that."

"Yes, of course, I'll help you. Whatever you need." Lakshmi bites her lip. "Diana, he's not asking you to sort this. You don't have to do this."

"But I do. I need to be prepared in case those people come looking for me. Imagine you discovered a letter like this from Ramesh. Would you put it away somewhere and forget about it?"

Lakshmi tugs at her braid. "I probably wouldn't be able to let it go."

"Why wouldn't you ignore it?"

"Because I love him."

"*And* because you'd have to understand why he didn't tell you about this before." The next part is hard to say out loud. Diana forces her-self to meet Lakshmi's gaze, instead of looking away. "There's another reason, too. The kids were there when I found the letter. I wouldn't let them see it, of course, but Duncan looked for it. I guess I hadn't hidden it well enough. I never thought he'd go through my room."

Lakshmi gasps. "He read it?"

Diana nods. "So I can't ignore it, even if I might want to. He misses Tom so much, and if I don't figure this out, his feelings about his father could become confused or twisted. He could grow to resent Tom because he kept a secret like this. I can't let that happen."

"Of course you can't," Lakshmi says, standing up from the table. "I think we need the wine after all."

Diana offers a small smile. "Maybe we do."

While Lakshmi rounds up the bottle and glasses, Diana turns on her laptop. She enters her password, JUNE30, Tom's birthday. A five-year-old photo of her family on a hike in the Berkshires fills the screen. A pigtailed Phoebe sits on Tom's shoulders; Diana and Duncan stand on either side, offering half-hearted grins.

Why did she select *this* photo as her screensaver? It hadn't been a happy day; that hike, in fact, had been a disaster.

That summer, Diana's parents had rented a bungalow on a small lake near Stockbridge for their vacation and planned to spend two weeks attending classical music concerts, visiting museums, and watching the sunrise from the dock behind the house. They invited Diana, Tom, and the kids for a long weekend, and Diana agreed without consulting Tom. He'd been withdrawn and unreachable for weeks. A relaxing time away, Diana had decided, was exactly what they all needed.

Tom, however, was unwilling to embrace a few lazy days on the lake and mapped out that hike for the four of them, confident the kids would be able to keep up. "They can handle it," he said when she protested. "The exercise will be good for them."

They spoke in biting whispers, the house too small for privacy. A heat wave had rolled through the area, and the bungalow, which had appeared so charming in its online posting, was suffocating with its tiny windows and lack of air-conditioning.

Arguments between Diana and Tom were rare; she could count on one hand the number of times they'd fought. Typically, Diana capitulated when Tom's position became unyielding, her desire for peace overriding her need to be right or to win. She gave in quickly and often, falling into this habit early on, somehow intuiting that her adaptability was a necessary ingredient in their relationship.

That day, however, a restless Phoebe had kept her up all night, and Diana's exhaustion superseded her instinct to compromise. "They're four and seven, for God's sake," she pressed. "The hike is too strenuous for little kids. They can stay with my parents, and we'll go."

"They are coming with us," he said. "I will get water bottles and snacks. You find the sunblock and hats."

"But Tom—"

He didn't give Diana the courtesy of listening to the rest of her sentence. Instead, he stalked out of the room and into the hallway, where he greeted her father with artificial cheerfulness and made small talk about the weather. She waited for him to come back and finish their conversation, but he never did.

Diana's assessment of the kids' perseverance was, in the end, accurate. The hike included bouldering up a steep incline, crossing a rickety bridge, and passing through a swarm of gnats that flew into their noses and ears. Phoebe, usually the most optimistic of children, fell apart after the bugs, refusing to walk a step farther until Tom put her on his shoulders. Duncan trailed behind, dragging his feet, his shirt drenched in sweat.

Diana kept her emotions in check for the kids' sake, smothering her anger like she would extinguish the last flames of a campfire, ensuring nothing remained, not even one small cinder. She fed Duncan gummy fruit snacks and promised him a new Lego set if he'd take a few more steps. They finished the hike, but it took twice as long as Tom expected, and Duncan threw up in the parking lot when they finally made it to the car.

The photo had been taken during one of their many pauses to let the kids rest. A young couple passing by, looking like an ad for an outdoor living magazine, not a bead of sweat anywhere, offered to snap a photo for them to "remember this awesome day." Diana forced a smile and thanked them for their thoughtfulness while avoiding eye contact with Tom.

That evening, while the kids slept in front of a window fan and Diana drank half a bottle of rosé on the dock, her feet submerged in the brisk, mountain-fed water, Tom made excuses. He did not apologize or acknowledge her feelings, assuming, perhaps, they'd subsided like they had after every other disagreement. Instead, he talked about a trial that had ended badly, with a judgment against his clients, a retired couple facing foreclosure. When he said they were going to lose their house, she thought he was going to cry, and she forgave his rigidity and remoteness, wrapping her arms around him. She let herself forget the kids' discomfort, her anger, and his unwillingness to listen to her, and instead embraced a positive memory of that hike, one that was good enough for her to select a photo from that day as her screen saver.

Lakshmi sits back down at the table and opens the wine bottle. "Where shall we start? Have you tried googling Tom?"

Diana clears her throat. "Yes, and it wasn't helpful. I couldn't find a way to begin an organized search. I thought you could help me do this with some amount of logic."

"Let's focus on what he's saying. What's a fact, not an emotion?" Lakshmi pours the wine and hands a glass to Diana. "Where did he live when he was eighteen?"

"Tom turned eighteen in 1982, the summer he relocated from Vermont to college in North Carolina."

"Where in Vermont? I never heard him talk about his hometown."

"Hamilton, a small ski town about four hours from here," Diana says. "Whatever this is, it must have happened there or at college."

Lakshmi takes a pad and pen from the basket in the center of the table and, on a clean sheet of paper, writes *North Carolina or Vermont?* She draws a line down the center, making two columns. "Write down what you know and who you could talk to from that time."

Diana takes the pen and pad from Lakshmi. Under "North Carolina," she writes the name of Tom's law partner and roommate during college and law school, Jonathan Hobart.

Under the *V* in "Vermont," Diana lists Tom's family: his cousin, Chris, and Tom's aunt and uncle, Teresa and Brian.

"Remind me where they live?" Lakshmi asks, reading over Diana's shoulder.

"They also live in Hamilton," Diana says. "You've met them, right? Chris used to visit every year, while Teresa and Brian came down a few times. Tom brought me to visit them in Hamilton once, before the kids were born."

"Only once in all these years?" Lakshmi again tugs at her braid.

They only went that one time because Tom said going home was too painful. To him, Hamilton was all about grief. His father, Gary, passed away when Tom was nine, the same age Phoebe is now. Tom's mother, Martha, died when he was in law school. Diana is no longer sure whether his reluctance to return home was because of the loss of his parents—or this secret from his past. Had he lied to her about that, too?

What Do I Know? Diana taps her pen against the table, as a list begins. She tries to break down the letter as if it's a problem at work, a project she is paid to fix. She scribbles across the bottom of the page:

He committed a crime.

People died.

"Does murder have a statute of limitations?"

Lakshmi puts down her wineglass. "While it's wise to explore all of the options, Tom didn't kill anyone."

"You can't be sure he didn't. It's possible. He could have done it, Lax. He could have hurt someone, accidentally or deliberately. Or—"

"Diana."

All it takes is for Lakshmi to say her name, each syllable filled with compassion, and Diana bursts into tears. She is exhausted by her emotions, by everything, really, but the crying brings release, too, as if a rainstorm has arrived to wash away the humidity of a stifling summer afternoon.

Slowly, Diana's weeping is replaced by a rattling wheeze and then hiccups. "Sorry," she says, wiping her face with the tissue Lakshmi hands her.

"No apologies. This is upsetting," Lakshmi says gently. She pushes the pad to Diana. "Let's come up with a plan. Who on this list can shed light on Tom at eighteen years old?"

From the tone of Tom's letter, it's clear someone has the information she needs—and they're not the sort she should trust. But maybe there are other people who have part of the story, who can help her piece this together.

"Jonathan would have insight into their freshman year of college when they were both eighteen. Chris would be able to fill in the time before Tom left Hamilton. Maybe Uncle Brian and Aunt Teresa could help, too."

"Anyone else?"

Diana covers the page with random squiggles and lines as she considers Lakshmi's question. "There's no one else. Except for me, and I have zilch." She throws down the pen, and it rolls across the table. "This is all too much."

"Tell me about finding the letter. Maybe there's a clue there."

Diana opens up about Phoebe finding the time capsule, her own concerns about the look back into the past, the joy at seeing glimpses of their life together, and Duncan's grief. "I thought life was getting better and then this"—she points to the letter—"comes along."

"Finding a letter like this would throw anyone."

"Even Celine?"

Lakshmi laughs, a full-belly chuckle that makes Diana smile. "You still have your sense of humor. That's a good sign. And, yes, even Celine."

Diana picks up the letter, looking at the last paragraph: *When you speak of me to Duncan and Phoebe, tell them their father was imperfect, but he loved them, and you, more than anything.*

"The idea he had secrets . . . It's terrifying. How could I be with a person who hid something like this? What does this say about me that I was so unaware?"

"Don't let yourself go there, Diana. None of this is your fault."

"That's debatable, though I appreciate your vote of confidence," Diana says, sighing. "Lax, I've hit my limit. This is all I can handle tonight."

Lakshmi squeezes Diana's shoulder. "We're not done. I'm with you all the way. We'll talk more tomorrow."

Diana packs up and walks across the darkened yard to her home. After flipping Duncan's basketball gear from the washer to the dryer, she checks in on the kids. Both are fast asleep. She pauses on the landing between their bedrooms, in front of the wall of family photos. In the center is a photo she and Tom took during their visit to Hamilton; they pose with Chris, Aunt Teresa, and Uncle Brian in a hastily taken snapshot before departing. Their parents' and grandparents' wedding portraits are here, along with a photo from their own wedding. A dozen pictures of Phoebe and Duncan over the years cluster on either side. Diana walks by those photos every day; she even occasionally dusts them. Yet they exist in the background, like a curtain behind actors on a stage, hiding the ladders and paint cans from the audience, disguising what is real from the story the audience is being told. It's as if her whole life with Tom is on this wall. A life she thought she understood.

But what is her marriage, her love for this man, if he kept such a secret from her?

Chapter Seven

The clock reads 1:02 a.m. "Goddammit," Diana says, rubbing her eyes.

She's been awake for hours, her mind churning. Somewhere, maybe around midnight, her sadness over Tom's letter transformed into a new emotion: anger. Fury throbs inside her, beating in time with her grief, red and pulsating. Her skin is hot to the touch, as if a fire has been lit inside her.

A memory comes to her, one she hasn't thought of in years. One that, after Tom's letter, now appears much different.

When she and Tom first lived together, before they were engaged but when they were talking around the subject, their home was an apartment in Brookline, a few streets away from chewy bagels, delicious Thai food, and a bookstore where they spent Sunday afternoons. From every room in the apartment, they could hear the clanging of the subway cars rattling up and down Beacon Street. The train stopped at crowded intersections, picking up passengers making their way into Boston in one direction, or out to the suburbs in the other. The location, and the time, had been a crossroads in their lives.

What made their apartment extraordinary was the five-foot-tall Palladian window in the bathroom. The arched window of stained glass was perfectly preserved. Green ivy wove its way up and down the sides, and a delicate pink oval, lined by opalescent spheres, floated in the center. During the day, the sun fell through the window and danced across the floor.

Thinking about that room, years later, fills Diana with peace, as if remembering the way the light reflected through the glass could bring her back to a time when everything good was still ahead of her.

A claw-foot tub, the other element that convinced them to hand over first and last months' rent, as well as a security deposit of an equal amount, occupied the space under the window. To its left was a dark-green velvet armchair Diana pilfered from her childhood bedroom. It was here she would perch to read the newspaper aloud to Tom, as he rested in the tub after a fourteen-hour day filing motions and doing the grunt work of a junior lawyer in a big firm. This was before he and Jonathan went into business together and back when he still smoked.

"Only occasionally, only one, and only when I really need it," he explained, aware she hated the habit. He stopped when she became pregnant with Duncan, but back then, he needed a cigarette more often than not, the stress of work eating at him. In the bath, he would settle into the cooling water, his ashes falling onto a small saucer on the windowsill, as Diana's voice filled the room, echoing off the solid surfaces.

One night, after Diana read Tom an article about autumn foliage, she asked about a trip north. The leaves were especially spectacular in Vermont; why didn't they go up to Hamilton that weekend? Visit his family and check out the changing colors? He immediately said no, citing the need to work on Saturday.

Hoping to change his mind, she stood up to show him the photo accompanying the article—a vibrant sugar maple, its leaves red and stunning. As she bent over, Tom's arms encircled her waist, pulling her into the tub. She shrieked in delight, as water sloshed over the sides, drenching the bath mat and the newspaper she'd dropped on the floor. Her champagne-colored nightgown stuck to her curves, her bottom resting against Tom's stomach.

He nibbled at her ear, making her laugh, and turned her over. His expression was serious, his eyes half closed, and she placed her hands on either side of his face and kissed him. He tasted like cigarettes, acidic and ashy. He peeled the nightgown down to her waist, kissing her as he went, nudging it off her body.

Diana still remembers that nightgown, wet and silky, against her skin.

He kissed her again, harder this time, and her neck pressed painfully against the side of the tub. As if he understood her discomfort, he lifted her up and settled his arm under her head, cushioning her. She relaxed against him and drew her legs across his back. Tom slid into her and groaned, the sound filling the bathroom. They moved together slowly at first, finding their rhythm, the water shifting with them. Their cadence became more intense, and she remembers never wanting the moment to end, hoping they'd forever be connected like that.

At last, though, Diana, feeling as if she might dissolve into the water, gasped and grabbed Tom's shoulders. He said her name, loud and rough, and was still.

They stayed in the tub afterward, wrapped around one another. They left only when their fingers and toes were shriveled and goose bumps dotted their skin. Naked, they cleaned up the room. He stuffed the wet newspaper in the trash can; she left the damp towels in the tub to deal with the next day.

Why this memory now? Diana flicks back through the past, like turning pages in a book, searching for what she's overlooked. She wanted to go leaf peeping. She suggested they visit where Tom grew up. He hadn't wanted to go, so he changed the subject, distracting her in the most obvious way.

How often had he done that? How many times had he directed her away from his past, away from what he had done?

She cries, her breath erratic. This grief is different: This is the loss of each memory of Tom. She no longer understands which ones are filled with love—or which ones are a manipulation.

Had there been clues he was hiding something? She tries to find evidence of this in her past, but her emotions make her memories indistinct, and she comes up empty.

Had she been too rigid in the way she saw Tom? Had she been too in love with the idea of the two of them together instead of creating a connection where they could be honest with one another?

What had she hidden from him?

She never deceived him about who she was. However, when they were first dating, she may have embellished a story or two to put herself in the best possible light. Even if these exaggerations weren't criminal, they're a sign she wasn't always truthful.

She quiets, exhausted by all the ways this letter has upset her life.

Still, sleep eludes her, and after too long staring into the dark and rehashing her life, Diana begins to wonder whether she might find the key to Tom's letter in her house.

One of the places she hasn't touched since his death is his bedside table. Inspired, she climbs out from under the covers and turns on the bedside lamp. As the room floods with light, an engine revs outside, an unexpected sound at this time of night. Diana moves to the window and peeks out from the curtain in time to see a car speed away from the curb in front of her house. Startled, she jumps back. Strange cars in front of her house in the middle of the night are not regular occurrences. "Nothing about my life is regular these days," she mutters, pressing a palm against her racing heart.

Concerned about what the car was doing outside her house, Diana inches down her creaky stairs into the darkened living room. In the front hall, she grabs Duncan's baseball bat from the closet. She makes a fast yet thorough sweep of the first floor and basement, checking that the doors and windows are locked. She finds nothing amiss, nothing broken, no evidence that the driver of that car, or anyone else, tried to enter her home. She even braves an opening of the front door to see if anything was left for her in the mailbox, but it's empty. The lid clanks shut as she returns inside and locks the front door.

"You're overreacting," she whispers, as she climbs back upstairs. "A good night's sleep will fix this."

Returning to her bedroom, she remembers her earlier idea to go through Tom's bedside table. She slides the bat under the bed—as a precaution, she tells herself—and dumps the contents of his top drawer onto the duvet. All she finds are the items he left behind: a pair of sunglasses, cuff links shaped like basketballs, and eye drops His cell phone and charger are in the second drawer; she placed them there after closing his account. She didn't even download his photos or read his texts. It was all too distressing.

In the bottom drawer is an unlined journal she's never seen before, drawings filling the pages. Tom had been a doodler, adding M.C. Escher–like geometric shapes to the corners of his legal briefs while in meetings and braiding together whorls and loops along the margins of their daily newspapers while he drank his morning coffee. The images in the journal, however, are new to Diana. She finds sketches of Phoebe as a baby and Duncan on the basketball court. She even finds herself in one picture, standing in profile in a doorway. Turning to the last pages, she finds a drawing of a woman she doesn't recognize, outlined in pencil, and dozens of horses, standing still, galloping, jumping.

Who is the woman? Why did Tom draw horses? He hadn't liked them. Once, after Diana's mother read Phoebe *Black Beauty*, the girl asked for horseback riding lessons, and Tom refused to discuss it. *Absolutely not,* he said, and immediately changed the subject.

"Tom, you have to help me," Diana says, as if he is only around the corner. She's never spoken out loud to him like this. She read about people who carry on conversations with their dead loved ones, keeping them alive and present, but thought it would be confusing to Duncan and Phoebe if they witnessed her conversing with Tom, so she's never tried.

She needs help, and maybe her husband, wherever he is, could send her a sign. "Now would be good, Tom."

She waits, looking around the silent room.

There's no answer, of course. Diana throws the notebook back into the drawer and grabs her laptop. "Let's try this again."

Thanks to her employee access to Alcott Memorial's interlibrary database system, she loses herself in back issues of Tom's college newspaper. She uncovers nothing scandalous in its pages, and a review of North Carolina news for the early 1980s also is unsuccessful in providing any clarity.

She discovers that the *Vermonter*, the largest newspaper in the state, has back issues online, but she needs more time to scan the headlines from June 1982 through June 1983, the year Tom was eighteen. She drills down to news in Hamilton and learns the *Hamilton Star* is the local news outlet. The *Star* comes out on Thursdays, and its web presence is minimal—she can find only issues since 2000 on its site. The paper covers local politics and prints a bare-bones police log centered on arrests for DUIs and wild animals trapped in garages.

The clock clicks by 4:00 a.m., then 4:30. Diana's eyes burn, and the battery life on the laptop whirls down to 2 percent. Looking for ways to cope with a brain that won't stop, she starts a list: *What Don't I Miss about Tom?*

He left his shoes on the stairs.

He never cleaned up the sink after he shaved.

He always forgot to pick up the dry cleaning.

He was stubborn.

No, she thinks, wrapping her arms around her chest, the laptop forgotten. She's disgusted with herself for giving any consideration to these meaningless pet peeves.

The truth is, Diana thinks, squeezing her eyes shut, *I miss everything about him. Every single thing.*

Chapter Eight

That Friday, four days after discovering Tom's letter, Diana is readying her house to host Family Dinner when she remembers the landline. Abandoning her plans to clean the bathroom, she instead kneels in front of the office bookshelf and pushes aside printer toner, watercolor paints, and a cast-off piggy bank shaped like a snail to unearth the phone and answering machine. Both had been Tom's in college. "They still work," he said when he set them up their first day in the house. "Why not use them?"

Both the answering machine and phone are filthy. "I really should clean more," Diana says, wiping away the grime. She's surprised by the Full Memory error message blinking across the answering machine's display screen. She sits on the floor with the machine in her lap, its wires twisted around her knees, and listens to the fifty messages that follow, all hang-ups. It's slow going to wait for the click of each hang-up, then delete the message, but she finds the process oddly soothing.

After the display finally arrives at zero, she plays the greeting and Tom's voice fills the office. *Hello! You've reached the Morgans. We're not available. Please leave a message.* Her stomach twists, hearing his voice for the first time in months, but she plays the greeting again and again, letting his words wash over her.

When her front door opens and she hears her name, Diana realizes she's lost track of the time. She hasn't set the table, finished tidying the house, or vacuumed. Her mother will notice.

"Be right there," Diana says, shoving the answering machine back onto the shelf.

She needs more information before she tells her family about Tom's letter, so tonight, she'll keep this news to herself. She hopes Duncan can do the same.

In the front hall, her father stands with his toolbox and a broad smile. "Hi, sweetheart," he says, enveloping her in a hug. Diana fits her head under his chin and rests against his coat, chilly from outside. With her ear against his steady heartbeat, she remembers how her father's hugs always fixed everything when she was a child. She wishes they had that power once again.

Francis breaks away when Diana's mother steps across the threshold, toting an overstuffed grocery bag.

"What's all this?" Diana lifts the bag from her mother's grasp. Inside she finds peanut butter, bread, and frozen broccoli. "Another shopping trip for me and the kids? Mom, it's too much."

"I thought you needed a few things," Vivian says, removing her perfectly tailored wool coat and hanging it in the front closet. "There's more in the car."

Vivian's voice is full of warmth, yet Diana hears the unspoken reprimand. Eager to greet Diana, Francis bounded into the house without bringing in any of his wife's many packages. *The General is not pleased,* Diana thinks, as her father heads outside again.

"Diana," Vivian says, peering closely at her as they walk into the kitchen. "Why do you look so tired?"

If Diana explains her recent turn toward insomnia, her mother will launch into a lecture about proper sleep hygiene and follow up tomorrow with an email linking to articles written by someone she says is a famous somnologist. The General may even recommend a visit to a sleep clinic. Diana has no time for any of those well-meaning, yet unhelpful, suggestions. "I woke up early. Must be that."

"I'll pick up some melatonin for you tomorrow." Vivian turns on the oven and looks around the room. "Where are my grandchildren?"

"Duncan's in his room. Phoebe's playing with Mira. I'll text Lakshmi to send her home." Diana picks up her phone from the counter. Please send P home. Grandparents are here.

Lakshmi's text arrives within seconds: Already on her way. Shall I call her back to tuck a bottle of vodka in her backpack? You might need some help to get through dinner.

Diana stifles a laugh. I'll call if I get desperate. She pockets her phone as her father returns with a gallon of milk and a large dish with a glass lid.

Diana reaches for the milk, but her mother swats her away. "I'll get everything organized and dinner underway. Your father will help. Go take care of yourself. Your sister and her crew will be here any minute."

The back door swings open, and Phoebe runs in. She heads straight for her grandmother. Vivian bends down to hug her only granddaughter, her silvery-gray head pressed against Phoebe's brown locks. They look like the same person, meeting herself at different ages.

Diana slips upstairs. After showering and running a brush through her hair, she changes into a red button-down her mother gave her for her last birthday and a pair of too-snug, dark jeans. *I have to cut back on the wine,* Diana thinks, applying cover-up to the seemingly permanent dark circles under her eyes. She hears her sister and her family arrive as she swipes mascara on her ever-thinning lashes.

On the stairs, she passes her five-year-old nephew, Noah, running up to fetch Duncan to set the table. She tousles his hair, but Noah doesn't stop for hello, yelling Duncan's name instead.

"There you are," Andrea says when Diana turns the corner toward the kitchen. "Let's get out of here before Mom asks us to help." She holds up a bottle of wine and two glasses. "Drink?"

Even though she's younger than Diana by three years, Andrea often acts like the older sibling. Her work as a psychiatrist for at-risk youth has trained her to evaluate and diagnose every situation, including Diana's life. Andrea likes to tell Diana what to do, and for years, this caused tension between them. Once Tom was diagnosed, Diana let her sister's natural authority lead the way. It's easier, she's learned.

"Did you watch the debate last night?" Andrea asks as they settle on the living room sofa. She doesn't wait for a response, immediately launching into an analysis of the presidential candidates.

On the other side of the room, Francis and Evan, still in his coat with condensation blurring his glasses, crouch in front of a silent radiator, engrossed in conversation. While the other radiators in the house hiss and clank, this one mysteriously stopped working a few days ago. Diana casually mentioned it to her father, and he brought his toolbox to fix the problem. Francis has recruited Evan, an emergency room physician, to help, assuming her brother-in-law's ability to patch a bullet hole and diagnose a myocardial infarction makes him qualified to fix machinery, too.

"Diana, you're registered to vote, right?" Andrea asks, still focused on her election monologue. "If not, I can sort that for you. Or maybe you want to vote by mail so you can get it done early?"

Phoebe skips across the room, stopping in front of Diana and Andrea to offer an elaborate curtsy. Dressed in a striped apron that brushes the floor, the girl wields a wooden spoon like a conductor in front of an orchestra. "Dinner is almost ready."

"Are you our maître d'?" Andrea asks. Andrea and Phoebe are both carbon copies of Vivian, with heart-shaped faces, dimples, and elegant fingers. Diana, on the other hand, resembles Francis, solid and Earth bound. She inherited his temperamental hair that frizzes in an ounce of humidity, his thick eyebrows, and his crooked smile.

"Your what?" Phoebe replies, cozying up to her aunt on the sofa.

"Our maître d', the person who's in charge of dinner and decides where everyone sits."

Phoebe jumps up on her toes and claps her hands. "Yes, follow me!"

Andrea and Diana trail after Phoebe as she twirls across the house, through the kitchen, and into the dining room, where The General supervises as Duncan lights the candles in the center of the table.

Diana notices her best blue tablecloth and long-unused china. Yellow roses in a crystal vase and gleaming stemware complete the table setting. "Mom, this is really nice. Why so fancy, though?"

Vivian places a cast iron trivet next to the candles as Francis and Evan enter. "Family Dinner is an important occasion."

Tom would have agreed. When it was their turn to host Family Dinner, he served as chef, the only meal he cooked outside of the occasional Saturday-morning pancakes. He made each dish more elaborate than the last. Coq au vin. Moussaka. Hand-rolled sushi. He was specific about how the table was to be set, which wine should be served, and when they could begin eating. Diana found his extravagant efforts endearing, believing he threw himself into the dinners because he missed his own family. Thoughts of how Family Dinner used to be— how much Tom had loved hosting—make his death feel fresh and new.

"It's good you stepped in," Diana says, hoping to prevent the enveloping snare of grief from taking hold. "If dinner had been left to me, I would have forgotten entirely to cook or we'd be scarfing down lukewarm take-out pizza on paper plates."

A brief frown appears on Vivian's face, but it's gone so fast only Francis and Diana catch it. "Children, please help me bring in the food," she says, returning to the kitchen.

"Your mother only wants to make tonight special, sweetheart," Francis says gently, taking her hand in his. "You don't need to make jokes or speak negatively about yourself. We know things are hard for you."

Diana's cheeks redden. Family Dinner stopped when Tom entered hospice. These gatherings are intended to be joyful, and there wasn't much joy for any of them then. Now, her mother is only trying to help. She is grieving, too. Sometimes Diana forgets Tom's death isn't hers alone.

Her father squeezes her hand, and Diana looks down at their intertwined fingers. She examines the dark, wiry hair on his thumb, the callus on his pointer finger, the faded scar along his wrist from the time he tried to repair a broken drainpipe. Has she ever noticed the story he carries on his strong fingers and the cracked skin over his knuckles? Could she conjure Tom's hands if she tried? She searches for his hands in her memory. They are out of reach, gone with the rest of him.

On the other side of the room, Andrea and Evan whisper to one another, their heads bent over Evan's phone. Evan points to the screen, and Andrea giggles. He kisses her, his hand against her cheek. When they break apart, Andrea meets Diana's eyes, and her smile disappears, guilt seeping into that moment of affection. Diana tilts her head to the side, as if to say, *"Go ahead, love him in front of me—it hurts, but this is my life,"* and after a beat, she turns away.

The General carries in the lasagna, and the tangy scent of her home-made sauce spreads throughout the room. The children trail behind her like brand-new chicks clucking after their mother hen, each holding an item for the meal.

"Thank you for this," Diana says, hoping her gratitude makes up for her earlier comment. "I appreciate it all."

"I'm happy to take care of it all, sweetheart." Vivian puts the lasagna on the trivet and helps the children add their contributions to the table. "Shall we eat?"

"We're waiting for our maître d' to tell us where to sit." Andrea gestures to Phoebe. "Mademoiselle? What would you like to do?"

Phoebe directs each family member to a chair, pausing at the seat next to her grandfather. "That's Daddy's seat, isn't it, Mama?"

Diana, with one blink, sees dozens, hundreds of meals at this table with Tom in that chair. She read somewhere grief isn't a straight line; there is no step one, two, three. Rather, it jumps around, remaining dormant for a time and then unexpectedly rearing up to cut at the heart, jagged and deep. Like now, at the start of Family Dinner.

Diana's family listens for her response, though they're pretending to be busy settling into their seats, pouring water, and filling wineglasses. She expects her mother and sister are readying follow-up comments in the event her words are insufficient.

"Phoebe," Diana says softly, "that *was* Daddy's chair for Family Dinner. He wouldn't want it to be empty forever. He'd want it to be yours. How does that sound?"

Phoebe nods and sits down, her mouth already stuffed with garlic bread. Vivian and Andrea relax, mirroring each other in the swift shift of their attention away from Diana and Phoebe and toward the meal before them.

Diana slumps into her chair. She can't follow the conversations that race around the table, so she focuses on her plate of food, relieved her family is too busy eating to ask how she is.

What Else Did Tom Lie About? That's a list she's resisted until now, too afraid to let the words join together.

All those nights he stayed late at the office. What if he wasn't working?

Those law conferences he attended. Was that what they really were?

He didn't ever want to talk about the past or share stories from his childhood. Why not?

He only brought me home to Hamilton once. Why?

Her father interrupts her list-making. "Are you with us, Diana?"

"What?" Everyone at the table stares at her, forks poised over their plates. Only Noah keeps munching, sauce streaked across his cheek.

"I asked you to pass the salad, sweetheart. Two times. You were miles away. Everything okay?"

"Of course." Diana hands him the hefty wooden bowl. "Here you go, Dad."

"Thank you," Francis says, as he piles greens onto his plate. "Evan and I are making progress on the radiator. We bled it and cleaned out some sludge built up inside. Next, we're going to turn off the heat and turn it back on again. If that doesn't fix it, we may need some outside help, I'm sorry to say."

Her father and brother-in-law keep Diana's house in working order, like it's an Olympic sport. One or both of them stops by each week to check on the boiler or the HVAC system. They wash her car, put air in the tires of the kids' bicycles, and clear snow from the roof. They do their best to fill the gap Tom left.

"Thanks for trying," Diana says, biting into the lasagna. Her mother gave her an end piece, her favorite, and the top cheesy layer is crunchy from the broiler and spiked with a welcome kick of oregano.

As Noah begins an involved story about a game he and his friends play during recess, Diana studies her parents. They've aged over the past year. The lines on either side of her father's mouth are more pronounced, and his hair has turned completely white. While he works part-time at a real estate firm in town, helping longtime clients sell the homes they raised their families in as they retire to Florida or move into assisted living, her mother has fully stepped back from teaching elementary school. Vivian has embraced days filled with exercise classes at Alcott's senior center and meetings of the Garden Club. What would their lives have been like if Tom hadn't died? Vivian has long wanted to visit the lavender fields of Provence; Francis talked about getting a place on the Cape. They put their plans on hold to look after their widowed daughter and grandchildren. When will they be able to live the lives they've imagined for themselves?

"Phoebe, you're up," Francis says. "What do you have to share?"

"We found the time capsule," she says, nearly shouting.

"Time capsule?" The General asks, looking at Diana for clarification. Diana busies herself with the last remaining shreds of arugula on her plate.

"We opened a Leap Day time capsule," Phoebe continues. "It's full of photos, newspapers, one of my drawings, and Duncan's homework. Stuff like that."

Duncan remains silent, looking at Diana with a blank stare. He's promised to keep the letter's contents to himself, and this is his first real test.

"There was a letter for Mommy from Daddy in it, too," Phoebe adds.

The noise in the room stops. Diana can practically see Andrea holding her breath for what comes next.

"It was a love letter," Diana lies.

Perhaps this cancer is the universe fixing my wrongs. If it is I under-stand, though I wish leaving you was not the debt I had to pay.

"That's remarkable," her mother says, and the room exhales. "And surprising, I would imagine."

"Very." Diana says.

Duncan drops his napkin onto his plate. "Grandma, can I be excused?"

Diana notices the slight: asking her mother for permission to leave the table, not her. She lets it go. Tonight is not the night to crit-icize her son.

"Me too!" shouts Noah.

"Clear your dishes first, please," The General orders.

The room fills with the clatter of silverware and plates. The chil-dren, freed from table manners and supervision, disappear, promising to come back for dessert. Francis returns to the stubborn heater for another attempt at a fix. "The garlic bread gave me an idea,' he says. Evan trails behind him, trying to hide his grin.

Diana remains at the table, finishing her wine and handing empty glasses to Andrea to bring into the kitchen.

"You didn't tell me about the letter," Andrea says on her third trip back to the table, the lasagna pan in her arms. "Do you want to talk about it?"

"It's what you would expect of a letter like that." Diana clears crumbs from the tablecloth. "We can't let Mom do the dishes alone. We won't hear the end of it." She stands up to blow out the candles and pick up the last of the plates. "I'll get the rest of this."

"Just don't finish the wine," Andrea says, laughing. "I'm off tomor-row and could really use another glass."

When she's alone in the room, Diana realizes she's trembling. She's never deliberately deceived her family before—"You're our open book," her father always says—and she's disturbed by how easy it is to hide things from them. She wonders if it was easy for Tom, too.

Chapter Nine

The Monday after Family Dinner finds Diana at the old Victorian that houses the law firm Tom and Jonathan Hobart started more than fifteen years ago. She's here to meet with Jonathan in the hope that he can provide insight into Tom's past. She texted him last night, after spending the weekend looking out for strange cars and agonizing over Tom's secrecy and her children's grief. Duncan's outpouring on the basketball court keeps coming back to her: *He gets fuzzier in my mind. Sometimes, I can't remember him on my own. Like he's only a story someone told me, not a real person.* She can't let this letter be the way Duncan remembers Tom. She needs answers for him—and for herself, too.

Diana surveys the building through her car window. Tom and Jonathan spent a year renovating this space, transforming it from a private residence into a quirky office building. They knocked down walls on the weekends and refinished the floors after spending the days writing briefs and meeting with clients. Tom came home many nights with sawdust in his hair and nails in his pockets. Diana and Jonathan's wife, Lily, in an effort to see their husbands, if only to feed them, took turns bringing Chinese takeout or pizza, sitting together on the front steps as the two men worked inside. They were there so often Duncan took his first steps in what is now the first-floor bathroom, all of them cheering the boy on as Diana knelt in front of him, arms outstretched.

The building, one town over from Alcott, is a fifteen-minute drive from her house, yet Diana hasn't been by since the day Tom was diagnosed. *Not that day,* she corrects herself, clutching and unclutching her hands from the steering wheel. *We never actually made it.*

She and Tom expected to return to work after his doctor's appointment. He had a strategy session for an upcoming court appearance; she was to oversee a budget meeting at the library. They made these plans because they were confident the news would be good, that the doctor would tell them his stomach pain and weight loss were stress-related, and that Tom only needed more sleep, vitamins, or maybe a vacation. He'd been tired and out of sorts for months but attributed it to the demands of his job, canceling the multiple medical appointments Diana scheduled for him until she decided the only way to get Tom to the doctor's was to take him there herself.

On the drive to the appointment, they discussed where they'd go on that much-needed vacation: someplace warm with palm trees, frozen pineapple cocktails with mini paper umbrellas, and water clear enough for snorkeling. The doctor stunned them, though Tom would later say he knew all along the news would be bad, by delivering the worst of the worst-case scenarios, the one that spiraled them from confidence into chaos.

The news that Tom had advanced pancreatic cancer made the blood pound in Diana's head. "He's only forty-nine," she said to the doctor, as if Tom were too young for bad news. "He'll be fifty in June."

She watched the doctor's mouth move, his eyes downcast behind wire-framed glasses, but his words were jumbled and wrong. All she could make out was the irregular inhale and exhale of her lungs, the rhythm too fast and the air too shallow. She felt she was falling down through icy, black water, all the sound muffled and distant. She focused on the doctor, scribbling what he said in her notebook; the next day, she would read what she wrote and none of it would make sense

They left his office armed with a "You have cancer—what next?" brochure and a follow-up appointment to discuss options, the few available. She didn't remember whether she and Tom spoke to one another in the slow elevator ride down to the harshly lit, claustrophobic hospital garage, or how they remembered where they'd parked their car. The shock blurred her memory of that visit. What was clear was what came after.

Instead of driving to their respective offices, they went to a hole-in-the-wall bar in Cambridge, a place they hadn't visited since before the kids were born. She remembered the silence of that car ride, the words fleeing from them as if terrified by what would be said. Tom steered the car through the congested streets, never glancing over to her. When Diana realized where he was headed, she texted her parents to get the kids from school and sent emails to their colleagues. Change in plans, she wrote to Camille. I need a personal day.

Tom found them a parking spot in front of the bar. Corralling quarters from the center console, Diana filled the parking meter to its maximum allotment. The irony of buying time wasn't lost on her.

In the bar, with its gray walls covered with black-and-white photos of the city before gentrification, they sat on two sticky, red vinyl stools and drank to forget. Getting drunk in the middle of the day was their way of avoiding Tom's diagnosis. Months, the doctor had said; maybe four, possibly six.

They asked for nachos and chicken wings, but the food sat uneaten in front of them. Blue cheese dressing for the wings pooled in an unappetizing clump as sunlight made its way through the half-open shades. Diana ordered tequila shots, her alcohol of choice when she was twenty-two with free time to waste on sleeping late, shopping for shoes she didn't need, and clubbing with girlfriends whose names she couldn't recall. She and Tom licked salt off their hands and threw back the sharp liquor. She dulled the tequila's burn by sucking on chunks of tart limes. Another shot followed and another. As Diana settled into the fog of intoxication, the booze filling her with a hazy, fictitious warmth, Tom ordered Manhattans, bitter and medicinal, a cocktail she always thought of as sophisticated but now made her sad.

"The hot water heater needs to be replaced," Tom said into the mirror behind the bar. He didn't look at her as he spoke, focusing instead on their reflections. "The roof needs to be checked, too. It could be time to replace it."

Diana didn't reply. What was there to say?

"I'll make a list. Of what I typically do. Like mow the lawn, put in the storm windows, clean out the gutters. I can teach you and Duncan." Tom's voice broke on Duncan's name, and he finished off his Manhattan in a swift, angry swallow. He gestured to the bartender for another, and Diana waited for him to continue. She knew there was more he wanted to say. She hoped there was enough time to hear all of it.

"Passwords," he said, after a prolonged silence. His shoulders were so tense they pulled up into his neck. She wanted to hold him, but she was afraid of what would happen if she did. Maybe he needed that pressure to keep himself together for a little while longer.

"We need to update passwords, to make sure you can get into all the accounts, including the ones that are my own." He looked at her. His eyes were red and sunk into his face.

He looks like he's dying, she thought.

"You'll need access to stupid stuff like frequent flyer miles and our Costco account. Important things, too." Tom's clammy hand grabbed hers. "I'll take care of what I can—before. You'll need—"

"I understand," Diana said. "We'll work it all out."

The bartender placed a Manhattan in front of Tom and left to assist another customer. "There's more," Tom said, releasing Diana to roll the drink between his hands. "When I was younger . . ." He paused to clear his throat. "When I was younger, I made mistakes. Bad ones that I've never told you about. I should have told. You deserve to—"

Diana placed her hand on his forearm. "All that matters is today and tomorrow and the days we have together." She leaned her forehead against his and let his warm breath slide over her skin. "I love you. I think I've loved you from the first moment we met."

"I love you, too," Tom said, sighing.

A Guinness, dark and creamy, sat in front of her when Andrea and Evan arrived, responding to a drunken text Diana had sent when

Tom was in the men's room. When they pushed open the heavy outer door, the sun had already set and the after-work crowd occupied the bar, orbiting around Diana and Tom the way a planet circles around a dying star. The other patrons seemed aware something was happening to them, an undoing of a kind, and they stayed as far away as possible, the unwritten code of all those who end up in a place like this, on a day like this.

One look at Andrea's anguished face, and Diana collapsed into her arms. Evan paid their tab and half carried them to his car. Andrea followed in their minivan, the back seat filled with booster seats, basketball sneakers, and half-eaten snacks. Tom didn't say a word during the trip home, through the windy one-way streets and the end-of-day traffic. As Diana wept, he held her and gazed out the window. At their front door, he waved off Andrea and Evan and helped Diana to bed, where she passed out, her clothes in a pile on the floor.

The next day, Tom returned to the office to clean out his desk and pass his client files to Jonathan. He was done with work, a decision he'd made so quickly Diana almost hadn't believed him. When she offered to accompany him to the office, he declined her help. "This is mine to do," he said.

"And now here I am," she says apprehensively, looking up at the building.

She realizes then that Tom wanted to open up about his past that day in the bar. He tried to tell her the truth, but she hadn't let him say the words.

Chapter Ten

Everything looks the same, smells the same, too. *Like Lemon Pledge and file folders,* Diana thinks as she stands in the foyer of Tom's old law firm, her hand on the brass doorknob.

The name on the sign behind reception is different, though. No more "Hobart and Morgan"—the firm is now "Hobart and Associates." Jonathan and the firm's employees bought out Tom soon after his diagnosis.

A young woman Diana doesn't recognize sits at reception. "May I help you?" she asks as Diana surveys the room. A cordless headset hooks onto the left side of her head, and her fingers clatter along the keys as she speaks.

"I have an appointment with Jonathan Hobart. I'm—"

"Diana!" Jonathan strides into the lobby and envelops her in a hug. Her face presses against his itchy blue suit jacket. "How are you? The kids? Everyone wants to say hello. We'll do the greetings after?"

"I'd appreciate that."

"Are you hungry or thirsty? How about a cappuccino?"

Jonathan makes arrangements with the receptionist, whose name Diana never gets, and steers her to his office. His phone rings as he closes his door. "Sorry, I have to take this. Won't take long."

Diana hasn't seen Jonathan in months; he looks good—thinner, more fit—though his hair is grayer at the temples. His office hasn't changed: Empty coffee cups line the windowsill, paperwork is piled on the floor by his desk, and lawbooks blanket the table in the corner. On a bookshelf near the door are an award from the bar association and photos of Lily and their kids. The original "Hobart and Morgan" sign sits on the top shelf, next to a framed photo of Jonathan and Tom cutting the ribbon for the building's grand opening. Diana takes it down for a closer look. She and Lily stand on the other side of their husbands; Duncan perches on Diana's hip, and Lily, largely pregnant with their second daughter, holds their toddler's hand. How young they were. How long ago this all feels. How much time has passed since Diana last spoke with Lily.

Lily and Diana were once close, a connection born of Jonathan and Tom's friendship and, later, their business partnership. Perhaps each woman subconsciously cultivated their relationship to keep harmony between the men in those years when starting the law firm called for long hours and sacrifice.

Their friendship had the added benefit of grounding Diana during the upheaval caused by Duncan's arrival. Amid the exhaustion of early motherhood, Diana and Lily regularly met up to push their children in clunky strollers along Alcott's bike path or to sit together at Sully's, the café in Alcott center. Together, overcaffeinated and sleep-deprived, they shared breastfeeding tips and whispered about the women who came in wearing kitten heels, with perfect makeup and impeccable blowouts. Diana envied how rested they looked, a sign they had time for themselves, a luxury that had disappeared for her with Duncan's birth. Lily, on the other hand, focused on their clothing and accessories, identifying the high-end brands each woman wore and calculating the cost of their ensembles.

Diana recalled those days as confusing; she was overjoyed with being a mother, yet she resented the loss of some essential part of herself, as if she'd sacrificed her own identity for her son. With Lily, Diana found the companionship she needed, and she looked forward to sharing the different phases of parenthood with her.

When Tom was diagnosed, however, Lily and Jonathan drifted from the center of Tom and Diana's friend group to its fringes. Consumed with Tom's needs, it took Diana a while to notice, and at first, she was stung they'd pulled away. Yet she wasn't shocked. People were afraid of Diana and Tom, as if spending time in their presence put them at higher risk for losing their own spouse or receiving a terminal diagnosis. It didn't change after Tom died either; people acted as if widowhood were communicable, or as if Diana were radioactive, exposed to too much pain and therefore dangerous.

Six months after Tom's funeral, in the hope of reconnecting, Diana called Lily. The coffee date that followed was memorable for its awkwardness. Lily jabbered away about a recent shopping trip to New York City and didn't ask once how Diana and the kids were managing without Tom.

"I miss him all the time," Jonathan says, coming up next to her. "But I'm happy to see you, Diana. What brings you here today?"

Diana puts the photo back on the shelf and turns to Jonathan. "I need your help."

❧

Twenty minutes later, she sips her cappuccino as Jonathan reads Tom's letter for the fourth time. "You found this where?" Jonathan asks. His lunch sits on the desk, untouched.

"In a Leap Day time capsule from 2012." He's asked her this question multiple times, and she's curious if this is an established lawyerly technique: Ask the same question over and over until the answer changes, or until the answer is finally believed.

"It's his handwriting, but it doesn't sound like him." Jonathan hands the letter to her and sits back, his arms crossed. "This isn't what I thought you wanted to talk about."

"What did you think I wanted?"

"The building. I thought maybe you wanted to sell."

Tom divested himself of the firm before he died but retained their co-ownership of the building. Jonathan and Lily own 50 percent; Tom and Diana—now Diana—own the other 50 percent. The rent checks from the building's other tenants are a stable source of income, especially since she's a single parent. "Keep the building for the short term," Tom said when they reviewed their finances before he entered hospice. "Someday, you might want to sell. Make sure you get a good deal."

Diana places her drink on the edge of Jonathan's desk. "That's not why I'm here. I need advice about this letter."

"Right."

She waits for him to say more, but he seems stuck, the silver-tongued attorney at a loss.

After an awkward silence, Jonathan picks up his salad, the plastic container squeaking as he wrenches it open. "What are your questions for me?"

"Did you know about this?"

"Did I know Tom committed a crime when he was eighteen?" Jonathan asks, swallowing a mouthful of lettuce.

"You were his best friend."

"You were his wife. I'm assuming, from the way the letter is written, you were oblivious to this as well."

Diana flinches.

"Shit, Diana, I'm sorry. I didn't mean it that way." Jonathan pushes away his salad, and the fork falls to the floor. "I don't know about any of this, including these people he mentions. The ones he says might come looking for you. Are you okay?"

"Nothing happened at college? Nothing out of the ordinary?" Tom and Jonathan met freshmen year, thrown together by the randomness of roommate assignments. They instantly became the best of friends, living together all the way through law school. "When you and Tom met, he was eighteen. Maybe he's referring to your first year of college?"

Jonathan stares up at the ceiling, squinting at the lavish crown molding lining the room. To Diana, it looks as if he's diving into his memories, holding each one up for a closer look.

"I don't remember Tom acting secretive about his past or anything that happened in college," he says slowly. "I never witnessed him doing anything illegal. He was never out of control. He was adamant about staying away from drugs, even pot. I have no idea what this letter means."

Diana believes him. "I have more questions."

"Go ahead."

"You're my lawyer? I probably should have asked you this first. We signed an agreement to that effect years ago. It's current? I'm still protected by attorney-client privilege?"

"Yes, yes." Jonathan responds to her question as if the answer is obvious. He leans down to pick up the plastic fork, throwing it in the trash. "Next?"

"Can my family be held responsible for this crime?"

"You can't be held responsible for something your dead husband did more than thirty years ago." Diana cringes at Jonathan's bluntness. He winces and mumbles an apology. "No matter what the crime was, unless, of course, you were involved in it in some way. Which is not the case here. It's possible Tom's estate could be sued, but I'd need more information about the crime, including what it was and where it took place."

"Do I have a responsibility to turn this letter over to the police?"

"Which police? Where?" Jonathan returns to his salad, taking a new fork from his desk. "Since you found the letter in your home, you can file a report with the Alcott police. Two possible outcomes could occur. First, your report would be relegated to the bottom of a very busy to-do pile, where it would remain indefinitely. How can they follow up on a crime that happened so long ago in an unknown place, even with Tom's claim people might be coming for you? They don't have the resources to investigate something so vague."

Diana can almost hear the squeal of that car pulling away from her house in the middle of the night. She pushes away the sound and focuses on Jonathan. "What's the other possibility?" she asks.

"Your report could end up in the police blotter in *The Alcott Chronicle*. Other media, or even those true crime fans, could get interested, and you'd have to contend with people snooping around your life, Tom's life. You don't want that. Not for you, not for the kids."

"I don't want this to become public. I don't even know what *this* is." She gestures to the page. "Maybe he remembered wrong? Maybe he dreamed this? Maybe it didn't happen?"

"Maybe."

Another question comes to her, one she didn't think of until now. "Is there anything about Tom's work here at the firm that might be relevant? Anything that could somehow be connected to this letter?"

Jonathan spears a cherry tomato with his fork and brings it up to his mouth. He holds it there for a second or two before dropping it back into the salad. "Why are you asking that?" His voice is strained, and she's immediately suspicious.

"It's a reasonable question."

"No, it's not. All client matters are confidential. You asked me about attorney-client privilege, after all. Regardless, there's nothing you need to know."

"If there's nothing I need to know, why are you upset?"

"I'm not upset," Jonathan replies.

Diana crosses her legs at her ankles and waits.

After a few minutes of poking his fork through his lettuce, Jonathan says, "After we bought out Tom, I had the accountants examine the books. It's a best practice when there's an ownership change." Abandoning his food, he peers out the window. "They came across a series of odd withdrawals Tom made over the years. I'm not sure why they weren't caught at the time. Maybe because he oversaw the books while I hustled for new business? Some of it, maybe half, was returned to the firm's account. There's no explanation about where the rest of it went."

"How much money are we talking about?" Most of their earnings went back into Tom's law school debt and their mortgage. Diana often joked that the only excessive expense in their budget was basketball gear for Duncan.

"I shouldn't have said anything about this. It's in the past."

"How much, Jonathan?"

He sighs. "A little over $60,000."

"$60,000? Are you sure?"

"Yes, I'm sure," Jonathan says grimly.

First the letter, now this missing money. She expected Jonathan to have answers, not more secrets. "I know nothing about that," Diana says, gripping the arms of the chair. "I can look through our bank account when I get home. I would have noticed an unexplained $60,000, though."

"This money could have been for the firm. It was withdrawn in varying amounts over several years, and like I said, some of it—about $30,000—was returned. The records are unclear, which is why I didn't bring it up sooner."

"You're mad about it." She sees Jonathan's anger in the set of his jaw and the blunt rhythm of his words.

"I'm confused, and I don't like to be confused about my business." Jonathan pauses. "I've decided if the money wasn't for the firm, it was for something else, something important to Tom."

As they talk, sunshine streams in through the window behind Jonathan's desk, temporarily blinding Diana. She's enveloped in the light, as if it is a living being she can touch. For a moment, Diana believes Tom is there with them, reaching out to her. What is he trying to say?

Jonathan clears his throat, and Diana remembers again that Tom is gone.

"Let me make a copy of this letter," Jonathan says. "I'll do a little research, though I advise you not to worry about this. Let sleeping dogs lie, as they say."

Diana smooths the letter across her lap. As she traces Tom's signature with the pointer finger on her right hand, she runs her left thumb over her engagement ring and the wedding band with their initials engraved inside. Telling Jonathan about the letter is one thing, but giving him a copy? She loses control of this if she does that.

"Diana." Jonathan's voice is silken and cajoling. "This letter doesn't match up with the man who was my best friend. I know—*I knew*—that Tom. He was a good man. Calm, steady. I never once saw him lose his temper. This letter doesn't change who he was to me. Nor should it change who he was to you."

Diana thought she'd accept whatever Jonathan recommended she do, like she had every time Tom offered advice. Something—her own instincts?—holds her back.

Jonathan rests his elbows on the glossy walnut top of his desk, his fingers reaching out toward Diana. "You came here for help. Let me help you."

"Okay," she says, and passes him the letter. She is unsure whether this is the right decision. Then again, what is the correct response to any of this?

"I'll keep this confidential, of course." Jonathan places the letter in the feeder of the printer next to his desk, and the machine slowly chirps and sputters as a copy appears in the output tray. Jonathan hands Diana the original and slides the copy into a folder on his desk. "This was years ago," he says. "Try to put it out of your mind."

Diana stands up. "Thanks for your time. Can you tell the rest of the staff I said hello? I have a meeting back at the office and have to get going."

Jonathan smiles, as if he senses her lie.

"How much do I owe you for the consult?" Diana says, pulling on her coat.

"Come on, you're family. The family price tag is a hug. How about that?" Jonathan steps around the desk and puts his arms around her.

She stands in his embrace, inhaling Jonathan's wool and coffee scent, her eyes closed tight. How she wishes he were Tom.

Chapter Eleven

Two days later, Lakshmi calls while Diana microwaves leftovers in the library's break room.

"Diana, did you hire a house cleaner?" Lakshmi's voice, typically calm and soothing, is frantic.

"Is this about my house's messiness? Lax, I get that enough from my mom; I can't believe you're starting in on me." Diana laughs as she removes her turkey meatloaf from the microwave and douses it with sriracha.

"Did you hire a house cleaner?" Lakshmi repeats.

Diana stills. "Why are you asking me this?"

"There's someone in your house. I was at my easel and saw something out of the corner of my eye. It was a person walking into your backyard. They were there for less than a minute before they went around to the front and unlocked the door."

Diana stills. Someone is in her *house*? Her breathing starts to hitch, and a lightheadedness fills her body. There's a pounding in her ears, and she wonders if this is the start of a panic attack.

"Should I call the police?" Lakshmi gasps. "Wait—the person's in the kitchen. I'm calling the police."

"No," Diana says. That one word comes out twisted, as if her body has figured out what she's about to say next and protests her decision. "Don't call the police. I'm coming home." She runs from the room.

"You're coming home? Why? To confront this person? That's not safe."

Diana grabs her keys and bag from her office. "Lax, listen to me, we're going to hang up, and you're going to record everything you see. Can you do that?"

"You think this is the person from Tom's letter?" Lakshmi says, fear shading her words.

"No matter who it is, video will be helpful. Can you do that? Record what you see?" Diana forgoes the elevator for the stairs, nearly leaping between the landings. "Or take photos, whatever is easier. I'll be there as fast as I can."

On the drive home, Diana hits every green light. She clenches her jaw to keep her molars from grinding against one another, all the while thinking of the conversation she had with Jonathan. She asked him about bringing Tom's letter to the police, and he warned her from doing so. *You'd have to contend with people snooping around your life, Tom's life. You don't want that. Not for you, not for the kids.* She's sure he'd change his advice if he knew there was an intruder in her house. Bringing in the police now would be the logical, smart decision. But if this intruder has anything to do with Tom, having law enforcement involved would only make getting answers about his past more difficult. She has to handle this herself.

When she pulls into her driveway, Lakshmi paces in her front yard. The front door to Diana's house is wide open.

"What happened?" Diana asks, as she throws herself from the car.

"I'm so sorry," Lakshmi says. She wears fuzzy slippers and her painting apron, the thick canvas stained with the colors of the rainbow. "I couldn't see the car's license plate from inside, so I came onto my porch. They must have spotted me through the window. They burst out of the house and drove away before I got to them."

Diana's shoulders sag, relief overtaking her adrenaline. She was so focused on getting here that she hadn't allowed herself to acknowledge her fear. She wanted to talk to this person and get answers, but she's grateful to avoid a confrontation.

"Did you record everything?"

Lakshmi removes her phone from her apron. "From the second we hung up until they turned the corner down the street. I really think we should call the police, Diana."

"Let's see if anything is missing first," Diana says, leading Lakshmi inside.

The house is eerily quiet, no hums or beeps of overworked appliances, no clanks or hisses from the radiators. If homes could talk, Diana's would say it was nervous or even scared. Or perhaps she's projecting her own thoughts. Either way, something is definitely off.

She walks through each room, opening closets and dresser drawers, Lakshmi silently following. The idea that a stranger walked through her space, poking around and invading her family's privacy, sets Diana on edge. She examines every corner of her house with a critical lens. Her house is tired, she sees. The baseboards are scuffed, paint has chipped away at the corners, and the windows could use a good scrub. No wonder Lakshmi's first instinct when she saw that person in her house was to ask if she'd hired a cleaner.

There's good news, though: Nothing appears to be missing. The laptop is on the coffee table where she left it last night; her jewelry, including Tom's wedding ring, is accounted for in the small leather case in her bedside table; and even her secret stash of cash, stuffed in a makeup bag under the bathroom sink, is untouched.

It's in the kitchen where Diana finds evidence of her uninvited visitor. At first glance, the room is the same as when she hustled Duncan and Phoebe out the door to school only hours earlier.

Then she sees the mug in the sink.

The mug is white, with a photo of Tom hugging the kids printed on its side, and We Love Daddy curved around the rim in green script. She and the kids gave the mug to Tom the Father's Day Duncan was five, Phoebe two. He used it every day, even with a chip in the handle, the result of an unfortunate clash with a frying pan. After Tom's death, Diana placed it in the hard-to-reach cabinet above the refrigerator, where it remained until now.

"They've been here before," Diana says.

"Why do you think that?" Lakshmi says, joining Diana at the sink.

"This mug was up there," Diana says, pointing to the cabinet, "behind old Tupperware and vases I never use. That person was in the house for about fifteen or twenty minutes, right? How did they know to go into that cabinet, all the way in the back? If they'd been looking to steal money or jewelry, my bedroom was where to start, but they didn't because everything is where it's supposed to be."

Lakshmi's eyes widen as she understands what Diana is saying. "They knew where your hidden key was."

Diana thought of that as soon as Lakshmi said the intruder went into her backyard. Under the deck is a fake stone that hides a backup key to the house. She placed it there herself when she and Tom first moved in.

"Or maybe it was a lucky guess?" Lakshmi continues. "Lots of people have hidden keys."

"Others know about my past," Diana recites. *"After my death, around the time you find this letter, when I hope you've moved on from me, they may come into your life."*

"Who knew about your hidden key?"

"Me, you, Ramesh, my parents, Duncan, Andrea, and Evan." Diana looks up at Lakshmi. "And Tom."

Lakshmi's eyes are unblinking. "You think *Tom* told this person about the key?"

"I have no idea," Diana says. She loads the mug into the dishwasher.

"Diana, call the police! They can dust that mug for prints. Maybe we can find out who that person was."

"No police. Or at least not yet." Diana shuts the dishwasher. "Let's look at your video."

Lakshmi's recording starts when the intruder passes by the dining room window, reappearing in the kitchen. Neither angle provides much detail. "Their hair is tucked under a beanie, and they're wearing big sunglasses. Maybe the person is five feet tall or so," Lakshmi says. "I think it's a woman."

"They could be male," Diana says, zooming in on the figure in the window.

"I'm confident it's a woman," Lakshmi says. "There's something about the way she carries herself that says female, though I guess you're right. It could be a man or even a teenager."

The video turns jerky as Lakshmi walks through her house and onto her porch. She centers her phone on the car parked in front of Diana's. "The car was an older gray sedan. There wasn't a license plate on the front bumper, so I wanted to see the back." Lakshmi points to the screen. "Here's when I'm spotted."

Diana's front door slams open, and the intruder dashes from the house, their hat pulled down, nearly covering their face. They wear a tan Carhartt jacket, buttoned up to the chin, jeans, and black sneakers. The intruder never looks at Lakshmi, not even when she runs down the steps and yells, "Stop, stop! I want to talk to you!" They jump into the car and race down the street, nearly colliding with a van pulling out of the school parking lot.

"You came home a few minutes later," Lakshmi says. "I'm sorry I didn't get more."

"No apologies. This is helpful, Lax. Thank you. It was a big risk." Diana texts the video to her number and returns Lakshmi's phone. "So now we know the people Tom mentioned in his letter are real. They know where my hidden house key is, or was, and they've probably been here before. What were they searching for? That's the question." She again looks around the kitchen, assessing whether anything else is different, and that's when she sees the empty space on the refrigerator.

A small square next to the ice machine is blank. Typically, Diana's refrigerator is covered with photos, Phoebe's drawings, and scribbled grocery lists. In that space should be a snapshot of Tom and the kids, taken on the playground across the street.

This is when Diana understands real terror. Her heart thudding in her chest, she drops to the floor. "Where's the photo?" She scans under the fridge and along the cabinet kickplate. "The one of Tom and the kids. Did they steal it? A photo of my *kids*?"

"I don't see it," Lakshmi says, crawling into the pantry. "Are you sure Duncan or Phoebe didn't take it? Maybe it's in their rooms?"

"The photo was here this morning," Diana whispers. She smiled at the photo when she returned the milk to the fridge after preparing the kids' breakfast. "I'm sure it was."

That night, Diana sleeps on her living room sofa, though "sleep" is a generous interpretation of her actions. Instead of falling into oblivion, she holds Duncan's baseball bat in her lap and stares at the front door, where she jammed a kitchen chair under the doorknob as an added safety measure. It doesn't offer the assurance she wants, and she jumps at every creak and sigh her house makes.

After her discovery of the missing photo, Diana and Lakshmi looked for the front door key, correctly assuming that the intruder didn't have a chance to return it to the fake stone before their hasty departure. It was nowhere to be found. That key is the main reason Diana settles onto her sofa for the night. The intruder, or anyone they're affiliated with, could return at any time. Tonight, tomorrow, next week.

How long can someone go without sleep, Diana googles, the light from her phone illuminating the darkened room. *After three or four days without sleep,* the internet tells her, *hallucinations may occur.* "If only this was a hallucination," Diana mutters.

The missing photo plagues her, tapping at the back of her mind like a metronome. She'd gotten so used to that photo on her refrigerator that she barely saw it; now, she struggles to recreate its image in her mind.

The photo had come in one of the condolence cards she received after Tom's death. Andrea opened the cards for her, sorting them into piles: cards that arrived with flowers or charitable donations and required a thank-you note; cards that included a story about Tom that Diana might want to read; cards from Tom's colleagues and clients; and cards from family and friends. Andrea sent all the necessary acknowledgments, and Diana read the cards only once before letting her sister pack them away.

Andrea separated the photo from the card it came with, hanging it on the refrigerator without explanation. Diana has no idea who sent it; all she remembers is that the photo was taken on the school playground and captured Duncan and Phoebe on the double swing, with Tom behind them, mid-push. It must have been taken during a school event and sent to her by a well-meaning parent or neighbor. She has thousands of photos of Tom and their children, yet this one haunts her. Was Phoebe laughing? Was her hair down or in a braid? Was Duncan wearing a red sweatshirt, or had it been blue? Where had she been when the photo was taken?

And why did the intruder steal it?

She accepts, for the first time since she opened that letter, that her home might not be safe. That perhaps she and her children are not safe either. She's shocked that her husband left her so vulnerable.

"I really didn't know him at all," she whispers, tightening her grip on the bat and staring at her front door.

Chapter Twelve

The referee's whistle screeches through the crowd's chatter. He calls a foul on Alcott's opponent, and Duncan's team takes possession of the ball. The whistle blows again, and Jadyn, Duncan's cocaptain, is a blur of elegant movement as he dribbles down the court, sneakers squeaking against the hardwood, the other players on his heels. Jadyn is too fast, though, and without any obstacles, he approaches the basket, shoots, and scores.

Across the stuffy gymnasium, Diana and Phoebe throw their hands in the air and cheer. Andrea and Evan join them in celebrating, stomping their feet against the bleachers. Noah jumps up, as he does every time Duncan or his teammates get near the ball, and shouts his approval. Having appointed himself Duncan's number one fan, Noah refuses to miss any of his games, even going so far as to wear a shirt with Duncan's number, eleven, written on the back in permanent marker. Duncan loves the attention, though he plays it cool for his cousin.

Diana is nervous, her jitteriness and agitation so palpable she feels as if she's guzzled multiple espressos. Her nerves are not for Duncan—he'll play his best and that's enough—but for another reason.

It's been three and a half weeks since she found Tom's letter, and while she's spent this time immersing herself in the complicated details of criminal law, studying felony and misdemeanor statutes in North Carolina and Vermont, and reading issues of the *Vermonter* from the early 1980s, she's no closer to understanding his message. Even when she leaves the letter at home, hidden away, Tom's secret weighs on her, like a snake encircling her chest, squeezing the air from her lungs. It's as if the efforts she's put into rebuilding her life are meaningless, lost to this unsettling yank into the past.

On the plus side, she's not had another uninvited guest. Diana called the locksmith the morning after the intruder's visit and paid extra to have him come immediately to replace every lock in the house. She also had him install bars over the basement windows. When she gave new keys to her parents, Andrea, and Evan, electing not to hide a spare in the backyard, she explained that she'd read an article advising widows to change their locks, a "best practice" for living alone, and they all nodded sympathetically. Only Lakshmi accepted the new key with concern etched across her face.

"If you still won't go to the police, how about getting an alarm system?" she asked. "I'll look into it for you."

Diana shook her head. "The new locks should be enough."

"New locks are not enough, and you know it," Lakshmi said, clearly frustrated. "Stop being stubborn about this. Think about your kids. You need to do more. If an alarm system freaks you out, how about one of those doorbell cameras? I'll order one for you and have Ramesh install it." Lakshmi put her hand on Diana's shoulder. "Say yes, if for no other reason than it will make *me* feel better. And I know you don't want to stress me out."

Diana gave in then, and Lakshmi had the new doorbell installed by the next afternoon.

These extra precautions haven't helped to alleviate Diana's worries. She's taken to looking over her shoulder when she walks down Alcott's Main Street, sleeping with Duncan's baseball bat next to her in bed, triple-checking that the doors and windows are locked before bed each night, and googling every call she receives on her landline. She checks the answering machine each evening, and the hang-ups have continued. So far, they've all come up as Unknown.

The letter is weighing on Duncan, too. He hasn't mentioned it since their talk on the basketball court, but this morning, Diana found a photo of Duncan and Tom in the trash, ripped into pieces. The photo of the two of them on a beautiful spring afternoon as they battled it out in a competitive game of H-O-R-S-E, their foreheads puckered in concentration, had been pinned to the bulletin board over his desk. When she asked him about it, he stalked off with a heartbroken look on his face. She saved the pieces in her jewelry box for the day when she has answers for her son.

Down below on the court, Duncan jumps into the air and sends the basketball into a perfect arc. The ball falls through the net, and the gym vibrates with chants of "Alcott! Alcott!"

Noah hops up from his seat, punching his fist into the air. "Yeah, Duncan!" Phoebe stands up, too, holding Bear Bear over her head and dancing.

"He's playing well," Andrea says, leaning behind Noah to speak to Diana. "Too bad The General and Dad missed that basket. Where are they, anyway?"

"Dad's closing ran over. They'll be here soon," Diana says, watching Duncan high-five his teammates.

Diana still hasn't told Andrea or her parents about Tom's letter or the break-in. At first, she thought she was holding off because her family would ask too many questions—questions she couldn't yet answer—but the truth is, she's still hiding herself from them. She's lost count of the number of times she's forced a smile on her face when all she wants to do is weep, or said everything is great when really, she's drowning.

"Pay attention, Noah," Andrea says, as she ties his sneaker laces. "You don't want to fall going up and down the bleachers."

"Yup," he says, keeping his eyes on the game. Andrea smiles and kisses him on the top of his head.

"Mom," Noah hisses, pushing Andrea away and scowling. "There's a game going on!"

"Okay, okay, no kisses from Mom during basketball, I get it," Andrea says. She catches Diana's eye and shakes her head. "I thought I had more time before he rejected me."

"You don't have anything to worry about," Diana says. "You're a good while away from being embarrassing just for existing."

"I hadn't planned on dealing with parental alienation for another eight to ten years."

Andrea is never without a plan. Diana knows of only two occasions on which she deviated from a plan she'd set into motion: when she chose psychiatry instead of the surgical career she always envisioned, explaining that she wanted to "understand what made people tick, not just cut them open," and when she gave up on the idea of a second child after barely surviving Noah's early years, which were marked by severe acid reflux, colic, and an inability to sleep through the night until he was three years old.

Diana admires Andrea's clear vision of the way her life is to unfold, though she doesn't completely understand it. She wonders whether her sister is closed off to spontaneity or unknown possibilities, but she's never shared those concerns. Their relationship doesn't work if they criticize one another's choices. They learned that the hard way.

Tom taught them that. Or more specifically, Diana's relationship with Tom was the catalyst for Diana's understanding that her relationship with her sister included areas where they could not tread. Within months of meeting, Tom and Diana were living together and talking about marriage. Andrea, who dated Evan for four years before agreeing to move in with him, and then only after drafting an extensive pro-con list, thought Diana was moving too fast toward a life-altering commitment. "What happened to moving abroad? Running your own library?"

Andrea posed these questions, her voice urgent and bewildered, while they helped their parents decorate their house for Christmas. Andrea and Diana stood in the stuffy attic, handing boxes down to their father. Their mother's directions floated up from the living room, where she commanded each step of the preparations.

Hunting amid the boxes for the angel to place on top of the tree, Diana shrugged and bent down to push a box of ornaments to the edge of the stairs, the cardboard scraping against the plywood floor. "I don't know. I'll figure that out. Or I won't. It doesn't matter."

"Doesn't matter? Your plans don't matter?"

"Everything okay up here?" Francis asked as he popped up through the attic opening.

"We're good, Dad. Still looking for that angel, though," Diana said. He nodded and left with the ornaments.

Andrea clutched Diana's arm. "You're moving too fast, Diana. You're not thinking this relationship through."

Diana slowly unpeeled her sister's fingers. "Andrea, I'm happy with Tom. That's what's important. Dreams change."

"You're making a mistake."

"No," Diana said softly. "I'm not."

They never spoke of that conversation again.

Phoebe taps Diana's elbow. "Can I have M&M's?" She gestures to a table in the corner of the gym where the booster club sells candy and bottled water.

"I want Twizzlers," says Noah, tugging on Andrea's arm.

Diana's phone buzzes, and she pulls it out of her coat pocket to find Jonathan's name on the screen. "I have to take this."

"Candy's on me," Andrea says, shepherding the children down the steps.

"Is this a good time?" Jonathan asks, as Diana hikes up the bleachers, passing families watching the action below and a group of giggling tween girls.

"I'm at Duncan's game, so it's a little noisy." Diana finds a seat in the nearly empty top row, near a curly-haired woman hunched over her phone.

"I did some research and wanted to update you."

Diana's stomach turns, and she presses the phone close to her ear. "What did you find out?"

He hesitates.

"Jonathan?" Diana's anxiety increases, her agitation returns. The woman with the curly hair looks at her from behind dark, round sunglasses, and Diana worries she's talking too loudly. "Tell me," she says quietly.

"The thing is, Diana, I didn't find anything. There's no record of Tom ever being arrested in Vermont. I checked Massachusetts and North Carolina, too, to cover all the bases. There's nothing."

"Nothing? That doesn't make sense."

"Doesn't it? In the letter, he mentions he never took responsibility for what he did. Therefore, there wouldn't be any arrest records." Jonathan's voice falls into a whisper as if someone is in the room, and she strains to hear him over the crowd. "I really think you should focus on the Tom you knew, not the one who wrote that confusing, and frankly, strange, confession."

A portion of the letter comes to Diana: *I never owned up to what I did, a decision that was another mistake.*

That woman with the curly hair and dark glasses is closer, only a foot or two away. Did she move, or did Diana shift without realizing it?

"Diana? Are you still there?"

"Yes, I'm here." She stares at the woman, trying to place her. "What about the money? I reviewed our bank accounts, and there wasn't anything out of the ordinary. No odd deposits or unexplained money in or out of our checking or savings accounts." Diana knew she wouldn't find anything; she was the one who paid the bills and balanced their checkbook. She would have noticed if something were off. She looked anyway, though.

"Don't worry about the money. It doesn't matter. Put it out of your mind. The letter, too. Can you do that? Can you try?"

Duncan's words come to her: *Sometimes, I can't remember him on my own. Like he's only a story someone told me, not a real person.* Diana thinks of Phoebe, too: how her daughter doesn't remember sledding with Tom, or how much he loved Family Dinner. As the memories of Tom fade, their children are losing him all over again.

"If I were you," Jonathan continues, "I'd let this all go and move on."

If I were you.

How easy it is to tell someone else what to do with their life. Jonathan doesn't have to live with the questions that trail along after the letter. The questions that will never get answered unless Diana makes uncovering the truth a priority.

She considers telling him about the intruder: the terror of having a stranger in her home, the worry about that missing photo no matter how many stories she concocts for why that person stole it, the constant fear they'll return. Jonathan might take her more seriously if she does, but he also won't keep it to himself, like Lakshmi has promised to do. He'll call the police or her parents; he'll force this latest development out into the open, and Diana will lose the little control she has over her life.

Her parents enter the gym through the side door, her father wearing a blue Alcott sweatshirt, her mother carrying a tote bag filled with what Diana anticipates will be healthy snacks for the kids and Gatorade for Duncan. The General will not be happy about Andrea's candy purchase. Evan waves to them, and they climb up the bleachers, holding hands.

Diana wishes Jonathan responded differently; she wishes he validated her growing interest in finding answers, like Lakshmi had.

The jittery feeling from before expands into the hum of rage. Sweat breaks out on her temples, and her hands clench. *Why didn't Tom take this secret with him? Why is this mine to deal with?*

"Diana, did I lose you?"

The humming fades, still in the background but quieter.

"I have to go. Phoebe's calling me," Diana says, looking at her daughter, M&M's clutched in her hand, following Andrea and Noah back to their seats. Diana says a fast goodbye and hangs up. She turns to the woman to ask why she was eavesdropping, but she's already down the bleachers, scurrying toward the door.

I'd let this all go and move on, Jonathan said.

As if it would be that easy.

As if she could ignore that Tom lied to her.

As if she could forget the intruder in her house, violating her privacy, her children's safety.

Her children . . . She sees how not wanting them to forget Tom and not fully knowing him are connected. The two ideas braid themselves together in a tight, thick rope of need she imagines winding around Duncan and Phoebe. That rope binds them to Tom, and she can't let it break.

A plan begins to form. If Jonathan can't find the information she needs, it's time to visit Tom's family in Vermont. Maybe they'll be open to talking about Tom's past. She can check out the archives of the *Hamilton Star* while she's in town, too.

Maybe I can get some answers, she thinks, energized by the hope this new idea offers.

As the game continues below, Diana turns back to her phone and texts Tom's cousin. **Hey Chris,** she begins.

Chapter Thirteen

The plan to go to Hamilton, Vermont, four hours north of Alcott, comes together in short order. Chris, Uncle Brian, and Aunt Teresa are free the following weekend, and Diana's parents offer to watch Duncan and Phoebe. "I'm glad you're taking time for yourself," Vivian says when she picks up the kids' overnight bags. "But why not a spa? Someplace where you can really unwind?"

"I told Chris I'd visit," Diana says, choosing her words with care.

Andrea calls later, in between patients. "I have to work Saturday or else I'd come with you."

"It's only a few days," Diana says, grateful for her sister's busy schedule. "You won't even realize I'm gone."

Diana makes the trip on a Friday, taking a day off from work. She gives Duncan a kiss before he leaves that morning, sticking twenty dollars in his pocket for emergencies. She waves goodbye as Phoebe walks across the street to school with Mira, the morning bell ringing throughout their neighborhood, the pom-poms on the girls' winter hats bouncing with each step. They'll be safe at her parents', she assures herself, repeating the sentence three times in the hope that the words are true.

As Diana throws a suitcase in her trunk, Lakshmi meets her in the driveway, holding a travel mug filled with coffee and a lunch sack.

"You didn't eat this morning, did you? Or pack food for the ride?"

Diana grins. "Of course I didn't. Thanks for always feeding me, Lax."

"Drive safely and text me with an update. I hope you find what you need."

⌒

The drive is easy: highways through Massachusetts and New Hampshire and into Vermont, back roads from Route 89 into Hamilton. But the farther she drives from home, the more Diana worries about what she'll discover.

Over the years, Tom kept his connection to Hamilton through his extended family. While Uncle Brian and Aunt Teresa came to Alcott a handful of times, Chris visited every winter. *Every winter, except the ones since Tom died,* Diana thinks.

Both only children, Tom and Chris grew up as the best of friends, cousins so close they thought of themselves as brothers. When they were boys, they spent countless hours playing ball and riding bicycles on the dirt roads weaving around their town. As adults, during Chris's trips to Alcott, he and Tom caught a Celtics or Bruins game, and afterward sat at the kitchen table late into the night, drinking and talking. Diana would pass Chris in the early morning, asleep on the sofa, still in his clothes from the night before. He always came alone.

Chris was briefly married to his college girlfriend, Becca. She left him years ago, moving to Los Angeles to try her hand at acting. He heard from her only once after she departed Vermont, Tom told Diana, when she filed for divorce.

Diana asked why Chris hadn't remarried or found someone else to love. He was a catch, she said. Tall and lanky, with black hair and kind hazel eyes, he had a good job running his own carpentry business. Tom dismissed Diana's question with a wave of his hand.

"Why not?" Diana persisted. "Isn't he lonely?"

"Lonely? I'd guess he doesn't allow himself to think much about that. Becca's leaving broke him. I'm not sure he'd ever risk himself like that again," Tom explained. "Don't try to be a matchmaker here, Diana. It won't go anywhere."

As the buildings of Hamilton take shape, a new list starts up: *What I Might Learn Today.*

Nothing. I'll find out nothing, and this trip will have been a waste.

Diana blinks and the list is gone, popping like a bubble. That doesn't usually happen, but it's appropriate, isn't it? This is her deepest fear, more than learning the awful thing Tom did. She is terrified she'll be left in this uncertain wasteland of enough information to make herself sick with worry and not enough to let go. She's worried about Duncan, too—both finding out answers for him and sharing what she learns. He's still a kid; she has to be mindful about what she reveals.

She told Chris she'd meet him for dinner, so her early arrival affords her time for research. She drives to the west side of town, past the high school, the lone supermarket, and a metal-clad diner in the shape of a railroad car. The streets here are lined with oak trees, the bare branches arching over the cars as if they're trying to reach one another, an embrace years in the making.

While spring is beginning in Alcott, here it's still winter, an overcast day that leaves Hamilton in gloomy darkness. And the snow: At home, it's gone; in Hamilton, piles hug the road, stubborn, mud-covered mounds of what had been bright white and new.

The *Star* is housed in a three-story building off Main Street. Painted cream with mullioned windows and tall columns in front, the building resembles a wedding cake. Diana parks in front and steps slowly up the ice-covered stairs to the front door. A large wooden desk sits inside, with the empty office in the rear. Diana expected more activity; she thought the *Star* would be like the newsrooms she's seen in the movies: a bustling space filled with reporters, arguing with editors waving red pens.

"Can I help you?" A woman emerges from behind a six-paneled door, wiping her hands on a paper towel. She is round, with gray hair cropped short. Eyeglasses hang on a beaded string around her neck.

"I'd like to take a look at your archives. Is there a fee to view them?"

"Only if you want to make copies, dear," the woman says, throwing the paper towel in a trash can next to the desk. "Follow me, and I'll set you up." She walks Diana into a small conference room. "What are you looking for?"

"Your issues from June to December 1982, please."

The heater under the window barely throws off any warmth. Even in her winter gear, Diana feels the chill. She zips her coat to her chin and follows the woman across the room. Open shelving covers two walls, and each shelf is filled with boxes labeled with dates. The woman climbs a rolling ladder and begins handing items to Diana.

When the last box has been stacked on the table, the woman steps off the ladder and brushes dust from her hands. "If you need more help, just give a shout. My name is Kara. Kara Marquis."

Kara's welcoming nature unnerves Diana. She expected this request to be more complicated, that she'd be interrogated and asked why she wants access to the back issues of the *Star*. "I'm Diana Morgan. Thanks for your help."

"Morgan?" Kara squints at Diana. "Any relation to Teresa Morgan?"

Diana should have realized Hamilton is like Alcott: Everyone knows everyone, everyone knows everyone else's business.

Instead of answering, she seizes onto an unexpected idea: She could pretend. She could lie to this stranger; she could imagine a different Diana Morgan, a version that has not been shattered by loss. Every ounce of her body covets this other life where her husband is alive, where her family is whole, where there aren't people breaking into her house.

What would this other Diana have done today instead of looking through old newspapers? Would she and Tom have made love when they woke, their bodies sticky with sweat, pressed together under the striped sheets he hated? Would they have cooked the kids blueberry pancakes for breakfast, laughing as Duncan read the comics and Phoebe told corny jokes, maple syrup smeared down the front of her pajamas?

Diana's desire for what she had before Tom's death flares within her, a seductive pain she finds herself craving.

But pretending won't bring him back.

Tom is gone.

Diana shakes off the last tendrils of that brutal fantasy and forces out a response. "Teresa is my husband's aunt."

"Husband's aunt?" When Kara realizes who Diana is, her eyes soften. "You must be Tom's wife then? I'm sorry for your loss." She bustles over to the table and picks up a box labeled MAY–JUNE 1982. She hands it to Diana. "You'll want this box to see his high school graduation. My niece graduated the same year as Tom. The *Star* did a nice summary of the ceremony, as it does for every senior class." As Kara leaves the room, she points to her desk. "I'm available if you need anything else, and the publisher should be in later if you have questions for her."

Once Kara leaves, Diana shifts the box containing Tom's graduation to the far end of the table. "First things first," she murmurs. Tom turned eighteen on June 30, after graduation, so that story will have to wait.

The first box she opens holds the July and August 1982 newspapers. It hits her then that she's looking for evidence to prove her husband committed a *crime*.

She knew this, of course, but the truth of it makes her nauseated, and she begins to shake. Needing to calm herself, Diana remembers how each session of that support group she hated began with a meditation. It was the only part of those meetings she liked. She sits on one of the conference room's hard wooden chairs, rests her hands in her lap, and inhales. She closes her eyes and lets out a slow exhale. She repeats this breathing four more times, and her agitation slowly ebbs.

On the last exhale, she opens her eyes and grabs a newspaper from the box. She reads about the search for an elementary school principal and the new parking guidelines for the local swimming hole. She pores over photos from the Fourth of July parade and town-wide picnic. The opinion page is filled with commentaries debating the merits of letting a Dunkin' Donuts franchise open in Hamilton, but the only crime she reads about is an article on page two of the last issue in July. A farm on the outskirts of town experienced a theft of equipment from its barn, when someone stole two saddles and several tools from an unlocked tack room. This was the fourth such burglary in the area since March, and the police requested assistance from anyone who had relevant information to help break the case.

Diana checks her watch; she's been at the *Star* offices for thirty minutes. She'll have to read faster if she's going to be on time to meet Chris.

She puts the July issues aside and turns to August, her fingers stained black from the newsprint. The first two weeks of the month are uneventful, filled with advertisements for back-to-school shopping, a reminder to contact Town Hall about broken water meters, and early predictions about the prospects of Hamilton High's football team.

The August 19, 1982, edition is different. On the top left corner of the page, printed above the fold to emphasize its must-read status, is a stark headline: **Barn Fire Kills One; Two Others Seriously Injured**.

Diana's hands tremble so violently the newspaper shifts across the table, almost falling to the floor. She grabs the corner and pulls back the paper, her eyes locked on the story under the headline.

An unidentified body has been found in the barn of Grace and William O'Connor, the article begins, **discovered by investigators after Hamilton's volunteer fire department put out a fire in the early hours of August 14. At this time, authorities are unable to say who the person was, if they had anything to do with the fire, or how the fire began.**

A film covers Diana's eyes, obscuring her vision. She blinks to clear them and turns to page three for the continued story. There she learns that the O'Connors both suffered life-threatening injuries and were taken to the hospital. Two horses also died in the blaze, and the barn was destroyed.

The last paragraph of the story ties the O'Connors to an earlier *Hamilton Star* story. In July, the O'Connors were burglarized. Several items went missing from their barn. That case, along with other area thefts, remains unsolved.

Large color photos of the barn, before and after the fire, fill the inside spread, along with profiles of the O'Connors. Grace and William were active in the community: William was a member of the vestry at the Episcopal Church, taught history at the high school, and sold the apples they grew on their land at the farmers market. With her sister, Grace ran a camp for disabled children on the farm, and her apple pie won second place in the 1981 Hamilton Autumn Festival.

Diana takes out her phone and snaps photos of the articles in case she needs to reference this news later. The next issue continues the front-page coverage of the fire and identifies the body as Carson Roy, a Hamilton High School graduate. The O'Connors, the *Star* reported, remain in the hospital.

Tom was eighteen that summer, home in Hamilton until his departure for college in August. The timing works. This fire could be part of Tom's secret.

"Keep going, Diana," she whispers, the words catching in her throat.

Throughout September, the paper reported how the town came together to help dispose of the timber and ash remaining on the O'Connors' property after the fire, how the townspeople raised money for William and Grace's medical care, and how Carson was buried in the town cemetery, next to his father and grandparents. His mother was his only survivor.

William O'Connor Dead, reads the front-page headline in an early-October issue. **Lifelong Hamilton Resident Was History Teacher and Farmer.** The article reports William never regained consciousness after the August fire, spending his last weeks in a medically induced coma. An infection overwhelmed his damaged body, and major organ failure followed. The doctors were unable to save him.

The newspaper includes a statement from the police chief. He explained that Carson Roy was responsible for the blaze. A search of his home uncovered items stolen from the O'Connors and others.

"Mr. Roy was found under a collapsed beam. He was killed by that impact and by smoke inhalation," the chief said. "Our theory is that he returned to the barn on August 14 to commit another crime and inadvertently started the fire that led to his and William O'Connor's deaths. This case is closed."

Diana is flooded with relief. This fire had nothing to do with Tom. Carson Roy was responsible, not Tom. She'll have to keep looking.

An update on Grace's condition is included in the same article. "She's getting better, though she has a long journey ahead of her," her sister Irene said. "We appreciate the continued prayers for her recovery."

The stories about the O'Connors dwindle by December, though there is a sweet story about a community effort to shovel their driveway that winter.

Kara calls to Diana from her desk. "Find what you're looking for?"

"Not sure. Can I look at 1983, too?"

"Of course, help yourself. Leave all those boxes on the table when you're done—I'll clean up later."

Once the 1983 boxes are on the table in front of her, Diana reads quickly, eager for more news, ideally a report of some other crime. The newspapers from January through May of that year are clear of any details that could explain Tom's letter. There's nothing out of the ordinary, nothing criminal beyond speeding tickets handed out by the Hamilton police and shoplifting reports from the local supermarket. It was a stretch anyway; Tom was away at college at that time, far from Hamilton, Vermont.

There's no more news about Carson Roy either. She does find an article about the O'Connors in June of that year, when the school committee announced a scholarship in William's memory for a deserving Hamilton High graduate. She reads through July, in case any news from June, when Tom was still eighteen, was reported later, but there's nothing of note.

As Diana snaps a photo of William O'Connor's obituary, Kara shuffles into the room, tugging a cardigan over her wool sweater. Diana hastily drops her phone into her pocket. She hasn't asked if taking photos is acceptable and doesn't want to strain Kara's good-natured assistance.

"It's cold in here all the time," Kara says. "I ask to increase the temperature, and the publisher says there's no money in the budget." She chuckles in a way that sounds like her opinion of the publisher is not high. "What do you have there?" She leans over the table. "Oh, William O'Connor. What a loss."

"You knew him?"

"We both taught at the high school. Home economics was my subject. William was the history teacher all the kids loved. I'm friendly with Grace through the Women's Club here in town."

"She still lives in Hamilton?" Kara stands so close Diana can smell her cloying perfume and another scent, one that clouds her nostrils. *Mothballs,* Diana thinks, taking a discreet sniff.

"Yes, though she no longer runs her land as a farm. No more horses either. Not since William died." Kara puts on her glasses to read the article, the beaded string swinging. "He was such a good man. That Carson Roy caused heartache for so many people."

For a moment, too quick to hold on to, Diana thinks Kara is talking about Tom, the past morphing right in front of her into an alternate reality. Woozy, she grips the edge of the table and squeezes so hard the blood leaves her fingers, while Kara chatters away next to her.

"Carson was an only child, and his dad left town before he was born," Kara says. "His mother died a few years after him. It was icy out, and she drove into a tree. The police ruled it accidental, but I'm not sure everyone believed that."

William O'Connor, Carson Roy, his mother, Tom: all dead.

Diana remembers Jonathan's phone call during Duncan's basketball game, when he told her he hadn't been able to find evidence that Tom had been arrested. *He never took responsibility for what he did,* Jonathan said. *Therefore, there wouldn't be any arrest records.*

Which means there probably wouldn't be any news stories either.

Has this visit to the *Star* been a waste of time?

Kara dabs at her eyes with a handkerchief from her cardigan pocket. "It was a difficult time for the whole town. William was a special person."

"I'm sorry. I didn't mean to upset you," Diana says automatically.

Kara waves at Diana, as if erasing the apology from the air. She smooths her hands over her generous belly and changes the subject. "Tell me, did you like the graduation coverage? The senior profiles are a very popular feature with our subscribers." When Diana looks at her blankly, Kara gestures to the box of May and June 1982 *Star* editions. "The story about your husband's high school graduation?"

Diana forgot about that box. She opens it now and flips through the issues until she comes to the June 17 paper, which features an in-depth profile of the senior class and their graduation ceremony. On the front page is a full-color shot of the graduates standing on the high school football field. She scans for Tom and finds him on the edge of the crowd. Dressed in jeans with his sandy hair cut in a shaggy mop, he's laughing, his head angled to the side. His right hand clasps the upper arm of a dark-haired teenager. Chris.

"There's my niece. She lives down in Norwich. Has twin boys." Kara points to a blurry girl in the front row. "There's Carson Roy." Kara's finger, the nail painted a pale pink, rests on a boy in the back row. He is turned away from the camera, his arms spread out as if he's planning to jump from the frame.

"They were in the same high school class?" Diana says, not realizing she's spoken the words out loud.

"Your Tom and Carson Roy? Why, yes, they were."

Diana opens the paper to the profiles of the ninety-one graduating seniors. She finds Tom on page three. His senior portrait, which she's never seen before, is printed in the top, left corner. Underneath, reminding Diana too much of Duncan's interview of Tom from the time capsule, is his profile:

Name: Thomas (Tom, Tommy, TM) Morgan

Favorite Subject: English

Favorite Memory: Lunch with Chris & skipping class
with Carson (sorry, Mom!)

Goals: College and travel

Parting Thoughts: Thanks to Mom, Uncle Brian, Aunt
Teresa, Mr. & Mrs. O'Connor! I couldn't have done this
without you!

Tom knew the O'Connors, enough to thank them in his senior profile, and he knew Carson—or, at least, *a* Carson.

"Were there any other Carsons in this graduating class, or perhaps in another grade?" Diana asks, her mouth so dry her tongue sticks to her teeth. *Please let there be another Carson,* she prays. *Please.*

"No, Carson Roy was the only Carson this town has ever had, as best as I know." Kara rereads Tom's senior comments. "That's interesting; it sounds like your husband and Carson were friends."

People died. It's all my fault.

Panicked, her pulse racing, Diana shoots up from the chair, nearly knocking into Kara. An overpowering urge to leave this place possesses her.

"I'm done." She grabs her purse and makes for the door. "Thanks for your help."

"You need anything else, please come back, dear."

Diana pushes through the front door as Kara climbs on the first rung of the ladder, a box balanced in her hand.

The air in Diana's car is so cold that her breath fogs up the windows. Some essential piece of information is outside of her grasp, and as she waits for the heat to come on, a *What Have I Learned?* list begins. She gives in to it, more than ever needing the comfort of old habits.

Tom did something terrible when he was eighteen.

He knew the O'Connors.

He was friends with Carson Roy in high school.

Carson died as a result of that fire. William, too.

Grace was seriously injured.

The O'Connors were important to Tom, enough for them to be listed in his senior profile, and yet he never told me about them.

Diana yanks off her scarf, perspiration pooling at the back of her neck. It's freezing, a New England cold that settles into her bones, but Diana is burning up, her body fighting dual impulses: to find out more and to flee.

"I'm not giving up," she says, more severely than she needs to, as if reprimanding herself for even a hint of indecision. She checks her watch; it's time to meet Chris. She turns on her blinker and merges onto the road, leaving the *Star* behind.

Chapter Fourteen

Diana's prior visit to Hamilton was a two-day trip when she and Tom were first engaged. She had wanted to go sooner but worried about inflaming his grief over his parents' deaths, so she shied away from pressuring him. Her parents, however, especially her father, found it strange she hadn't been to Tom's hometown or met his extended family beyond Chris.

"Why haven't you gone to Hamilton?" Francis asked. He'd canceled a client meeting and driven into Boston to, as he described it, "talk some sense" into her. They met for lunch at a bistro on Newbury Street. "If you're going to build a life with this man, you should meet his family. You can't be introduced for the first time on your wedding day. Your family matters in your relationship. His does, too."

Diana trusted her father's advice but had been nervous to talk to Tom. "I want to see where you grew up," she said the following night over dinner, twisting spaghetti around her fork and avoiding his eyes. "I want to know everything about you. Can't we visit at least once?"

Tom was quiet for a long time, so long she almost told him to forget about it. "Fine," he finally said, his face paler than usual. He called his aunt and uncle that night and made arrangements. They went up the next weekend.

Now, driving the streets of Hamilton, Diana realizes Tom never dissuaded her from believing that his reluctance to visit Hamilton was related to anything other than the loss of his parents. He encouraged that perception, in fact. He filled their visit with memories of them, putting his parents at the center of nearly every conversation, leaving little space for much else.

Hoping to organize her thoughts, Diana begins a list: *What Do I Remember from That Visit?*

Tension. Tom was tense the whole time we were in Hamilton.

He showed me the parking lot where his father taught him to ride a bike.

We visited his parents' graves, and he put flowers on their headstones.

He never mentioned the O'Connors, the fire, or Carson Roy.

No one did.

She stops her list when she reaches Chris's home. During one of his annual visits to Alcott, Chris drew an outline of the porch he'd designed for his cabin, his pencil scratching across the page. The addition took shape on the blank paper as he explained it would be where he'd sit to drink his coffee in the morning and watch the sunset each evening.

After the porch, Chris turned his attention to building a barn on a crest to the left of the house. She finds him there, leaning over a metal workbench, sandpaper in hand, his arms in motion. She's startled by how much he's like Tom—a dark-haired version of her husband. Tom is in the outline of Chris's sinewy muscles under his shirt, the way his jeans hug his hips, and the broad planes of his cheekbones. In the past, he and Tom joked about their resemblance, but Diana could never see it. Now, the similarities between the real man in front of her and the memory of her dead husband are uncanny. This is the closest, outside of being with Duncan, she'll ever get to Tom, and she's nervous. Thrilled, too.

"Diana," Chris says, looking up from his work. He drops the sandpaper and removes his safety goggles. There's an indentation around his eyes, a bruise left by the goggles, and Diana stuffs her hands in her pockets to avoid running her fingers along those marks.

"How are you? The kids?" Chris's unshaven chin scrapes against her skin as he kisses her cheek, and all she can think about is how he smells like sawdust.

"Duncan and Phoebe?"

"Yes, Duncan and Phoebe," Chris says, laughing. "You have other kids I haven't met?"

Diana blushes, embarrassed by her attraction to Chris. "They're okay." Maybe in the past she was reserved with Chris since their connection was through Tom, not independent of him. She shared only the positive side of her life, the same way she did with her family. She doesn't want to pretend anymore. "We're all still hurting."

Chris's voice quiets. "I still can't believe he's gone."

"Me either."

He drags two wooden stools across the concrete floor. He sits on one and gestures for Diana to take the other. "While I'm glad you came for a visit, I wish you'd brought them."

"Next time," Diana says, climbing onto the stool as its uneven legs rock. "What are you making?"

"An Adirondack chair for my porch."

"Only one?"

"I only need one," Chris says, shrugging. "Duncan still playing basketball?"

"You can't get the ball out of his hands. Want to see him in action?"

She and Chris hunch over her phone as she shares a grainy clip of Duncan practicing layups on the court across the street from their house.

"He's got good form," Chris observes.

"Definitely inherited from Tom."

"There was this game when we were in the tenth grade; Tom made a basket right before the buzzer." Chris grins. "I remember it all: the way the ball flew through the air, the screams when it made it through the net, the excitement when everyone realized we'd won. The team hoisted Tom on their shoulders and carried him around the gym, yelling his name. It was amazing."

"I've heard that story before," Diana says, thankful the memory Chris shared isn't a surprise. "But I like hearing it again."

Chris's phone beeps. "My mother," he says, checking the screen, "is asking if you've arrived. We should probably get to their house, or I'll never hear the end of how I made you late for dinner."

Diana hops off the stool. "You don't mind I'm staying with them? They have more room, and I thought it would be easier."

"No problem." Chris lifts his coat from a hook by the door and turns off the overhead light as they step outside. "My mom's a better cook anyway."

Six cars are parked in front of Uncle Brian and Aunt Teresa's when Diana follows Chris's truck up the driveway. He meets her as she exits her car. "Half of Hamilton must be here tonight," he jokes. "My mother does not shy away from a chance to entertain."

Diana takes a bouquet of lilies for Teresa from the trunk. She also has a bottle of bourbon for Brian. Chris suggested it when she texted him for gift ideas.

"She told me they had dinner plans when we talked about me coming up this weekend," Diana says, as she shuts the trunk. "Glad I stopped at your place first, though. It gave me a quieter arrival."

An early-April snowfall crunches underfoot as Diana and Chris walk to the house. "What's it like to be here?" Chris asks.

"Strange," she whispers. "I wish Tom was with me. Then again, I wish that every day."

Aunt Teresa stands in the doorway. Before any hellos are shared, she hugs Diana. The lilies crush between them, their sickly-sweet smell filling Diana's nose. With her gray hair piled on her head, Teresa barely comes up to Diana's chin. The embrace goes on longer than expected, and Diana understands Teresa is hugging Tom, too.

When Teresa eventually lets go, Diana hands Tom's aunt the flowers. "Thank you for having me."

"Lilies, my favorite." Aunt Teresa dips her face into the fragrant blossoms, and her hazel eyes, so similar to Chris's, shine. "Come," she says. "Brian wants to say hello." Chris and Diana pile their coats on an overstuffed rack in the corner and follow her down the hall.

The aromatic scents of cumin and cayenne greet them in the warm kitchen. Two women chat by the table, as one slices red peppers and the other pours juice for a group of waiting children. Aunt Teresa introduces Diana to her guests and moves into the dining room, where she makes room amid the cutlery and cloth napkins for Diana's lilies. Chris grabs a beer from a cooler in the corner.

"My son gets a drink before he greets me," calls out Brian. "Where are your manners, Christopher?"

The room erupts into laughter and banter Diana can't follow. She's disoriented; she remembers Uncle Brian and Aunt Teresa's house from her previous visit, but the sounds and smells are different now. The room is too full of people, and yet she's painfully aware of the empty space at her side where Tom should be.

Standing still will only increase her nerves, so Diana threads her way around the kitchen, forcing herself to greet one person after another, including a stocky man wearing a Bernie Sanders sweatshirt who vigorously shakes her hand and asks if she's registered to vote. When she manages to break away, Diana makes a straight line for Brian.

Tall like Chris but with silver-streaked hair, Uncle Brian commands dinner preparations from his spot in front of the stove. He stirs the peppers into the simmering pot of chili as he kisses Diana's cheek. She puts the bourbon in its gray velvet bag on the counter next to him. "For me?" Brian asks. He unwraps the bottle and examines the label. "Now we have a celebration."

More guests enter the house, and Diana is swept into the dining room. She forgets the name of each new person she meets as soon as they are introduced, with the exception of Kara Marquis from the *Hamilton Star*, who smiles shyly and takes a seat on the other end of the table. These new friends bring home-brewed beer and chocolate cupcakes, and none of them mention Tom. There are no expressions of sympathy or inquiries about her well-being, and Diana finds relief in this normalcy.

The dinner that follows is raucous, voices competing to be heard, one-liners and puns thrown back and forth. Diana spends the meal listening to the Bernie Sanders fan, who has much to say about local skiing conditions and the increasing interest in the area from out-of-state tourists. She nods along to his monologue, as she drinks the multiple glasses of wine Uncle Brian pours for her and watches the other guests through the candlelight.

Before she knows it, the evening is over, and sleepy children are hustled into the dark for their parents to drive them home through the starlit night. The dining room table's lace tablecloth is covered in chili stains and cornbread crumbs, and chocolate icing is smeared across abandoned dessert plates. Empty wine bottles gather on the sideboard. Etiquette tells Diana she should aid in the cleanup, but it's been a long time since she felt this relaxed, and she's loath to move.

"Teresa!" Brian yells, a little drunk.

"What do you need, my love?" Teresa asks, returning from the kitchen. She dries her hands on her apron and looks at him, half with irritation and half with the sated look of a hostess whose dinner has gone off well.

"Sit and drink this bourbon Diana brought." Brian's voice is gruff, and his eyes are full of mischief. He holds out his hand to his wife. "Come."

Teresa stoops so her face is level with his. Brian places his hands on her hips and kisses her. Their embrace breaks apart only when she giggles.

"You two," Chris says. He grabs for the bourbon, but his father nabs it first.

"Fifty-three years of marriage, Christopher, is a precious gift," Brian says. He opens the bottle and sniffs. With a delighted smile, he pours the amber-colored liquor into four etched tumblers and nudges them across the table.

"What shall we toast?" Teresa says.

"Diana, of course," Brian says. "It's been a long time since you've crossed our door, and we love that you're here."

Chris and Teresa echo Brian, raising their glasses to Diana.

"To Tom," Chris says, meeting Diana's eyes. The bourbon hits the back of her throat, sweet and woody, as Teresa and Brian repeat Tom's name.

Brian leans over to Teresa. "A toast to my love," he says, as they clink their glasses. They hold their heads together, Brian whispering into Teresa's ear. Teresa blushes and swats his arm.

Diana managed to keep thoughts of Tom away while she sat surrounded by his family and their friends. Now, envy rises up. Fifty-three years of marriage. She'll never have that.

She lifts her glass. "To Teresa and Brian."

∽

Aunt Teresa and Uncle Brian's guest room, above their garage, has white walls and pale-blue carpeting. Two sets of bunk beds sit in the corners, and a queen platform bed rests in the center under a large skylight. "Like being in a tree house," Diana says when Teresa escorts her to the room, both unsteady on their feet. "Like we're above the world."

The view outside, overlooking the snow-covered backyard dotted with evergreens, does give the impression of flying, of being disconnected from the earth.

"Sleep well, Diana," Teresa says, closing the door behind her.

As she settles into bed for the night, Diana's thoughts drift to her visit to the *Hamilton Star*. A nagging feeling presses at the center of all she learned today. She's missing something. What is it?

She rolls over and takes her phone from the bedside table. She checks the app that controls her new doorbell camera and is grateful to see her empty front porch, no intruders in sight. She next sorts through the day, beginning with her arrival at the *Star*. She relives meeting Kara and opening that first box, reading the newspapers, and discovering the stories about the fire. Diana scrolls through the pictures she took in the newspaper's conference room: a photo of the ashy shell of the O'Connor barn, the fire chief's statement that Carson Roy was responsible for the fire, William O'Connor's obituary.

Or, more precisely, William Duncan O'Connor's obituary.

It comes to her then, so forcefully she sits up in bed, choking.

Duncan.

William Duncan O'Connor.

That's it: *William Duncan.*

Her son is *Duncan William.*

In the weeks before the baby was born, she and Tom bantered names back and forth, Diana set on Lachlan or Aiden. Maybe Miles. Tom was unconvinced.

"How about William Duncan?" he said one night as they walked home from getting ice cream, Diana's craving for mint chocolate chip having established a nightly ritual they both enjoyed.

"You don't want to name the baby after your dad?" Diana asked, licking ice cream from the corner of her mouth.

"Gary?" Tom wrinkled his nose. "I can't imagine that as a baby name."

"In that case, what about Duncan William?" Diana said. "I like that better."

Tom stopped in the middle of the sidewalk. "You asked about my dad; what about yours? Would he be hurt if the baby isn't named after him?"

"Francis would be better as a middle name." Diana finished off her cone with a triumphant crunch. "We can reserve it for baby number two."

"Planning ahead, are you?" Tom smiled. "I like it."

"So it's settled: Duncan William, if it's a boy." Diana smiled back, satisfied. "We should come up with a girl's name, to be safe, but I'm ninety-nine percent sure it's a boy."

"I bet you're right." Tom took her hand in his and didn't let go until they walked through their front door.

He never explained the significance of that name. Another secret.

"Goddammit, Tom," Diana says, smacking her hand against the mattress. "That's my *son*." Quaking with anger, her fingers tighten into a fist, and she punches the mattress, leaving a dent behind. Her muscles clench as she continues pounding, yanking the sheet off from the corner. Each slam rings through her like a scream. *"My son."*

She hits the mattress until her arm muscles spasm. Exhausted, she falls back against the pillow, tears sliding down her cheeks and pooling on her neck.

Why had he *deceived* her?

What if he *had* left the letter out of spite?

What if the love they shared was the *real* lie?

Diana keeps her body rigid for several minutes, until the idea Tom didn't love her, had wanted to hurt her, disappears into that place inside her where she keeps the hardest of things. Then she sinks into the mattress and waits for morning.

Chapter Fifteen

Hours later, Diana stands in Aunt Teresa and Uncle Brian's kitchen looking for coffee. Chris wants to get an early start for snowshoeing, an invitation Diana agreed to last night after her second glass of bourbon. She needs caffeine to be able to participate in the adventure he's planned. As she searches through the cabinets, Teresa enters the room, her slippers shuffling against the tile floor.

"I was coming to start breakfast, but you beat me to it," Teresa says sleepily, flipping on the overhead light. As if reading Diana's mind, Teresa opens a cupboard next to the stove and selects a bag of organic beans. "Let me do this."

The kitchen fills with the angry protest of the coffee grinder and the heavenly scent of coffee. "Any chance you have Tylenol?" Diana asks. "I have a killer headache."

Teresa points to a cabinet across the room. "Get me some, too? I don't usually drink bourbon."

Inside the cabinet Diana finds a photo taped to the door. Chris and Tom, dressed in orange hunting jackets, standing in front of a woodpile. The image is blurry, but their smiles make Diana grin in response.

Teresa steps behind her. "That was taken when the boys were around fifteen. They were supposed to go hunting with Brian, but they goofed around so much he got frustrated and left without them. They thought they were so clever. Brian wasn't having it. He grounded Chris for being rude. Tom, as I recall, talked his mother out of any punishment. 'I wasn't being disrespectful to Uncle Brian,' he argued. 'I was exercising my right to bear, or not bear, arms.'" Teresa chuckles. "It was a ridiculous argument, but Martha could never say no to Tom, especially not after Gary died."

Diana removes the bottle of Tylenol and selects pills for herself and Teresa. "I've never heard that story before."

"I suppose you wouldn't have."

"Why do you say that?" Diana asks.

Teresa pours them each water in the tumblers from last night. "We didn't see you much up here, did we? Only that one visit. When Brian and I visited you and Tom for the kids' christenings or for Easter, it was always so busy that there wasn't enough time to share stories. And I doubt Tom talked much about his past."

"What do you mean?" Diana asks, dread inching down her spine. "Why wouldn't Tom talk about the past?"

Teresa slugs back the water and the medicine Diana hands her. "I should really get breakfast going," she says, putting the tumbler in the sink and opening the refrigerator. "I hope you're hungry."

Diana remains in front of the cabinet, thinking of the photo of her children and Tom that the intruder stole from her home. Is it a clue to Tom's secret? Or is it, like this photo of teenage Chris and Tom, a glimpse into a life that's long gone?

⌇

Chris arrives with the snowshoes as Teresa puts a plate of steaming waffles on the kitchen table. "Perfect timing," she says.

Chris stomps snow off his boots. "Always, when your cooking is involved, Mom." He accepts a cup of coffee from Diana and looks around. "Where's Dad?"

"Sleeping off Diana's bourbon, I'm afraid," Teresa says. "He misjudged his tolerance for the good stuff."

They take seats at the Formica table, Diana across from Teresa and Chris to her left. She watches them under half-closed eyes as they slide waffles onto their plates, pour syrup, and sip coffee. Her face flushes with anticipation. Before she considers the best way to phrase her question, the words blurt out. "Does the name Carson Roy mean anything to you?"

"Sure, Tom and I went to school with him," Chris says.

"And the O'Connors? Grace and William O'Connor?"

Teresa puts down her fork and focuses on her son.

"Mr. O'Connor, our history teacher?" Chris rolls the words around, as if he's tasting them.

"Tom worked for the O'Connors, didn't he?"

Chris nods and shovels waffles into his mouth, syrup dripping onto the table, leaving a sticky puddle behind. Diana waits. He'll be suspicious if she pushes.

"Mr. O'Connor and his wife had the farm over on Route 119," Chris says after he swallows. "Tom helped take care of their animals and did some yard work, stuff like that."

Pieces of this story are falling into place.

"Tom liked it there, and he was close with Mr. O'Connor. Right, Mom?"

Teresa refills Chris's mug. "Yes, that's correct."

"What's all this about Carson and the O'Connors?" Chris scrapes his fork across the plate to pick up the remaining crumbs. Licking the tines, he looks at Diana. "That was years ago."

"There was a fire? Carson and William died?"

"Yeah, it was terrible," Chris says.

"Did you know the O'Connors, Teresa?"

"We didn't socialize, if that's what you mean. This is a small community, so of course, I knew who they were." Wariness creeps into Teresa's voice. "Why are you asking about them?"

"I came across their names in Tom's papers." It isn't a lie, but it isn't the complete truth either. "I hoped you could tell me who they were to him."

Chris glances between Teresa and Diana.

"As Chris explained, this was many years ago," Teresa says. "Plus, Tom was a private person, even with us. We won't be able to help you with your questions."

Diana is bewildered by Teresa's reluctance to offer up even one detail. She looks at Chris for help, but his eyes are firmly locked on his coffee. "If you aren't able to tell me about Tom and the other people in his life," Diana asks, "who can?"

"These questions should have been asked of Tom, not us," Teresa says quietly, not giving an inch.

Diana thinks of Duncan lying on her bedroom floor holding Tom's letter, the intruder entering her house and stealing that photograph, and Tom naming their son after William O'Connor, and she loses all sense of restraint. "I would *love* to ask Tom," she says, an edge to her words, "but he's *dead*. I have no choice other than asking you. I don't want to make things awkward between us, I just want to understand who my husband was."

The room goes silent, with only the hum of the refrigerator in the background. Diana watches Tom's aunt and cousin for what feel like the longest minutes of her life. The waffles sit heavily in her stomach. She's about to apologize and explain the stress she's been under when Teresa stands up and drops her napkin on her chair.

"Tom was a good man who loved you and your children. That should be enough." Teresa clears her throat. "You'll have to excuse me; I really should check on Brian." She leaves the room so quickly Diana doesn't have time to respond.

Chris is also up, balancing the plates and silverware into an unstable pile. "We should get moving if we want to get a parking space close to the trail head."

Diana brings her plate to him at the sink. "I—"

"Let's get going."

She nods, frustration lurking. They're clearly hiding something, but what? And why?

Chris and Diana snowshoe for two hours, up the back of Hamilton's ski slope, the sun so bright Diana squints behind her sunglasses. She treks behind Chris, her shorter legs struggling to keep up, her snowshoes filling neatly in his tracks. Neither of them speaks. Diana fears she'll never get him to open up, and that concern carries her all the way up the mountain.

Chris stops at a plateau overlooking the valley, where the air smells crisp and sweet. Rugged mountains surround them on all sides, and pine trees hug the steep landscape. Diana surveys the trails below, watching the skiers and snowboarders in their vividly colored jackets speed down the mountain, their movements seemingly choreographed.

"When Becca left, it took me a long time to not see her in every corner," Chris says, pulling a water bottle from his backpack. He takes a swig and offers it to Diana. "I thought about her all the time. It's not the same as losing Tom, of course, yet the hole is still there."

The water is cool down her throat, quenching a thirst Diana didn't realize she had. "How much time passed before you were yourself again?" she asks. Chris has never spoken about Becca before. She wonders what it's like to have your marriage end with your partner choosing to leave you. Is it harder, or is the pain the same as losing a spouse via death: impossible yet inescapable?

"I never went back to being the old me. For better or worse, her leaving changed me." Chris looks sadly at Diana. "I was different before. More carefree, my mother says."

Diana thinks about sharing Tom's letter with him. Would it do to him what it's done to her? Would it leave him confused about the truth, about who Tom really was?

"People always say time heals all wounds. Yet when you're in it, in that mess, you want it to be better. Immediately." Chris jams the water bottle back in his pack, yanking the zipper closed. "But the truth is, that old saying is right. The hurt does diminish in time. Everything's different with time."

"Time can also bring clarity to the past," Diana says.

"You're asking questions about Tom, I get it. His death is a terrible loss, and you're trying to hold on to him. I did that with Becca. It didn't get me anywhere. I ran around in circles for years, grieving, imagining what might have been, hoping she'd come back. It's better to look ahead, Diana. There's nothing in the past that's important. For you or the kids."

"Chris—"

"We should start back down." He swings the pack onto his shoulders and begins his descent. She waits for him to turn around and ask why she isn't walking, but he doesn't. Instead, his snowshoes crunch against the snow until he's enveloped by the pine trees, and she's alone.

Diana reluctantly follows his trail down the hill, certain with each step that whatever Chris isn't telling her has been bothering him for a long time.

Chapter Sixteen

The O'Connor farm is so hidden from the street Diana almost misses it. A shiny red "For Sale" sign is her only indication a home is nearby. A photo of a real estate agent with perfect teeth peers out from the bottom of the sign as it swings in a slight breeze. OPEN HOUSE TODAY, reads a placard affixed across the top.

Diana stops her car in front of the sign. For sale? Another surprise in an unending list of surprises.

She's supposed to be on her way back from the store. She offered to restock Aunt Teresa and Uncle Brian's wine after it was depleted during last night's dinner party. Really, she wanted an excuse to get out of the house, away from the awkwardness caused by her questions about Carson Roy and the O'Connors.

If Chris and Teresa won't open up, maybe there's information here. While Diana isn't interested in getting arrested for snooping around someone's private property, an open house is an invitation to come inside, isn't it?

She considers leaving, returning to Aunt Teresa and Uncle Brian's to uncork the bottle of merlot in her trunk and drink away all her questions about Tom, but Duncan's words come back to her: *How am I supposed to remember him if he was someone else?*

Diana presses on the gas and turns onto the property. The winter has left deep grooves in the gravel driveway, and her tires grind against the stones, the sound reverberating in her head. Her palms are wet, and under her arms, a cold sweat spreads.

On her left is a dense forest of birch trees, naked in the afternoon light. To the right, the branches of a willow tree reach nearly to the ground. She slows the car to a crawl, following the drive around a bend. The house, painted white with a covered porch and smoke puffing out from a brick chimney, backs up against an expansive yard rimmed by a slight hill where apple trees stand at attention, forming a barrier against the wild Vermont land beyond.

Diana parks at the rear of the driveway, next to a silver Mercedes and a yellow Volvo station wagon. She steps from the car, slinging her purse across her chest. Can she find Tom here? Are bits of him left in this place? That's why she came: to see whether the O'Connor farm offers answers or some remaining echo of her husband.

She shuffles across the cold, unyielding ground to the remains of a circular paddock. Only a portion of the fence remains, and its rotted wood indicates years of neglect. Diana grips the brittle railing as the wind glides across her face and through her hair. The air feels wet; more precipitation will come later. She inhales, letting her lungs fill with the chilled air.

The back door swings open, and a coiffed, middle-aged woman emerges from the house. Dressed in a navy-blue pantsuit and striped blouse, she marches to the Mercedes and takes a box from the back seat. As she closes the door, she notices Diana standing in the yard.

"Are you here for the open house?" the woman calls.

Unprepared for another person's questions, though Diana's brain tells her a simple yes is all that's required, she panics. She looks around the backyard, stalling for time, trying to come up with an answer.

"It's okay that you're early," the woman says. "I'm ready for you."

Diana lets go of the fence. As she approaches the house, the woman tucks the box under her arm and sticks out her hand, a gold bracelet sliding down her wrist.

"Stacy Sousa. I'm the agent representing the seller. Welcome." She shakes Diana's hand, and Diana recognizes her from the photo on the for-sale sign. "Let's go inside." Stacy turns back to the house, talking to Diana over her shoulder. "Did you have any trouble finding the place? It's secluded, isn't it? Like an oasis."

"Yes . . . I mean no. I used the GPS on my phone."

"Those apps are a godsend. What did we ever do without them?" Stacy holds open the porch door for Diana as she leads the way inside.

A generous mudroom flows into the kitchen, where a fire crackles in the stone hearth. Above the mantel hangs a large seascape of a lone boat tossed over storm-driven waves, the horizon dark and menacing.

"This is the kitchen," Stacy announces unnecessarily, dumping her box next to a plate of sugar cookies on the rectangular table. She removes the listing brochures and sign-in sheet from her box. With a gesture, she invites Diana to the table.

Diana scribbles her name, the signature messy and difficult to read, and picks up a brochure.

Stacy glances at the sheet. "Donna, is it? Have you been looking long for a place?"

Donna it is. It's a needless deceit, but one that steadies Diana. She stands in front of the fireplace, warming her hands and examining the seascape. The painting is sad: the moment before a terrible event happens. "My search is very recent."

"You're welcome to look around." Stacy gestures to a doorway in the far corner of the room, then turns back to her brochures, spreading them out across the table. "Before I forget: The owner is home. Wasn't feeling well. Nothing contagious, nothing you need to worry about. She's in the sunporch. Won't bother you at all. I thought it best to continue since we did so much advertising. Hope you don't mind."

Diana trips over the threshold and grabs the wall to keep from falling. She didn't expect to meet Grace O'Connor today, and she finds herself frozen, uncertain whether she should proceed or come up with another plan.

Stacy looks up eagerly from her spot at the table. "Yes, Donna? Do you have a question?"

"No, no question." Suddenly hot, Diana unbuttons her coat and loosens her scarf. *Everything will be fine,* she thinks, fanning herself with the brochure and moving away from Stacy Sousa and her efficient real estate instincts. *I came all this way for answers. Now's not the time to waver.*

Diana enters a large hallway with a set of stairs in the middle and walks through the closest door. A bare desk sits under a window of wavy glass, and a tan love seat covered in chintz pillows occupies the far corner. The bookshelves are what prompt her to cross the room; all the way to the ceiling they go. Diana trails her fingers along the spines of the books. Ward, García Márquez, Woolf, Thoreau, Atwood, Didion. The books are neat and dust-free and clearly have some kind of organization to their placement Diana can't decipher. Perhaps by how much the reader loves them—that's her favorite system. One shelf is dedicated to Bibles: King James, Coverdale, Inclusive, Modern English, and several others; another to animal husbandry, with a focus on horses; and yet another is filled with manuals about wildflowers and apple-growing techniques.

Diana returns to the hallway, where a woven, L-shaped basket rests on the two bottom stairs. Her grandmother used one of these. It's a catchall for items that need to go upstairs. Diana hasn't seen one in years, not since her grandmother passed away when she was in middle school. Inside is a set of knitting needles and a copy of *National Geographic* magazine. She's curious why Stacy Sousa hasn't squirreled the basket away somewhere.

She climbs the stairs, her hand trailing up the banister. The wall to her left is covered in photographs. Some are old, black-and-white portraits of serious-looking men and women, children standing frozen at their side. In the center hangs a large picture of a young woman in a gold, glass-less frame. She sits astride a brown horse in front of a red barn, its doors open to a paddock.

In another photo, several people crowd together on the house's front porch. Is the couple in the back the O'Connors? The others, an older woman and a teenage girl with curly hair, are a mystery. On the end, though, leaning against the porch railing, a baseball cap pulled down across his eyes, is Tom. Diana recognizes the slant of the shoulders, the long legs. She sees this boy in Duncan every day.

She stares at the photo—why has all this been unknown to her?—until she hears the kitchen door open and close. Stacy Sousa loudly offers greetings. Someone else answers. Diana isn't the only visitor to this open house.

She hastens up the stairs and into the empty hallway. She passes sparsely furnished bedrooms, stopping at what she guesses to be Grace's room. A bed covered in a pink, quilted satin comforter is positioned under two windows overlooking the backyard. An Impressionistic painting of a riderless horse galloping through a forest, the sky luminous with morning light, hangs across the room. On either side of the bed are Shaker-style tables. One holds a glass lamp, a digital clock, and a pile of books; the other is bare.

On the dresser is a black-and-white photo of a young man in a suit and tie, a younger version of the man whose obituary Diana found while reviewing the archives at the *Hamilton Star*. William Duncan O'Connor. Other personal items have been cleared away so that people like Diana—trespassers—can envision living here, so they aren't distracted by someone else's life. What would strangers say about her bedroom? Would her too-big bed and closet still filled with Tom's clothes say "widow"? "Lonely"? "Grief-stricken"?

"I have to get out of here," Diana says. As she walks down the staircase, she notices the steps here squeak like the ones she has at home.

At the bottom, standing next to the basket, Diana pauses. Stacy Sousa and the new arrivals are still in the kitchen, blocking her exit.

"These windows! Aren't they special? They're original to the house. They don't make them like this anymore." The real estate agent's voice rises and falls. "This house has so much space. It'll be perfect for a family. How many children did you say you have?"

Diana escapes down the hall, away from the kitchen. Turned about in the house's mazelike layout, she tries another door, only to find herself standing in the pantry. Mason jars of jam and cans of soup are stacked on one side; toilet tissue is on the floor next to a bag of dog food. Most of the shelves are bare. This is the opposite from Diana's pantry, which overflows with options to feed her kids and their friends.

She tries one more door, hoping it leads outside. As the door opens, Diana realizes she's in the sunporch, looking right at Grace O'Connor.

The older woman is propped up on a wicker sofa, a knitted afghan spread across her lap. A black Labrador perches at her feet. He lazily raises himself and sniffs as Diana enters. Through the window, Diana spies her car, a few hundred feet away.

Grace is an older version of the woman on the horse in the photograph, with tapered cheekbones and gray hair in a loose bun. Diana's first impression is that Grace is unhappy. She understands, of course; she'd be pissed off having strangers stomping around her house, poking in her closets and drawers, and examining her life.

"I thought this was the door to the outside. I didn't mean to disturb you," Diana stammers, clutching the real estate brochure in her hand, folding the corner back and forth to stave off her nerves.

"It's not a problem," Grace replies, patting her dog's head until he lies down again. "The seller isn't supposed to be home during an open house, isn't that right?"

"Your house is lovely," Diana says impulsively. "How did you come to live here?"

"My husband grew up in Hamilton, and he took over this farm from his uncle when we were newlyweds. It's my favorite in the spring, when wildflowers bloom in the yard and the land comes alive, especially the apple trees."

"What kind of apples did you grow?"

"McIntosh," Grace says. "Do you have any questions about the house? Anything the very efficient Ms. Sousa couldn't answer for you?"

Diana can tell Stacy Sousa isn't Grace's favorite person; how can you possibly like someone who is working to dismantle your life? She saw Tom's hospice nurses the same way. She appreciated their help as her world fell apart, and she hated them, too. Hated they were in her life because Tom was dying.

Diana gestures to the backyard. "What was the fence for?"

Grace frowns. "A paddock. It was next to a barn my husband built for me. I used to raise and train horses. Local folks boarded their horses with us, too."

"What happened to the barn?"

"There was a fire, many years ago."

Diana mops sweat from her forehead with the back of her hand. "I'm sorry," she says. "What happened to the horses?"

"We saved most of them. Opened the doors and they went running out into the fields. Took hours to catch them again."

We saved most of them, Diana repeats to herself. The coverage of the fire in the *Hamilton Star* indicated two horses perished in the flames.

"You didn't rebuild?"

"William put up that barn for me." Grace tucks the afghan around her body. "I couldn't accept another building in its place."

Diana asks the question that's been nagging at her since she first learned about the fire: "How did it start?" The *Star's* reporting indicated the police thought Carson had set the fire, but not how he did it. Understanding her inquiry is so close to bringing up William's death, which she knows all too well can be painful, Diana adds an apology of sorts. "If you don't mind me asking, that is."

"The fire wasn't caused by faulty wiring, if that's what you're asking. The authorities ruled that out." Grace's dog lifts his head to rest on her knees, and she rubs behind his ears.

"I wonder if I could ask—"

"I must let you return to your tour," Grace interrupts. "If you go through that door on your left, you'll be at the back porch by the kitchen. Ms. Sousa will be there, I assume, and she can answer any other queries you may have."

Grace's formal tone tells Diana she is dismissed. She reluctantly leaves, looking back only as she closes the door. When Grace believes she's alone, her posture gives way. She collapses against the cushions; her eyes close and her hands fall into her lap. Diana suppresses the urge to comfort the older woman, forcing herself to continue walking across the porch.

The temperature dropped while she was inside. Diana zips up her coat and stuffs the real estate listing into her pocket. She strides through the yard and around the paddock, past an old tree stump and a pile of abandoned ladders, until she comes to the barn's crumbling foundation.

She's frustrated she didn't ask Grace more questions, that she didn't push harder, that the answers to Tom's letter still aren't clear. And she is sad. So sad he didn't confide in her.

Her phone swooshes, indicating the arrival of a text. Diana fishes it out of her purse; she missed several messages while she was in Grace's house.

From Chris: Hey, where'd you get to? Dad has the steaks ready to go.

From Lakshmi: How are you? What did you find out? I've been keeping an eye on your house. So far, no visitors.

From Jonathan: Just checking in. Have time for a chat?

From Andrea: Hope you're having a good visit. Can you bring me home some maple syrup?

Instead of responding, Diana sticks the phone back in her purse and bends down. Among the remaining chunks of the foundation, she selects a small, bronze-colored rock with gold streaks, smooth on one end, pointed on the other. She clenches it tightly as she stands up, and the rock pierces her skin, making her gasp. Drops of blood rise to the surface. Hypnotized, Diana stares at her palm as a red puddle forms.

An upstairs window slides open, and Stacy Sousa's voice rings into the yard. Diana blinks and remembers where she is. Swiftly moving toward her car, she keeps a tight hold on the rock as droplets of her blood stain the snow underfoot.

Chapter Seventeen

After an uncomfortable dinner, during which Chris is distracted, Aunt Teresa is quiet, and Uncle Brian explains in excruciating detail the process of tapping the trees in his yard for maple syrup, Diana excuses herself to pack for home. As she lies on the bed, her clothes scattered across the floor, she contemplates what she's learned and how she'll explain it to Duncan and Lakshmi. She can't even explain it to herself.

Her uncertainty calls for a list, of course, and the one that comes to her is inevitable: *What Is Tom's Secret?*

He said, "People died. It's all my fault."

Does this have to do with the O'Connors?

But Carson Roy started that fire.

Why would he do that?

Or was it someone else?

Was it—

Diana's questions are interrupted by a knock, and she opens the door to find Aunt Teresa on the landing, jogging in place in a light snowfall to keep herself warm. She holds out a large leather-bound book. "I wanted to give you this."

The book is heavy, and the leather along the spine is split. An overflow of pages prevents it from closing properly, forcing the volume into the shape of a right triangle.

"What is it?" Diana asks, wiping melting snowflakes from the cover.

"Tom's childhood photo album. I should have passed this on years ago. It didn't come to mind until after breakfast this morning. Maybe you'd like to take it home and share it with Duncan and Phoebe."

"Oh, Teresa." Diana delicately pulls back the cover, the leather sighing with the relief of being opened. The cellophane covering the first page crackles, and she smooths its folds and tatters to get a clear view of the photo beneath. There is infant Tom, lying on a white blanket, his chubby legs kicking in the air. "He looks like Duncan and Phoebe at that age." She smiles, her vision cloudy. "Thank you."

"Come back and join us, if you'd like. We still have more bourbon."

Diana hugs the album to her chest. She recognizes this gift as Teresa's peace offering, but it's not enough. "Will you tell me what I want to know? Will you answer my questions?"

Teresa's eyes take on a faraway look Diana can't decipher. "This . . . this is all we can do. Be content with what you have, Diana." She turns and walks carefully down the stairs and across the driveway, the snow covering her hair in a fine white film.

Diana expects to be angry at Tom's family's unwillingness to help her; instead, disappointment floods her veins. *This must have been what Tom was afraid of,* she thinks. *That I'd turn away from him if he told me.*

She spends hours reviewing the photos. She finds nothing that helps her search, though the pictures of Tom's senior prom make for a sidesplitting laugh. His slicked-back mullet and his date's teased-out lion's mane of hair will be the first items she shows the kids when she arrives back in Alcott.

The album is not a complete bust, though. At some point, between photos of Tom at his sixth birthday party and his first day of middle school, Diana comes up with a plan for her next steps. She has to return to the O'Connor farm to talk to Grace.

The next morning, after a late breakfast, Diana says goodbye to Aunt Teresa and Uncle Brian on their front stoop. "We're grateful you came to Hamilton, Diana," Teresa whispers in her ear.

"Please visit with the children. Maybe this summer?" Brian says, gently hugging her before stepping back to take Teresa's hand.

Chris scrapes the last of the snow off her windshield. "Look out for ice until you're clear of the mountain," he says, brushing his lips against her cheek.

Fifteen minutes later, Diana's tires turn against Grace's gravel driveway, nausea flaring in her abdomen. She parks in the empty drive and steps out before she second-guesses herself. In her coat pocket, she carries the rock she picked up at the open house. She rubs the pointed edge, careful to avoid snagging it on the scab that's beginning to form over the small cut on her palm.

She climbs the porch steps and pauses before knocking on the kitchen door. Would the front door be a more respectful choice? She walks across the covered porch, bypassing piles of cardboard boxes that weren't there yesterday. One of the top boxes is labeled "Donate" in large black letters. Tennis rackets stick out at odd angles, as if waving at her to stop. Or to keep going? As she continues forward, Diana peeks back at the kitchen door, still deciding what to do.

She crashes into a stack of boxes and stumbles back. "Ouch!" Boxes spill over the porch. Dozens of books lay scattered. Diana rubs her hip and picks up a hefty volume of Vermont history and *The Brothers Karamazov*. "Klutz," she mutters.

She is returning the last of the books to the boxes when Grace O'Connor drives up, stopping her station wagon near Diana's car. She gets out slowly, her eyes on Diana. Grace opens the back car door, and her dog jumps from the seat.

Diana waves. "Mrs. O'Connor, I'm Diana Morgan. I came to the open house yesterday, and I'd appreciate a chance to talk with you again."

Grace steps onto the porch, the dog at her side. "You really should direct any questions to Ms. Sousa. I have an offer already from a couple from Rutland, looking for space to expand their artisanal cheese business." She seems neither sad nor angry, but resigned.

"I'm not interested in the house. I need to speak with you."

"About what?"

"Tom Morgan."

Grace's eyes narrow. "What's your connection to Tom?"

"He was my husband."

The muscles along Grace's jaw flex slightly. "I heard he died. I'm sorry for your loss."

"Thank you," Diana says, grief rippling through her body, the way it always does when she has to acknowledge his death. "That's why I'm here. I want to talk to you about the time Tom spent on your farm."

"That was long ago. I have no wish to revisit it." The dog nuzzles the backs of Grace's knees. "Now, you'll excuse me. I have much to do."

Diana hasn't let herself consider that Grace might turn her away. "This is important. You'll want to hear me out."

"*I'll* want to hear you out?" Grace wrenches open the door and shoos the dog inside. Her face is red, and her arm shakes as she holds on to the knob. "You don't know me, and all I know about you is that you came to my home yesterday under what appear to be false pretenses. You've returned today, invading my privacy and demanding I talk about a difficult time without any regard for my feelings. You should leave." She follows the dog inside, slamming the door behind her.

Diana sinks onto the steps, holding her head in her hands. Shame coats her skin like an oily film. Grace is right: She never once thought about this other woman's feelings. Not once.

Diana doesn't look at her watch or her phone as she remains on the steps, so she's not certain how much time passes. Fifteen minutes? Thirty? An hour? All she thinks about is how cold she is, how quiet it is here on the farm, how stiff her back is from sitting hunched over, how she should leave this place and head home to her children. But she doesn't move, paralyzed by the idea of departing without answers.

She's counting the apple trees when Grace opens the door.

"You're still here."

Diana stands, her back muscles twitching. "I'm sorry. I shouldn't have come to the open house. Or at least I should have told you yesterday who I was." Duncan's face flashes in her mind, and Diana stiffens her shoulders, trying to mimic her son's stance when he argues with her. "I'm here because I made a promise to my son"—Diana's voice cracks—"and I won't disappoint him."

Frowning, Grace stares at her feet. Diana holds her breath, hoping what she's said is persuasive. The pressure makes her lungs seize and her eyes water, and she fears she'll pass out there on the porch.

Diana exhales only when Grace looks up, meeting her eyes with an unreadable glare. Without a word, the older woman spins around and returns inside, closing the door behind her.

Diana holds on to the porch railing to keep herself from collapsing. Maybe this is as far as she can take this. Maybe she'll have to learn to live without answers.

Yet she's so close.

With each second Diana remains on the porch, her hope that Grace might help her fades. Finally, Diana's shoulders cave in, and she steps down onto the walkway. *I'm sorry,* she thinks, though to whom she sends the apology, she's not sure.

That's when the kitchen door opens again, and Grace emerges holding her coat. Her dog is at her heels. "Would you like to join Scout and me for a walk?" Grace asks, gesturing across her property. "If we're going to do this, I need to be outside."

"A walk would be good," Diana answers, hope rising within her once again.

Grace joins Diana on the path. Despite the chill, she refrains from putting on her coat. She stands with the enviable posture of a ballet dancer, her spine locked, her head held high. A black headband holds her thick gray hair off her face. Her nose is straight and narrow, and tortoiseshell eyeglasses hang from the pocket of her chambray shirt. With the sleeves rolled up, she looks exactly like a small-town farmer, competent and practical, prepared to bale hay, ride a horse, or clean out a dusty attic. So different from yesterday.

It takes Diana a few seconds to notice what else is different about Grace, and when she does, when she sees Grace's arms, she bites the inside of her mouth, the metallic taste of blood mixing with saliva.

The skin on the underside of Grace's forearms is puckered and red. The scarring reappears on her neck, stopping below her chin. Her right ear is smaller than the left, as if part of it has disappeared or, more likely in Grace's case, has been burned away.

Diana read about Grace's injuries in the newspaper, but in person, they are staggering. During the open house, Grace was bundled up in a knit blanket, so Diana hadn't taken in the damage. Now, she can't pull her eyes away.

Grace is showing Diana what was done to her by the fire to make a point, to send a message, and Diana grasps for what to say. "I hope you're better today. Yesterday . . ."

Grace shrugs on her coat as Diana's words die off. "Go," she says to Scout, and the dog takes off to chase an unlucky squirrel.

The two women walk, their steps slow but steady. Neither speaks. While Grace appears content with the silence, Diana is agitated, understanding she's on unstable ground. She has so many questions, such an acute need for Grace to tell her what happened all those years ago, but now, here, in this other woman's sadness, she's not sure how to begin, which question to ask first.

Scout trots back to Grace, panting, the squirrel long gone. Grace bends down to pick up a gnarled stick and tosses it a few feet to the right. Scout races off after it, his tail wagging with excitement.

As Grace stands up, a twinge of pain flickers across her face. Diana recognizes the melancholy this other woman carries. It's in her profile, the downward slant of her mouth, and the way the air around her is laden with pain and regret.

Grace gestures to the broken paddock fence. "This all looked different when Tom was with us. William and some friends built the barn that first summer we were on the farm. He carved our initials into the rafters and promised we'd grow old here together."

In her coat pocket, Diana clenches the rock from Grace's yard, focusing on the sharp point digging into her skin, letting the pain keep her upright.

"Why did you come back?" Grace asks.

"I wanted to ask you about Tom and the time he worked for you and your husband."

"Why? Because of this promise to your son?"

"Tom had a secret," Diana says. "Something terrible he did when he was a teenager. I need to know what it was." She unzips her purse and pulls out a photocopy of the letter. She thought about bringing the original with her to Hamilton but, at the last minute, slid a copy into her purse instead.

"Tom's death . . . It feels like both long ago and only yesterday. He had what people said was a courageous battle with cancer." Diana frowns. "I hate when people equate cancer with war. It's too simplistic, too violent. Though the treatment is its own kind of violence, I guess." She tucks her hair behind her ears and tries to slow down her words. "Plus it sounds as if there could have been a different outcome, that Tom had options, that he could have lived, but his cancer was too advanced. I understand now that he saw his death as a debt he owed. To the universe, maybe to you and your husband."

Diana lets her sentences spill out, one after another, so Grace won't interrupt. She's afraid she'll lose her nerve if she pauses even for a moment.

"I didn't know you existed until two days ago. Which is strange, because Tom and I were together for twenty years. We told each other everything."

Diana looks up from the letter. "Well, I *thought* we told each other everything. From what I've been able to piece together, that time Tom worked for you during high school was important to him. Formative.

You and your husband were special to him, too. So special our son is named Duncan William, after, I believe, your husband."

There's a sharp intake of breath from Grace. "I think this letter has to do with your fire," Diana continues. "With your injuries and your husband's death. The authorities said Carson Roy started the fire, but I have this feeling Tom was involved somehow."

As Grace considers the paper in Diana's outstretched hand, her apprehension, so clearly reflected in her face, morphs into fear, and finally, to curiosity. Scout is at her side again, licking her hand. She pats him and takes the letter.

Grace reaches for her glasses, placing them on her face with a precise sweep of her arm. She is so still when she reads that Diana cannot help but fidget. She shifts her weight from one foot to the other; she squeezes the rock before letting it drop to the bottom of her pocket. She zips and unzips her coat.

When Grace finishes reading, she takes off her glasses and sticks them back into her pocket. "I can't help you," she says, returning the letter to Diana. "I know nothing about this secret or about what Tom says he did."

The hope Diana had clung to disintegrates, desperation filling its place. "No, I'm sure you know something. If you can talk about the time he worked here, about the fire, too, it might be what I need."

"I don't talk about that time." Grace starts walking, and Diana hurries to catch up.

"The only thing that will make sense of all of this is the truth, no matter what it is," Diana says, so fast the words spiral and jump, making her voice thready and unfamiliar. "I was so certain of Tom and of the life we built together . . . Now, I don't know what to believe. I don't know what my life is anymore."

Grace stops abruptly, her back to Diana. She peers up through the brilliant winter light to watch a robin fly overhead. The air vibrates with its song, clear and welcoming.

Diana clutches the letter. "Whatever you can tell me. Any detail. *Please.*"

Chapter Eighteen

Scout moves closer to Grace, placing himself between his owner and Diana, a low growl in his throat. Diana steps back, her hands up.

"It's all right, Scout," Grace says, turning around. Her gaze fixes on Diana. "What do you mean by 'I don't know what my life is anymore'?"

Diana stuffs her hands into her coat pockets, her fingers seeking out that rock, squeezing it tight. "Losing Tom was devastating. Is *still* devastating. Learning he kept things from me? It's as if the ground underneath me isn't there anymore. It's an awful feeling, and I can't live like this."

Grace slowly nods. "That's similar to how I've felt all these years without William. Like I can't hold on to anything. How did I get here, I ask myself. How is *this* my life?"

Diana takes in the view before them: the stark trees, the emptiness, the quiet. William's absence defines this land and, to an extent, Grace. This scares Diana—the way Grace hasn't moved on. This could be her life, too. "I wish . . . I wish for so much I can't have."

There's a pause while Grace's eyes sweep across the yard, landing first on a small thicket of evergreens and then on Scout rolling around on the ground. She again begins to walk, setting a faster pace than before, her boots crushing ice and snow with each step.

"Tom worked for us part-time during the school year and full-time during breaks and the summer," Grace begins. "My sister Irene and I ran an equine therapy camp here during the summers. We offered programs for children and teens with all different kinds of disabilities; some faced physical challenges, a few had developmental delays. Irene was a special needs teacher in Burlington, and the camp was her idea.

"William and I were skeptical at first. Money was scarce, and a lot needed to be done to get the camp up and running. Reinforcing the paddock, buying special saddles, increasing our insurance. I agreed because Irene was coming off a bad divorce and I thought the camp would be a helpful distraction. Plus, it was a good way to get the animals exercised, and it felt like we were giving back."

"How did Tom come to work here?" Diana keeps up with Grace's steady pace, though her hamstrings ache from yesterday's hike with Chris.

"Jimmy McCarthy, the owner of the Hamilton General Store, recommended him. Tom applied for a job there, but Jimmy didn't have any openings. When William stopped by and mentioned we needed an extra set of hands to help around the farm, Jimmy pulled Tom's application off a pile in his office. William had taught Tom in history class and remembered him fondly, so he called him up."

Grace steers Diana away from a steep slope along the tree line. "Jimmy died a few years ago. His kids run the store now. I stop there on Fridays for a turkey sandwich and their fudge. They make the best fudge. Secret family recipe, Jimmy said." Grace's words fade to a whisper. Diana understands what she's feeling: the joy of remembering, and the pain, too.

"What happened when William called Tom?"

"Tom rode his bike over a few days later to talk with us, and William hired him on the spot. He was at that age when he was growing into himself, all gangly limbs and awkwardness. His hair always needed cutting, if my memory is correct."

In Grace's description, Diana sees Duncan.

"Tom's job was to help William. Together they managed the horses, mowed the lawn, insulated the attic, built fences, tended to the apple trees—whatever needed to be done. William would tell me they talked as they worked, about nothing and everything. Tom, as I recall, loved basketball."

Some things don't change, Diana thinks.

Grace stops in front of an iron bench under a large maple tree. She sits, motioning to Diana to join her. Diana shivers as her body makes contact with the cold metal. The house is off to the left, a crest of trees is in the distance to the right, and the mountains are on the far horizon. West, she realizes. The bench faces west to take in the sunset. This spot must have been where Grace and William together ended each day, and she bites down the sadness that surges within her.

Grace continues, "William encouraged Tom's plans after high school; he even wrote him recommendations for college. William saw Tom as an adopted son of a sort. We never had children, and while William said he was at peace with that, a part of him still dreamed for a son. Tom's father was gone. It's almost as if they needed each other.

"Our niece, Jessica, was here that summer. She's the daughter of William's brother. A handful, that one was. She'd been talking back to her parents and hanging out with the wrong sort of kids. Her parents were worried she was getting into drugs, so they asked if she could come here for the summer. They had four younger children at home in Portland and needed help. William and I said yes, of course. We thought the farm would be good for her."

"Was it?" Diana realizes who Jessica is: She's the first person Tom ever slept with, possibly his first love. He never said much about her, certainly not her name, only that his first time had been the summer before college with a girl from Maine. He dismissed Diana when she asked for specifics, back in the early days of their relationship. *This was years ago,* he said. *I barely remember her.*

"At first, Jessica seemed happy. She listened to us, did as we asked. Then we discovered she was sneaking out of her room at night. To go where, we never knew," Grace says. "Did anything happen between Jessica and Tom? William thought yes; I wasn't sure. Tom was easygoing and never gave us any trouble. Jessica? She was angry at the world."

Diana remembers the rage she felt over Tom's letter. How easy it is to be angry, a much more attractive option than being sad.

"When I look back, I realize Jessica was clever, biding time with us until she could go back home. She never gave being here a chance. I suspect, if I'd been a sixteen-year-old girl sent off into exile, I wouldn't have either. At the time, I didn't identify with Jessica's anger. It wasn't until later, after I got out of the hospital and returned here, that I began to see how anger could be all-consuming," Grace says, echoing Diana's thoughts.

"And the fire?" Diana appreciates these details but anticipates there's a limit to how long Grace will talk. Diana is afraid if she doesn't ask directly, Grace will avoid the topic altogether.

Grace begins to walk again. Diana follows, her purse swinging with each step. Grace pauses briefly by the birch trees to pick up bark lying in the snow. As she begins recounting the night of the fire, she shreds the bark into silvery, gray curls that fall at their feet, making Diana think of the breadcrumbs Hansel and Gretel leave behind in the witch's forest to find their way home.

"When the fire started, William and I were sleeping. It was hot, and we'd left our windows open to let the breeze circle through. Something, maybe a noise, woke me up. The moment I opened my eyes, I knew something was wrong. There was too much light, and the air was filled with smoke. At first, I thought I'd left food on the grill, but I remembered scraping it clean, removing the burned ends of the chicken we'd eaten for dinner. I looked over William, through the open window, and I could see the barn was on fire." Grace shudders and her sure steps falter.

"I shook William awake, and he ran to the window. He stood there, clenching the sill for a second or two, before he raced from the room, yelling for me to call the fire department. I could hear his footsteps pounding down the stairs, and a crash followed, the sound of glass breaking. I fumbled for the phone on the bedside table and called for help."

Terrified that William had gone ahead without her, Grace retains no memory of the phone call. "Though I do have a very specific recollection of running after William and finding him in the yard. I stopped at his side and watched the flames consume the barn. It was clear the Hamilton volunteer fire department wouldn't arrive in time to save the building. I didn't understand William had already formulated a plan. An insane, risky plan. That night, though, it was the only option." Grace's voice catches but she continues: "He said that he had to get the horses. Before I could say anything, he turned, pulled open the doors, and plunged inside."

Smoke poured out into the night. The barn sizzled and burst as the beams and siding caught and then exploded. The fire threw off so much heat that, even at a distance, Grace's skin tightened, as if she were at the end of a long day at the beach, a sunburn blistering across her chest.

Suddenly, above the flames, Grace heard a crash, and two horses ran out through the smoke, their gasps frantic and shallow. They galloped across the yard, as far away from the barn as they could get. "I watched them melt into the darkness. I knew I should follow them, to make sure they didn't run back toward the blaze, but I couldn't move. That's when William fell down next to me, coughing. I crouched beside him and cleaned off soot from his face. I was so grateful he was alive."

Grace stops, her hands continuing to strip the bark, her eyes looking back to the broken paddock fence. "Four more horses remained in the barn. William was wheezing so hard it was difficult for him to speak. He managed to explain that he hadn't been able to get to them." Grace shakes her head. "Those poor, poor animals. They were so good. They didn't deserve to die like that.

"I didn't deliberate over what happened next; rather, my body chose for me, instinct taking over. I kissed William and ran into the barn."

All Grace remembers from being inside the blaze is darkness and heat. Fear, too. So much fear.

She saved two of the horses. When Grace tells that part to Diana, she flexes her hands, the skin layered in scars, scorched by the metal locks of their stalls.

"The other horses, a gelding Irene recently brought to the farm and Daisy, my favorite of the mares . . . I couldn't get to them. I can still hear their screams, high-pitched and ear-piercing. The fire was too hot, too fast, and the smoke was everywhere."

When Grace was well enough, her sister filled in what happened next, repeatedly detailing what she knew, so by the time Grace was discharged from the rehabilitation facility, she assumed Irene's stories as her own memories.

William somehow found her lying on the barn floor, unconscious. He carried her out onto the grass, beating the fire from her body with his own hands.

"Then my beautiful, stubborn husband went inside one more time. When the firefighters rescued him, he was a few feet away from Daisy's stall, barely alive. Carson's body wasn't far from William's, but the smoke likely prevented the two of them from seeing one another."

The pain hovering around the older woman intensifies, thickening the air with a grief so endless Diana finds it hard to breathe. Her instincts tell her to comfort Grace, to tell her she's said enough; yet a hungry, reckless voice whispers that doing so would put her own healing at risk. So Diana remains silent, pushing down her rising guilt to listen to the rest of Grace's story.

"The fire ruined our lives," Grace says. "My sister said it was like William and I were a building in the middle of an earthquake. We held together as best as we could, until our broken pieces collapsed onto one another, and only the memory remains. William's death, months after the fire, was when everything fell apart.

"I meant to be with him, but my doctors were concerned that my own healing was behind schedule. They'd convinced me to go to physical therapy. One morning away from William would be fine, they assured me. They were wrong. As I struggled to get my damaged legs to remember how to walk, William's heart gave out. By the time I made it back to his room, he was gone."

Grace finishes talking, and the last splinter of bark lies shredded at her feet. She tips back her head, the sun highlighting the lines on her face and the scars on her neck.

Diana is speechless, which, for the first time, gives her sympathy for all those people who shied away from her after Tom died. Some of them, she guesses, had been scared off; others, she suspects, had no idea what to say that wouldn't sound trite or useless.

"Everyone—the doctors, the nurses, Irene—worried I wouldn't make it, that losing William would be a setback I wouldn't be able to survive," Grace says. "I pushed my grief to the back of my mind, choosing to deal with it later. I never really did, though."

"I'm so sorry, Grace," Diana says, offering words of compassion yet knowing, from her own experience, that they won't quench the pain.

"I couldn't then, and still struggle now, to look too closely at everything that happened. At the fire. At William's death. At this lonely life I've led ever since." Grace's posture loosens as she speaks, transforming her competence and independence into frailty. "Sometimes, not looking too closely is the only way to get through a terrible time. Yet after William's death, I began to remember more about that night. I would smell smoke; it was as if my body was still back in the barn. I'd wake up at night, my clothes soaked, dreaming I was on fire, flames all over my skin."

Grace bites out her words. "I was so angry. I *am* still so angry. This didn't need to be my life. I wanted to be with William, to grow old with him here." She kicks at the bark, scattering the pieces. "I haven't been able to let my anger or pain go. You should."

"Someday, maybe," Diana says, "but I can't do that until I understand the letter."

Grace leads her to the remains of the barn. "I never met Carson Roy. I knew his mother, though. She was the receptionist for the local dentist, and every time I went in for a cleaning, we'd chat about the weather and the latest town gossip. William probably had Carson in class. It wasn't a large high school, and he taught every student at some point. Carson wasn't anyone William mentored or ever talked about. Maybe that's why he stole from us? Maybe William gave him a bad grade? Or did he resent not having William's attention?"

Diana imagines that a map of Grace's telling of this story would be shaped in spirals and swirls, the sentences swooping around one another, obscuring the facts, hiding away the truth, keeping her from understanding.

"The police said Carson started the fire," Diana says. "How did he do it?"

"When he came to steal from us, he dropped a lit cigarette inside the barn. I'm sure he never meant for things to get as out of control as they did." Grace scratches behind Scout's ears. "That summer was the first time we ever worried about a fire. A few times, in the early morning, William thought the back stall smelled like tobacco. Other times, marijuana. He was furious; smoking in a barn like ours was dangerous. It wouldn't take much to cause a fire. He told Jessica and Tom to go somewhere else if they needed to smoke. Jessica denied doing anything wrong. Tom was agreeable enough that William didn't suspect he was the problem."

Diana sees Tom in the tub in their Brookline apartment, smoking his one cigarette to decompress from the stress of work, so careful to dispose of the ashes, never leaving a lit cigarette unattended. He started smoking in high school, he told her. *Oh, Tom,* she thinks, covering her face with her hands.

"Are you all right?"

Diana lifts her head. "If there was a cigarette, why don't the police test it for DNA now? I've read about how people have gotten out of jail when old evidence is examined with modern techniques."

"Why bother? It was an open-and-shut case. Everything pointed to Carson. Even if there was *some* question about that, there was a flood at the police station back in '98 or '99, and all the old evidence was destroyed. The *Hamilton Star* did a big story about it, and I remember how they said all cold cases would have to be closed out because of the water damage. My fire wasn't a cold case, but the flood definitely ended any possibility that new information would be found."

Diana lets her hands drop. "What about Jessica? What happened to her?"

"Jessica's had a challenging life. There was a boyfriend who went to prison for armed robbery. She developed a serious drug problem. She has a little girl. Ava, who must be about eleven. Jessica's parents are raising her. Not sure they planned on parenting in their seventies, but the child needed them. I talk to them every couple of months. They've been good about staying in touch all these years."

With her boot, Grace pushes aside remnants of the barn's foundation. "You know, I never heard from Tom after the fire. He never came by the hospital, never sent a note, never checked in on us. He didn't come to William's funeral either, which was hurtful since they were close, but I always chalked that up to youth and inexperience, not a crime."

Diana thinks of Jonathan and Lily pulling away when Tom was diagnosed, unable or unwilling to be a part of his death. Why would Tom cut Grace out of his life? Grief, perhaps? Or guilt?

"Was there ever any talk of someone else," Diana asks, struggling to get out the words, "other than Carson, being involved in the fire?"

"I've never had any reason to disbelieve the police investigation, Diana. Never thought it was anyone but Carson who caused my husband's death. I don't think Tom's letter has anything to do with what happened to William and me."

Diana reviews all Grace has told her so far, the facts sorting themselves like cards in a deck, stacking against one another and rapidly shuffling past. Grace's story hasn't offered the clarity she hoped for; instead, it's left her with more questions. Was Carson really responsible for the fire? Was it accidental or deliberate? What was Tom's role?

Or maybe she's wrong about all this. Frustration glimmers at the edge of her vision, sending her pulse into an unsteady beat.

"After the fire, Irene tried to get me to rebuild the barn and continue William's plans to cultivate our orchard," Grace says. "She was afraid not doing so meant I'd given up. Letting nature take this space back has been a gift of a kind. I like it untamed and messy, like the way it had been, I suppose, before people came to this valley. Of course, abandoning William's dreams for our trees was painful. I just couldn't do it without him." She points to the apple trees, their wizened branches empty of the plans William once had for them. "Though Irene was right: Sometimes, I did want to give up. Yesterday was like that. I told Ms. Sousa I was ill, but it was more like I was heartsick. My heart broke when William died, and it has never healed back to what it was before."

Diana knows that feeling. "How did you move on?" she asks, hoping Grace has the answer for her.

"I haven't. That's the truth of it. I'm eighty-one years old next month, and every day for the past thirty-four years, I wake up expecting William to be next to me. Then I remember he's gone."

⌐

Before Diana leaves, Grace invites her inside. From a cramped kitchen drawer, the older woman fishes out her worn address book, its pages stained and ripped from years of use, and copies Jessica's address and phone number onto a scrap of paper.

"When was the last time you saw Jessica?" Diana asks.

"Fifteen years ago, maybe," Grace explains. "The last update I received about her was from her parents. They said she lives in Nashua, New Hampshire, and calls every Sunday at 11:00 a.m., after her parents get home from church, to catch up with Ava."

"Thank you, Grace. For talking to me today, for opening up." Diana gives Grace a smile she hopes conveys that, while their meeting wasn't easy, it was more than she'd hoped for.

"I still don't think that letter is about William and me, though I guess it's worth asking Jessica what she remembers from that time." Dropping the address book back in place, Grace closes the drawer with a swift push. "Promise you'll tell me if you uncover anything that's relevant to me. I wrote my address in Florida on that paper, too. I'm moving to a retirement community where my sister lives. It's not my farm, but it will be easier to manage."

"I promise," Diana says, taking Grace's hand, carefully holding the older woman's thin, ruined skin. She expects she'll never see Grace again after today, and she finds herself surprisingly sad about that. She would have liked to have had this woman in her life for much longer—as a connection to Tom, as a reminder of the quicksand of grief, and most of all, as a friend.

Chapter Nineteen

Sitting on a tree trunk, Diana stares at the frozen pond below. A crowd huddles on the shore; teenagers tie their laces, and parents help children wobble on skates across the uneven surface. In the center of the ice, a young girl extends her arms and spins, her laughter rising up through the pine-scented air.

Diana planned to drive straight home from the O'Connor farm, but she didn't anticipate how Grace's story would make her feel, how it would settle under her skin and wedge in between her lungs. After nearly rear-ending a truck a mile back, her mind not focused on the road in front of her, Diana stopped in the parking lot of Hamilton's main ice-skating spot, crowded today with families taking advantage of the overnight chill for an outdoor skate. A short walk into the woods to clear her head brought her here.

Grace's words haunt her: *I was so angry. I am still so angry. This didn't need to be my life.* How easy it would be for Diana to share Grace's path. Her widowhood could define her entire life; Diana could forever be as she is now: hurt, sad, searching for answers.

A list forms: *What Would Have Happened If Tom Had Come Clean? Maybe we wouldn't have met or fallen in love or made a family together. I might not have Duncan or Phoebe.*

She imagines Duncan and Phoebe disappearing from her life, like an eraser skimming the surface of a chalkboard, removing her children with each stroke. The idea of such a loss terrifies her.

"Enough," she says, forcing away the vision.

Diana wants to believe if Tom had shared his secret with her, she would have advocated for him to own up to whatever he did and go to the police.

Yet the terrible truth is, if he'd asked her to keep his story private, never to tell anyone, she would have. She wouldn't have challenged him, just as she'd avoided arguing with him so many times before. She would have agreed the past stays in the past, a phrase he often said to her, and she never would have spoken about this ever again.

Diana shifts on the tree trunk and watches two adults, with a young boy between them, hold hands as they skate along the pond's edge.

She misses her children. This weekend away is the first time she's been separated from them in over two years, and their absence hurts, like thousands of small needles pressing into her skin, setting her nervous system into overdrive.

Diana presses a hand against the roots of a nearby tree to steady herself, and mud encases her fingers, dark and gooey. Wiping it off on the snow only makes it worse, and she manages to spread the mud over both of her hands. Frustrated, she hikes down through the trees.

In a small creek feeding the pond, Diana finds a break in the ice. Balancing on a slippery rock, she sticks her hands in the water and scrubs. Her fingers become numb, and wavy marks appear on the tips as her skin prunes up. Her wedding band and engagement ring refract the light through the water's surface, and she remembers Tom's proposal during an autumn hike up Mount Washington and the confidence she had in him, in their life together.

Without much thought, acting only on instinct, Diana slides off the rings. She clutches them in her right hand, as she wiggles her left hand under the water. She's astonished that her fingers look normal—not naked or different or lost. Normal.

She unhooks the gold chain she wears around her neck, a birthday gift from Tom years ago. She weaves the chain through the rings and clasps the necklace back around her neck. The metal is cold and wet against her skin, sending a shiver down to her toes.

She still has unanswered questions. Everything she's uncovered is circumstantial, facts hanging together without the connecting thread. She needs to make that connection for all this to make sense. And she knows who to turn to next.

When she calls Chris, she can tell by the way he pauses before responding that he's surprised to hear from her. Surprised she's still in Hamilton, too. "I'll explain when I get there," she says.

She stops first at the Hamilton General Store to pick up maple syrup for Andrea and the fudge Grace raved about, along with two bottles of sauvignon blanc and a six-pack of a local IPA. Having decided to tell Chris the sum of what she's learned, she may need alcohol to make the talking easier.

When she arrives, the sky behind Chris's cabin is beginning its descent into night, the blue of the day replaced with shades of vivid coral that seem to throb with joy. As she approaches the house, the screen door scrapes open and slaps against the wood frame. Chris meets her on the edge of the porch.

Diana shifts the general store bag to her hip and points up. "It's magnificent."

"The finest sunsets in the world are in Vermont, so they say."

"Who are 'they'?"

"Rudyard Kipling, though he was talking about sunsets over Lake Champlain. He must have never caught one over the Green Mountains."

A wind chime hanging off the porch rings in the breeze, the metal tubes gently bumping against one another, sending out a plaintive song into the evening. "I was about to make dinner," Chris says. "You hungry?"

Diana nods, her stomach grumbling at the question. She hands Chris the bag and follows him inside.

They keep the conversation light as Chris grills salmon and asparagus, and Diana pours wine and assembles a green salad with slices of crisp cucumbers and ripe avocado. They meet at a table already set for two. New, tapered white candles in brass holders sit next to matching plates and silverware. This is much fancier than Diana expected from Chris; she anticipated pizza or burgers, a greasy take-out box on the counter. As he dishes out the salad, Diana realizes Chris is wearing an ironed button-down, and his face is clean-shaven. She was so caught up in what she learned about Tom she didn't really see Chris until this moment.

"This dinner was for someone else," she says. "A date?"

Chris focuses on cutting his asparagus into small pieces. "It's for you."

"Chris," Diana says. She's not sure what to make of this effort or how he pulled it together so quickly.

"You don't deserve a nice dinner?" A tinge of pink appears on Chris's cheeks. "Why don't you tell me why you're here? You missed me, is that it? Couldn't stay away?"

Diana smiles. How kind he is. Handsome, too. She's always known this, of course, but there's something different about him this visit. She can't quite put her finger on what it is.

Chris clears his throat, and Diana realizes she's been staring at him. She shifts her eyes to her wineglass, trailing her fingers down its stem. "I went to visit Grace O'Connor," she begins. "She told me about Tom, or at least the Tom she knew from thirty-five years ago."

"Why did you need to talk to her? Tom hadn't mentioned her or Mr. O'Connor in years. At least not to me."

Diana removes Tom's letter from her purse hanging off the back of her chair. "You might want to read this and listen to what I've learned."

As Chris reads, Diana downs her wine. He's quiet, but midway through, he inhales sharply, and his eyes flare. When he's finished, his face is grim.

She begins with the time capsule, mentions the money missing from Tom's law practice, and moves back all the way to the fire and the O'Connors. Chris doesn't say anything while she talks, nor does he ask any questions.

When Diana finishes, the food on her plate is cold, while an empty plate sits in front of Chris. His appetite wasn't interrupted by her truth-telling; in fact, he had seconds. "Why aren't you upset?" she asks.

"I knew pieces of this story." He says the words with compassion, but they slice through her. "I suppose if I wanted to look close enough, I could have figured out the rest, but I never did."

"Why didn't you?" Diana asks, though Grace already told her the answer: *Sometimes, not looking too closely is the only way to get through a terrible time.*

"Tom didn't want to talk about it."

"Why didn't you *make* him talk?"

"If Tom had wanted to open up, I would have listened. He knew that."

"Are you sure?"

Chris's eyes narrow. "You don't think he knew I was there for him?"

"We both loved him, and yet he didn't tell either of us. He didn't tell Jonathan. We were all people he trusted, yet he kept this part of himself hidden. He shared his darkest secret in this letter for me to find after he's gone. That doesn't read as trust to me, this from-the-grave mea culpa."

"His mother knew. Mine did, too."

Chris's words slam into her chest, sparking and crackling, as if they're alive. She reminds herself to breathe.

"I'll tell you what I know, if that's what you want." Chris meets Diana's eyes. "Are you sure?"

"Why does everyone keep asking me that?" Diana shouts. "I *want* to know. I *have* to know." She slams her hand against the table, and the plates shift along the smooth wood. The tears are hot against her cheeks, and she's furious for losing her composure, furious all over again that she found the letter in the first place.

"This was a long time ago," he says softly.

"It's not long ago anymore. This letter makes Tom's past my present. Maybe my future, too," she says, hugging her arms around her chest. "Tell me."

Settling back in his chair, Chris runs his hand in his hair, and the ends stand up in front. "Everything was changing that summer," he says. "Tom and I were getting ready to leave for college, and each day felt both too fast and incredibly slow. Work took up most of our time. I washed dishes at the diner in town. Tom was at the O'Connors' farm. We barely saw one another.

"A few days after the fire, Tom and Aunt Martha loaded his stuff into her truck and said they were going to head out early to college. They wanted to take a leisurely drive to North Carolina. He seemed distracted. I thought it was the jitters about leaving home and starting college. I had them, too, although I was only going up to UVM. This was before texting, FaceTime, and even email, remember?"

Diana thinks back to her years at college, when she stayed in touch with friends and family through late-night phone calls, the cord of the telephone curling around her hands as she sat in her cinder-block-lined dorm room.

"Tom and I didn't really connect those first months away. We called but never caught one another. At Christmas, he went on a service project. Aunt Martha was so proud of him that no one was upset that he hadn't come home."

"A service project? Where?" As soon as Diana asks the question, she knows it isn't relevant; those aren't the details that will explain what happened the night of the fire.

"Alabama, maybe? Or Texas? I wasn't really paying attention. Becca and I were together, and we spent most of that break in Burlington. That first Christmas set a pattern. Whenever Tom had time off and could come home, he didn't. More service projects followed. Internships.

Study abroad. He was never here." Chris empties the wine bottle into his glass. "Want me to open another one?"

Diana holds up her hand, impatient. "I've had enough."

"I probably have, too," Chris says, though he drinks anyway. "The Christmas after Aunt Martha died, Tom again said he wasn't coming home for the holidays. This was maybe six or seven years after the fire. I made some smart remark about how he was too good for us. My mom said I was wrong; it was best, she said, if Tom didn't come home at all."

Everyone knew about this except for me, Diana thinks.

"My mom said Tom had been at the O'Connors' the night of the fire. When he came home the next morning, he wouldn't tell Aunt Martha what happened. He did ask her to say, if the police came around, that he'd been home with her. She agreed, though she was frustrated he wouldn't tell her why."

"So he *was* at the farm that night." This is the first piece of information that directly links Tom to the fire. Everything before this moment could have been explained away. But not this.

"The police chief and Aunt Martha were old friends, so he told her about the investigation," Chris says. "He mentioned a cigarette started the fire before it was released to the public. That was when Aunt Martha decided Tom needed some distance from Hamilton. Even though the chief had pinned this on Carson, Aunt Martha didn't want anyone to look closely at Tom. She knew he smoked—she nagged him about it all the time—and she was suspicious. Or frightened. Probably both. She begged my mom not to tell this to anyone, not even my dad. My mom didn't talk about it until after Aunt Martha died."

"If this secret was so important, why did your mom tell you? Why didn't she keep it to herself?" Diana's brain is sluggish and filled with questions.

"My mom said I needed to know, that I couldn't say anything to anyone. Maybe this insight would help me find a way to reconnect with Tom. Strangely enough, it did. I called him up, and it was like no time had passed. This was all before you two met."

"Did you ever ask him about the fire or Carson or the O'Connors?"

Chris shakes his head. "I tried. He always changed the subject. Once, he even told me to shut up and back off. So I did. Our lives were so different. I guess I didn't want to lose what we had."

"What about your mom and Martha? Why did Martha tell your mom? I'm not following all of this."

"You know Aunt Martha had heart failure? She needed a transplant but was too sick to qualify for one. She told my mom all of this before she died, when it was clear she didn't have much time left. My mom and Aunt Martha were best friends since childhood, practically real sisters. My mom was a second mother to Tom, like Aunt Martha was for me. I guess Aunt Martha didn't want Tom to be alone in this and hoped my mom would support him."

Deathbed confessions are a tradition in this family, thinks Diana, though she's glad she has the good sense to keep this comment to herself.

Chris continues, "Aunt Martha didn't tell Tom how bad her illness was. My mom had enough of that and called him up. Tom was in law school. My mom said he had to get his ass to the hospital to be with his mother. She was the one who told him his mother was dying. He was sitting at Aunt Martha's bedside when my mom arrived at the hospital the next morning. Aunt Martha passed away four days later.'

"What about Carson?"

"I haven't thought about Carson Roy in years." Chris tips his chair back onto its rear legs. "We played Little League together. He was a good shortstop. By high school, he was high all the time."

"And Tom was friends with him." Diana is having a hard time concealing her annoyance with the pace by which this story is unfolding and that the answers aren't immediately available. *That's how this secret stayed hidden,* she realizes. *If it was easy to see, I might have noticed something a long time ago.*

"Were they friends?" Chris again rubs his hands through his hair. "Are people friends with their dealers? Maybe?"

"Dealer?"

"Carson was Alcott High's resident drug dealer. Pot. Cocaine. Pills. It's a miracle he never got arrested. I still can't figure out how he managed that."

Diana stares at Chris. Did she mishear him? Did he say "dealer"?

"Tom never talked about high school?" Chris asks.

"He told me he played basketball, that's about it."

"Tom was a big partier. Occasionally I joined him, but getting high and trying every kind of illegal drug out there wasn't my thing. During the school year, his partying was only on the weekends. Since our grades were good and we managed to avoid real trouble, our parents gave us a lot of leeway. Aunt Martha wasn't really on top of him, anyway. Those days, she worked two jobs, trying to save up for his college. More and more during our senior year, it was a mystery where Tom was or what he was up to. It was like whatever he was doing, he knew I wouldn't approve, so he cut me out."

The room starts to whirl, and Diana's vision fogs. Wheezing, she bends down and puts her head between her knees.

Chris is around the table in an instant, crouching by her head. "What's happening?"

"He . . . he didn't tell me any of this," she says, the words coming out in a staccato beat between gasps. "Why didn't he tell me?"

"Let me get you water." Chris runs into the kitchen and returns with a glass filled to the brim. "Can you sit up?"

Diana slowly raises her head and sips the tepid water Chris offers her. The room is still again, but his words echo. *Tom was a big partier. Occasionally I joined him, but getting high and trying every kind of illegal drug out there wasn't my thing.*

"I don't know why he didn't tell you," Chris says. "It doesn't matter, does it?"

Diana is lining up the pieces of this story, one by one. "Tom said coming home to Hamilton was painful, which is why we stayed away. I thought this place held too many bad memories for him." She snorts. "I guess I was right."

"Diana—"

"He didn't tell me about who he'd been in high school because he was afraid it would lead back to the fire." She is making conclusions, but that's what she has to do. Assemble what she's learned and try to sort through all the different versions of Tom—the star basketball player, son, cousin, friend, responsible business owner, possible thief, successful lawyer, beloved husband and father—to discover his core truth.

She continues, "One of the qualities about Tom that I found most endearing was how good he was. He was always calm and in control. Everything he did fit the image he wanted me and everyone else to believe. Tom, the driven lawyer committed to defending against injustice. Golden and good."

"He *was* a good person, Diana."

"Was he like that because it was his true nature? Or because he had to be that way to make amends for a mistake he never owned up to?"

Chris returns to his chair. "Maybe Tom was there with Carson that night, maybe he was at the farm for a completely innocent reason. Or maybe we're wrong, and this isn't even the story Tom meant in his letter."

"The timing lines up, Chris. He did something he was ashamed of—*haunted by*—when he was eighteen. He never visited the O'Connors in the hospital or contacted Grace later to check on her. He left town earlier than planned. He avoided returning home for years afterward. These are signs of someone who—"

"Had something to hide," Chris finishes, frowning.

The rage that threatened to consume Diana in Uncle Brian and Aunt Teresa's guest room, after she'd learned the origins of Duncan's name, flares back up again, bright and searing. "What did he *do*?" Diana stands up from the table, kicking aside the chair. It skitters across the floor, bumping into Chris's sofa. "Not only did Tom leave this secret for me to unravel, but these people he mentions . . ."

The missing photo of Tom and the kids flashes across Diana's vision. She can't get enough air into her lungs. Dizzy, she sinks to the floor, arms wrapped over her head, panting. Chris comes to her side and pulls her into his lap. He holds her gently, murmuring her name.

After several minutes, Diana's breathing settles. She slowly releases her arms and tucks herself against his chest. Chris pushes her hair from her face, and his calloused fingers are rough against her overheated skin. Her stomach tightens in response. Diana looks into Chris's eyes and sees not the sympathy she'd expect from someone who just watched her fall apart, but something completely different. Desire.

She didn't understand until this moment how much she needs a man to look at her the way Chris is looking at her now. Her body sings with her attraction to him. She heard this song yesterday when she first arrived at his home, and it's still there, urging her on. She doesn't care that Chris is Tom's cousin, that he looks so much like her husband, that acting on his desire and her own need is likely a bad idea. She wants him to hold her closer, to touch her. How she craves to be touched.

Letting his sawdust and cotton scent fill her lungs, Diana traces her fingers along his cheekbone and down to his mouth, pausing to rub her thumb against his bottom lip. Chris's hazel eyes are wide and glowing.

She slides her hand to the back of his neck, and his arms tighten around her. Diana's lips are only inches away from his.

"Diana," Chris whispers.

She presses her mouth against his, and he holds still for the briefest of seconds. She nudges his lips with her tongue, and when he responds, Diana forgets everything that happened before this moment. She thinks only of how Chris tastes like wine, how good he feels against her, and how he'd feel inside her. She runs her hands down his chest, unbuttoning his shirt. When her fingers dance across his bare skin, Chris groans and pulls her onto her feet. His lips never leave hers as they maneuver toward his bedroom, shedding their clothes with each step.

Chapter Twenty

Diana curls against Chris's chest. For the first time in weeks—*or years,* she thinks—she's at ease. The strain she always carries is gone, and she relishes the feeling of Chris's hand on her hip, warm and sure. He nuzzles her neck, and she rolls over to face him. She takes in his bare chest and the hollow of his collarbone where, she's recently learned, he very much likes to be kissed.

Chris smiles and pulls the blanket over her shoulders. "You okay?"

Diana weaves her legs through his. "That was good."

"Good?" Chris arches an eyebrow. "That salmon was good. The wine was good. What we did? It was *much* better than good."

Diana laughs. "Okay, it was great."

"Was that"—Chris pauses—"the first time since Tom?"

"It was that obvious?"

"Not at all," he says, winding his fingers through her hair. "I only wondered if you'd been . . . out there yet."

"Out there?" Diana frowns. "I'm a single mom with two kids, a demanding, full-time job, a mortgage, and a husband who haunts me from the grave. I have no time to be 'out there.'"

Chris blinks at the bitterness in her voice. "Your life is complicated." He gestures to the two of them. "This is only difficult if we let it be, and we don't have to."

"Okay, so we won't," Diana says, though she has no idea if that will be possible.

Chris kisses her temple, and his hand moves down her back in long, lazy strokes. She feels sleep beckoning.

"You're welcome to stay the night," Chris whispers. "I'd like you to. Plus it's late, and you have a long drive home."

"Yes," she sighs. "I'd like that." She ignores her practical, responsible side that says each moment in this bed is a mistake, one that will demand time and energy she doesn't have. *This is for me,* she thinks, unable to remember the last time she did something that wasn't for someone else—her colleagues, her extended family, Tom, her children.

Her children.

Diana sits up, Chris rising with her, a question on his face. "I have to call home, and I should get my stuff from the car," she explains. She picks up Chris's shirt from the bedroom floor and pads out into the main room of the cabin, where traces of their meal remain. Her chair is askew; their plates and empty wineglasses are abandoned on the table.

"I'll take care of this," Chris says. He's followed her out of the bedroom, wearing only a pair of boxers, and Diana swallows hard when she sees him in the bright light.

As he stacks their dishes and heads into the kitchen, she slides on her coat and boots, the door banging shut behind her. In the harsh porch light, the cold makes her breath float on the air like golden clouds, and goose bumps dot her bare legs. She runs her fingers along the rough siding of the cabin, trying to center herself.

This evening has not turned out how I expected, Diana thinks, spying Chris through the kitchen window. *How do I explain what happened with Chris? Or what he told me about Tom? Or why my husband kept so much to himself? What will Lakshmi say? Andrea? My parents? What do I tell the kids about what I've learned?*

Her children . . . The pain of missing Phoebe and Duncan still pricks at Diana. She needs to make sure they're safe. Diana pulls out her phone to call home.

When her mother answers, Diana hears voices in the background, indistinct and agitated.

"Diana, your father and I brought the children home so they'd be able to go from here to school tomorrow." The background noise quiets as a door closes. "Where are you?"

"Still in Hamilton." Diana cringes. She should have called her mother earlier. "Chris and I got to talking, and I lost track of time."

"When do you expect to arrive in Alcott? Midnight? That's late to be driving."

"I thought I'd sleep here tonight. I'll get up early. I should arrive home as Duncan and Phoebe leave for school. Can you or Dad stay with them tonight?"

"Of course."

"I'm sorry for the delay, Mom."

"It's no trouble at all, sweetheart. It's the safe choice." Vivian pauses. "Was the visit helpful?"

Helpful? In a world-shattering, my-husband-lied-to-me-and-I-slept-with-his-cousin kind of way, Diana thinks, though she realizes her mother is referring to her grieving process, not Tom's secret. "It's good I came here."

"I'm glad to hear it." Vivian sighs. "I don't want to worry you, but there's something I should tell you."

Fully alert now, the euphoria of lovemaking dissipating, Diana imagines her parents and children arriving at her house to find the front door unlocked, the house ransacked, and all their photographs missing. "What happened?"

"When we got to your house, Duncan asked if he could use the computer before bed. He wanted to watch a video of his last basketball game to prepare for this week's practice. He said something about how the bigger screen of the computer makes it easier to view everyone's footwork. Your dad agreed. About fifteen minutes later, your father left the kitchen to turn off the outside lights and lock up, and when he came back in, Duncan was agitated and crying. I was helping Phoebe wash her hair, so I wasn't there."

Dammit.

Diana knows exactly what happened. She used the laptop she and the kids share to research Tom, always closing out of the browser when she was finished. Except she hadn't cleared her search history. Duncan could see what she looked up: all the Thomas Morgans and their crimes, Tom's college newspaper, criminal statutes in North Carolina and Vermont, and much more. It's one thing to be told she's investigating Tom's past; it's another to stumble upon evidence of that search. How could she have been so careless?

"Can I talk to him?"

"He's with your father in his bedroom. Talk to him tomorrow. I wanted to give you a heads-up, that's all. Let him get some rest."

This is why The General is such an apt nickname for her mother. Vivian prides herself on her ability to address a problem and identify the solution, often before Diana processes what's happening. Duncan is her son, her responsibility. *Hers.*

Tom managed her like that, too, didn't he? He took over the decision-making, shutting her out. He avoided asking her opinion on matters big and small, like which color they should paint the house or which car they should buy to replace Diana's old sedan. When he decided Duncan would play basketball instead of baseball or hockey. When they named Duncan after a person Diana didn't know. When he left her that goddamn letter.

Why hadn't she been mad when Tom made decisions without her? Why hadn't she spoken up? Maybe if she had, things would be different.

"Diana? Are you still there?"

If she makes her mother put Duncan on the phone, it might make this situation worse. "Yes, I must have cut out. Cell service up here is terrible. I'll talk to him tomorrow."

"Drive safely, and we'll see you in the morning."

"Thanks, Mom. I love you."

"Good night, Diana. I love you, too."

After the phone call with her mother, Diana slides back into bed with Chris. They make love again, this time with an intensity that makes Diana already regret having to leave in the morning.

Afterward, she lies in his arms, her head next to his on the pillow. "Now *that* was great," he says, his lips on hers as his fingers trace circles across her thighs.

"Better than great," she murmurs before falling into a dreamless sleep.

Diana wakes before dawn, the alarm on her phone beeping insistently. She tiptoes out of Chris's bedroom. He follows, pulling on his boxers again. "Do you want me to make you coffee or breakfast before you go?"

"No, thanks," Diana says, looking for her clothes. "I'll stop somewhere." She finds her underwear first, in the hallway.

"Can I ask a favor?" Chris says as she hooks on her bra, his eyes lingering on her chest.

Diana's skin warms under his attention, and she reluctantly pulls on her sweater. "Yes," she says, uncertain what she's agreeing to, but they're in a precarious place. Their relationship—Dalliance? Affair? She's not sure what to call it—can be easy or very, very difficult. She already has enough problems in her life; she'd much prefer easy.

"If you have other questions about Tom, come to me. I promise I'll help in any way I can. My mom was upset after your questions, and I'd like to leave her and my dad out of this."

As much as she would love to get Teresa and Brian to talk to her, Diana would ask the same to protect her parents. "Okay," she agrees, yanking on her jeans. "But there is someone else."

"Who? They're all dead," he says, grimacing. "Everyone else you could talk to is gone."

"Remember Jessica?" Diana locates one of her socks under the dining table and another, oddly enough, under the sofa. "The O'Connors' niece? She might have the answers I need. I have her address in New Hampshire."

"You know, I met her."

Diana stills. "What was she like?"

"A few times that summer, she came into the diner with Tom. I wasn't supposed to leave the kitchen, so I'd say hello and go back to work. They'd sit at the counter and get something to eat. I thought she was a casual friend, maybe a summer fling. No one of consequence in his life," says Chris, running his hand through his sleep-tousled hair. "I don't think I ever asked any questions about her."

Would Diana have uncovered all this sooner had she asked Tom different questions? Or been more observant?

She stuffs her feet into her boots and grabs her coat. "Why did you tell me all of this? You didn't have to."

Chris collects her purse from the dining room chair. "For years, I was angry about Tom's distance from our family. I need to let go of that." He hands the purse to Diana and tucks her hair behind her ears. "And that letter? He said hurtful things in it. I can't fathom what it felt like to read it. I want to help."

He kisses her, and his sawdust and cotton scent lingers. She'll smell him on her skin all the way home.

"Thank you," he says with a mischievous grin, "for a *great* night."

Diana's body pulls toward Chris. She wants to drag him down the hall and tumble back into his bed. She should tell him last night can't happen again, but she finds that those words aren't what she wants to say. "I'm happy about being with you"—Chris's hands tighten on her waist—"though I'm not sure what comes next."

"We'll see each other again." Chris smiles. "And who knows?"

"And who knows," she agrees, kissing him goodbye.

⌒

The sun rises in Diana's rearview mirror as she crosses the border into Massachusetts. Swallowing bitter rest-stop coffee she picked up outside

Hamilton, she increases her speed past the posted limit. She is nervous to see Duncan and uncertain what to say about her trip to Hamilton.

A list, naturally, would be helpful. This habit of hers is becoming increasingly useful in sifting through these questions about Tom. Distracting, too. *Not distracting, distancing. It allows me to stay removed, maybe only a fraction of an inch, but that gap is there,* she thinks. *That may not be good for me, but I can't give it up—at least, not yet.*

"What will the list be today, Diana?" In the quiet of the car, she carries on a conversation with herself, not caring what drivers passing her by might think. "All the mistakes I've made? What a mess of a parent I am? Chris?"

What Would I Say to Tom?

Ah, there it is. What would she say if he were sitting in the seat next to her?

It's good to see you.

He's there, in the corner of her eye. The Tom she remembers: vibrant with health, his skin golden, his hair curling around his ears. She wants to touch him, to smell him again.

I miss you so much.

Sleeping with Chris might not have been my smartest decision, but it wasn't a betrayal.

I don't understand why you didn't tell me about this when you were alive.

She considers pulling over into the breakdown lane to let it all out. She can't, though; Duncan and Phoebe are waiting.

I don't understand why you left me this letter to find after you died.

I'm angry with you. So angry.

Duncan's name? It's manipulative. I will never say his name without remembering you lied to me.

How can I love you so much and be so mad at you at the same time? How can you be gone and still hurt me?

She exits the highway then, parking in an empty turnoff for trucks along a dented guardrail. She leans back against the headrest and lets herself cry.

When Diana arrives home, her father meets her at the front door. "Do you have any idea why Duncan's upset? He won't tell us."

"I'll sort it, Dad. Thanks for trying."

Diana shifts past him into the kitchen. Duncan and Phoebe sit at the table, eating scrambled eggs and bacon, Bear Bear on the chair next to Phoebe. Diana notices Phoebe is dressed for school with her hair neatly braided—thirty minutes before she needs to leave. *The General,* she thinks.

Diana kisses Phoebe's forehead, spending an extra few seconds with her lips pressed against her daughter's smooth skin. "Look at you already set for school. I love your outfit." She gestures to Phoebe's yellow dress and green leggings. "You look like a flower."

"Grandma helped me pick it out." Phoebe turns to Vivian. "Can I have more bacon?"

"*May I* have more bacon, and yes, you may," Vivian says from across the room. "Diana, would you like some breakfast?"

"No, thanks." Diana tries to embrace Duncan, but he stands up and moves out of her grasp. "I missed you, Duncan."

"I have to leave." He carries his plate to the counter, handing it to Vivian. "Thanks, Grandma."

"Let's talk after school," Diana says.

"When after school? There's a teacher in-service, so I have a half day. Will you be here when I get home?"

"A half day?" Diana looks at the calendar on her phone. Both kids have half days. Phoebe's aftercare will fill the hours; Duncan is without a plan for the afternoon.

"You forgot."

Of course she forgot, but she'll keep that to herself.

"Why don't we hang out, Duncan?" Francis says as he pours himself a cup of coffee. "I'll pick you up from school. I can help you with your homework, or we can shoot some hoops."

"I have this, Dad," Diana says. As Duncan passes by on his way to the front door, she places a hand on his back. "Let's meet at Sully's for lunch. It's a short walk from school. Afterward, you can finish your homework at the library before we pick up Phoebe."

He frowns, his forehead wrinkled in deliberation.

"We'll catch up. We're overdue, yes?" Diana stares intently at Duncan, hoping to convey her message telepathically: *I'll explain. Be patient.* "Meet you there at noon?"

"Fine." He waves to his grandparents and leaves, coat in hand, without kissing Diana goodbye. It's the first time he hasn't reached out for her in months. The absence of that gesture hurts more than expected. She wraps her arms around Phoebe to steady herself, burying her face in her daughter's hair.

Chapter Twenty-One

Diana has frequented Sully's since she was a child. Located down the street from the library, Sully's was always a greasy dive, famous for its bacon-and-sausage breakfast sandwich, until ten years ago, when Sully retired to Fort Myers to watch the Red Sox spring training, and his daughter Stephanie, Diana's high school classmate, took over. Stephanie added kale salads and fruit smoothies to the menu and upgraded the Sanka-like coffee to fair trade beans from South America. Despite the changes, Sully's remains the go-to spot in town.

When Diana enters the crowded café, she greets Stephanie and compliments her new electric-blue hair, the latest in a string of ever-changing coiffure colors. After placing a lunch order for herself and Duncan and picking up a large coffee, Diana sits at an empty table in the corner. Thanks to Sully's seven-foot-tall, leafy ficus tree on one side and Stephanie's prized Italian espresso machine on the other, the booth has the benefit of being insulated from other customers, a fact Diana realizes is important since she's here to talk to her son.

She's early to meet Duncan, and he's likely taking his time. She could use the extra few minutes to settle herself. Diana didn't accomplish anything at work this morning. The trip to Hamilton and the prospect of having to explain it—or at least part of it—to Duncan distracted her, making concentrating on library matters impossible. Plus, his basketball coach called earlier with upsetting news that she has to discuss with him.

Diana's phone buzzes, and when she checks the screen, she finds a message from Chris. Hi—I wanted to make sure you got home safely. She wonders how long he spent on those ten words.

She reads and rereads Chris's text, remembering his sawdust scent and the feeling of his skin against hers, how comfortable she was with him—never once worrying about the softness of her belly or her stretch marks. Her cheeks flush as she thinks about how easily her body responded to his, how longed for Chris made her feel.

Diana always saw Tom as her great, once-in-a-lifetime love. That she can delight in another man is astonishing. Strange, too. It's as if she's woken up with wings and suddenly can fly. She's not sure she recognizes herself.

Chris texts again. This time he sends a photo of a sunrise peaking over Hamilton. Saw this beauty on my way to work this morning. Made me think of you.

Diana smiles, and a wave of incandescent happiness sweeps over her. She toys with several possible responses, and after too much deliberation, chooses to go with direct: We don't have sunrises like that in Alcott. Drive was fine—no traffic. Thanks for checking in. She hits Send before she overthinks her response and places her phone face down on the table.

She's blowing on her coffee when she hears the beep of another text, and in her haste to see if this new message is from Chris, she knocks over her drink, and a puddle of much-needed caffeine pools across the table.

Oh, this is going to be a problem, Diana thinks, grabbing napkins from the dispenser on the counter. A list presents itself—*What Am I Going to Do About Chris?*—and she's grateful for a way to sort through this particular challenge.

I don't have to do anything. It was just sex. Great sex.
He's my husband's cousin, which makes him my cousin, too.
This is definitely a moral gray area.
I like him.

Liking him doesn't mean I have to have a relationship with him.

I'm not ready for a relationship.

I shouldn't tell anyone about this.

She tosses the sodden napkins into a nearby trash can and returns to the table. She flips over her phone to a pang of disappointment. The new text is from Jonathan, not Chris. Do you have time to talk today? Or tomorrow? I have something I want to discuss with you.

She's still frustrated by Jonathan's response to Tom's letter—*I'd let this all go and move on*—and isn't up to talking to him right now. When she sees Duncan enter Sully's, Diana slides the phone back into her pocket without answering.

As Duncan walks the perimeter of the café, Diana switches to mom mode and takes in her son. What joy it is to see him like this, independent and separate, yet part of her. Part of Tom, too.

She hopes Duncan's anger toward her has worn away during the shortened school day, but it's clear it hasn't when he throws down his backpack and falls onto the bench without speaking. He slumps against the window, tapping on his phone.

Diana assesses her approach. Should she dish back some of the anger he clearly has for her? Play it cool and calm? Cry? She's never thought of manipulation as a tool in her parenting arsenal. Cajoling and persuading, yes, but not manipulation.

She decides to proceed with calm and honesty, the hardest of the options before her. "Grandma told me you were upset last night. She said it had to do with the computer. You want to tell me what happened?"

He stops tapping and makes eye contact for the first time since he walked through the door. "Grandma told you that?"

"Of course she did. She was worried and knew that I needed to know what's going on with you."

Before Duncan replies, Stephanie approaches with their food. "Roast beef panini and strawberry smoothie for you, Duncan. Chef's salad for Diana. Enjoy."

Duncan opens the bag of potato chips that accompanies his sandwich, the plastic wrapping squelching as he pulls apart the sides. He stuffs the chips in his mouth, crunching loudly and staring at Diana.

"You need to know what's going on with me?" Duncan says in between swallows. "What about what's going on with you and Dad's letter? You haven't told me anything. You've been looking into this, Mom. I saw your search history."

Diana senses the pressure of his need for answers; it's a burden that can't be put down, a hunger that can't be sated. She's somewhat managed that need within herself by searching for those answers, but Duncan hasn't had the benefit of doing something to understand Tom's final message. Instead, he's waited for her to offer an explanation, and she has yet to come through for him. Duncan will be disappointed when she tells him that her time in Hamilton left her no closer to the truth, only with more questions.

"I'll explain what's going on after you drop the attitude." Diana rubs berry-flavored Chapstick, from a tube she borrowed from Phoebe's backpack, off the rim of her mug. "Attacking me isn't going to get you information, nor is it going to make either of us feel better."

"Sorry," he says, his cheeks turning red. He balls up the empty chip bag and drops it on the table.

Diana picks up the chips and looks inside. "I can't believe you didn't leave any for me, not even one."

He smirks and picks up his sandwich. "You're too slow."

"Definitely not as fast as you."

She watches him eat. He needs a haircut, and his arms are too long for his shirt. Every day he changes, and she doesn't notice. Too close, too distracted. *That's how Tom managed to never tell me,* she realizes, an electric shock of awareness running through her. *I saw only a slice of him, never his whole self.*

"Mom?"

This is one of those moments Duncan will always remember, and Diana wills herself not to let him down.

She shares only the essential facts, hewing as close as possible to the truth: Tom may have been involved in a fire—the details of which are unclear. Two men died, and a woman was injured. She doesn't talk about the horses, the barn turning to ash, or the impact of William's loss on Grace. She definitely avoids telling him about the person who broke into their house and her now constant worry that she and the kids are unsafe.

Duncan holds it together at first. But William's and Carson's deaths, even with her lack of detail, make his chin quiver and his eyes glass over.

She scoots around the bench, and he crumples against her. His tears drip onto her chest, her hands still his fists. "It's okay, honey. It's okay," she says into his ear. He smells like coconut and sunshine; her mother must have forced sunblock on him that morning.

It was a mistake to come here. The others she shared Tom's story with had been in private when they heard the news. None of them is a child, none of them is Tom's son. She's messed this up.

At that moment, Stephanie peeks around the corner, coffeepot in hand, her blue ponytail bobbing up and down. She sees Duncan in Diana's arms and leaves, only to return seconds later sliding an oversize armchair across the floor. She positions it next to the ficus, hiding them from curious customers. Diana bends her head in a silent thank-you.

A few minutes pass before Duncan sits up, wiping his eyes. "What's next?"

"'What's next?' That's the first thing you say to me? 'What's next?'" No parenting handbook she ever read prepared her for this conversation. "You don't want to disagree with me and tell me I must be wrong about what your father did?"

"Why would you lie to me?"

Someday, Duncan will understand how easy it is to deceive, Diana thinks. *How people use half-truths to protect themselves. Maybe then he'll look back and realize how screwed up it was Tom left that letter.*

"I have to find Jessica, your dad's friend from that time." She doesn't explain how they were involved. Sex and drugs are topics for another day; death is enough for today. "Or I could stop here, and we can put all of this behind us."

"You can't stop, Mom. You need to find this Jessica person."

"It's not going to be easy."

"You tell me the hard stuff is worth it. Don't give up and all that. Well, you can't either," Duncan says. "I bet a private detective could find her. You can have my allowance to hire one, if it's too expensive."

"A private detective? We don't have to do that." Diana pushes his hair off his face. "You keep your allowance. Aren't you saving up for a new Celtics jersey?"

"Maybe Grandma and Grandpa will get it for me for my birthday. It doesn't matter. Figuring this out is way more important."

What a burden her son carries because of Tom. Because of her, too. "I'll find her. Please don't worry about it," she adds, though she knows he'll worry. In that way, he resembles her more than Tom.

He shrugs and sucks on the straw in his smoothie until only ice remains. He picks up his sandwich and is about to take a bite when Diana changes the subject.

"Your coach called me today."

"He did?"

"You're not turning in your homework, and you've been goofing off at practice. He wanted to give me a heads-up. Duncan, if this continues, you're going to lose your cocaptain position, and you could be cut from the team."

Duncan lowers the sandwich to his plate.

"Our deal was that you'd focus on school, right? And I'd take care of the rest?" Diana places her hand over his and squeezes. "I asked him to give you time to improve, and he agreed."

It hadn't taken much to convince the coach to give Duncan another chance. All she had to say was "grief" and "missing his dad," and the coach had done everything possible to end the call. Sometimes, the loss card did work in their favor.

"You have two weeks to get back on track," she continues. "Two weeks, okay?"

"Okay," he croaks. He swipes a lone tear from under his left eye and attacks his sandwich. As she finishes her coffee, she promises herself she'll check in more regularly on his homework.

When only a lime-green pickle remains on Duncan's plate, he lowers his voice and leans over to her. "Mom? We shouldn't tell Phoebe about any of this."

"No, absolutely not."

"Did you tell Grandma and Grandpa?"

"Not yet. I'll share this with them when the time is right."

Will he resent her for telling him all this? Is this too much for him to carry? Like those stories she heard in that support group had been too much for her?

Maybe she'll ask him when this is over, when Duncan is grown, if she should have told him a different story about his father, not the truth.

Chapter Twenty-Two

It's Phoebe who next brings up Tom. That evening, after dinner, she sits on the window bench on their second-floor landing, waiting for Duncan to come out of the shower. Diana is around the corner in her bedroom, changing the linens on her bed. Her mother, with her strict rules for hosting, stripped the bed that morning, but wasn't able to remake it before she left for her Garden Club meeting. Vivian was more put out by her inability to fully complete that task than she was by Diana's delayed arrival home from Vermont.

"You appear to be behind in your laundry, Diana, so I washed all of your sheets," Vivian explained before she departed. "I took care of the towels your father and I used as well. You'll find everything in the dryer. Please be sure to put everything in the linen closet so I can find it next time."

Diana, grateful for her parents' help, responded to her mother's comment with a heartfelt hug and let the criticism wash over her, understanding The General's need for control is her way of managing life's uncertainties.

As Diana tucks the crisp sheet around her bed, the bathroom door opens. "You were in there a long time," Phoebe says to Duncan.

"Timing me?"

"I was waiting for you," Phoebe says. "I wanted to show you this."

Duncan's footsteps thump across the wooden floor. "What's that?"

"Daddy's photo album from when he was a kid. I asked Mama if she'd brought me back a present from Vermont. She gave me this."

"Move over."

Diana picks up a pillow and its case from her bed and creeps across her room to stand behind her partially open door. She spies Duncan's leg through the gap between the door and its frame.

"Is that Dad?" he asks.

"And Chris," Phoebe answers. "They're my age in this photo, don't you think?"

"Maybe."

"It would be better to look at this with Daddy. He could tell us who these people are and what was happening when the photo was taken. I wish he was here."

Diana crushes the pillow against her belly and leans against her bedroom wall. Tom should be sitting with Duncan and Phoebe, telling them about his childhood. He should have shown his children this book years ago. He shouldn't have hidden who he was from the three of them.

Especially not from me.

Duncan and Phoebe are silent for several minutes, as they turn the album's pages, the plastic covering crinkling with each movement.

"Who's that?" Phoebe asks.

"Our grandparents, I think." Duncan disappears from Diana's sight line, and his footsteps start back up again as he moves across the landing to the wall of photos. "See here? In this old wedding photo? These were Dad's parents."

"Did you meet them when you were little? When I was a baby?"

"No," Duncan says, returning to the window seat. "They died a long time ago. Mom didn't even meet them."

Sadness washes over Diana. She misses Tom's parents, Gary and Martha. What a strange kind of loss it is to mourn these people she never had the opportunity to know.

"Look, Duncan, here's Daddy playing basketball." Phoebe leans over to her brother, and Diana can make out the corner of the photo album, the top of Phoebe's head, her daughter's graceful hand pointing at the page. "He looks like you!"

"Or maybe I look like him," he says.

"I wish I remembered him more."

"Me too," Duncan says, wrapping his arm around his sister.

Diana resists joining her children on the window bench. Moments where her children connect like this are becoming less and less frequent as Duncan approaches his teenage years. If talking about Tom is the way they strengthen their bond, she has to let that conversation happen, even if it hurts.

⌁

A few hours later, Diana sits at Lakshmi's kitchen table, fussing with the fruit bowl. She piles the oranges and mangoes into a lopsided pyramid. One of the oranges bounces to the floor, forcing her onto her hands and knees to rescue it before it rolls under Lakshmi's china cabinet. All the while, she talks, updating Lakshmi about everything that's happened.

The more Diana tries to remember that photo the intruder stole, the fuzzier the image becomes. Hoping she saved a snap of it on her phone, after lunch with Duncan, she scrolled through her photo app, going all the way back to the last months of Tom's life. She'd never looked that far back before, and she wasn't surprised to find very few photos from that time. The ones she scrolled by—Mira and Phoebe on the jungle gym across the street, a bowl of cucumbers from her mother's garden, a pie her sister baked—gave no indication Tom was dying at the time they were taken. The last photo of her husband was from their final Cape Cod vacation. He stood at the stove of their rental house, showing Duncan how to cook scrambled eggs, their boy at his side, both of them turned away from the camera.

Diana did find a picture from about six months ago with the missing photo in the background. In it, Phoebe leans against the refrigerator, demonstrating the handstand she learned that day in gym class.

Diana zoomed in for a closer look, her fingers hovering over the screen, and spotted the missing photo in the small gap between her daughter's upturned legs, but the image was too pixelated for her to see it clearly.

As Diana talks, Lakshmi cleans up from dinner, while Ramesh reads to Mira upstairs, his voice a hushed chant in the background. Next door, Diana's kids are already asleep. She tucked them into bed before she left, kissing their cheeks and wondering what they, especially Duncan, might dream about tonight. She worried about leaving them alone but checked all the locks before she came here and positioned herself in front of the window with a clear view of her front door.

"I'm going to Jessica's place this Sunday. My parents are babysitting Noah since both Evan and Andrea have weekend shifts, so they were happy to take Duncan and Phoebe, too. I'm planning to be at Jessica's apartment at 10:45 a.m. Grace said Jessica calls her daughter every Sunday at 11:00 a.m. I figure they must talk for, what? Twenty minutes? Maybe thirty? At 11:30, I'll ring her bell and hopefully get some answers. I know it's a long shot. With a cell phone, Jessica could call her daughter from anywhere. But it's the only lead I have right now." Diana pauses, gently holding a mango, the weight of the fruit heavy in her hands, its green skin smooth to the touch. "Is this a good idea? Or am I crazy to show up unannounced?"

Lakshmi twists her braid around her fingers and tugs, her gaze thoughtful. It's her tic, Diana realizes, the subconscious quirk that shows Lakshmi is nervous or about to make a decision. Chris has one, too: He runs his fingers through his hair, making the ends stand up. How funny it is to discover something new about people you've known for a long time. Diana grins at the observation, thankful that this bit of learning isn't upsetting.

"Why are you smiling?" Lakshmi's forehead wrinkles in confusion.

Diana rolls the mango between her hands. "Nothing important." She keeps her thoughts to herself, just like how she hasn't yet told Lakshmi about the evening she spent with Chris. That development in her already complex life isn't ready to share, not even with her best friend.

"I'm coming with you. You have no idea what you're walking into," Lakshmi says. "This woman has a history of addiction. She could be unstable. You can't predict how she'll react to your questions. Plus, after that intruder . . . you can't be too careful."

Diana is ready to argue, to persuade Lakshmi she can do this on her own, when she realizes the opposite: She doesn't want to go by herself. "Okay."

"I thought it was going to be harder to convince you."

"What can I say?" Diana drops the mango back in the bowl. "I'm open-minded these days."

"Good, because I have another concern." Lakshmi selects an orange and peels its dimpled skin. The rind falls on the table, scenting the air with citrus.

"Makes me think of summer," Diana says, accepting a segment from Lakshmi and popping it into her mouth. The orange is tart and sweet, and she savors the taste, curious how she'll feel about all this when summer arrives. "What's your concern?"

"Have you considered this has been too easy?" Lakshmi shakes her head. "That came out badly. This clearly hasn't been easy for you, or now, for Duncan. What I mean is everyone, except Teresa, has been willing to talk with you. It might have taken some persuasion, but no one threw up an insurmountable roadblock, or even, as much as you can tell, lied to you. Isn't that odd?"

Diana frowns. "This hasn't been easy at all. It's been the opposite: scary and disorienting. I'm really stupid not to have picked up on the fact Tom had a secret."

"No, that's not what I mean at all." Lakshmi takes Diana's hand, her fingers sticky with juice. "Wait—your rings."

Diana extracts her necklace from under her shirt. "It was time."

Lakshmi holds Diana's wedding and engagement rings between her fingers. "You all right?"

"Yes, surprisingly."

"This is a big step. I'm glad you felt ready." Lakshmi gently lets the necklace fall back against Diana's collarbone. "It must be strange. Like letting go of him again."

"It wasn't as hard as I thought it would be," Diana says, thinking again of Chris.

"That's a good sign, Diana." Lakshmi shifts in her seat, flicking her braid over her shoulder. "Which is why I want to make a case for caution and for being practical. It may not be straightforward with Jessica. I want you to be prepared."

"Yeah, all good points. I'll be prepared. Or as prepared as I can be."

"And I'll be there."

"And you'll be there."

Chapter Twenty-Three

Jessica's apartment is on a dead-end street, bookended by a sub shop on one corner and a package store on the other. Triple-decker houses make up the rest of the blighted neighborhood. Each building is in a different stage of neglect, from plywood-covered windows and graffiti-tagged siding to broken fencing and sagging front porches.

Diana spent the drive here trying to figure out what to say to Jessica. *"Hi, I'm the widow of the guy you slept with in 1982, and you may have information about a crime he committed"* doesn't sound appealing. She makes a list to manage her unsettled mind, setting her expectations low: *What Are All the Ways This Could Go Wrong?*

Jessica could slam the door in my face and refuse to talk to me.

Jessica could tell me she doesn't remember Tom.

She could tell me Carson was solely responsible for the fire and for William's death, which means Tom wasn't involved in the fire and I have no idea what his letter is about.

Lakshmi parks across from number twenty-five, in front of a fire hydrant, the only free spot. Grace said Jessica lives in apartment two, which Diana assumes is on the second floor. The windows are dark, curtains pulled tight. Diana was too nervous to eat before they left home, and hunger makes her stomach ache, spasms shooting through her midsection.

"What do you want to do?" Lakshmi asks, looking at her watch. "It's 10:53 a.m."

"Wait thirty minutes or so, until she's had time to call her daughter."

Lakshmi taps her paint-stained fingers on the steering wheel. "How about we check to make sure this is her place? If we have to wait, we should be sure this is where she lives."

"How would we do that?"

"I go up to the house to look at the mailbox."

This suggestion makes Diana's heartbeat speed up. "Maybe we should stay here."

"If that's what you want." Lakshmi's tapping slowly progresses to full-on drumming, the rhythmic beat pulsing out a message. *Go, go, go.*

"Okay, fine," Diana says, unable to stand the tension anymore.

Lakshmi leaps out of the car and steals across the street, weaving between the other parked cars, several of which look as if they've been in their spots for years, their windows crusted with dirt. She steps gingerly up the front stairs and stands in front of the door. A moment later the car door opens, and Lakshmi hands Diana her phone. On the screen is a photo of the mailbox.

Apartment 1: Kuras
Apartment 2: O'Connor/Desjardins
Apartment 3: Sampaio

"Who's Desjardins?" Lakshmi asks.

"A roommate? A boyfriend? I have no idea."

"Now we wait."

"Yes, we wait." Diana rolls down her window. The sky is clear, but the air feels heavy, the barometric pressure dropping at an uncomfortable rate. She estimates she can sit here for one hour before she begs Lakshmi to put the car in Drive and flee. She mulls over the prospect of leaving without talking to Jessica but remembers Duncan's words: *You tell me the hard stuff is worth it. Don't give up and all that. Well, you can't either.* She has to stay, for her children's sake and for Grace's. And for herself.

"One thing's been bothering me," Lakshmi says.

"Only one?"

"Yes, well, this is the biggest one. Why did Tom leave you the letter? In the time capsule, of all places? I can't sort that one out."

"I can't either." Diana has wrestled with this one and been unable to come up with a satisfactory explanation. "I wish—"

She is interrupted by a thud as the door to number twenty-five opens and crashes against the house. Diana crouches in her seat, watching from the corner of her eye. Lakshmi shifts closer. A man stomps down the front steps. His hair is stuffed into an unkempt ponytail, and he wears a sleeveless shirt and jeans. His arms are covered in tattoos. He lights a cigarette and takes a long drag, slowly blowing out the smoke. He spits onto the sidewalk and staggers away from the house, moving as if being vertical is a new concept.

"Is he Sampaio or Kuras?" Lakshmi whispers.

"Or Desjardins? The possible roommate/boyfriend? I hadn't thought about there being someone else."

"I did."

"That's why you came, isn't it?" Diana asks.

"Let's hope Mr. Cigarette stays out of the house."

When the clock on Diana's phone indicates it's 11:20 a.m., she pulls down the car's visor to check her makeup. She's chewed off her lipstick, so she takes a few seconds to reapply, hoping the dark-pink color makes her look less pale and nervous. She drops the lipstick back in her purse, zips it closed, and tucks her hair behind her ears. "It's time. You stay here, Lax. It might intimidate her if there's two of us."

"No way. I'm coming with you."

Diana smiles gratefully and walks with Lakshmi to the house and through the unlocked front door. Diana listens to Lakshmi's sure steps behind her as they climb the stairs.

A crooked silver metal *2* hangs on a door on the second-floor landing. Diana touches the number and knocks, tentative at first and then with force.

There's a slow shuffling as someone comes to the other side of the door. The deadbolt clanks, and the latch turns. The door swings open to reveal a tall, rangy woman wearing a black camisole and underwear, her bleached hair hanging limply around her pinched face.

"Who are you?" The woman squints at Diana and Lakshmi, her eyes darting between the two women. "What do you want?"

She imagined Jessica differently. More solid, less worn.

"Are you Jessica O'Connor?"

"Fuck no, I'm Nikki. You looking for Jess? I haven't seen her in months."

Diana hadn't considered Grace's information could be inaccurate. "She's not here? Where did she go?"

"No idea. She moved out last year. She disappeared one day while I was at work. She left behind a bunch of furniture. Even some clothes." Nikki speaks deliberately, enunciating each word, her tongue clicking against the roof of her mouth. "I tried calling her, like, five times but could never get a hold of her."

"Do you have her forwarding address?" Lakshmi asks.

"No, she left without telling me anything." Scowling, Nikki opens an overflowing drawer in a dresser by the front door and grabs a stack of paper. She thrusts it at Diana. "She got mail here for a while after. You give it to her. I don't want it."

Heavy footsteps clump up the stairs. Lakshmi puts her hand on Diana's arm.

"What's going on?"

Mr. Cigarette appears on the landing, carrying a six-pack of beer and a plastic bag imprinted with the name of the corner sub shop. As he slouches past Diana, she smells his body odor and a strong vinegar scent and reflexively steps back, bumping into Lakshmi.

"These people are looking for Jess," Nikki explains as he joins her inside the apartment. "I told them she's gone and we haven't heard from her."

Mr. Cigarette puts his arm around Nikki, and her face is in his armpit. Diana squeezes Lakshmi's hand to keep from retching. "She was a real partier, wasn't she, babe? You guys into that?" His eyes trail up Diana's body and then Lakshmi's. When he notices Diana watching him, he winks. "Why don't you come on in?"

Lakshmi yanks Diana toward the stairs. "Not our scene, thanks."

Diana glances back when she and Lakshmi reach the front door. Nikki and Mr. Cigarette stand in the apartment doorway. When they notice Diana looking, they slam the door shut, and the crooked *2* swings.

Lakshmi propels Diana across the street and into the car. Of all the outcomes Diana fantasized about, not being able to find Jessica hadn't crossed her mind. It isn't until she and Lakshmi are inside the car, with the doors locked, she realizes she's still holding Jessica's mail.

"What am I going to do with this?" Diana flips through the pile. Most of it is junk, but at the bottom is a cell phone bill.

Lakshmi points to the bill's postmark. "This is from thirteen months ago. Tell me again: Why did you believe she lived here?"

"Grace said she lived in Nashua and called her daughter every Sunday morning. I assumed her information was accurate. That was so stupid of me. Jessica could be anywhere, Lax."

"This isn't—"

Diana rips open the envelope.

"Wait!" Lakshmi says. "It's a crime to open someone else's mail."

"I'm amazed Nikki and Mr. Cigarette never opened it." Diana scans the pages. "I didn't think people got paper copies of their bills anymore. You'd think she'd have signed up for electronic statements."

"Diana!"

"Okay, okay," she says, skimming the pages. "There are a bunch of numbers here with Massachusetts area codes: 617, 781, 413."

"That doesn't mean she's nearby," Lakshmi says. "You have her number, don't you?"

Diana removes the paper with Jessica's phone number from her purse and compares it to the last four digits on the bill. "It's the same.

Strange that Grace had the right phone number but was wrong about where Jessica lives."

"Call her. Or text her."

"And say what? Coming here was hard enough. I thought if she saw me, maybe I could convince her to tell me what she knows. Via text, she could ignore me. Or block me. Like she's clearly doing to Nikki."

"Come on, call her. Give it a try."

"I'm not sure that's a good idea."

Lakshmi waits, her head tilted to the side. She starts humming, a smile growing on her face.

Diana groans. "Celine Dion?"

"It's about not giving up." Lakshmi claps her hands. "Would you like me to sing? My voice isn't as good as Celine's, of course."

"Point made," Diana concedes. "I'll call her. Just don't sing."

As she dials, her stomachache from earlier returns. With the last number, a beep sounds. *This number is not in service.*

"A dead end." Diana hands the phone to Lakshmi and collapses against the seat. All the adrenaline that pumped through her as she climbed the stairs is gone, and she's drained. It's time to go home.

Lakshmi listens to the recording and returns the phone to Diana. "It's not a dead end. It's a bump in the road. You're going to have to figure out another way to get to her. That's all."

"I—"

"You what?"

"Nothing."

"Hmm," Lakshmi says, waiting for what else Diana has to say.

Diana fiddles with the pile of mail. "I thought I knew Tom. I thought he trusted me. That what we had was real."

Lakshmi's seat squeaks as she shifts to face Diana. "Your marriage was real. He did love you."

"Why didn't he tell me about all of this when he was alive?"

"Maybe he couldn't?"

"What do you mean?"

"We keep part of ourselves secret, Diana. All of us do. I think of how desperately I wanted to quit my job. I wanted that for years, but I didn't want to disappoint Ramesh. I convinced myself he'd think less of me if I wasn't a successful lawyer. It took that harassment suit for me to see how stupid that was. He was thrilled when I told him I wanted to try a new career. He'd been worried for some time that I wasn't happy at work. I had no idea he felt that way. Opening up earlier would have been better for both of us." Lakshmi tugs at her braid. "My story isn't the same as Tom's, of course, but the idea we all keep a part of ourselves hidden is true, isn't it? Maybe there are always limits to knowing someone else. Even when we love them."

"That means everyone is keeping secrets." Diana is keeping a secret, too, isn't she? Chris. He called last night, and they talked for an hour after the kids went to bed. While neither of them made any promises, he did ask to see her again. Diana used Duncan and Phoebe as an excuse to put him off, though that will only work for so long.

"Is it a secret?" Lakshmi continues. "Or is it protecting a part of yourself you're not ready to show? I keep coming back to the purpose of the letter. What did he want you to do with it? Did he expect you to track down Grace and Jessica? Or did he only want to warn you about those 'other people'? Though if it was the latter, a direct approach would have been much better."

"I have no idea," Diana sighs.

"Maybe Jessica is the key to all of this."

"Maybe." Diana stuffs Jessica's mail and the paper with Jessica's contact details into her purse and drops it on the car floor.

"I need you to make me a promise," Lakshmi says, as she clips in her seat belt. "Mr. Cigarette and Nikki were . . . concerning. I'm worried about your safety as you take this forward. Promise me you'll be careful."

"I'll be careful."

"You have to tell someone where you are, okay? No looking for Jessica without telling me or your family how to find you."

"I promise."

"And we're going to enable location sharing on our phones so I can always find you."

"I already have that set up with my parents and Andrea, but, yes, we can do that, too." Diana squeezes Lakshmi's forearm. "I'm really grateful for your help."

Lakshmi offers a small smile and restarts the car. As she drives them out of the neighborhood, toward Alcott, Diana keeps her eyes fixed on number twenty-five.

Chapter Twenty-Four

The next day finds Diana back at Sully's for lunch. As she waits for her order, she checks out the announcements pinned to the bulletin board by the front door.

"Do you think they ever found this cat?" A woman to her left, wearing dark sunglasses and a wool coat, her head swaddled in a plaid scarf, points to a "Lost and Found" notice for a missing cat named Belle. "The date on this is a month ago. Maybe she came home?"

"Maybe," Diana says.

"I always wanted a cat. Do you have one?"

"When I was little, my family had a cat named Pearl." Diana smiles. "She liked to eat blueberries and sleep on my pillow."

"And now?"

Diana turns to the woman. She looks familiar, but it's hard to tell with the scarf and sunglasses obscuring her face and hair. It's strange she's so bundled up on this warm day. "No, my husband was allergic to cats."

"Diana, your order's up!" Stephanie calls from the counter.

"Excuse me," the woman says. She slides past Diana on her way out the door, leaving behind the faint smell of cigarettes.

I must have met her at the library, Diana thinks, as she turns back to the "Lost and Found" notice. Printed in large text across the posting, above a photo of a black cat with elongated whiskers, is a plea: WE MUST FIND HER.

Just as I must find Jessica, Diana thinks. *What if I can't?*

This question occupies her as she picks up her sandwich and her second large cappuccino of the day and walks down Main Street, past the post office, the florist, and Alcott Bank. *What Are the Consequences If I Don't Find Jessica?*

She sips her drink, and the ideas come to her, one by one:

If I don't find Jessica, this will be all I have: a story without an ending.

There will be gaps. Always.

I'd never know the full truth.

I'll never understand why Tom left me that letter.

Her phone rings, and Diana stops in front of the library's garden, where the tulip bed is already filled with green stems, a sure sign spring is on its way. She drops her sandwich into her tote and retrieves her phone from her jacket pocket.

Alcott Elementary School. "Dammit," she says, answering the call with a frantic jab at the screen.

"Mrs. Morgan? Hi, it's Rosemary Sekella."

"Is Phoebe okay?" Diana doesn't offer a greeting; calls from Phoebe's teacher in the middle of the school day are never a good sign.

"Phoebe had a little scuffle on the playground during recess. She's physically fine, but she's been upset since and can't settle. Are you available to pick her up?"

"On my way."

As Diana runs to her minivan, she reviews her schedule for the rest of the day. Two meetings, a conference call, an overpacked to-do list. Maybe she can take the call from home, after she figures out what's wrong with Phoebe. Or maybe work will have to wait. It wouldn't be the first time.

In the months after Tom's death, when everyone tried to help her transition to widowhood, Diana was introduced to the niece of a friend of Vivian's whose husband had also died young. She was supposed to offer Diana helpful tips for navigating her new life, but the two had little in common other than their loss. Without children or family nearby, the woman worked eighty-hour weeks and spent her free time doing yoga. "My body is amazing, and I can do the one-handed tree pose," she shared during their one phone call. "But I'm miserable. If only we'd had a baby."

Diana tries to remember that woman when the kids don't listen or fight with one another. Or need to be picked up early from school.

Situations like this make living across from Alcott Elementary School convenient. Diana parks in her own driveway, leaving her cooling cappuccino in the cup holder, and sprints to the school's front door. As she waits to be buzzed in, she texts Camille. **Sick kid. Working from home rest of today.**

Phoebe waits on the bench outside the nurse's office, clutching her backpack and coat and sniffling. "Mama," she says, holding out her arms. Her face is covered by a large bandage and white surgical tape.

"What's going on, Pheebs? Why are you out here?"

"A kindergartner came in throwing up. The nurse said I should stay in the hall."

"Good idea," Diana says, sitting next to her. "I'm going to look at your face, okay?"

Diana pulls off the tape, and Phoebe gasps as her hair sticks to the adhesive. Diana inhales sharply when she sees her daughter's wound, a bloody streak from chin to cheekbone. "Does it hurt?"

"Not really. Only when I smile."

"So no smiling, kid."

Phoebe grins and then winces. Diana adheres the bandage back in place and kisses her nose. "Want to tell me how you got this scratch?"

"Mrs. Morgan, good, I caught you." Rosemary Sekella comes around the corner, stopping in front of the bench. "The office told me you were here, and the children are at music, so I was able to come talk to you."

"What happened?" Diana likes Mrs. Sekella. She taught Duncan, too, and Diana had found her fair and encouraging. Duncan still talks about the lizards she keeps in her classroom.

"During recess, Phoebe and another student bumped into each other, and Phoebe fell face-first on the blacktop." Rosemary scrunches up her face in sympathy. "Phoebe got the brunt of it, I'm afraid. The other child was unharmed."

Diana picks up Phoebe's backpack and takes her hand. "Thanks, Mrs. Sekella. I'm sure she'll be at school tomorrow."

Diana decides an afternoon of recuperation is in order: unlimited cartoons, along with Oreos and orange juice spiked with seltzer, served with Phoebe's favorite pink metal straw. Diana is in the kitchen preparing the snack when the landline rings. She forgot to turn the ringer off when she last checked the messages, and before she can get to the phone, Tom's voice fills the house. *Hello! You've reached the Morgans. We're not—*

"Hello?" Phoebe says, interrupting the recording. "Hello?"

When Diana enters the office, Phoebe is holding the phone, a quizzical look on her face. "Mama, no one's talking."

"Let me have that, honey. You go lie down." Diana places the phone next to her ear. "Hello?"

There's silence on the other end, though it's not the typical delay that comes before a political campaign robocall or telemarketing appeal kicks in. Instead, Diana swears she hears someone breathing. "Who is this?"

She hears a click, and the line disconnects. Diana turns to the answering machine and presses play. The twenty-three messages that follow are all hang-ups, and each is from an unknown caller. For the first time, Diana pays attention to when the calls came in and discovers that each was made on a weekday while she was at work and the kids at school. She dials *69, a trick she remembers from the pre–cell phone days, but it doesn't go through. Whoever is calling has blocked their line.

Are these calls from the people Tom warned her about? Is it the intruder? Diana quickly steps away from the window, as if the caller might be parked in front of her house.

"Mama?" Phoebe yells from the living room. "Can I have my Oreos?"

"Yes, honey. One minute." Diana turns down the phone's ringer and stacks a box of pencils on top of the answering machine, preferring to keep the machine hidden from her children. *There's nothing to do about this now, but be vigilant,* she tells herself, closing the shades in the office and moving into the living room to shut the drapes. After all, these could be wrong numbers.

Diana settles Phoebe on the sofa with her cookies and drink and covers her with a blanket. "Need anything else?"

"Bear Bear. He's in my room."

"Of course, Bear Bear," Diana says, as she checks the lock on the French doors to the backyard. "How could I forget him?" She runs up the stairs and grabs the stuffed animal from Phoebe's bed.

Confused by Bear Bear's heft, Diana turns him upside down. A lump shifts inside. She lifts Bear Bear's shirt. On his belly, a large safety pin closes together a ragged gash. Diana unhooks the pin and peels back the fur. In between the stuffing are dozens of small copper disks. Pennies.

"What the hell?" Diana walks slowly down the stairs, poking her finger inside Bear Bear's belly. When she reaches the living room, she deposits Bear Bear on the coffee table and removes the pennies.

"Phoebe, what are these doing in here?" Diana starts counting, as if the number of pennies will give her an answer.

"Mama, you aren't supposed to see them."

"What do you mean? Why are there pennies inside Bear Bear?"

"They're from Daddy." Phoebe speaks in a rush of words. "Grandma said sometimes when people die, they send us messages. These pennies are Daddy's message to me."

Diana's heart stutters, as she clutches some of the pennies in her hand. Others spill out into her lap. She loses count at thirty-six.

"Daddy always picked up pennies when he saw them on the ground. He put them in his pocket for later. So now I look for pennies. They're everywhere, Mama. Everywhere!" Phoebe smiles, her eyes squinting as she strains her cheek muscles. Her hand flies up to her bandaged cheek. "Ow. I forgot."

Diana tries to hide her twitching mouth. She has no memory of Tom picking up pennies.

"It's why I fell today. At recess." Phoebe looks so tiny, curled up under the blanket, with her long hair spread across the pillow and the bandage obscuring half of her face. "I saw a penny on the blacktop and ran to get it. A fourth grader was running to catch a football, and we crashed into each other. He fell on his butt, and I fell on my face." Phoebe digs her hand into the pocket of her jeans. She holds up a penny. "But I got it."

Don't cry. Do not cry, Diana thinks. "You love Bear Bear. Why would you cut him open like this?"

"He's my most special stuffie in the whole world. That makes him the best place for my pennies."

"How about a piggy bank instead?"

"No, Bear Bear." Phoebe rubs his ear between her fingers. "Can you close him up? I'd like to snuggle with him."

"All right," Diana says, unprepared for how exhausted this conversation has made her.

"You can have some of my pennies, if you want, Mama. I'm sure it would be good with Daddy."

Parenthood is challenging enough, Diana thinks as she busies herself putting the pennies back into Bear Bear. *But handling this on my own? When will it all stop?*

After fixing the safety pin in place, Diana hands Bear Bear to Phoebe. "You keep the pennies, honey," she says, grief coloring each word. "I think that's what Daddy would want."

At bedtime, Diana finds Phoebe in her room, reading to Bear Bear, the bedside table lamp dropping a halo of light around them. Diana stops in the doorway and assesses her daughter. A new emotion surfaced with the discovery of the pennies: guilt. For all she's missed and keeps missing.

"It's time for sleep." Diana enters the room and takes the book from Phoebe, setting it on her bedside table. "First, though, I have something for you."

"A present?"

In Phoebe's hands, Diana places the small blue ceramic dish Tom kept in their bedroom. It was where he emptied his discarded change before bed each day. Diana hadn't touched it since his death. After dinner, though, she dusted it off and dumped it onto her bed to sort the coins. To her astonishment, the dish was filled only with pennies, dozens of them.

"These were your dad's last pennies. You should have them."

Phoebe brings the dish up to her face and closes her eyes. She looks like she's praying, or sending a message. She inhales and her eyelids pop open. "Thank you, Mama," she says, her voice full of awe. Phoebe makes space next to the lamp for the dish and settles back against the pillow. "See? It's a sign!"

"A sign?"

"I wanted a message from Daddy, and these pennies are the message."

Diana wants to run away. Drop everything, leap up and out the door into the night. Run and keep running until all this is over, until moments like this one can't crush her anymore.

"What's the message, honey?" she chokes out instead.

"He loves me. More than anything."

When she's halfway down the stairs, Diana recognizes the familiarity of Phoebe's words. *When you speak of me to Duncan and Phoebe, tell them their father was imperfect, but he loved them, and you, more than anything.*

A coincidence? A higher power? Or are the words common enough? Diana doesn't know what to believe, though she admires and is even a bit envious of Phoebe's faith.

Chapter Twenty-Five

When Diana arrives at work the following morning, Camille waits in her office. Two large Sully's coffee cups sit in the middle of the desk. Diana pauses in the hallway and tries to guess why Camille is here. Is Camille angry she worked from home yesterday? Did she forget a deadline or a meeting? *Anything is possible,* Diana thinks.

"There you are," Camille says, standing up and smiling.

She wouldn't be smiling if I messed up. Or bringing me coffee.

"Did we have a meeting? I'm sorry I forgot, Camille."

"No, no, I wanted to talk with you before we both got busy with our days." She points to the desk. "I got you a cappuccino."

Dropping her bag on her desk, Diana picks up the drink. Still hot. Camille hasn't been waiting long. "Thank you. What can I do for you?"

Instead of responding, Camille closes Diana's office door.

Maybe I did screw up, Diana thinks.

Camille sits back down, and Diana follows suit. She slowly places the cappuccino on the desk. *I shouldn't hold a hot drink if I'm about to hear bad news.*

"I'll get right to it. Are you planning to attend the Spring Fling next week? Paul has a last-minute business trip, so he's out," Camille says. "I'll be solo and could use backup."

The Spring Fling, the library's annual fundraiser, is one area where Diana doesn't get involved, except to approve the vendor contracts and make sure the bills are paid. "Is there an issue with the budget?"

"The budget is under our projections, actually. I'm asking if you're planning to attend. You skipped it last year, which was the right thing to do. How about going this year? It'll be good for you to be out there, talking to people. You may even have fun." Camille finishes with a theatrical swoop of her arms.

Diana grimaces. She hasn't been to a party since before Tom's death. Is she ready to put herself out there?

When she returned to work after Tom's funeral, putting herself out there, even talking to anyone, was too much, and Diana retreated. She barely made eye contact with her coworkers, and she avoided the library's patrons, taking the service stairs to her office instead of walking by the main desk. She ate lunch in her office with the door closed and declined as many meeting invitations as she could.

She would have stayed like that forever had it not been for Camille. After the third time of Diana giving her regrets to the all-staff meeting, Camille came into her office and made it clear the time had come to reengage. "Diana," she said. "Enough hiding."

Diana looked up from the quarter-end financial statements. Camille had an expression Diana hadn't seen since before Tom was diagnosed. She was irritated, and Diana was relieved to be the recipient of an emotion other than pity. She thought of her coworkers, how they donated vacation and sick time to her so she could spend Tom's last days at his side, how they dropped off food while he was in hospice, how they crowded the church at his funeral. She had been hiding from them.

She acquiesced to Camille's demand, but that first all-staff meeting had been brutal. The hugs from the children's library staff, the way Leonard in security patted her shoulder without saying a word, the promises of ongoing prayers from Ruth, the head of janitorial—they all did her in, and as soon as she could, Diana escaped back to her office.

She hadn't heard her door open. She hadn't realized Camille was there, until her strong arms wrapped around her.

"It will get easier," Camille whispered, perhaps anticipating the end of Diana's suffering, a time when grief wasn't her first thought in the morning and her last late at night. "It will."

Eventually Camille was right: It did get easier. Diana stopped collapsing after chats with colleagues, even with Ruth's continued prayers and Leonard's sorrowful shoulder taps. By the first anniversary of Tom's death, minutes could go by when she wouldn't think of him. Sometimes, hours went by before he came to mind. She didn't realize the change at first, only that she felt lighter and that the days passed by more quickly.

But now, because of that letter, she's back to focusing on Tom all the time. The loss of him is a ringing in her ears and a jabbing, sharp pain in her ribs, as if her body is punishing her for having put him aside.

Camille speaks again, bringing Diana back from the past. "I have another motive for having you join me: I want you to run next year's Spring Fling committee."

"You've got to be kidding."

"This fundraiser is one of the last areas where you can build experience, and it's time for you to get involved. Staffing the Spring Fling is the perfect first step." Camille's serious expression and the firm set of her chin indicate she's made her decision, and no one, including Diana, will be able to change her mind. Diana attempts to anyway.

"Camille, the Spring Fling is your baby. Having both of us working on it is duplicative, a waste of resources," Diana says, fully aware of how much Camille hates wasted resources.

"Nice try," Camille says, with laughter in her voice. "You're going to fly this one on your own, so someday you can run the entire library."

"What are you saying?"

"With Malcolm off to college this fall and Paul eligible for retirement next summer, we've been talking about moving back to Atlanta. Our extended family is in Georgia, and I'd like to trade in my boots and parka for Sunday lunch with my sisters. I need to get my affairs in order here at the library. That includes getting you ready to take over as director."

Diana freezes, the shock of Camille's news overwhelming her thoughts.

"You don't need to make any decisions about this today," Camille continues. "I can't give the job to you, of course. You'll have to apply and go through the interviewing process. Having the board on your side would be advantageous, which means you need more face time with them. Say yes to this, Diana."

If Camille had presented this suggestion before—when Tom was still alive—Diana would have immediately declined, Tom's career demands taking priority over hers.

It hits her like a clap of thunder on a spectacularly sunny day: She is different. Losing Tom, being on her own, learning he kept secrets from her—all that has changed her. She wants *more*. She's not sure what that *more* might be, but she lets that idea linger.

"Diana?"

"If my parents can watch the kids, I'll come."

"Excellent. Ask your mom."

"Come on, don't you have better things to do? Like oversee the library? Check on the staff? Do literally anything else?"

"No, actually, I do not."

Diana fishes her phone out of her bag and texts her mother. Library fundraiser next Friday night. Any chance kids can stay with you and Dad?

"Done," she says, holding out her phone to Camille.

"Good, *now* I can go run the library," Camille says, turning to leave.

Diana's phone buzzes. Yes, of course. We'll make it a sleepover.

Camille stops, her hand on the doorframe. "And?"

"She said yes, so I will be your wingman. Or is it wingwoman? Whatever it is, I'll be there," Diana says, though she fears attending the Spring Fling will be a mistake.

Camille gives her a thumbs-up and disappears out the door, the sound of her silver bracelets ringing behind her.

Once she's alone, Diana removes the lid from her coffee and licks the cappuccino's foam. She hadn't anticipated this conversation with

Camille, but it's intriguing. She'll have to give the idea of being library director more thought.

As for the Spring Fling, the last time Diana attended was two years ago, with Tom. She remembers him asking why the event was scheduled for outside in April, when the probability of a winter chill or a blizzard was a reality. "Wouldn't a hotel be smarter?" he said, as he knotted his tie in front of the bedroom mirror.

Diana was in the bathroom applying her makeup, trying for the third time to give herself a smoky eye that didn't look like she'd been punched in the face. "I've asked about moving it to June, even September. When I do, I'm told that it wouldn't be the Spring Fling and what people want is the *Spring Fling*."

They hadn't yet known he was sick; that would come the following month, like a torpedo stealthily making its way through the cold, dark ocean to its target.

The rest of the night comes to her in bursts of memory: Tom spinning her across the dance floor; kissing him against the leafless maple tree across from Alcott Pond on their walk home; the tree branch that left a large purple bruise on her lower back; and Tom's fingers holding her chin as he whispered, "I want you." His voice was urgent and demanding, and they ran home, her feet slipping in her high heels, their hands clasped together. They left their clothes in a pile by the front door, and after, they fell asleep on the floor of the living room, a scratchy blanket from the back of the sofa thrown hastily over them, Tom's arm under her shoulder, the other across her waist.

Five months later, he was dead.

Diana stands up and walks across the room to the windows. She presses her fingers against the glass, watching people stroll along the sidewalk below. She needs to look at something else, something real. She focuses on a budding forsythia bush in front of the post office until the memories of that night fade.

Chapter Twenty-Six

Duncan lopes down the stairs clad in a Red Sox sweatshirt and jeans. "I'm ready," he says to Diana and her father as he stuffs his feet into his sneakers, laces untied.

"We're going to pick up Evan and Noah and head into Fenway," Francis says. "We should make it in time for the first pitch."

Diana couldn't have dreamed there was more her already hands-on father could do for her kids, but once Francis heard about the call from Duncan's basketball coach, he managed to find new ways to be involved. Over the past week, he helped Duncan with his history project on the electoral college, taught him how to fix the dishwasher, and planned this night out at the Red Sox game. It's been good for both of them.

As they drive away, Diana remains on the threshold, scanning the street for strangers and inhaling the lush scent of early spring. Around her, the neighborhood settles into evening. She hears Lakshmi and Ramesh talking through an open window, neighborhood kids yelling to one another on the playground across the street, and a dog barking off in the distance.

She remembers the time she chaperoned Duncan's fourth-grade field trip to the Museum of Science. At the reptile exhibit, they learned how snakes shed their skins, leaving the old one behind, slithering off into the sun as a new version of themselves. Diana recognizes a change is up ahead: her own new skin. Ever since she returned from Vermont, she's felt different, as if looking into Tom's past has shifted the direction of her future. This excites her, this unexplored possibility. It scares her, too.

When she hears Phoebe call her name, Diana reluctantly closes the door and returns to the kitchen, where preparations for a girls-only Family Dinner are underway. Her daughter balances on a stool, watching Vivian make pesto. Phoebe's cheek is healing nicely, the angry red scrape fading each day.

Diana pours apple juice and uncorks a bottle of chenin blanc, looking up when she hears the front door open. "A stealthy arrival. I didn't hear your car."

"I rode my bike. Needed the exercise," Andrea says. "How can I help?"

"Set the table, please," The General answers for Diana. "We'll be ready to eat soon."

"She really does like to tell us what to do," Andrea mutters to Diana. "I'll get right on it, Mom," she says to Vivian, pulling the silverware from the drawer.

~

After dinner, as Vivian contends with Phoebe's bedtime routine, Diana kneels in front of the fireplace, adding newspaper, kindling, and a large log to the hearth. This is the last of the fires she'll make until autumn arrives, and she wants the blaze to last.

The fireplace was what sold them on the house. "We'll sit in front of it with our kids," Tom said. Duncan wasn't conceived yet, but the idea of him was on their minds. "Movie nights, Christmases, birthdays. All here."

"I've never built a fire," Diana said. She saw the rest of her life taking shape in that house, and she was left breathless, like she was free-falling off a cliff.

"I'll do it," Tom said. "I'll take care of it, of us." And he had, for as long as he could.

After his diagnosis, he taught her how to use the snowblower, light the boiler, and check for ice dams—chores for which he had been responsible. One of the last duties he passed on was the fireplace, and together, one early-summer evening, they built a fire. Diana learned to open the flue, check for squirrels stuck in the chimney, and clean out the grate. Tom was patient throughout the lesson. She cried the whole time, barely listening, imagining herself throwing the poker through the window in frustration.

As the wood catches fire, Diana closes the mesh safety screen and moves to the sofa. Andrea leans against her, and Diana inhales the scent of her sister's lemongrass shampoo. Andrea takes her left hand and rubs the empty spot on Diana's ring finger. "This still okay?" she whispers. Diana's mother and sister immediately noticed the missing rings, each looking at her with the same worried forehead crinkle, each checking in several times since she returned from Vermont to make sure she didn't regret the decision.

"Yes, Andie, it is." Diana slides her arm around her sister, and the only sound in the room is the ticking of the clock on the mantel.

Vivian enters the living room a few minutes later. "I don't know how Phoebe did it, but she convinced me to read three books, despite my firm declaration I had a limit of two." She lowers onto the leather chair next to the fireplace. "Diana, how was your visit with Tom's family? You haven't talked much about it."

"Chris and I went snowshoeing," Diana says, electing not to tell her mother and sister what else she and Chris did. "It was good to spend time with Teresa and Brian, and Teresa passed on Tom's childhood photo album."

She fantasizes what it would be like to tell her mother and sister about the letter. She sees herself stand up, walk into the office, open the bottom desk drawer, and pull out the fireproof box, where she placed the letter after Duncan's discovery and the intruder's unwelcome visit. Diana imagines unlocking the box with the gold key hidden in the jar of paper clips on top of the desk, removing Tom's letter, and handing it to her mother.

"Diana?" her mother asks. "Are you okay?"

Diana decides to plunge ahead although the outcome is uncertain. "Remember that letter Phoebe mentioned a few weeks ago at Family Dinner? The one Tom wrote me before he died? It wasn't a love letter, and it's the real reason I went to Vermont."

Andrea sits up, her feet hitting the floor. "That was weeks ago," she says. "You've kept this from us all this time? What does it say?"

"It's complicated." Diana returns to the fireplace to select another log from the brass bin under the window.

"Loss *is* complicated, sweetheart," Vivian says. "When my mother died, I found the immediate months after were focused on planning the funeral, cleaning out her house, and dealing with paperwork. It took some time for me to be able to articulate what it meant for me to no longer have her in my life. Maybe that's where you are? And why you didn't mention this letter sooner?"

"That's some of it." Diana recognizes the relief in her mother's eyes: problem identified and solution offered.

"What about the letter?" Andrea asks. "What does it say?"

"You don't have to tell us, if you don't want to," Vivian says. "If it's difficult for you, I mean."

"You already know about it," Diana says, heading toward the office. "You might as well read it."

~

After Vivian skims the letter, she hands it to Andrea, who, in her eagerness, nearly snatches it from her mother's hands. Andrea finishes the letter in record time, and her reaction includes several exclamations of "you're making this up" and "this is bullshit."

Before their questions begin, Diana tells them the rest of the story: the time capsule, her late-night internet searches, Lakshmi's help, her meeting with Jonathan and the missing money, her fact-finding trip to the *Hamilton Star*, the visit to the O'Connor farm, the additional pieces of the story Chris knew all along, and her journey to Nashua to look for Jessica.

Vivian scoots to the edge of her chair and points to the letter. "Diana, I'm most concerned about these people he mentions. Have you noticed anything strange? Maybe you should go to the police."

The car driving by late at night. The intruder. The missing key and photo. The phone calls. Those incidents will only alarm her mother and Andrea, and calling the police will make this whole situation more complicated. "We're good, Mom. You don't need to worry."

Vivian nods and shifts back in her chair.

"You told Lakshmi about this before you told us? And Jonathan?" Andrea asks. "Lakshmi, I understand, but not Jonathan. I'm kind of pissed about that."

"I thought I should get a legal opinion, that's all."

"He and Lily ghosted you after Tom died. He doesn't have your back."

"Tom trusted him. I can trust him, too."

"Is he going to tell Lily about this?"

Diana considers her sister's question. "He promised to keep this confidential. I assume he won't tell Lily, but I didn't ask that specifically."

"I never liked her," Andrea says, her voice bitter. "She's shallow and materialistic."

"Andrea," Vivian interrupts, "this isn't the time to discuss Lily Hobart."

"Fine." Andrea reads the letter again, her fingers bending the page, making Diana twitch. "But Tom was on a lot of pain meds in those last days. Maybe it's not true. Maybe it was a hallucination."

If she hadn't met Grace or talked to Chris, Diana might have agreed with Andrea, but she's learned too much to discount Tom's message.

Andrea continues, "On the other hand, chalking this up to pain meds is a kind response. It could be Tom was an asshole. Leaving you this letter to find like that? It's a sucker punch. Cruel, even."

"Andrea!" Vivian says.

"He wasn't a cruel person," Diana says, pained she has to defend Tom. "You know that."

"Do I?" Andrea waves the letter in the air, pointing to the longest paragraph. "What's all this crap about this being your fault? It's ridiculous."

The passage in question has kept Diana awake nearly every night since she found the letter. The words are among the worst: *If we had been different people, or maybe if our relationship had been different, I might have told you all this sooner. I tried, but I wasn't sure how you'd react. Would you have been disappointed in me? Or angry? How could you trust me for lying to you for our entire relationship? For so long, I blamed you for my inability to come clean. I saw you as the obstacle to being truthful when it clearly was me. I'm sorry for so much.*

"Why the cloak and dagger?" Andrea says, dropping the letter onto the coffee table. "Why is he so evasive? He's telling you something bad happened, but not what the something bad is. That's designed to dig its hook into you and keep you in place."

"I'm sure he had his reasons," Diana says, though it's difficult to understand what those reasons might be. She stalks around the room, avoiding eye contact with her mother and sister and replaying Andrea's words: *Leaving you this letter to find like that? It's a sucker punch. Cruel, even.* Diana feels raw, as if the bandage she carefully placed over the wound left by Tom's death has been ripped off without her permission. She stops at the French doors leading to the deck. The darkness outside and light inside make it impossible for her to see anything other than her own reflection, rippled and dim.

"You're a lot like him, acting secretive, hiding this from us," Andrea says.

Diana wipes tears from her face. How is it that they still come? It's impossible she can still produce them, that her body isn't worn out from all the crying.

"Andie, so much of my life these past few years has been controlled by others," she says, still looking at her reflection. "By doctors, nurses, Tom, the kids. By you, Mom, and Dad. There was a time, after Tom died, when I needed you to take care of me, to get me out of bed and make me shower, to get me to work on time and remind me how to function in the world." She chokes out the words. "That's not who I am anymore. This is *my* story, *my life*. It's not yours to live."

Andrea comes to Diana's side and tries to embrace her, but Diana holds up a hand as if to stop her sister. "Don't touch me," she says, her voice brimming with hurt.

Her rejection flickers across Andrea's face. "You're right. We have been doing all of that these past few years," her sister says, "living your life, taking care of you and your family. You've been everyone's priority."

"That's not true," Vivian says.

"It is. It's *always* Diana first."

"Andrea, your father and I love you both equally," Vivian says. "We support you both, we care for you both. Where is this coming from?"

"Diana sucks all your time. Your decisions revolve around her."

"Your sister has been through a terrible loss—"

"It's been eighteen months, Mom. I thought it was getting better, that maybe Diana's emotional well-being wouldn't continue to be the engine that fuels this family."

Diana turns around. "You can't talk to Mom like this. Or me."

"I'm done with my life being determined by your grief, Diana," Andrea whispers. "I know what I'm saying is harsh, and I'm sorry for that." Andrea reaches for her again, but Diana steps back. Her sister's voice rises in response. "You need to get rid of the delusion Tom was such a perfect guy. For God's sake, he says in that letter that you're the reason he never spoke about what he did. *That's cruel.* Leaving you a message like that—which is consuming your life—is such a Tom move."

"Such a Tom move?"

"Diana, can't you see? Everything was about him. You catered to him. His needs, his wants, his preferences. And this family went along. No one else's opinion mattered."

"I have no idea what you're talking about."

Andrea returns to the coffee table for her wine, finishing off her glass as Diana and Vivian watch. "It was all the small things: what we ate for Family Dinner, what we talked about at dinner, which game we played after. Always Monopoly. Do you know Evan hates Monopoly? With a passion. Me too, yet anytime we suggested a different activity, Tom shot us down."

"You're mad about Monopoly?" Diana asks. She looks at her mother for help, but Vivian is staring at Andrea.

"Since the night you met Tom," Andrea says, taking a deep breath, "every decision you've made has been for him. Not for yourself, not for anyone else in this family. Your career was second to Tom's. Your dreams didn't matter."

Andrea mops her face on the sleeve of her sweatshirt, a sign she is deeply upset. She only cries when she gets mad, as if her emotional temperature has bubbled over like a pot on the stove, unable to be contained.

"I didn't want him to die, Diana. For you and the kids, I wanted a miracle. When he didn't make it, I thought maybe you'd find your way again on your own. That things would be better. Then you discover a letter from him that sets you on a wild-goose chase. And you hide it from us! You're consumed with finding out who he was and what he did. The truth is right in front of you: He was selfish and self-absorbed, and even after his death, he's still dictating your life and your choices."

Diana wants to scream at Andrea, to tell her to shut up, to slap her, to make her stop talking. Except . . . is her sister right? Did she only ever make decisions that benefited Tom? Did she lose her way? Not all of what Andrea said is true, but enough of it is that Diana can't move, her feet glued to the floor. She flattens her hand against the door, and the glass is cool against her palm. "This attack of yours isn't helpful, Andie. I shouldn't have told you anything about this."

"It's time to put Tom behind you," Andrea says. "To live your life for yourself."

"Enough," Vivian says. "Andrea, back to the sofa. Diana, come here. Please."

Diana joins her mother in front of the fire, sitting at her feet.

"The letter is yours, Diana. The decisions related to it are also yours." Vivian holds up a hand when Andrea attempts to interject. "Let it go, Andrea."

Andrea folds her arms across her chest but remains silent.

"I have no idea what it's like to lose a spouse," Vivian continues, "though I do know what it's like to disappoint the person you love the most, to forever change the way he perceives you."

"What are you talking about?"

"Maybe my experience will help you." Vivian sighs, and as the air flows out of her body, she deflates, like a balloon days after a child's birthday, the joy of the celebration gone forever. "I don't drink alcohol because I've told you that I'm allergic—"

"You're not allergic?" Diana interrupts, confused.

"That's what I told you. But it's not true."

Chapter Twenty-Seven

Perhaps this is the change that's up ahead. Perhaps whatever her mother has to say will offer the answers Diana seeks. Andrea seems to sense it, too. Her sister unfolds herself from the sofa and joins Diana on the floor, her bottom lip caught between her teeth and a puzzled expression on her face.

"Andrea, you talk about how wearying it is to parent. You complain, a bit more than I would like, about motherhood. It's not, though, that I can't empathize.

"When you two were small, your father worked all the time, trying to make his real estate business a success. I'd quit my teaching job to stay home with you. We'd recently moved to Alcott, and I didn't have many friends. Today, you'd say I was depressed. Back then, though, depression wasn't something people talked about.

"I started to drink. A glass of wine after dinner. Two glasses. It wasn't long before it escalated, and I was drinking at lunch, at breakfast. I'd pull out the wine as soon as your father got in the car to leave for work. I didn't even wait for him to drive away," Vivian says dully.

"Mom, I don't—"

"You were a toddler, Diana. Andrea was a baby. It would have remained my secret, had it not gotten worse."

"Worse?" Andrea says, her voice cracking.

"One night, it was about an hour before dinner, after I had finished off an entire bottle of wine." Vivian shudders. "I realized we were out of milk. *My babies need milk,* I thought. Your father was at a meeting, and I didn't expect him until late. I bundled you both up in your coats—it was winter, a bitterly cold night—and put you in your car seats."

Diana has never seen her mother so vulnerable before. She depends upon Vivian's strength and competence. That her mother is a flawed human being isn't a reality she wants to face.

"We were only going down to the grocery. A two-mile drive at best, but the roads were slick with ice, and I started out too fast . . ." Vivian's voice trails off. She clears her throat and finishes, "I backed out of the driveway and rammed into a tree."

"Oh, Mom," Andrea says.

"It was a terrible scene. The fender was mangled, and the crash made such a noise. The tree was in the front yard of the house across the street from us. The Thompsons lived there then; they came running out into the cold. The wife wanted to call the police, but the husband must have smelled the alcohol on me and convinced her not to. He somehow moved my car back into our driveway. He never said a word to me. I was so ashamed.

"After I got you both inside and into bed, I dumped all the alcohol down the drain. Your father came home while I was pouring out an expensive bottle of port, a gift from a client. He wasn't happy about that. He was even less happy when I explained what happened. How I had been drinking too much. How I had tried to drive while drunk. How I could have hurt the two of you."

"What did he say?" Diana whispers, taking her mother's hands in her own. Her heart is beating too fast, and she hates that she unintentionally drew her mother into a conversation that caused her to reveal her own secret.

"He had no idea I was miserable. He was blinded by his work and the pressure of supporting our family. I should have told him earlier; he should have paid attention." Vivian smiles sadly at her daughters. "I vowed never to drink again, and we agreed I would go back to work. I started substitute teaching that spring and had a full-time position for the new school year. I've never had a drop of alcohol since that night."

"Mom, I had no idea." Diana looks directly at Andrea for the first time since her sister's hurtful attack. "We had no idea."

"Every day of my life, I see that tree—it's misshapen and never grew right after I hit it—and I am reminded you two could have died. We were lucky. I made a mistake. I hid what was going on from the person I loved the most, which was another mistake. Your father, fortunately, forgave me. It took a long time, but one day, I forgave myself, too."

Vivian lets go of Diana's hands and gestures to the letter. "People make mistakes. When we love them, we forgive them, even if they take a very long time to tell us what they did."

Diana thinks of Lakshmi's theory that there are limits to knowing another person. Of Grace and how many years she's suffered without William, reliving the loss of him every day. And of Duncan: lying on the floor of her bedroom, Tom's letter in his hand.

"Mom, should I keep trying to figure out the rest of the story?" What a relief it would be for her mother to tell her what to do. That is one of the hardest parts about being a widow: all the solitary choices, not sharing the responsibility of making decisions with someone else.

"That's your call. Not mine. Not Andrea's. Whatever you do, I'll support you. But," Vivian says, unable to entirely refrain from offering an opinion, "when I read this letter, I see a man trying to make amends, albeit in a clumsy way, but still, trying."

The intimacy of their conversation is disrupted by the beep of Andrea's phone. "It's Evan. They're almost home. I should go." She nods at Diana and kisses Vivian's cheek. "See you tomorrow at Noah's soccer game, Mom." Then she leaves, escaping the emotions bouncing around the room. The door clicks shut behind her, and the house is quiet again, save for the pop of the fire as a log breaks from the heat.

That did not go well, Diana thinks. Andrea didn't even comment on their mother's revelations or ask how Diana feels about the letter, whether finding it reignited her grief, or whether she's hurt to find out Tom kept secrets.

Vivian checks her watch. "We have some time before your dad and Duncan get back. Let's have a cup of tea."

Diana follows her mother into the kitchen, where Vivian takes the kettle from the stove to fill it with water.

"Thank you for telling us your story, Mom. It's so not how I see you, but I guess that was your point."

"A rather obvious 'nail on the head.'"

"Will you tell Dad about Tom's letter?"

Vivian turns on the burner, centering the kettle over the flame. "This is too important to keep from him. That's not how our marriage works."

Diana doesn't respond to the subtle dig at her relationship with Tom; instead, she busies herself gathering mugs and spoons for their tea.

"I'm sorry. That came out wrong," Vivian says. "I didn't mean it as a criticism about you and Tom. Having open communication is a priority for your father and me, and I have to honor that. You didn't ask me to keep this to myself, and I hope you won't ask me to do so now."

Diana imagines her parents sitting together at their kitchen table after the accident, opening up about her mother's secret. They were tested, and they chose honesty as their marital currency. She and Tom didn't ever discuss their relationship to honesty; she assumed they'd tell the truth. Clearly they each interpreted telling the truth differently.

"Will Dad be upset I didn't tell him myself?"

"He'll understand this is difficult for you. He'll be glad to know what's going on, and he'll be sad Tom didn't feel safe enough to tell any of us what happened."

"Didn't feel safe?" Diana says, putting rooibos tea bags in the mugs. "That's an interesting kimterpretation."

"There must have been a good reason why he didn't tell you earlier."

"A reason I'll never discover."

"I wish you didn't find that letter and that this whole mess would go away. You have enough on your plate with the kids and work."

"Are *you* telling me to forget about all of this?"

"No, not at all. It's only . . ." Vivian sighs. "Have you thought through the consequences of keeping at this?"

"I can't stop looking for answers because it might be uncomfortable. The kids and I bear the biggest burden from all of this, and I'll make sure we're okay." Diana hopes she sounds confident.

"What about your sister? Clearly, she is hurting and is in pain."

"That's my responsibility? She said awful things about Tom, and about you, Dad, and me. It was too much."

I'm done with my life being determined by your grief, Andrea said. Diana wishes she could forget her sister's insults, but they are as clear to her as the lines from Tom's letter. *You need to get rid of the delusion Tom was such a perfect guy.*

"I predict you'll hear from Andrea in the morning. She'll regret what she said and need support."

Diana could make a case for needing support as well, but if Andrea is right and her needs have driven their family for the past two years, this is not the time for that comment. "Do you agree with her?"

"I don't agree with how she came after you. That was wrong of her." Vivian picks up the whistling kettle from the stove and pours the boiling water into the mugs as Diana takes the honey from the cupboard. "Tom was complicated, sweetheart."

"Complicated?" Somehow that description hurts as badly as Andrea's comments.

"My calling him complicated isn't distressing, is it? You two loved one another, a fact I don't have any doubt about. But he did demand a lot of you, didn't he? He was so focused on what he wanted. He worked all the time. I worried about that. Your sister saw Tom differently than you or I did, and the letter set her off. She's concerned about you and the kids."

"She has an unusual way of showing her concern."

"Try to forgive her. I'm asking a lot, but our family can't have a rift between you two."

"I'll think about it. That's the best I can offer." Diana stirs a spoonful of honey in her tea and blows on the hot liquid. "You know, the person I would have forgiven, without any hesitation, was Tom. Even for committing a crime. *I know I would have.* Which is why all of this is so—"

"Upsetting. Disappointing. Frustrating. Worrisome. Maddening." Vivian, never one to keep her opinions to herself, jumps in to finish Diana's sentence.

"Yes, all of that. Maybe he was being selfish and hurtful, like Andie said."

"That's not the Tom your father and I knew. He was complicated, Diana, not malicious."

"Why couldn't he bring himself to tell me until he was dead?"

"Oh, Diana, he was ashamed. Two men died! Tom was afraid of losing you and the children. Losing his career and reputation, too."

"I wouldn't have left him over this, Mom."

"This doesn't have *anything* to do with you. That's tough to wrap your head around. Tom not telling you was rooted in his own fear and shame. He probably couldn't get out of his own way to realize it would be all right—challenging, but all right—if he opened up."

"What about leaving the letter for me to find in the time capsule?"

"We can have theories about why he did that, but you're going to have to find an answer you can live with."

"You're not going to share your thoughts?" Diana asks. "That's out of character."

"Ah, yes, The General always tells you what to do." Vivian chuckles at Diana's wide eyes and open mouth. "You're surprised I figured out you and your sister call me The General behind my back? Give me some credit."

"How did you do it?"

"To be an effective general, one must never reveal one's intelligence sources. Let's say it didn't require a complicated military operation to figure out."

They both laugh, and the sound is magnetic, propelling them across the room to one another. Vivian, only a few inches taller, wraps her arms around Diana. Diana relaxes against her mother, inhaling her rose perfume, grateful she's been loved by this woman all her life.

"Your sister came up with the nickname, didn't she?" Vivian asks when she releases Diana from their hug. "I can count on Andrea for the incisive remark."

"It's said with admiration. You're efficient. Organized. You hold the family together. I couldn't have made it through Tom's illness, his death, or all these past months without him if you and Dad hadn't been there."

"It's what we do for the people we love, sweetheart."

"Of course, but Mom? It's time for me to take care of myself, to not rely so much on you, Dad, and everyone else." As she speaks, Diana feels a shift, as if a power long dormant has woken up.

A look comes over Vivian's face, one Diana hasn't seen in some time. It's pride, as if she's been waiting for Diana to arrive at this moment. "What will you do about this letter?"

"Find Jessica," Diana says. "Thanks to my online sleuthing, I came across arrest records for her in New Hampshire and Massachusetts, plus a high school graduation listing and her parents' address in Maine. I sent a letter to her at their house, in case she visits."

"You've done so much to find her."

"I also came across Carson Roy's obituary. His only survivor was his mother, which I already knew. The obituary mentioned he dreamed of opening his own garage. Apparently, he'd been rebuilding motorcycles since he was a kid." Diana has never ridden on a motorcycle. Had Tom? She has no idea. "I wrote to Grace, too, with an update, but there's been no word back yet. I figured a letter would be easier than a phone call. This way, she can decide when to read it. Or *if* to read it."

Diana is relieved she's told her mother what's going on, but she's still angry at Andrea. Sometimes families make things difficult.

"Will you ever tell the children?" Vivian muses. "Maybe when they're grown, like I did?"

"Duncan knows."

"Duncan? Wait, does that have anything to do with what happened when you were in Hamilton?"

In the past, Diana might have shielded herself against criticism about her parenting; tonight she holds her ground. "He figured some of it out, so I had to update him. I didn't tell him all of it, only the details that are most relevant. He's okay."

"That's why you're not giving up," Vivian says, understanding filling her eyes.

"Yes, for both Duncan and Phoebe. For me, too. And for Tom."

Chapter Twenty-Eight

As Diana's mother predicted, Andrea is full of regret after their fight and desperate for forgiveness. Diana, however, can't stop rehashing what Andrea said: *You're consumed with finding out who he was and what he did. The truth is right in front of you: He was selfish and self-absorbed, and even after his death, he's still dictating your life and your choices.*

In the days that follow, Diana erases Andrea's voicemails without listening to them. She ignores her sister's texts, which include earnest apologies, accompanied by photos of the two of them as children or GIFs of people sobbing. Diana distributes the gifts Andrea leaves on her doorstep to others; the bouquet of tulips goes to Lakshmi, and she leaves the basket of homemade toffee brownies in the library break room for her coworkers to enjoy.

Soon, Diana thinks. *Soon, I'll be ready to talk.*

Though she has nothing new to report to Duncan, one evening, as she drives him home from basketball practice, she updates him on her efforts to find Jessica. She tells him that she's written to Grace and Jessica's parents and found some old information online about Jessica. "I don't hear back from her parents soon, I'll call them."

"What about her social media?" Duncan asks, holding up his phone. "She's around your age, right? She's probably on Facebook, or maybe Instagram."

"Trying to say something about me being old?" Diana says with a laugh as she merges into traffic. He wiggles his tongue at her. "That's a good idea, though. I should have thought of it."

That night, after she's locked the windows and doors and made sure her children are asleep, Diana sits at her kitchen table and opens the shared laptop. She wishes she still had access to Tom's email. He deleted his email and social media soon after his diagnosis. "I'm doing this so you don't have to," he explained when Diana asked why he was even bothering. It would be helpful now to access his messages. She thought he took care of these details as a courtesy to her, but she's not sure about that anymore.

A few clicks, and she's on Facebook. She scans her news feed and finds posts announcing that the Spring Fling is sold out and those still in need of tickets can be added to a waiting list, missives about the upcoming presidential primaries, and a call for volunteers for Alcott Middle School's teacher appreciation breakfast.

Diana enters "Jessica O'Connor" into the search bar, and dozens of options fill her screen. Thumbnail-size photos of women of all ages, young to middle-aged, smile back at her. Some cuddle fuzzy-haired dogs, others stand bikini-clad on sandy beaches, and some have replaced their avatars with images of Ruth Bader Ginsburg or Hillary Clinton.

"Which one are you?" Diana says, moving down the page.

After several dead ends, she clicks on a profile for a Jessica O'Connor from New Hampshire who has never turned on her privacy settings. Her most recent post is a four-year-old photo in which she poses with a young girl in front of a pink azalea bush. Both wear heart-shaped sunglasses and sundresses. **Celebrating Ava's birthday**, reads the caption.

Jessica's daughter is named Ava. This must be her.

Diana can't get a sense of Jessica from the photo; her hair is tucked under a bandana, and she stands slightly behind the little girl. Who took the photo? Where were they? Why does it say she lives in New Hampshire when she moved out of the apartment in Nashua? Does she still live in the state? Why hasn't she posted any updates since this photo?

Although this Jessica hasn't maintained her profile, it's possible she visits the site, lurking about to read friends' posts, so Diana writes a private message she hopes will earn a response: Dear Jessica, My name is Diana Morgan. You and my husband, Tom, worked together one summer on your aunt and uncle's farm in Hamilton, Vermont. I have some questions about that time and would appreciate talking with you. Thank you. Diana includes her phone number and hits send.

It's then she allows herself to click over to Tom's Team, the Facebook group she created as news spread about Tom's diagnosis. She used the group to share brief updates, photos of their last vacation to Cape Cod for his fiftieth birthday, and, at the end, inform everyone he was gone. The group was easier to manage than fielding countless emails, calls, and texts. After he died, though, the thought of keeping it going distressed Diana. She didn't respond to any of the sympathy messages decorated with broken-heart emojis; instead, she closed out of the site and deleted the app from her phone.

The profile pictures of old friends, neighbors, work colleagues, and a few of Tom's former clients blend together as she reads their posts. Such a loss. What an outstanding man. May your memories be a blessing.

What memories of Tom do these people hold? Did they really know him?

Because after all, Diana hadn't really known him, had she?

～

Grace's response to Diana's letter arrives the following week, the day before the Spring Fling, stacked in the mailbox with the latest issue of *The Alcott Chronicle* and the water bill. Diana finds the letter when she arrives home from work. Her worry manifests into yet another list: *What Have I Done to Grace?*

I've disappointed her by not yet talking with Jessica.

I've wrenched up the past and added to her grief.

I've made her angry, and she wants me to stop searching.

"Get it together. She wouldn't want you to give up," Diana mutters. It's the perfect time to read Grace's message. Both kids are at her parents' house, lured by their dinner invitation and the promise of a trip to the ice cream shop in Alcott's town center. There's no reason to wait. Diana opens the letter and begins to read.

Dear Diana,

I've been eager to learn what happened when you found Jessica. I was, at first, concerned I had out-of-date contact information for her, but I shouldn't have been. Jessica's whereabouts and her life in general have been a mystery for some time. That's why her parents took in her daughter, who, I am glad to report, is thriving. I called Jessica's father after I received your letter. He told me she's back in Portland and provided me with an updated phone number for her. I've included it below.

Thank you for asking about my move. I miss the farm very much. My new home is comfortable, though I wish my sister would stop brooding over my well-being so much.

Yours,

Grace

Underneath Jessica's new phone number, printed carefully so there's no way Diana could misunderstand the digits, is a postscript:

P.S. I've enclosed a photo of Tom and Jessica I found while unpacking. Thought you might like to have it.

The photo is faded and worn smooth by time. Tom holds a rake in one hand and a baseball cap in the other. His hair is lighter than Diana remembers, bleached by the sun. He looks beautiful. Young, healthy, and *alive.* Diana welcomes the swell of grief that rushes over her.

At his side stands Jessica. She barely comes up to the middle of his chest, and in her arms, she carries a large wooden bucket. She's attractive, with full cheeks and an explosion of curly brown hair. She looks like someone Diana has seen before, and at first, she assumes it's because Jessica was in the photo on Grace's wall, the group shot on the porch that included Tom, or because she found her profile on Facebook.

But that's not it.

The answer comes to her like a snare drum beating out a steady rhythm, slowly and then faster until it builds into a resounding crescendo. She runs up the stairs to her bedroom, her feet skipping the top step. Kneeling on the floor, Diana yanks open the bottom drawer of Tom's bedside table.

The notebook with his sketches.

The woman on one of the back pages.

Diana holds the photograph next to the sketch. The woman in the notebook is older, with a thinner face and faint lines around her eyes, but it's her: Jessica.

She assumed Jessica and Tom lost touch after that summer at the farm. This sketch makes her think they saw one another again. Or that Tom thought about Jessica enough to have been inspired to envision her as she might look in the present day. Either way, Jessica appears to have been more important to Tom than Diana knew.

Diana has been wrong about so much.

She doesn't wail or curse or punch her fist against her bed. At the beginning, in those early weeks after finding the time capsule, she would have done all those things.

Instead, she thinks of Tom's letter: *I should have accepted responsibility a long time ago, before I met you. Maybe if I tell you now, it will be enough. It's also possible I'm making things worse for you by writing this letter.*

Diana takes one long look at the sketch and places the notebook back in the bedside table. She stands up, tucks her hair behind her ears, and fiddles with the leather buttons on her cardigan. She reviews her options, and a list slowly forms: *What Should I Do Next?*

"I don't need a list for this," she says.

Diana returns to the kitchen, where she collects her phone and enters Jessica's new number. The phone rings two, three, five times before the voicemail kicks in with the default greeting, robotic and impersonal.

Startled, Diana hangs up. She hasn't rehearsed a message. She stares at the phone in her hand. "That was dumb."

What is it that Duncan says? Only old people use voicemail? Diana clicks over to her text messaging app and starts typing.

Hi Jessica—Grace O'Connor gave me your number. I'm Tom Morgan's widow. I'm looking for information about the time you spent with him on your aunt and uncle's farm when you were in high school. Can we talk? I'd meet you, too, if that would be easier. I live outside Boston. Thank you—Diana

As the text swooshes away, Diana's stomach drops. *What have I done? What makes me think she'll respond?*

She waits, her fingers mapping the edge of the phone, hoping for an answer, but nothing comes.

Chapter Twenty-Nine

As the Alcott Memorial Library Spring Fling begins, Diana is in the women's bathroom forcing her hips into a black sheath dress she found in the back of her closet but didn't try on until now. As she grabs for the zipper, the satiny fabric tugs and pulls, leaving bulges across her midsection.

The last time she wore this dress was Tom's funeral; after weeks of subsisting only on coffee, the dress was loose. Since there's no time to go home and get another option, she can wear this dress or her work clothes, a sensible navy skirt and cotton sweater, which are all wrong for the Spring Fling. She curses and yanks the zipper closed. This dress will have to do.

In the past, Diana and Andrea would have chosen dresses to wear to the event together, squeezing into a changing room at the mall and laughing about the unflattering lighting. But Andrea is working tonight, and Diana isn't sure she's up for dancing with her sister. She still hasn't been able to let go of the hurt caused by Andrea's reaction to Tom's letter.

For the hundredth time that day, Diana checks her phone. After reviewing the feed from her doorbell camera app and confirming no one is currently trying to break into her house, she looks for a response from Jessica. *Nothing.* Ever since she reached out, Diana has been hyperaware of her phone's beeps and buzzes. She's slept with her phone under her pillow and once tried to take it into the shower.

There is, however, a text from Chris—Have fun tonight! Wish I was there with you—that makes her stomach wobble. Attending the Spring Fling with Chris would be a date, and she is absolutely not ready to date anyone, not even him.

Or is she?

Diana scans the text thread she and Chris share. Since she returned from Vermont, they've sent hundreds of texts to one another, from early-morning hellos to late-night check-ins. Their connection has been such a surprise, and she isn't sure what to do about it. She's still in love with Tom; how can she have feelings for Chris, too?

Her phone alarm beeps, a reminder she's due to meet up with Camille and get to the party. Diana texts Chris a dancing emoji and drops her phone into her tote. Tonight, wearing an ill-fitting dress without pockets means the phone will have to stay behind.

"There you are!" Camille says when Diana steps into the hallway. "I was looking for you."

Diana suspects Camille was worried she'd skip out on the fundraiser. She considered it, making a list of reasons she could offer up as an excuse: *migraine, food poisoning, basement flood, Legionnaires' disease.* Since Diana is more afraid of disappointing Camille than she is of navigating this event, she's pushed aside the excuses to show up.

"You look amazing," Diana says. Shimmery bangles replace the customary silver bracelets at Camille's wrists, and her braids are held off her face by a band of rhinestones. Her gold-and-silver dress has bell-shaped sleeves, with alternating stripes on the bodice.

"Yes, I do," Camille says, smiling. "You look ready, though I'm not sure about all black." She unties a gold silk scarf from her neck. "May I?"

Camille concentrates on adjusting the scarf around Diana, as if she's sending her off into battle with the silk as a shield against the arrows that might come her way. Yet the gossamer fabric is too delicate, too transparent, and too beautiful, and it can't safeguard Diana.

"That's better." Camille nods appreciatively. "Let's drop off your bag and get to the party."

When Camille and Diana arrive at the Spring Fling tent—the event having long ago become too large to be held inside the library—the DJ, who spends his days as the high school lacrosse coach, blasts "YMCA" by the Village People from a stage in the corner. Diana waves to Stephanie, whose hair tonight is fluorescent pink. Stephanie smiles and gestures to the dance floor, but Diana mouths "later" and follows Camille through the crowd.

When Camille pauses to answer a question from the caterer, Diana continues on, keeping her eyes down. She looks up once or twice in the hope that she finds someone to talk to who won't demand anything of her.

As if she conjured up Lakshmi and Ramesh, they appear at her side, holding hands. Each time Diana sees the two of them together, she's reminded that some people have more luck than others, that they can find their forever love and hold on to one another, never having to face life's ups and downs alone.

"How are you?" Lakshmi says, as she kisses Diana's cheek. Lakshmi smells like jasmine and turpentine, and Diana finds the combination comforting.

Since Lakshmi is one of the people in Diana's life who can see through any pretense, she says what is true. "I wish I was anywhere except here."

"You're not on your own, are you? I thought you were with Camille," Ramesh asks. His dark eyes scan the room as he moves to Diana's right elbow. "You must stay with us."

"You two are not going to babysit me all night." Diana's voice is prickly, and Ramesh and Lakshmi share a look. "Truly," she adds. "Please have fun, and don't worry about me."

"We're here if you need us," says Lakshmi.

Spying Camille waiting for her, Diana forces a smile and maneuvers through the crowd.

The next hour blurs as Diana and Camille greet the library's largest donors and the town's leadership. The chair of Alcott Bank asks after Diana's parents, and the Alcott Historical Society's executive director talks about a book he recently borrowed from the library. It's Elizabeth Donahue, the president of the library board, who asks about Tom.

"You've had such a difficult time, Diana. I remember what it was like when my husband died. The grief can be debilitating. How are you? Your children? How are they faring without their father?" Elizabeth takes Diana's hands in hers, holding them together as if in prayer.

While Diana assumes Elizabeth means well—or, at least, she can convince herself the questions are asked with kindness—she's had enough. She jerks her hands away, causing Elizabeth to stop midsentence. "Losing my husband has been awful," she concedes. "Thank you for asking after me and my children. We're doing a little better every day."

"It gets easier with time," Elizabeth says.

"That's what people tell me. It's still the hardest thing I've ever done."

Diana excuses herself. *Maybe that's the answer,* she thinks as she walks away. *Not hiding from the truth but owning it.*

She accepts a glass of wine from a passing server and looks around. She expected to be exhausted after talking to so many people; instead, she's alert and full of energy. She feels victorious, as if she's overcome a demanding challenge and claimed a hard-fought medal.

She locates Jonathan on the other side of the dance floor, standing on the edge of a group of men. She walks nearby, to a high-top table covered in half-drunk champagne glasses, and catches his eye.

When he joins her, Jonathan says, "You saved me from a boring conversation about golf. Thank you."

"You don't like golf?"

"I like it, but I don't need to hear every detail of other people's golf vacations."

"Where's Lily?"

"Dancing." Jonathan points to the dance floor, where a group of women in strapless dresses undulates to "Walk Like an Egyptian" by the Bangles. Lily and her friends square their hands to imitate hieroglyphics and shimmy across the floor. "She's had a few cocktails."

"Looks like she's having fun." Diana swallows a lump in her throat. How fortunate Lily is to have everything she wants. "Sorry I haven't responded to your texts. What did you want?"

"I wanted to see how you're doing."

"Right." She decides then to voice the question she should have asked the minute she returned from Vermont: "What can you tell me about Jessica O'Connor?"

Jonathan doesn't respond, but she can tell by the pulsing vein along his brow that he's heard her question. He lifts his cocktail—vodka on the rocks with a twist of lime, Diana remembers, that's his drink—and empties the glass, placing it next to hers. She wasn't sure he knew about Jessica until he met her question with silence.

"Do you really want to talk about this now?"

"No," Diana answers truthfully, "but you're here. And I'm here. This is as good a time as any."

Jonathan gestures to a café table at the perimeter of the tent. "Shall we sit? It might be quieter over there."

"Stop delaying," Diana snaps.

"You didn't ignore Tom's letter."

"Of course I didn't. Now tell me about Jessica."

Jonathan avoids looking at her, focusing instead on pulling at his shirtsleeves and lining up his cuffs with the edge of his jacket. "I never met her. Never even knew who she was until Tom took her on as a pro bono client. All he said about her was that she was a single mom who had gotten in trouble—drug charges, I think."

"What kind of charges?"

"Possession, maybe? I don't remember the details. After you visited, I went through our old files to see what we had documented about her case, but there wasn't anything there."

"Don't you typically have files on all your clients?"

"Yes, we do. Or we *should.*" Jonathan clears his throat. "It's possible Tom never opened a file for her, or it was destroyed at some point. Either way, at the time, all I knew was that he wanted to help her. I had a feeling he'd known her before, but nothing then made me suspicious."

"Nothing *then?* When did you start to question their relationship?"

"I always knew something was off about it. We were open about our clients. We bounced ideas off one another all the time, but he was vague about Jessica. It was almost like he made a point not to talk about her. It didn't worry me until afterward."

"The money." Diana wishes she'd sat down as he suggested. "You think she might have been the something important that drove him to steal from the firm."

The vein in Jonathan's brow pulses again. "It's all in the past. I really mean that."

The DJ switches to "At Last" by Etta James, and as the ballad fills the tent, couples gravitate to the dance floor. Ramesh leads Lakshmi to a spot near Lily and her friends, all of whom are being claimed by their significant others.

"If this *is* all in the past, I'd like that copy of the letter back." Diana hadn't expected to ask for it, but it's the right decision. The message was for her, not Jonathan.

Jonathan waves at Lily as she beckons him onto the dance floor. "I promised to keep it confidential." His voice is brisk and businesslike, and Diana senses he's hurt by her request. "I would never violate my oath. You have my word."

"If this really means nothing to you, you don't need to keep it, right?"

"I can destroy it for you. We have a service we use to dispose of our papers. They're reputable."

"No, I want my letter back," Diana says, trying to forget that "At Last" was the first song she and Tom danced to at their wedding. "I can swing by the office on Monday to pick it up. When's a good time?"

"I'll drop it off at your house. This weekend." She thinks he's going to say something else, but instead he leaves her alone at the table to join his wife.

He takes Lily by the hand and spins her around before pulling her close. They sway in sync, Lily's head on Jonathan's chest. He presses his lips against her hair, and the crowd surrounds them, hiding them from Diana.

She takes it as a sign to leave. She spies an opening in the corner, where the catering staff enters with trays of canapés, and she's through the tent flap before anyone engages her in conversation.

Too wired to go home, Diana settles on the stairs leading up to the library's main entrance. She tucks Camille's lovely scarf tight around her body and makes her list: *What Could I Have Done Tonight Instead of Attend This Party?*

I could have cleaned out the refrigerator.

I could have started that novel Mom keeps telling me to read.

I could have gone to sleep early.

Diana finishes off the last of her wine and sets down the glass, knocking it against the marble step. A crack appears down the middle. She holds up the glass in the dim light to look more closely at the breaking point. So fragile, so broken. How is it still together?

The DJ makes the odd choice to segue from Etta James to Def Leppard, and "Pour Some Sugar on Me" pounds through the speakers. As the servers go in and out of the tent, the light from the party and the unrelenting cheers from the dance floor rise up and recede. Diana catches brief glimpses of the partygoers: women on the dance floor, arms above their heads, mouths open to the ceiling; men, ties undone, laughing; a couple locked in an amorous embrace. It's like she's looking through a children's viewfinder toy, the images frozen in time, each clicking ahead one by one. She wonders who here tonight is truly happy, who is here because their spouse forced them to attend, and who is keeping a secret from the person they love most.

Diana stands up, swaying on her feet. "He could have been honest with me, instead of leaving that letter."

She throws her glass. It leaves her hand easily, disappearing between the bushes lining the stairs. She doesn't wait for it to hit the ground and shatter into pieces. Instead, she turns away from the party and runs down the steps, plunging into the darkness.

Chapter Thirty

The morning after the Spring Fling is gray and foggy, a souvenir of a night of rain that started after the party ended. Enveloped in Tom's flannel robe, Diana stands in her kitchen, rolling the rock she took from Grace's farm in her hand, rubbing her thumb along its rough texture and pointed end. She hopes the rain began after the Spring Fling, imagining the tents filling with water and sequin-covered women hurrying home through the deluge. Rain was definitely not on the invitation list.

She's reaching for the coffeepot when, through the window, she sees a car slow down in front of her house. Diana freezes. The back of her neck prickles with anticipation, and she fears the people Tom warned her about are here again.

Wishing Duncan's baseball bat were in the hall closet and not under her bed upstairs, Diana creeps to the front window. Fully expecting to find a stranger in her yard, she instead sees a newspaper, wrapped in a blue plastic bag, fly out the car's window. "The paper," she says, as relief floods her veins. "Get yourself together, Diana."

She stuffs her bare feet into Duncan's rain boots, her skin screeching in protest against the sleek rubber, and heads outside. She crosses the wet grass to rescue the newspaper from a puddle along the walk, careful to avoid the unfurling hyacinths her mother and Phoebe planted last year. She notices the buds on her magnolia tree, a promise of the beauty that will grace her yard in a few short weeks. New life surrounds her. It's not held back by unanswered questions, unreturned text messages, or uncertain relationships. Everything keeps moving forward. The surety of this cycle of growth might have filled Diana with despair a year or two ago, as she anticipated Tom's death and then struggled to live without him, but in this moment, it hits differently.

Now Diana sees possibility, and maybe even hope. Tom's letter has forced her to engage with the past in a way she avoided so completely after his death. By looking backward, by trying to understand him better, she's found that moving forward might not be as frightening as she once thought it would be.

Diana is halfway through the newspaper when her doorbell rings. A quick glance at her phone tells her it's not even 8:00 a.m., but she has an idea who it is.

"I was on my way to the gym," Jonathan says when she opens the front door. "I wondered if you have a minute."

At her invitation, he steps into the foyer but declines her offer of coffee or to sit on the sofa. He thrusts a manila folder at her. "Tom's letter," he says. "You want it back because you don't trust me."

"I want it back"—Diana pauses briefly—"because it's mine. I'm sorry about the money and that he kept secrets from you, too."

"I'm not expecting that money to be returned. It's in the past. I really believe that."

"Maybe you can live without knowing what he was hiding," Diana says, as she tucks the folder under her left arm. "I can't."

"It's your choice," he says, tiredly. This is the last time they'll talk about the letter, and that's for the best. "Since I've already explained to you about that money and Jessica O'Connor, I might as well tell you everything."

Fear shoots through Diana, setting her body on high alert. "Tell me everything? What do you mean?" She reflexively steps forward, her right hand outstretched.

Jonathan backs up against the door, his arms crossed at his chest. She interprets his movement as self-protective, designed to keep a barrier between them. He'll stop talking, Diana intuits, if she gets too emotional. She pulls her hand back to her body and drops her voice to a whisper. "What is it, Jonathan?"

He looks past her into the living room, at the fireplace, or perhaps through the French doors into the backyard. It doesn't matter where; he just won't look at her.

"When Tom sold the firm, he had some of his proceeds—I mean, some of your proceeds—sent to another person." Jonathan swallows. "He asked me not to tell you about it. Made me promise, actually, that I'd never tell you."

"Who?" Diana squeezes that folder between her hands. "It was Jessica O'Connor, wasn't it?"

When he looks at her, she sees how much breaking his promise to Tom is killing him. She doesn't care how much it hurts, though. She really couldn't care less how bad Jonathan feels for telling her the truth.

"How much money was it?" When Tom told her about the sale of their ownership stake in the firm, Diana had been disappointed by the amount he and Jonathan had agreed upon; she'd expected more and told Tom so. He explained that overhead and staff expenses, plus some client collections problems, had been a factor in the final numbers. "This is a fair deal, Diana," he said as he gave her the papers to sign. She believed him.

The vein along Jonathan's brow pulses. "He really wanted this to be confidential."

"So why are you telling me?"

"I didn't realize Jessica might be involved in whatever that letter is"—he points to the folder she's continued to twist and reshape—"until last night. Since you asked about her, it's all I can think about."

Diana really has to find Jessica. "Why didn't you mention all of this when I came to your office?"

Jonathan shrugs. "I promised him, Diana."

"Your promise to a dead man was more important than telling me the truth?"

"That's not fair. He was my best friend. He asked for my help."

Anger gathers under Diana's skin. "I thought we were friends, too. How much did he give her?"

Jonathan hesitates.

"Come on, Jonathan. You came here with the express purpose of sharing this. Don't chicken out now."

Jonathan blinks at the harshness of her tone. He sticks his hands into his jacket pockets and clears his throat. "$250,000."

"$250,000?" Diana repeats. "Why did he give it to her?"

"He didn't explain. He *wouldn't* explain. One of the last things he did at the firm was to set up a trust with her as the sole beneficiary. He asked me to wire the money into it when the sale was complete."

"This is . . . I have no idea what to say about this." A thick numbness settles over Diana's limbs, the weight of this truth overwhelming her body.

The vein along Jonathan's brow is pulsing even faster, and he presses his fingers against it, as if it's possible to smooth down the telltale sign he's upset. "There's something else I wanted to say. You *are* my friend, Diana. And as your friend, I should have been around more, checking in on you and the kids. Helping out. Lily, too. I got all caught up in my own stuff and kind of disappeared. I let my discomfort over the missing money and the promise I made to Tom impact me more than I realized. I'm sorry. I should have been a better support to you."

"Yes, you should have."

Jonathan's eyes widen. He must have thought she'd tell him everything's okay, and she's not disappointed in him, but honesty, Diana has learned, is best shared.

"Would Duncan like to catch a Celtics game with me sometime? Tom would have wanted me to be there for him. You and Phoebe, too."

"I don't think so, Jonathan."

I'd let this all go and move on, he once told her. Jonathan meant those words to dissuade her search into Tom's past, but they apply better to the friendship they once shared. She might have forgiven him had he not kept so much from her when she first asked for his help; she can't find it in her to do that now.

He opens his mouth to say something, but stops himself, shaking his head. "Of course. I'm sorry I didn't do more, Diana. If you change your mind, my offer will always stand."

He leaves her house without waiting for her response, walking swiftly to his car. Diana watches him drive up the street, back to a life apart from her own.

❧

Diana sends a second text to Jessica that morning: Hi there, Contacting you again to ask if we can meet. Or talk. I'd be grateful for any amount of time you can give me. Thank you, Diana Morgan. She attaches a snap of the photo Grace sent her; perhaps it will jog Jessica's memory.

Three weeks go by without a response. During that time, Diana phones Jessica's parents and leaves two voicemails asking for their help. They don't call back. Concerned she's at an impasse, Diana begins to research private investigators. She feels silly looking for a PI—that's for fictional characters on television or in books, not real people like her— but at this point, Diana can't say no to any option that will bring her closer to the truth, no matter how far it is outside of her comfort zone.

In the end, though, she doesn't need to hire an investigator.

When Jessica's text finally pops up on her screen, Diana is preparing lunch, slicing yellow peppers while watching Phoebe and Mira make slime at her kitchen table. Through the open window, Duncan and Jadyn run drills on the playground court, swerving around one another and jumping up to toss the ball into the basket.

I knew Tom. What do you want?

Right to the point, Diana thinks, wiping her hands on a kitchen towel. *I can do that, too.*

I need you to tell me about the fire.

Diana waits. Blue dots bubble on the screen.
"Mama?"
"One second."

Why are you asking me?

Grace says you might have information and that you might be willing to help me.

Phoebe continues to talk, but her words stay in the background, fuzzy and unclear, as Diana clenches the phone and wills Jessica to write again.

Saturday. Noon. I'll text you where in a few days.

Thank you. I really appreciate this.

"I'm hungry," Duncan says, entering through the back door with Jadyn at his heels.
"Can I stay for lunch?" Mira asks.
"Me too?" asks Jadyn. "My mom said I can."
"We're having veggie burgers. Mira, I'll tell your mom you're join-ing us." Diana sends a fast text to Lakshmi. "Girls, clean up that slime, and all of you, wash your hands." Diana puts her hand in her pocket and rubs her thumb against what she's come to think of as Grace's rock. *Soon,* she thinks.

The night before she's scheduled to meet Jessica, as Diana lies awake, watching the minutes click by on the bedside clock, she remembers another night in this bed. It was about a month after Tom's diagnosis, and she could see he was changing, pulling away. All she wanted was to keep him here, make it so he could stay with her.

She turned over, and he grabbed her, pulling her across the bed and into his arms. He'd stopped shaving, so when he kissed her, his stubble chafed her chin. His body threw off such heat, such life; how could he be sick?

They paused only to remove their clothes. Neither spoke as he rolled on top of her. She clasped his increasingly angular, thin body, enveloping him with her curves, her vitality. *If only I can make him well,* Diana thought as tears slid down her cheeks. Tom licked the wetness away and gently kissed along her eyebrows, down to her cheekbones, then to her mouth again, urgently this time. She ran her fingers down his back, his skin smooth under her touch. He shifted to look at her, and he kept her gaze as he entered her, his eyes full of love. She buried her face in the crook of his neck, inhaling his snowfall-tinged scent, promising herself she'd remember.

It was the last time they made love.

Now, alone in their bed, her hands empty, she wishes again they had more time. That he trusted her with all of himself.

And she wonders what Jessica will tell her.

Chapter Thirty-One

Diana parks her car in front of a dented "Reserved for Fiona's Customers Only" sign. With a faded sticker warning against drunk driving affixed across its bottom third, the sign cantilevers over a modest patch of grass filled with trash: empty Dunkin' Donuts cups, crushed beer cans, and torn plastic bags, the forgotten fragments of urban life.

Remembering her promise to Lakshmi, Diana takes her phone from its dashboard perch—she needed the GPS app to get here, the narrow and circuitous streets in this part of Boston unfamiliar to her—and makes sure someone knows where she is. **Hey Lax,** she texts. **Meeting Jessica at a bar in South Boston called Fiona's. Fill you in after xo.** She doesn't wait for a response, dropping the phone in her purse and listening to it bang against Grace's rock.

Diana steps out of her minivan into a perfect spring day masquerading as summer. The sky overhead is a sunny, cloudless blue, and the air is brand new, even in the middle of the city. The forecast calls for a high of eighty-five, a wave of heat that regularly comes this time of year, making late May feel more like August.

Figuring out what to wear to meet Jessica was a challenge. Nothing too obvious or desperate, nothing that indicates how nervous she is either. Diana settled on a blue cotton dress with a braided rattan belt, bare legs with brown leather boots, and gold hoop earrings. She centers her belt on her waist and prays she comes across as presentable and, hopefully, sympathetic.

Pushing her sunglasses down from the top of her head, Diana takes in her surroundings. Fiona's is housed in a squat, windowless brick bunker. In front, traffic backs up for more than a block, cars honking at the intersection, drivers anxious to make it through before the light turns from amber to red. The weekend is underway, and everyone wants to be somewhere else.

Getting here called for subterfuge, an approach Diana found all too easy. She concocted a story about needing to catch up at work, and as predicted, before she even asked, her father offered to take the kids for the day. "We'll go fishing," he said. "Your mother will pack a picnic. We'll make it an adventure."

Diana didn't need to lie to her parents. She can't let Duncan get too caught up in her search for Jessica, but her parents would have helped had they known where she was headed. Deceit—or, at least, hiding the truth—is second nature to her now.

She stumbles at this realization, righting herself before she falls. How much she's changed since she found Tom's letter.

Or perhaps she's finally seeing herself clearly.

A metal plate reading FIONA'S is bolted in place at eye level on the bar's front door, and the outline of what appears to be a fist is smashed in above the doorknob. Diana slings her purse onto her shoulder and opens the door.

Fiona's is exactly what she thought a South Boston bar on a Saturday morning would be like: dimly lit, the air thick with the yeasty smell of beer, the walls covered in Boston sports team posters. A large pool table takes up the far left corner, with round tables scattered around the scuffed linoleum floor. Hugging the right side of the space is a wraparound bar, where a man slumps on a stool, gawking at the wall-mounted television turned to a twenty-four-hour news channel.

He turns away from the screen to squint at Diana, blinded by the sunlight accompanying her inside. She steps forward and lets the door swing shut. The man returns to his half-full—or is it half-empty?—beer.

Diana doesn't know whether she should look for an optimistic slant on what has clearly begun as morning drinking.

In truth, she has no idea what's brought this stranger to Fiona's. Maybe it's the end of his day, a backbreaking night shift behind him. Maybe it's nonalcoholic beer. Or maybe it's one of a dozen other possibilities. Diana's nervousness is causing her to make assumptions, which she can't do if she's going to connect with Jessica. She offers a silent apology to Fiona's only other customer and takes a seat at a table next to a shrine to the 2004 Boston Red Sox.

As she drops her sunglasses into her dress pocket, a woman enters through a set of swinging doors. Diana twists her neck to peer at her. Is this Jessica? She asked to meet here; she didn't say whether she would be a customer or an employee.

When the woman turns, Diana is presented with a clear view of her face. *Not Jessica,* she thinks, recalling the photo Grace sent her, which she carries in the zipped pocket of her purse. The woman puts a plate of food in front of the beer drinker, and they speak briefly, their voices low. She glances at Diana, wipes her hands on a towel hanging from the waistband of her jeans, and comes out from behind the bar.

"You order at the bar at this time of day. No waitstaff for the tables," the woman says, stopping a few feet from Diana. Her dull blond hair is cut into a chin-length bob, and her voice is rough, the Boston accent swallowing up the *r* in each word.

Yah ordah at the bah, Diana hears. She's never, despite growing up outside the city, been able to mimic the accent.

"You want a drink?" The woman—Diana decides she must be Fiona—cocks her hip and pushes up her shirtsleeves, gestures that indicate she isn't up for arguments or complaints.

"A seltzer, please." Diana follows Fiona across the room, eyeing the door as a glass of carbonated water shifts across the bar, bubbly drops falling on the polished wood.

"Waiting for someone?" Fiona asks. Diana nods and opens up her purse to pay, but the bartender waves her away. "Get me on your way out."

As she returns to her table, Diana's phone buzzes. She opens her purse to see who texted. It's Lakshmi: **Be safe.**

A new list starts—*What Will I Do If Jessica Stands Me Up?*—but Diana is stopped by the loud screech of the front door's rusty hinges. Sunlight pours in, and it's her turn to blink against the glare.

A slight shape pauses in the threshold.

"Here she is," Diana murmurs, her heart racing.

Jessica scans the bar and acknowledges Fiona with a swing of her head so quick as to be missed in the reflex of blinking. She skips over the man at the bar and lands, at last, on Diana.

Diana holds up her hand. "Jessica?"

Jessica nods but walks over to Fiona. The two women chat, and Fiona hands Jessica a drink in a tall glass. Diana can't tell whether they're friends or meeting for the first time. She doesn't know whether Jessica is a frequent visitor to Fiona's. Or how she gets by. Or really anything about her.

Jessica is not what Diana expected. After hearing about Jessica from Grace and meeting Nikki, Diana anticipated Tom's ex would present with obvious signs of addiction, someone clearly struggling to function in the world.

This Jessica is the opposite.

Pretty, with a generous mouth and wide-set eyes, Jessica looks like one of the moms who meet for coffee at Sully's, straight from school drop-off. She's petite, barely five feet. Her hair runs to the middle of her back, and her corkscrew curls gently bounce as she moves. She wears a denim jacket, skinny black jeans, and ankle boots. Under her jacket is a green, striped blouse Diana immediately recognizes; she bought the same shirt last week. Jessica looks a lot like the girl from the photo: radiant and healthy. Diana has been more judgmental than she realized; she expected someone entirely different.

Jessica joins Diana at the table and, in a sustained chug, gulps down a third of her glass. Diana suspects Jessica's drink of choice is soda, though she wouldn't blame her if it included a shot of something strong and alcoholic. Stress practically radiates off her.

An ornate tattoo of the name Ava peeks out from the edge of Jessica's sleeve, its chunky lines twisting around her forearm. Her eyes, a rich brown, close briefly and then flutter open. "So you're Tom's wife."

Jessica's voice is low-pitched and raspy, as if she's been standing at the edge of a stage, screaming at her favorite band to play one more song. She locks her eyes with Diana, but Diana doesn't look away.

With each passing second, a realization comes to her, a connection she should have made sooner, perhaps when she saw the photo with Grace's letter or when she looked again at Tom's drawings. She's been a beat behind this entire time, so it's not a surprise she missed this.

"We've met before," Diana says.

Jessica blinks rapidly.

"Yes," Diana says slowly, heat rising in her body, turning her cheeks red. "We've met. At Sully's. The missing cat. That was you. That wasn't the only time, was it? I've seen you before."

Jessica drinks instead of responding.

"How often? How often have you been there and I didn't see you?" Lakshmi was correct about Diana's safety being a concern. Diana pushes her chair away from the table. "Have you been *following* me?"

Jessica slides her hand into her pocket, and when her fist exits her jacket, her fingers are curved, hiding something. Diana is unable to make out what it is, and she stiffens, fearing the worst. "I'm sorry," Jessica says.

Diana glances down and gasps. Her house key and the missing photo of Tom and their kids lie in front of her.

Her heart hammers in her chest, and she snaps her gaze to Jessica. This other woman—*the intruder*—stares back at her, regret in her eyes.

Diana has been looking for Jessica in the hope that Tom's ex can explain his past; perhaps she shouldn't be shocked about Jessica's involvement in her own present.

Diana claims the missing photo, taking a long look at the children she loves with a fierceness she can't adequately explain, and the husband who led her to this chair, to this bar, to this woman. She clamps down so tightly on the key that its grooves pinch against her skin. "Why?" she asks, the one word summarizing the many questions that fly through her mind.

"I wanted to see where Tom lived. I came down a few times and drove around your town. I saw places he mentioned, like that café and the library. Your house. I knew your son played basketball and guessed he was on the middle school team. I figured out the schedule and went to one of his games."

There's a ringing in Diana's ears, her body alerting her to how wrong all this is. Sully's wasn't the first time she saw Jessica. She remembers taking a phone call from Jonathan at Duncan's last game before she left for Vermont and noticing a woman who sat too close, almost as if she'd been listening to their conversation. Diana holds still trying to keep herself from bursting apart.

Jessica sips her drink. "I knew where the key to your house was. Once, I was on the phone with Tom when he came home from a run and realized you'd gone out with the kids. He didn't have his key and was locked out. It wasn't a big deal because there was one under the deck."

Diana glances at the door, trying to guess how many steps it would take to get outside. "If you've been following me, why did it take you so long to respond to my text? I assume you wanted to talk to me."

"I'd like a chance to explain," Jessica says, wrapping her hands around her glass and squeezing so tightly her knuckles turn white. "For Tom."

Diana flinches as Tom's name again comes out of Jessica's mouth, but she decides to play along. After all, she doesn't have other options.

"I didn't intend to go into your house. It just kind of . . . happened." Jessica shifts in her chair. "No, that's not a good explanation. The truth is I wanted to see his home."

"Do you have any idea how terrifying it was to have a stranger in my house? You took a photo of *my children*." Diana's voice rises, and the man at the bar turns around to look at them. She silently counts to five. "How many times did you use that key to go into my house?"

Jessica looks down at her lap. "The day I took the photo was the third time."

How had Diana not realized someone had been in her house, looking through her things, invading her privacy? Her safety? This could have ended much worse for her and her children. Diana wants to ask Jessica exactly what she did on each visit—each *intrusion*—but she also doesn't want to know. She wouldn't ever feel the same about her house if she knew.

The conversation is delayed by a plate of french fries clanking down on the table along with a bottle of ketchup. "Anything else?" Fiona asks, looking from Jessica to Diana. They decline her offer, and the woman withdraws to fill the glass of the man at the bar yet again.

Jessica smacks the bottle, and the condiment oozes out in a watery pile on the rim of her plate. "I didn't respond to your text right away, or the voicemail messages you left with my parents or the letter you sent them, because I wasn't sure if it was a good idea. I'm in recovery. Getting clean has been hard, and I didn't want to risk a relapse." She pushes the fries around the plate. "I knew Tom was married and had kids, but he didn't tell me much about you except that he was proud of your life together. I've always been jealous of that . . . and of you."

The truths keep coming, Diana thinks, securing the photo and key in her purse. "If meeting me was so hard, why are you here? And why this place?" Diana looks around Fiona's, taking in the pool table, the liquor bottles behind the bar, a broken mirror on the wall. "Why would someone in recovery want to spend time in a bar?"

"I used to come here a lot. Before I got clean. It's familiar." Jessica holds up two fries, dripping with ketchup, and then drops them onto the plate, uneaten.

"I need you to tell me what happened that summer you and Tom were on Grace and William's farm," Diana says. "And now, apparently, why you've been following me. You owe me that. For breaking into my house, if for no other reason."

Jessica nods.

"Let's start with you and Tom," Diana says. "Had you been in touch since that summer on the farm, or did you reconnect at some point?"

"I bumped into him at the courthouse in Lowell about twelve or thirteen years ago. I was there for a friend's trial. Tom was walking down the hall, like a dream." Jessica shifts the plate of fries off to the side. "We caught up. Exchanged numbers, that sort of thing."

Thirteen years ago, Diana was pregnant with Duncan, buying onesies and painting clouds on the walls of his nursery. Tom telling her he saw an old girlfriend wouldn't have been a threat to their marriage. To explain Jessica, however, would have meant opening up about the fire. He hadn't wanted to do that, so Jessica, too, had to remain a secret.

"Later, I got arrested for possession and needed a lawyer. Tom helped get me probation."

"You only saw him when he represented you?"

"Do you want to know about that summer?" Jessica's voice, which softened as she remembered reconnecting with Tom, grows stony again.

"I'm listening," Diana says. She notices Jessica didn't answer her question about how often she saw Tom.

"My parents sent me to Vermont that summer because they'd found coke in my backpack and freaked out. They thought a few months on a farm in the middle of nowhere would straighten me out. It wasn't awful. Uncle William and Aunt Grace didn't hang all over me like my parents did. They gave me chores but mostly left me alone. And there was Tom. I could tell he was into me." Jessica looks up, as if expecting

Diana to be mad. But Diana is too close to the truth to get upset about things that don't matter.

"He followed me around, trying to talk to me, even doing my chores. I had a boyfriend at home; it was his coke my parents found. He dumped me soon after I got to Vermont. I had a habit of dating guys who were losers. It took me years to figure that out." Jessica's tough exterior slips away, providing Diana with a glimpse of the insecure woman beneath. "Tom was different. He listened when I talked. He was funny, too, and kind."

He always was the same person. From his teenage years through to adulthood, he was always Tom—even if he kept part of himself from her. The essence of him was there. If Jessica says nothing else, Diana will be grateful for this revelation.

"I was the one who kissed him." Jessica finishes off her soda and sits back in her chair, her attention completely on Diana. "We were in the barn, cleaning out the stables. It was an oven in there, and the shovels were heavy, so we were taking a break in the middle of the horse shit and hay. A bird had gotten stuck inside and couldn't find its way out. Tom said it was a mourning dove. He could tell by the sound it made—kind of sad, like it was looking for someone."

Diana crushes her hands together so she won't be undone by Jessica's memory. She pictures it all: the breeze sweeping the bird through the barn; dust gliding along the sunlight; the rough, splintery wood of the shovel handle in her hand. She sees Tom, not yet the man she will love but on his way to that person, to that future with her.

"Tom stood next to me, staring at that damn bird. I remember the sweat trickling down the side of his face. He wiped it away and turned to me. He tasted like salt. I remember that." Jessica pulls a pack of cigarettes from her jacket pocket and taps it against her wrist.

Diana licks her lips, and salt is on her tongue. The stale-beer odor of the bar is replaced with the loamy smell of dirt and hay and horses. She's lightheaded and eager. She hadn't expected Jessica to make Tom come alive like this. *Tell me more,* she thinks.

Instead of more, though, Diana is jarred back into her chair by Fiona's return to their table. "You can't smoke in here," she says. Fiona picks up the plate and glasses, her eyes on Jessica.

Frowning, Jessica stuffs the cigarettes into her pocket and strides to the bathroom.

"She can smoke in the parking lot," Fiona continues. "Just pay your tab first."

Standing at the bar, distracted by Jessica's description of Tom, Diana is unable to accurately calculate percentages and leaves an extravagant tip for their order of carbonated beverages and french fries. Fiona reviews the receipt and disappears through the swinging doors. The beer-drinking man ignores Diana, his eyes on his rapidly emptying glass.

Diana contemplates the door to the women's bathroom. Should she go in and check on Jessica? While Jessica said she's clean, she also mentioned she was worried about holding on to her sobriety. Diana should have expected this and asked Andrea for guidance. Her sister's medical training would have been helpful today.

No matter what's happened, Diana needs her sister. She will make things right with Andrea when she gets home. It's time.

The bathroom door flings open, and Jessica emerges. When she doesn't see Diana at the table, confusion—and perhaps disappointment—ripples across her face.

"I paid our bill," Diana says, waving. "Do you want to go outside? We can talk while you smoke." Diana isn't confident being alone with Tom's ex is a good idea, but she has to take that risk if she wants to hear Jessica's story.

Jessica nods and opens the door with her hip.

Once outside, Diana stops, holding her face away from the sun to let her eyes adjust. It's then she spies a gleaming copper penny on the ground. She thinks of Phoebe and the pennies she hid inside Bear Bear. *A message from Tom,* she said. Maybe it is. Diana bends down to pick up the coin, holding it between her fingers, the metal hot with sunshine, before dropping it into her purse.

Chapter Thirty-Two

With Diana close behind, Jessica trudges through the parking lot and around a cluster of beat-up garbage cans to the rear of the bar. She selects a plastic crate from a stack along the chain-link fence and drops it next to the back door, where it clatters to the ground. She sits, stretching her legs out onto the gravel, and lights up a cigarette. "I gave up drugs and alcohol, but I can't quit cigarettes. I've tried, believe me."

The air here smells musty and pungent, making Diana gag. Thinking wistfully of their scarred wooden table inside Fiona's, she grabs a crate and places it next to Jessica, away from the smoke but close enough to hear.

After Jessica takes a long drag and exhales, she addresses Diana. "Why did you want to talk to me?"

"Tom left me a letter to read after his death, and in it, he says he did something criminal, something terrible," Diana says, impressed with her ability to keep her voice steady. "I think it's connected to Grace and William's fire and that you have the details."

Jessica removes her cigarette from her lips. "So he wrote you a letter."

Diana straightens, her body in a tight line. "You know about the letter?"

Jessica taps ash onto the ground, barely missing her foot. "Like I said, Tom didn't really talk about you. There was one time when he said he'd tried to tell you all of this but couldn't do it. A letter, I said. Write her a letter."

Since finding that letter, Diana has pictured so many scenarios about her husband's past; that he had a secret relationship with Jessica, and followed her advice, wasn't one of them. This startling truth chisels its way through her protective outer shell, cutting into the soft parts she tries to protect. She presses her fingernails into her palm to keep from lashing out, and her skin puckers under the pressure, dark-red half-moons arcing along her lifeline. "When did you tell him this? How often did you see him?"

Jessica glances across the trash cans and back toward the front of the bar, shame coloring her cheeks. "We met up every couple of months. It started when we bumped into each other in the courthouse."

"You met every couple of months? For *thirteen* years?" Diana is certain she's going to vomit. The heat, the trash smells, the cigarette smoke, Jessica telling her she and Tom were in touch all this time—it's too much. To avoid thinking about the bile burning her esophagus, Diana imagines leaving this place. She sees herself jump up and race to her car, jamming the key in the ignition and driving far away. She feels the weight of her keys in her hand and the pressure of her foot on the gas pedal.

"I told him to tell you about me," Jessica says defensively, interrupting Diana's daydream.

Diana tries a new tactic, putting aside Jessica and Tom's relationship for the moment. "I saw Grace. She hasn't been able to move on from William's death. She can't get resolution without you, Jessica."

At Grace's name, a noise comes out of Jessica that sounds like glass shattering, abrupt and stinging. The sobs that follow are aching and full of hurt.

I'm close, Diana thinks. *I'm almost there.* She removes tissues from her purse and gently lays the packet onto Jessica's knee. "Please tell me what you know."

Several minutes pass before Jessica speaks. "My parents sent me to my aunt and uncle that summer because they didn't want me around my younger brothers and sisters. I was trouble, they said." Her raspy voice grows brittle. "I could tell by the way Grace and William talked to me, the questions they asked, that they thought I was trouble, too. They wouldn't have liked it if Tom and I were involved. They would have been afraid a relationship with me would mess him up."

Jessica scrubs at her eyes, and makeup streaks across her cheeks. Her cigarette is forgotten, crushed under her shoe. "So I slept with him. Our first time was in the hayloft in the barn. He kept asking if I was sure. Didn't I want to wait to go someplace nice? I didn't care. I wanted to make a point. Not to Tom. To my parents, to everyone."

Jessica grips her knees, knocking Diana's tissues to the ground. "It's the kind of stupid stuff you do when you're sixteen. If my parents or Grace and William had known, so what? I did exactly what they thought I would do: seduce the good boy everybody loved. A self-fulfilling prophecy, that's all I was then. Maybe still am."

She returns to tapping her cigarette pack against her wrist, putting a dull thud behind her words. "When we were done with our chores, we'd meet up in the hayloft, or Tom would take me for walks in the woods. We'd lie by the apple trees and talk about where we wanted to travel, what we dreamed about. No one ever listened to me like he did."

Diana's fingers locate her wedding and engagement rings on the chain around her neck, the jewelry warm and reassuring against her damp skin.

Jessica lights another cigarette, the smoke curling in the air. "There was this one day when Tom said he wanted to plan a romantic evening for me because I was special. He said that: *I was special.*"

Had Tom loved Jessica? Had he hoped for a future with her? There are so many questions to which Diana will never have answers.

"My parents called as I was heading out to meet him. I was still mad they'd sent me to Hamilton, and I'd been avoiding them. Grace didn't like that we weren't getting along and made me get on the phone.

I don't remember what we talked about, probably nothing important. The call made me late to meet Tom. I was worried he'd left, but I found him outside the barn, waiting for me." Jessica smiles then, a woman remembering a teenage girl's joy. "He grabbed me by the hand, and we ran through the apple trees to a pond, in the woods about a mile from the farm."

The plastic crate presses against Diana's buttocks and thighs, and a trail of sweat slides between her breasts.

"He'd brought me there before to swim and look at the stars. He'd have a backpack with beer and a map of the night sky." Jessica doesn't say the pond was where they met to have sex, but the way she pauses when she speaks, as if she's editing herself, makes Diana believe they had. "We'd sit by the water and drink while he pointed out constellations I'd never heard of before. He'd tell me about the stories behind each one. The princesses and heroes and the gods who turned them into stars."

Diana sees Jessica and Tom lose track of time out there in the woods, the cool water lapping against their bodies. When they climb out of the watering hole, their feet squish in the swampy grass along the edge, and heat swirls over their skin. With their hair dripping wet down their backs, Tom kisses Jessica, an ardent embrace that engulfs Diana with envy.

"I loved that spot," Jessica continues. "I hated the pond, though. There were these plants that grew at the bottom and snagged your legs as you swam. I didn't tell Tom they bothered me; I wanted him to like me, so I always followed him in. I'd stay at the surface and float along until he was ready to get out."

"What does this have to do with the fire?" Diana is hesitant to interrupt this memory, but she's concerned Jessica is drifting into sentimentality.

"Like I said, Grace and William didn't know we were dating. Sneaking around made our relationship more exciting for Tom, I think.

That's why he waited for me in the barn while I was on the phone with my parents instead of knocking on the door.

"All these years, I've thought about the ways Tom and I could have prevented what happened." Jessica ticks the options off on her fingers one by one. "If I'd never gone to Hamilton that summer. If Tom hadn't worked for Grace and William. If we hadn't slept together. If we hadn't kept our relationship a secret. If we'd done something different that night, like go to the movies or visit his cousin at the diner. We had so many opportunities to make different choices."

A list comes to Diana: *How Could I Have Prevented Being Here Right Now?*

I couldn't have, she thinks. *Maybe that's one of the saddest truths of all this: Tom didn't understand I loved him too much to let his secret go without answers.*

Jessica holds her cigarette between her lips as she digs into her pockets. She produces a worn elastic hair tie and piles her curls into a tight bun. She instantly ages, giving the impression of being closer to the end of her story than to the beginning.

"We'd smoked in the barn before. It drove William crazy, but we knew how to safely put out the cigarette and stick the butt in the back pocket of our jeans so there wouldn't be any evidence. That night, though, Tom wasn't as cautious as he should have been." She jumps up to kick stones against the trash cans and pace across the small space. "Tom's cigarette started the fire. He didn't mean for it to happen, but it made him responsible. Me too. I was the one who first smoked in the barn and got him to do it. That's what he couldn't tell you. That people died because of him. Because of *us.*"

I owe it to you to tell you the kind of man I really was, Tom wrote.

Diana fights the instinct to collapse. Her body is heavy, and she struggles from the burden of staying upright, her head dipping down, and her shoulders curving inward. When she found Tom's letter, she described it as a storm, splintering her into pieces. How right she'd been in that description.

Jessica stops in front of Diana, her hands out, her cigarette dangling between her fingers. "So, Tom's wife, is this what you wanted?"

"I wanted the truth," Diana says softly. "Is this it?"

"Yes, it's the truth," Jessica sneers, her bloodshot eyes narrowing. "You don't believe me? You know, I didn't have to come here and talk to you."

Jessica wants Diana to attack, to distract her from the pain she's carried all these years. To do that, though, will only make Jessica walk away, and Diana isn't done asking questions.

"You're right." Diana keeps her voice calm and forces herself to sit up. "You could have ignored me, though I would have kept looking for you."

"I heard those voicemails you left my parents. It sounded like you wouldn't give up. That's one reason why I'm here."

"What's the other reason? Or reasons? There must be more, or else why were you following me around?"

"I wasn't following you around."

Diana can't help it, but she rolls her eyes. "Coming to my son's basketball game and driving by my house in the middle of the night? *Breaking into my house?* What else would you call it? Maybe 'stalking' is a better word?"

"I just . . . I just wanted to understand his life. If I saw where he lived and heard his voice, maybe he wasn't really gone."

"His *voice?*" Diana inhales sharply. "Oh my God, I am *so stupid* not to put all of this together. *You're* the one who's been calling my house. Those hang-ups are *you.*"

"It was the only way I could hear him," Jessica says, her voice cracking. "It started when I was in rehab, after Tom died. I'd gotten rid of my phone so I wouldn't be tempted to call any of my old friends. There was a pay phone for patients to use, and I'd call your answering machine to hear him say hello. It felt like he was talking to me. When I got back home, I kept calling." Jessica looks down at her feet, averting her eyes from Diana. "I loved him, too."

Diana bites her lip so she won't react to Jessica's declaration of love for her husband. She focuses instead on sorting through everything Jessica has told her so far. It's terrible, enough to fuel years of anguish, yet the story, she intuits, is incomplete. The rest is hiding along the edge of Jessica's words, shadowed and disguised.

"That's why you took the photo. Not because my children were in it, but because he was."

Jessica nods.

"But you're holding something back, aren't you?" Diana says, at first speaking hesitantly, and then with more confidence. Her question is directed to Jessica, but really, it's for Tom, wherever he is. "I need you to tell me all of it. Go all the way, Jessica. No more hiding."

Chapter Thirty-Three

At Diana's words, Jessica recoils, dropping her cigarette. Red-faced and choking, she spins around and grabs at the chain-link fence. The reflex of motherhood takes over, and Diana is at Jessica's side, tracing circles on her back, a soothing gesture that always works for Duncan and Phoebe.

Through Jessica's denim jacket, Diana makes out the curves of her rib cage, the unevenness of her breath, her fragility. She rubs Jessica's back until her hand goes numb. Right before she stops, Jessica, as if sensing a rearrangement of Diana's sympathies, steps away. Diana's arm falls, her tendons and nerves sparking with distress. She swings her limb, and the blood rushes down, setting her fingers afire.

Jessica plucks another cigarette from the pack and lights it with trembling hands. "Yes. There's more."

Holding tight to her purse straps, Diana returns to the plastic crate. "Go ahead."

"That conversation with my parents took forever. I could not get them off the phone." Jessica exhales off to the side, away from Diana. "When I met Tom outside the barn, he didn't say a word. He reached for my hand and pulled me into the woods. He ran so fast I could barely keep up. For some reason, this made me laugh. That's one of my clearest memories of that night: running through the woods with Tom and not being able to stop laughing. I was happy. Happy to be with him, to be in the woods, to have a whole night ahead of us.

"We stopped in the clearing next to the pond, and Tom fell to the ground. I thought he'd been laughing on our run to the pond, too, but really, he was crying. Maybe because I had been on the phone with my parents, I thought Tom was upset about his mom. I met her once when she came by the farm to drop off his lunch," Jessica says, tapping ash onto the ground. "I knew he was nervous about leaving her behind when he went to college, but his reaction seemed extreme for that."

Diana hates that Jessica met Tom's mother and she never did, that her children never did either.

Jessica remembers the pond was loud that night: Mosquitoes buzzed in her ears, and frogs croaked from their lily pads along the shoreline. The humidity was sticky and oppressive, and Jessica was considering taking off her sneakers to dip her feet into the water when Tom finally spoke.

"He was mumbling, and I couldn't understand what he was saying. I tried to comfort him, but he pushed me away. Eventually, I heard him say, 'It happened so fast. I didn't mean it. I didn't.' I asked him what happened, and it all came out."

Tom had been in the barn, finishing off a cigarette, when he heard a noise. It was a small sound—the clink of metal on metal—but it was wrong for the barn at that time of night.

The noise was followed by a voice calling his name. Tom turned around. In the low light, he couldn't see Carson at first.

"Carson shouldn't have been there, and he looked weird, with one shoulder larger than the other," Jessica says. "Tom stepped deeper into the barn and reached out into the shadows. When he felt leather, he understood Carson had William and Grace's saddles thrown over his shoulder. Carson wasn't used to carrying tack. His grip was wrong, and the weight forced him off kilter.

"Tom remembered an earlier theft from the barn and how upset William had been. He guessed this wasn't the first time Carson had stolen from my aunt and uncle, and he was mad. He told Carson to put everything back. Carson wouldn't, though. Tom reached for the saddles and tugged. Carson shoved Tom, and Tom fell. He crashed into a post and hurt his knee."

A memory comes to Diana through a stab of sorrow: Tom coaching Duncan on how to defend himself when he was picked on by another kid during the fourth grade. "Never turn away from a bully," Tom said. "Try reasoning with him first, and if that doesn't work, defend yourself in any way possible."

Jessica continues, "Carson tried to distract Tom. He said he had weed in his car and a case of beer. He knew of a party they could be at in fifteen minutes. Tom said no, and he got up from the ground and hit Carson while he was still talking. Even though they were friends, Tom had a limit of how much he could take from Carson, and learning he'd been stealing from people, especially Grace and William, was too much.

"Carson hit him back, and then Tom swung again, but he lost any advantage he had when Carson put him into a headlock so tight Tom thought he'd suffocate. He broke free by stomping on Carson's foot. Carson asked him to forget about all of this, but Tom didn't let him finish. He'd fallen next to William's tools. He picked up the shovel and swung. Tom said that when the shovel smashed into Carson's head it made a hollow *thunk*, like he'd kicked a pumpkin."

Diana wraps her hands around her face and presses against her mouth, willing herself not to retch. She wants to respond, to say something, anything, but she can't find words, she can't form a sentence.

"I was," Jessica says, "well, I don't know what I was. Stunned? Of course. Scared of Tom? Never. He was provoked. He tried to protect William and Grace. Things got out of hand." Jessica is adamant, her voice getting louder with each word. "You have to hear me on this: Carson attacked him. Tom never would have started a fight with anyone. He definitely wouldn't have with Carson. They were *friends*."

Jessica doesn't know how long she and Tom stayed at the side of the pond. "I told him we needed to call the paramedics. The police, too. We couldn't leave Carson in the barn. There was a chance he was still alive. Tom didn't agree at first. I got through to him when I pointed out that if we didn't do anything, William or Grace would find Carson. He couldn't do that to them."

They walked back through the woods, and Diana imagines it was so quiet the sticks and branches cracking under their feet sounded like thunder. They held hands, she thinks, Tom keeping Jessica close.

As they approached the farm, Jessica explained, a heaviness coated the air and the smell of smoke was everywhere. Tom took off, leaving her alone in the dark. "I caught up with him at the tree line. I got there as William ran into the barn. I couldn't believe he went in. The fire was so hot. And the noise. It was terrifying."

Jessica kept looking at the door, waiting for William to return to safety. Instead, two horses galloped out, past where Grace stood in the yard. Jessica remembers Grace turning to watch them as Tom slipped into the trees. "He was talking, but I couldn't hear him over the fire, so I got closer. 'No, no, no,' he kept saying. 'No, no, no.'"

William exited the barn and fell at Grace's feet. Tom gripped Jessica's arm, his fingers digging into her skin. "I blinked and Grace was gone, into the fire. I screamed at Tom to let me go. I wanted to open the side door to the barn and help. By then I'd figured out they were trying to save the horses."

Diana's hands fall into her lap. The harsh sun of the alley makes shimmering diamonds appear at the corner of her vision, and she wonders whether she's about to faint. She'd welcome unconsciousness, a chance to forget all this. She closes her eyes and waits for a reprieve from Jessica's truth-telling, but it doesn't come.

"I tried to get away from him," Jessica says, "but Tom was bigger than me, and I couldn't break free. It wasn't until William came out carrying Grace that Tom released me and ran. Even though I wanted to help them, I couldn't seem to make any decision other than to follow him to his car. He'd left it along the road, about a quarter mile from the farm. Tom drove us to the high school and parked in a far corner, under a tree. He left the car running, and I turned on the interior light so we could see each other while we talked. That's when I noticed his torn jeans and the blood splattered across his shirt."

Diana opens her eyes. "Why didn't you get help?" Her throat aches from holding in the screams she needs to release.

"At first, we were both freaking out," Jessica says. She is crying again, her cigarette abandoned on the ground, the tip still burning. "There was a lot of yelling. I wanted to go back to the farm. Tom kept banging the dashboard, saying, 'It's my fault, it's my fault.'" Jessica's strangled voice reminds Diana of the howl of a dying animal, its leg caught in a cold steel trap. "After an hour or two, Tom said he had a plan. The fire offered him a chance to avoid taking responsibility for Carson. He didn't have to tell the police he'd killed him. No one needed to know the truth. Except for me, and all I had to do was stay quiet."

"No." Diana says. She tries to visualize this younger version of her husband who made such a terrible decision, but she's afraid if she does, her Tom will be lost forever.

"If we were asked, we'd say we were at his house watching television. His mom would cover for us."

"She could have gotten into serious trouble for lying like that."

"You have kids. Wouldn't you do the same for them? I may not be the best mother, but I'd lie for Ava. I'd do anything for her."

Diana, too, would do anything for Duncan and Phoebe. She has more in common with Jessica than she first understood.

"We stayed in the car, not talking, until the sun came up. That's when Tom brought me to the farm. Irene, Grace's sister, was there getting Grace and William's things for the hospital. She said they'd been badly hurt. When we last saw them, they were outside of the barn. I still can't believe William went back in." Jessica runs her nails up and down her thighs, her black jeans shadowed where her fingers leave their mark. "Irene didn't even ask where I'd been all night; it was like she'd forgotten about me. I decided to go home, and Irene seemed relieved she didn't have to take care of me. She drove me to the bus station and offered to call my parents. She had to tell them about Grace and William anyway."

"That's it? You just went home?"

"About a week later, cops came to interview me in Portland. I said what Tom told me to say: I was with him that night, watching TV at his house. They believed me. It was my parents who suspected I was lying, and they grounded me for months because they thought I was hiding something. I left home as soon as I finished high school." Jessica continues scraping her nails across her body, focusing on her neck, leaving red welts across her skin. She shifts closer to Diana, only inches away. Diana smells cigarettes and Jessica's citrusy perfume. "All these years, Tom and I both kept this secret. I'm only here, telling you all of this, because he's gone."

He really is gone, Diana understands. And there is no way to get back the Tom she knew before all this started, before she found that letter.

Her next question shocks them both. "Who's Ava's father?"

"Diana," Jessica says, using her name for the first time. "Tom loved you. Even from the little he said about you, I knew he loved you."

He told her that he loved her every day, didn't he? Before he left for work each morning, before he fell asleep at night. And in the letter, too: *When you speak of me to Duncan and Phoebe, tell them their father was imperfect, but he loved them, and you, more than anything.*

Diana clutches the plastic crate to keep her body upright. "You didn't answer my question. Tom is Ava's father, isn't he? That's why he gave you that money: $60,000 over the years and $250,000 right before he died."

In the distance, Diana hears cars honk and voices call out. On the other side of the bar, people are going about their days, driving through traffic, listening to the radio. Here, a woman she's only just met is about to confirm another terrible secret, one that will obliterate Diana's understanding of her husband and her marriage. Her stomach twists, and though she knows she's right, she waits for Jessica to say the words.

"When Tom and I reconnected that day in the courthouse, I wasn't in a good place," Jessica whispers. "He tried to help me. The money he gave me was for rent and groceries, my phone bill, my car. I never used it for drugs."

Jonathan's words return to her: *I've decided if the money wasn't for the firm, it was for something else, something important to Tom.* Jessica *was* important to Tom, enough for him to steal from Jonathan and lie to everyone. Diana lets go of the crate and wraps her arms around her roiling midsection.

"Sometimes, I think Tom only tolerated me because of what I knew about Carson," Jessica continues. "Other times, I thought he cared for me. We slept together a few times, always when he was upset about something. A case at work, his guilt about the fire, a fight with you. He was always mad at me afterward, and I wouldn't hear from him for weeks. When he found out I was pregnant, he was furious. He wanted me to get rid of it. I wouldn't, though. I wanted the baby."

Diana feels a shooting pain in her chest, as if one of the last strands holding her together has snapped, and she falls against the building, breathing heavily. The brick wall grazes her skin through her thin cotton dress, and the nausea increases.

"Tom wouldn't have anything to do with me after Ava was born. I didn't see him again until she was about six months old and had gone to live with my parents. Raising her on my own was too hard, and I was still using. It wasn't safe for Ava to be with me." Jessica shakes her head so hard at some unspoken memory of Ava's infancy that the bun on her head falls, and curls spring loose around her ears.

"After that, Tom and I saw each other every few months or so. When Ava was around seven, I got arrested for possession. Tom got me probation, and that's when I broke it off. I was so screwed up. I couldn't face him anymore."

Jessica brushes away her tears, taking off the last of her makeup. "Before he died, Tom called me three or four times. In his voicemails, he said it was important. He was sick and had to speak to me. I thought maybe he finally wanted to meet Ava, so the next time he called, I answered. We didn't speak for long. You'd gone out on a walk with your sister, he said. Your brother-in-law was downstairs watching the kids. Tom was supposed to be napping. He laughed about that. He said what was the point of napping when he'd be dead soon enough?"

Diana so rarely left Tom's side after his diagnosis. She should remember taking a walk with Andrea and asking Evan to look after Duncan and Phoebe, but she cannot find that time in her memory.

"He called because he needed another favor. The first favor I'd done for him was keeping his secret all these years. The next was to get well. He asked me if I couldn't get clean for myself, could I do it for him? He'd pay for it. He didn't tell me where the money was coming from, and I didn't ask. He'd found a place in Arizona that was going to have openings that fall. It was a big commitment. Inpatient and a few months in a halfway house. I'd be gone for more than a year. He'd already talked to my parents about it, and they were willing to do whatever was needed to help me, including managing the money he wanted to give me."

Diana is finding answers to questions she didn't even dream of asking, connecting the facts of this story together, one fitting into another with a sharp click.

"I used all that money for rehab and therapy for me and my daughter," Jessica says. "Do you want me to pay you back? I live with my parents and Ava in Portland and wait tables. The tips are good, but I can't even afford my own place, much less come up with that much money."

Diana's eyes sting from the strain of holding in her tears. "Tom wanted you to have it so you'd get well. And you're better, right?"

Pride shines in Jessica's eyes. "I am better. He never saw me like this. He only ever knew the broken version of me."

Tom might have been happy with this version of Jessica. After all, she kept his terrible secret all these years and loved him despite his mistakes. She never stopped seeing him as that boy who walked her through the apple trees.

Tom never gave Diana the chance to understand who he really was. Perhaps he'd been right in his letter, after all: *If we had been different people, or maybe if our relationship had been different, I might have told you all this sooner. I tried, but I wasn't sure how you'd react.*

Remembering the contents of that letter brings Diana another realization. "Tom said other people knew what he did that night at the farm and that they might come looking for me. That was you, right? There isn't anyone else?"

"Not that I know of."

"He wrote that letter because he thought you'd find me after you were done with rehab. He told you to stay away from me and my children, didn't he? He made you promise?"

Jessica nods.

"But he was concerned you wouldn't stay away, so he had to scare me. He needed to make sure I'd be too frightened to talk to you. That way I wouldn't learn about your affair and Ava." Diana clears her throat. "He took a big risk with that letter, and it backfired spectacularly."

"I told Tom he should be honest with you, with everyone," Jessica says. "He said—and I remember this because I thought he was wrong then and still think he's wrong—'The past stays in the past.' We might want the past to stay there, but it never does, you know? The past is always with us."

Neither woman says anything for several minutes. Jessica stands up and stretches her arms over her head, the firm skin of her stomach flashing above her jeans.

"Is that it?" Diana asked, rising up next to her and very much hoping that's everything.

"Yes, that's it." Jessica steps so close that Diana sees the gold flecks in her brown eyes. "Who else are *you* going to tell? Or are you going to keep all of this a secret, too?"

"I . . . I've been so worried about finding out the truth that I haven't thought about what happens after," Diana says carefully. "If I go to the police, you might get in trouble for not coming forward sooner or for lying to them about the fire."

Jessica tosses her cigarette pack into the trash. "That's your call. I just hope you can do right by me."

They return to the front parking lot, standing together in the unrelenting sun. "Thank you for talking to me," Diana says. "Can I give you a ride somewhere?" Driving off to the suburbs and leaving Jessica here alone seems wrong, an inadequate response to the courage it took for her to open up, even if what she said has broken apart Diana's world.

"No, thanks." Jessica stuffs her hands in her jacket pockets and walks off without saying goodbye. She crosses the street and moves deliberately up the hill. Diana watches her until she turns left and disappears.

Chapter Thirty-Four

Instead of returning home, where she'd be surrounded by the reminders of her marriage—the photos, Tom's closet full of clothes, their bed—Diana finds herself at Alcott Pond.

When the kids were younger, she and Tom used to take walks here, pushing Phoebe in the stroller while Duncan waddled along, stopping every few feet to examine an iridescent bug or yelp at the chipmunks. As she circles the pond, Diana's mind crowds with images, as if a camera captured Jessica's story in a series of rapid-fire snapshots summer's nighttime constellations, a scuffed leather saddle, the burning barn against the night sky, ripples of water across the pond's surface, Tom's car speeding away from the farm.

On an empty bench next to a blooming lilac bush, the air filled with its sweet, floral scent, she sits down and unzips her boots. She removes her feet, wet with perspiration, a blister already forming on her left heel.

Finally, Diana has uncovered what Tom did. He killed Carson and never held himself accountable, nor did he tell the truth to the authorities. He started the fire that resulted in William's death, Grace's injuries, and the destruction of the O'Connors' dream. His choice to abandon William and Grace that night, to wait for dawn without calling for help, and to ask his mother to lie for him were also part of his guilt.

He slept with Jessica and had a child with her. He stole to support his lover and fund her recovery.

Before all this, Diana would have said Tom was dedicated, focused, hardworking, honest. Now? A murderer. A liar. A cheat. She could add her mother's "complicated" and her sister's "cruel." "Secretive," too.

Diana might have expected to need time to decide what to do next, but her path appears clearly before her, as if it has been waiting for her all along. She will keep Tom's truth to herself, telling no one, not Grace or her family, not Chris, not even Lakshmi, who so kindly helped her on her search. The burden of who Tom was will be hers alone. Or, at least, hers and Jessica's.

But Duncan is different. Her son—*their son*—deserves some slice of this story, enough to satisfy his curiosity, yet not so much as to irrevocably harm him.

As for the police, at its best, a visit to the Hamilton police department would be perfunctory: an update to a long-ago closed case file. At its worst, the police could investigate Jessica. While she gave Diana the distinct impression any punishment meted out by the justice system would pale in comparison to what she's put herself through all these years, Diana isn't interested in exposing Jessica to law enforcement.

It's then, when she thinks of Jessica's efforts to make amends, Diana realizes Tom was looking for absolution at the end.

That last night he was conscious, Tom asked Diana to sit on the deck with him. It was one of those perfect summer nights: a slight breeze, crickets chirping in the distance, fireflies dancing through the twilight. A half-moon hovered on the horizon, waiting in the spreading darkness for its turn. Duncan and Phoebe were at Diana's parents' for a sleepover. They had carefully hugged their father before they left. No one knew it was the last goodbye, though now Diana understands Tom had already decided it was time to go.

Diana stretched out next to him on the chaise, her head resting lightly on his chest. "What do you remember about our wedding?"

"I remember the whole day. Every second."

"Tom, come on." Diana was compelled to hear his answer, the need thrumming inside her. She would be, far too soon, facing years without him. Carrying his memories would help her to keep going, to ground herself in what was, so what could have been didn't become all she thought about.

"I definitely remember your mom's friend, the one who got very drunk and cornered us on the dance floor."

"She kept telling us to 'have babies, have babies right away!'" Diana laughed. "She was willing to explain how to make those babies if we wanted."

"We didn't need her help, did we?" Tom asked.

She looked up to find him staring at her, as if he were memorizing her angles, her skin, the way her hair fell around her shoulders. She responded by kissing him tentatively, and then with more urgency. She slid her arms around him, and the kiss was both endless and not enough.

"Diana, this life we have . . . It's fantastic, extraordinary. I—"

"*Shhh*, Tom."

"Let me say this." He swallowed, his tongue darting out to lick his lips. "I could have been a better person. I've let down so many people, including you. Forgive me. I never meant for it to happen. I'm so sorry."

"It's okay. I promise it's all okay." Diana wondered if it was normal for those who were dying to worry their loved ones were angry at them for getting sick and leaving. She poured a glass of water from a carafe on the table and helped him drink, his profile outlined by the light shining through the French doors.

"I love you," he whispered.

Diana took the glass from his hands and kissed him. "I love you, too."

They lay together on the chaise, Diana dozing off next to him. When she woke, Tom was staring overhead at the Milky Way. "I need help getting up."

"Yes, of course," she said with a jerk of awareness.

Once, helping him—his broad, strong body—would have crushed her, his weight pushing her down. That night, he was light, barely there, stumbling at the door, needing Diana to catch him.

"I'll sleep here." Tom gestured to the hospital bed the hospice nurse had arranged in the office. Before, he had refused to stay there, painfully climbing the stairs to their bedroom every night with Diana by his side.

This was different. Final.

She helped him into the bed, taking off his shoes and baseball cap and tucking a blanket around his chest. She gave him another sip of water and a painkiller, and he put his hand on her arm.

"Stay with me."

"Give me a minute to get ready."

Tom closed his eyes, falling asleep before she left the room.

Diana staggered into the kitchen and leaned against the wall. She bit her fist and slid to the floor. She heard a moan.

Is it Tom? Does he need me?

No, she understood—the moan had come from her; she was making that noise.

She grabbed her phone from the counter and texted Andrea. I think this is it, she typed, her fingers hovering over the keys.

She looked at the message for an agonizing moment before deleting it, her finger hesitantly pressing the backspace until the screen was blank.

She made herself return to the office and climb into bed next to Tom. He didn't stir.

Diana cradled him in her arms, listening to his slow heartbeat and feeling the all-consuming reach of grief surround her.

Sometime in the dark of the night, when even the stars disappeared, the silence in between each of Tom's breaths extended an impossibly long time. Diana pressed her cheek against his and counted each of his inhales and exhales, until they stopped, and she was alone.

I could have been a better person. I've let down so many people, including you. Forgive me. I never meant for it to happen. I'm so sorry.

Even at the end, he'd tried to tell her. He *had* wanted her to know.

She thinks of that list she started on the drive back from Vermont: *What Would I Say to Tom?* Some revisions are needed, she decides.

I love you.

I miss you. I always will.

Minutes or even an hour later, as sweat pools along her hairline, Diana feels the last ties to Tom's burden slip away.

She rubs her toes against the feathery green grass and watches a blue jay fly overhead. The sun makes her skin tender and hot to the touch.

She feels completely alive.

And remarkably, unexpectedly calm.

She lifts her phone out of her purse and shifts her attention to the present. She begins by sending a text to Andrea: How about you, Evan & Noah come over tonight for dinner?

The second, to her parents, will likely arrive as they pack up from the fishing trip: What's your ETA? I'll make dinner. xo

The third goes to Lakshmi: Free for a BBQ?

These messages are signs of the Diana she wants to be, a woman who throws spontaneous parties and looks for answers to hard questions; a woman who understands that, while her grief and pain may always be silent and persistent companions, they need not define her life. If she's learned anything from meeting Jessica and Grace and uncovering Tom's secrets, it's that she has a choice in who she becomes. She can, like that snake at the science museum, become a new, changed version of herself. She can heal and maybe, someday, forgive.

Responses arrive within seconds: a thumbs-up emoji from Lakshmi, followed by a short note (What happened with Jessica?!?!; a formal missive from her mother, replete with proper punctuation and grammar (Your father and I would be delighted to join you. We'll be home closer to 5 p.m.); and when Andrea's text comes, the swoosh tugs at Diana's heart (Yes to dinner. Can't wait. Love you.).

As her lips spread in a grateful smile, Diana zips her feet back into her boots and starts toward home.

The barbecue is precisely what Diana hoped it would be: The kids run around the yard, screeching and shooting one another with water guns; her father and Ramesh take over grilling duties; Evan mixes gin and tonics; Lakshmi entertains her mother with stories about her painting students; and Diana and Andrea reconcile.

It's simple: Andrea walks through the front door, salsa and chips in her hands, and bursts into tears. Diana wraps her arms around her sister, and they each whisper apologies. In the middle of their reunion, Evan takes the snacks from Andrea's grip and sends them outside with the kids, while the other adults disappear into the kitchen to give the sisters privacy. When Diana and Andrea reappear into the bustle of their loved ones, Diana notices how relieved their parents look.

Lakshmi asks to talk to Diana next, and they find a quiet space in front of the French doors, the children munching on chips on the other side, leaving crumbs for the waiting birds. Lakshmi hands Diana a small package wrapped in a paisley scarf. "For you."

"A painting?" Diana rubs the grooves of a wooden frame through the silk. She unties the knot in the corner, and the scarf falls away, landing at her feet in a radiant pile. The painting is of Tom, dressed in a white shirt, standing against a sapphire-colored sky. An invisible wind blows wisps of hair around his head, giving him the illusion of flight, of lightness, of otherworldliness. "Oh, Lax."

"Do you like it? Is it too much?"

"It's perfect. I didn't know you were painting him."

"Remember that piece I was working on of Ramesh?"

Diana summons that night, two days after she found Tom's letter, when she sought out Lakshmi for help. She tastes Lakshmi's sweet and spicy chai as she recalls the canvas in progress on her friend's easel. Was it only three months ago?

"Something about it wasn't working. One day, Ram looked at it and noticed it looked nothing like him, but so much like Tom. It all fell together after that."

"The sky—"

"The Cape, the last vacation you took."

"I love it. He would have loved it, too. Though he would have made a crack about how young you made him. No gray hair or wrinkles."

"This is how I remember him."

How I remember him, Diana thinks. *That's it. How I choose to remember him is up to me.* Wordlessly, she embraces Lakshmi, the painting tight in her hand.

Chapter Thirty-Five

After dinner, everyone settles in for the evening, as if leaving Diana's house will break a magical spell. The kids pile on the sofa to watch a superhero movie, while her father plays poker with Lakshmi, Ramesh, and Evan at the dining room table. Her mother remains in the kitchen, scrubbing it to spotless perfection and listening as Francis loses hand after hand. Andrea and Diana go upstairs to clean out Tom's closet.

"Three piles." Diana gestures to the bed. "Keep, donate, and trash."

"What do you want to keep?" Andrea snaps open a black trash bag and kneels in front of the shoes.

Diana pulls out Tom's flannel robe and the blue L.L. Bean fleece he wore on winter weekends, along with the cashmere sweater from their first official date. She puts aside his ties for Duncan and a law school sweatshirt for Phoebe. "The rest goes."

She and Andrea get to work, speaking only when Andrea has a question about an item. It will take a while for the free-for-all of sisterhood to return; eventually, they will find their rhythm again, though it will be different between them. Andrea has grown too accustomed to being the one who has it together, the one who "fixes" Diana's life.

My life doesn't need fixing, Diana thinks. *Or at least, not the kind of fixing anyone can do except for me.*

Andrea opens a new bag for Tom's baseball caps. Diana rescues his favorite Red Sox cap for the keep pile, along with his last pair of running sneakers.

"I've been meaning to tell you," Andrea says. "We got a letter from Noah's teacher. She's putting together a time capsule for the kids to open when they graduate high school. Could parents please contribute a letter for their child? Can you believe it? The last thing this family needs is another time capsule." Chuckling, she adds the bag to the growing pile in the corner of the room.

Diana offers a small smile. "Even though my experience with time capsules has been"—she pauses to find the right word—"unconventional, that doesn't mean they're bad. It's quite a nice idea."

"'Unconventional' is an understatement. More like 'screwed up.'"

Diana pulls Duncan's baseball bat from under her bed and leans it in the corner by the door so she'll remember to put it back in the downstairs closet. "You should write the letter, Andie. Include a photo of the kids from earlier today, playing in the yard. It will be good to remember."

⌐⌐

It's past midnight when everyone finally departs. The light under Duncan's door tells Diana he's still awake, and when she enters his bedroom, she finds him propped up against the headboard, watching the door. She sits next to him, and the mattress shifts with her weight. She hands him the photo she found in the trash of himself and Tom on the basketball court. She's taped it together; strips of cellophane crisscross their bodies. Their faces are intact, but the basketball is lost in the gash across the middle. "I thought you'd want this back."

He carefully holds the photo in his palm. "You found Jessica, didn't you?"

"I met her while you and Phoebe went fishing with Grandma and Grandpa."

"And?" His tone is so eager, so trusting. "What did she say about Dad?"

Diana taps the rings hanging around her neck. Tom should have told her the truth years ago. If he had, Duncan wouldn't be part of this story now. She'll never be able to forgive him for that. "Many years ago, your father made a terrible mistake. He could never move past it, but we're not going to hold on to it anymore."

Duncan listens as she recounts an abridged telling of Tom's role in the fire, deliberately omitting his culpability in Carson's death. She can't do that to her son.

When she finishes, he drops his head on her shoulder, and they sit quietly, holding hands. Diana is curious how he's matching this new vision of Tom with his memories of his father, but she doesn't ask. Maybe later she will.

Duncan breaks their silence with the phrase they'll think a thousand times, at birthdays and basketball games, on special occasions and ordinary days. "I miss him."

"Me too." She understands that Duncan will revisit the story she's told him again and again. Probably for the rest of his life. "Remember that your dad loved you. He was so proud to be your father."

"I love him, too." His voice is drowsy, and soon, Duncan's deep and even breathing tells her he's fallen asleep. She shifts him onto the pillow and turns off the light.

She should go to bed, too, but she's kept alert by memories: her own, and now Jessica's. They met only this morning, but already, the specifics are distorted, as if they're underwater, worn away by the waves into something colorless and delicate.

Downstairs in the office, Diana turns on the computer and slides the cursor across the screen to a folder titled "Our Wedding." She sets the images to slideshow, and her screen fills with a photo of Chris and Tom putting on boutonnieres and grinning. Another of Aunt Teresa and Uncle Brian walking into the church with Tom. Diana and Andrea, standing in their parents' yard on that steamy summer day in front of a row of blue hydrangeas, heavy with flowers shaped like stars.

She should be mad at Tom, furious and raging at his betrayal. Those feelings kindle inside her, a fire seeking to ignite. Before they blaze, however, Diana remembers Grace's description of anger's addictive qualities, how it could become all-consuming: *I haven't been able to let my anger or pain go,* Grace said. *You should.*

"I'll try," Diana murmurs, focusing on dousing those embers of pain, one by one.

Another photo appears on the screen. This one is of Diana alone. She remembers her mother waiting behind the photographer, powder in hand, ready for touch-ups, and the way her thighs, slick with sweat, stuck together as she adjusted her skirt. She remembers running her hands across the bodice of her dress, the lace tickling her fingers.

She enlarges the image, her face filling the screen. This Diana was passive. She never questioned Tom too closely about anything, not his family history, not his long hours at work, and not the reasons why he was reluctant to return to Hamilton. That Diana didn't demand much from those around her. If only she'd been different then. If only he had, too.

Diana removes the letter and its copies from her pocket and unfolds the pages on the desk. Would Tom have ever told her about Jessica if he'd had more time?

This thread of the story is unresolved, tied up in a knot she will never unravel. It will always tug at her, especially when she feels his loss most keenly.

The photos continue to advance: Tom and Diana's first dance, the wedding cake covered in sugar-spun flowers, the crystal chandelier above the dance floor glowing in the sun that streamed through the leaded windows. The slideshow ends on a black-and-white photo of Tom and Diana posing at the foot of a staircase, both unaware of how life would turn them about.

Her fingers clamp onto the letter. By now, the words are second nature to her. She repeats them like a prayer, her lips moving silently:

When I was 18 years old, I did something criminal. Something so terrible I can't even write the details here. People died. It's all my fault.

The answer of what to do next comes to Diana like a door opening from a darkened house into a bright day, bringing light to where there was an untenable murkiness. She opens the desk drawer and takes out the folder containing her research: the items she photographed while visiting the *Hamilton Star*, the brochure for the O'Connor farm sale, printouts from the internet, Jessica's cell phone bill, the paper from Grace with Jessica's Nashua address scribbled in blue ink, the sketches from Tom's notebook of Jessica and the horses, and Grace's photo of Tom and Jessica. Inside she puts the original letter and its two copies and leaves the office.

In the kitchen, she takes the original letter from the folder, tracing Tom's signature one last time. She drops the folder into the sink and opens the small drawer where she keeps odds and ends. Hidden under a coupon for Sully's breakfast sandwiches, she finds a matchbook. She opens the cardboard flap and pulls out one match, igniting it with an efficient switch of her hand.

The red-blue flame dances in front of her. She lets it burn until the heat licks at her fingers. She drops the match, and the pages smolder, sending off a stinging odor that reminds Diana of almonds. She lights another match, bringing it to the edge of the folder. The flames jump across. She sees letters—a *D* here, a *J* there—as the papers curl up into themselves and disappear.

After a last look at the letter Tom wrote, the one he held in his hands and left for her to find, she lights another match and positions it at the letter's corner. A narrow corkscrew of smoke rises up and out the window. She holds the letter over the sink, the fire closing in on her skin. When she can hold on no longer, she drops the paper, watching it fall into the sink and disintegrate.

Diana shovels the ash into a pile, scooping it onto a paper towel. She gathers up what remains and goes outside.

With her phone's flashlight, she finds a rusty trowel in a bucket of tools on the corner of the deck and walks across the lawn to the garden. Amid the ever-spreading mint and her temperamental rosebush, she digs. A few inches down, Diana places the ashes.

She reaches into her pocket for Grace's rock. She rolls it around, running her fingers along its rough surface and pointed end one last time. She places the rock on top of the pile of ashes and sinks both into the ground, her hands settling into the damp dirt.

Diana silently fills the hole, patting the ground with her palms, before standing up to return inside.

≈

The next day, Diana surprises Duncan and Phoebe with a trip to the ocean. The forecast calls for a scorcher, so she wakes them early to get a parking space at Good Harbor Beach before the crowds arrive. The kids tumble into the minivan with sleep still in the corners of their eyes.

They build sandcastles where the waves turn to foam around their feet. At low tide, they wade out to Salt Island in the frigid water, their lips turning blue, Diana holding Phoebe's hand as they follow Duncan over the rocks. After a short rest on damp towels to eat peanut butter sandwiches, the kids return to the water to try out the boogie boards Diana found in the basement. As Diana stands on the shore, they swim through the chilly Atlantic, Duncan waiting for Phoebe as she works to keep up with him. Afterward, salt still stuck to their skin, they sit outside at a seaside restaurant, eating fried clams and onion rings, ketchup dripping down their chins.

With achingly full bellies, empty plates in front of them, Diana tells her children that when Tom was a teenager, he worked on a horse farm. "Remember when I went up to Vermont? I met the lady who owned the farm. She said your dad even cleaned the horses' stalls, though I bet he didn't like that too much. Cleaning wasn't his thing. Remember how he always left his dirty socks all over the house?"

"I like it when you talk about Daddy," Phoebe says.

When you speak of me to Duncan and Phoebe, tell them their father was imperfect, but he loved them, and you, more than anything.

"I do, too," Diana says. "I'm going to be better at telling stories about him."

Duncan rubs his palm across his eyes. Diana reaches for his other hand and gives it a squeeze. "That work for you, Duncan?"

He nods quickly and beams a smile at Phoebe. "I think we need ice cream. What do you say?"

"A chocolate and vanilla twist with sprinkles," Phoebe agrees. She looks up at Diana. "Want one, Mama?"

Diana laughs as she pulls a credit card out of her wallet and hands it to Duncan. "I'm too full. I'll just taste yours." The kids scramble off the bench. "A small cone is enough!"

As her children weave between the other tables to a window through which teenage waitstaff sell frozen confections, Diana thinks of Ava. Someday, she'll tell Duncan and Phoebe about their half sister. Perhaps a trip to Maine would be good for all of them.

Thinking of the future inspires her to pull her phone from her shorts pocket and send a text that is long overdue. Camille, she writes, I'm interested in the library director job, and I'd love to talk with you about it.

Camille's response is instantaneous: About time I heard from you, I'll send a meeting invite for this week. We have a lot of planning to do.

Diana looks over to the window to find Phoebe's face obscured by what is most definitely not a small cone. Duncan, holding aloft his equally oversize ice cream, shrugs as if to say, *You said large, right?*

Diana shakes her head, laughing, and her children's smiles are so wide and so joyful that her heart aches in response.

Her phone buzzes, and Diana looks down to find a message from Chris, accompanied by a photo of a pile of wood. I'm making a second Adirondack chair for my porch. Should be ready in a week or so. Think you might like to break it in?

Diana swears she can smell sawdust. *I'd like that very much,* she texts back.

"Mama," Phoebe says as she approaches their table, Duncan at her heels. "We figured you'd want more than a taste." She licks melting ice cream from her hand. "Want to share with us?"

"Absolutely," Diana says. She wraps her arm around her daughter, kissing Phoebe behind her ear, where she smells of the sea, of childhood, and of everything Diana loves most in the world. "There's nothing I want more."

Acknowledgments

I begin my acknowledgments with—as befits this novel—a confession: Whenever I start a new book, I flip to the back to read this section first. I am always intrigued by how an author's thank-yous offer insight into their writing life and publishing journey, and I love carrying this behind-the-scenes look with me as I immerse myself in their story.

Whether you're reading these acknowledgments before or after you read *What Remains of You* (thank you for doing so, by the way!), I hope you take away from these pages the boundless gratitude I have for each person who said "keep going" and "I can't wait to read your book." It made all the difference.

My thanks begin with my agent, Jill Marsal: for her belief in me and for her wise counsel. Thank you to my editor Marilyn Brigham for bringing me into the Lake Union family and for advocating for me and my work; to Clete Barrett Smith for his smart and thoughtful edits that made this book all the better; to Joanne O'Neill for the beautiful cover; and to Angela Elson, Karen Brown, Kellie Osborne, Jessica Poore, and the rest of the Lake Union team for the dedication and expertise they brought to this book.

I didn't realize that, when I began to write this novel, I'd join such a vibrant literary community that would sustain me through the long path from idea to publication. Thank you to Henriette Lazaridis, in whose writing class at Grub Street I realized the project I'd been working on might actually be a book, and to Ursula DeYoung, who published an early version of this novel's first chapter, which provided encouragement exactly when I needed it.

My endless appreciation to Jenna Blum, who champions, cajoles, and motivates in equal measure and who shines a bright light on her writers and friends. Thank you to all those I met in Jenna's novel-writing class, an extraordinary bunch of writers who have become friends: Trisha Blanchet, Hillary Casavant, Mark Cecil, Tom Champoux, Jennifer De Leon, Chuck Garabedian, Julie Gerstenbatt, Edwin Hill, Sonya Larson, Joe Moldover, Jenna Paone, Jane Roper, Whitney Scharer, Adam Stumacher, Alex Sunshine, Grace Talusan, and Kate Woodworth. How lucky I am to have met all of you.

Thanks to the team at A Mighty Blaze, especially Jenna Blum and Caroline Leavitt, for giving me the opportunity to interview writers and booksellers for *Authors Love Bookstores*; to Joe Moldover for being the best cohost I ever could have asked for; and to all our guests who offered us a master class in writing and publishing each week.

Special appreciation goes to Donna Freitas and Marjan Kamali for their faith in me and my work and for their excellent feedback; to Julie Gerstenblatt for answering my endless questions and always knowing exactly when to text a much-needed pep talk; and to Kerry Savage for our writing sessions and Zoom calls, and for loving these characters as much as I do.

Thank you to Michelle Hoover, Jillian Jackson, Anson Wright, and Lynn Sheridan, for early, insightful reads; to Kerri Maher and Weina Dai Randel for perfectly timed advice; to Hank Phillippi Ryan for her support; and to Jennifer Koch, Anne Meade, and Joshua Pakstis, for answering my questions about psychiatry, horses, and the law, respectively. Any errors in this book related to these topics are all mine.

I'm forever indebted to my dear friends whose excitement for this book fed my soul each step of the way: to Megan McCormick, Gethin, Rie, and Laszlo Aldous; to Michael, Lindsey, Abby, and Jane Schrader; and to Louise Barbic, Sue Fish, Elisa Hurley, Maria Lang,

Phyllis Myung, Victoria Nessen, and Laura Weinstein. To my book club, which repeatedly asked to read my novel: Here you go!

It is not an overstatement to say that this book would not be in your hands were it not for the support of my family. To my mother, Judi Hensle, who instilled in me a lifelong love of books, storytelling, and libraries, and to my father, Emil Hensle, who was my biggest fan and taught me the value of persistence: I am so fortunate to be your daughter. I miss you every day.

To my beloved sisters-in-law, Roopal Patel and Sarah Hensle: Thank you for your friendship, for our travels, and for being the best sounding boards.

To my treasured brother, Michael Hensle; to my nephews, Kai, Jorin, and Tyler; to my brother-in-law, Dave Lowrance, and mother-in-law, Christie Lowrance; and to my extended Comer, Lowrance, Palmer, and Patel family—thank you.

To my children, Robert and Gwendolyn: You are my delight and joy, and my greatest inspiration. I adore being your mom, and I hope you take from my hustle to bring this story to life that working hard for your goals is well worth the effort. I love you to the end of the universe and back.

And finally, to my husband, Rob: Thank you for your steadfast care of my dreams. You never let me waver from my desire to become a novelist, always encouraging me and always cheering me on. Marrying you was the best decision I've ever made. I love you always.

Book Club Questions

1. What would you do if you found a letter from a partner, family member, or friend like the one Diana finds from Tom? Would you ignore the message or investigate? Could you live with not understanding what the message means?

2. Diana's family and friends each respond differently to Tom's letter. Lakshmi offers to help her figure out the truth, Duncan's grief is brought to the forefront, Jonathan tells her to "let this all go and move on," Andrea lashes out, and Vivian worries about the impact of the letter on Diana and her children. What do you think of each character's reaction? Which response did you identify with the most? How do you think you would respond if a friend or loved one showed such a letter to you?

3. After Diana's home is burgled, she elects not to reach out to law enforcement for help, nor does she bring the letter to the police. What do you think of these decisions? What would you have done if you were in her place?

4. When Diana and Grace talk about the fire and William's death, Grace explains: "Sometimes, not looking too closely is the only way to get through a terrible time." What do you think about this statement? Is Grace's coping mechanism healthy, or does it exacerbate her grief?

5. After Diana and Lakshmi fail to find Jessica in Nashua, they discuss the possible reasons Tom didn't tell Diana the truth

when he was alive. Lakshmi says: "We keep part of ourselves secret . . . Maybe there are always limits to knowing someone else. Even when we love them." Do you agree with Lakshmi that there can be limits to knowing our loved ones? Do you agree that we all keep parts of ourselves secret? If so, how do these barriers affect our connections to one another?

6. To both Diana and Jessica, Tom said the "past stays in the past." What do you think he meant by this statement? Do our past actions and experiences really stay in the rearview mirror, or are they always with us?

7. Have you ever learned a secret about a friend, family member, or coworker that completely changed how you saw them? How did you respond to this new information? How did it influence your relationship?

8. Grief and loss play a central role in this story. They are "silent and persistent companions" for several characters. What do you think about this novel's depiction of grief? Does it change how you might approach someone experiencing loss?

9. After finally uncovering Tom's truth, Diana elects to keep what she's learned to herself, with the exception of telling her son an abridged version of what his father did. Do you agree with her decision to tell Duncan some of Tom's story? Would you have made the same choice? If not, how would you have responded?

10. At the end of the book, Diana realizes that, now that she knows the truth, how she sees Tom is up to her: *How I remember him,* she thinks. *That's it. How I choose to remember him is up to me.* If you learned news that broke your world apart, like the news Diana learns about Tom, would you be able to choose how to remember the person who caused the pain? Could you separate the person you love from their actions? Could you forgive them? Do you think Diana will be able to forgive Tom and move on?

About the Author

Photo © 2025 Andre Toro

Kimberly Hensle Lowrance graduated from Boston University and the Harvard Graduate School of Education. A former nonprofit professional, she lives in Massachusetts with her family and their very shy rescue dog. *What Remains of You* is her first novel. For more information, visit www.kimberlyhensle.com.